A Very Merry ENEMY

VERY MERRY BOOK THREE

LYRA PARISH

Copyright © 2025 Lyra Parish
www.lyraparish.com

A Very Merry Enemy
Very Merry, #3

Cover Designer: Black Widow Designs
Character Illustrator: Qamber Designs
Editing: CM Wheary Editing
Proofreading: Marla Esposito

All rights reserved. No parts of the book may be used or reproduced in any manner without written permission from the author, except for the inclusion of brief quotations in a review. This book is a work of fiction created without the use of AI technology. Names, characters, establishments, organizations, and incidents are either products of the author's imagination or are used fictitiously to give a sense of authenticity. Any resemblance to actual persons, living or dead, events, or locales is entirely coincidental. No part of this book may be used to create, feed, or refine artificial intelligence models for any purpose without written permission from the author.

OFFICIAL PLAYLIST

- Christmas Tree Cluster - Deep Sky Dude
- About You - The 1975
- Enjoy the Silence - Depeche Mode
- Problem - Ariana Grande, Iggy Azalea
- Nobody Gets Me - SZA
- One I've Been Missing - Little Mix
- 'tis the damn season - Taylor Swift
- Cozy With Me - kenzie, Ant Saunders
- It's All Coming Back To Me Now - Céline Dion
- Underneath the Tree - Kelly Clarkson
- Rockin' Around The Christmas Tree - Brenda Lee
- Still into You - Paramore
- imperfect for you - Ariana Grande
- Don't Take It Personally - Selena Gomez, benny b
- white xmas - Sabrina Carpenter
- WAP - Cardi B, Megan Thee Stallion
- cardigan - Taylor Swift
- Diet Pepsi - Addison Rae
- Kiss Me - Sixpence None The Richer
- Main I Need - Olivia Dean
- All I Want for Christmas Is You - Mariah Carey
- Red Dress - Nova Miller
- Jingle Bell Rock - Bobby Helms
- buy me presents - Sabrina Carpenter
- When It's December - Savannah Sgro
- Have Yourself A Merry Little Christmas - Frank Sinatra

LISTEN TO THIS PLAYLIST ON SPOTIFY:
https://bit.ly/averymerryenemyplaylist

If you were ever made to feel small by someone you once trusted, this one is for you.

Babe, YOU are the secret recipe.
Don't you <u>ever</u> forget it.

CHAPTER 1

HOLIDAY

The bell over the glass door jingles with too much cheer. Happiness spreads like a never-ending laugh track. The air smells like cinnamon as Christmas music plays from a speaker shaped like a snowman that's hidden in the corner of Jolly Cookie Shop. A pine wreath hangs in the front window, glitter catching the early morning sunlight.

I adjust the row of peppermint snowflake decorations on the marble countertop, then take a step back to look at the case full of beautifully decorated pastries that I worked my ass off to make, starting at four this morning. There are sugar ribbons on gingerbread bows, star cookies with cranberry jam shining inside like stained glass, and my famous shortbread dipped in white chocolate and crushed candy canes.

Baking has always been my escape. Now is no different.

My hands shake for three seconds, and I press them against my apron, breathe through it, and pretend they're steady. I can do hard things. I have done really hard things. Returning to Merryville after fifteen years of avoiding this place is at the very top of my list.

Through the front windows of the bakery, I can see that the tree lot is already busy with employees setting up before customers arrive. Lucas is out there right now with his chain saw and bad attitude, pretending I don't exist, fifty yards away.

Or worse...wishing I didn't exist.

"You're a pastry godsend," Emma says from the doorway of the kitchen, one hand on her belly. Only Emma Jolly would stubbornly open a brand-new bakery on one of the busiest Christmas tree farms in Texas while pregnant with twins. "No way I could've pulled this off without you, Holiday. I'm so grateful."

She's married to Lucas's older brother, Hudson. They met last year, and with some help from the magic of Merryville, fell madly in love. Emma always talks about how much she adores Hudson and his five-year-old son Colby. They're the perfect little family.

"Yeah," I say. Can't say I love the circumstances that brought me back, but I'm happy to be useful to someone. "Hudson's mama wouldn't have let you fail. Neither would his cookie queen champion of a grandmother. Jake and Claire would've helped you, too."

I give her a smile. Jake is the middle Jolly brother who's marrying her sister Claire the weekend of Thanksgiving. I grew up with all the Jollys. Lucas was my twin brother Sammy's best friend first, but it quickly became the three of us.

Lucas is the same man who never wants to see my face again.

After all these years, I'd hoped he'd at least be indifferent. But indifference would require him to stop caring about what happened when we were eighteen. If I've learned anything, it's that Lucas Jolly holds grudges like his actual life depends on it.

He will never forgive me, and I accepted that a long time ago.

"Are you nervous about today?" Emma asks, her red glitter headband sparkling under the lights.

"No. I was born for this. I managed one of the greatest bakeries in Paris, which employed world-renowned pastry chefs.

I competed professionally and baked with the best. Tree season doesn't intimidate me."

I straighten cookies in the glass case, breathing in sugar and butter and the hint of peppermint. The smell is full of nostalgia and reminds me of being young and in culinary school. That was the last time my life felt like it was mine. Before everything got complicated and out of control.

The door jingles, and Mrs. Edna Parker walks in with her two sisters, Melinda and Brenda. The official Merryville Gossip Squad are wearing matching sweaters with sparkly reindeer.

"Holiday," Edna announces, leaning across the counter, glancing at my left hand. At one point, there was a big shiny ring on it. Not anymore. All that's left is a tan line where it was. "Welcome home. It's been far too long, honey."

"Thanks, Mrs. Parker."

She was my middle school home economics teacher, the one who helped me realize how much I loved to bake. At thirteen, I'd won the pie contest at the county fair. I still have the trophy.

Brenda leans over and points at a cookie through the glass. "What do you call these? They look too pretty to eat."

I laugh. "Cranberry star windows." I slide the case open. "They taste like snow days and good life choices. With coffee, it's an experience."

Melinda makes a clicking sound with her tongue. "I usually like a simple sugar cookie with sprinkles."

"Live a little. I'll let you try one," I say, because my pastries are like a drug. Once the sugar touches their tongue, the brain instantly wants more.

"Me too," both of her sisters say, and Edna laughs, knowing where this is leading.

"Why did you laugh?" Brenda asks Edna.

She chuckles again. "Holiday has a special skill. One taste is all it takes."

"I should make that my personal slogan," I say with a smirk. It's true, especially when it comes to men.

The sisters each take a bite, chew, and swallow. Their eyes widen.

"I've eaten so many of Holiday's cookies while we worked on the menu," Emma says from the chair behind me, "I think when the babies come, they'll call her mama."

I snort. "I'll cater their first birthday party."

"I'm going to hold you to that," Emma says. "Edna is my witness."

"I heard it," my old teacher confirms.

Once the cookie is gone, the three sisters pull out their credit cards and each asks for a dozen.

I sigh. "Wow, looks like I only have ten dozen left of these for the rest of the day."

"I'll take them all," they say in unison.

"We can split them," Edna explains. "Down the middle."

They nod, and I load every star window cookie into three large boxes. All that's left is powdered sugar and crumbs.

When they leave, Emma's shocked. "How did you do that?"

"Not to be cocky, but I'm good at what I do. You said as soon as everything was sold out, I could go home. I give it an hour."

Emma gasps. "No way. You baked five hundred cookies."

"I did. And they just bought one hundred fifty-six of them. Five minutes and word will spread. Edna will give every kid she sees a cookie. Just watch." I lean against the counter, my eyes on an analog clock with candy cane arms above the door.

At the four-minute mark, a line forms at the counter.

Bethany comes out from the back, eyes wide. "Um. Where did all those cookies go?"

My sixteen-year-old niece—my older sister Tricia's daughter—is doing half days here for school job credit. With a thirteen-year age gap between me and my sister, Bethany feels more like a little sister than a niece.

"Sold 'em," I tell her. "Run the register, just like I taught you. I'll box orders."

"Okay," she says, still looking confused. It's her first real job, and I'm trying not to be too militant even though professionalism has been drilled into me. I want her to have fun and learn what it takes to grow a start-up.

For thirty minutes, I place dozens of cookies into boxes until we sell out completely. The line is out the door, but all that's left are crumbs.

I clear my throat. "Okay, everyone, I'm sorry! We're sold out for the day. You'll have to come back tomorrow at nine when we open."

The groans are loud.

"We'll have a new menu, too. Once they're gone, they're gone for good!" I say.

I move everyone out of the shop and lock the door. I flip the sign over to "Sold Out."

"I don't know what to say. You just sold five hundred cookies in an hour. That's…unheard of," Emma says.

"Isn't that incredible?" I grin. "I think we need to triple our amount. While it seems like a lot, there are hundreds of people who visit the farm throughout the season. You couldn't have picked a better location, but you might want to consider getting two more ovens. Bethany, Bella, and Wendy can handle it this season."

"Okay." She opens the register and pulls out the money we earned for the day. "This is for you."

"What? Absolutely not."

"Yes, because you're going to be busting your ass for two months to keep up with this demand," she says.

"No. I'd do this for free," I tell her, not taking the cash. "Become a sensation and sell out every day, then we expand in town, then worldwide."

Emma blinks at me. "How are you so good at this?"

Bethany laughs. "She worked in Paris at a fancy-schmancy luxury bakery. For, like, over a decade!"

I roll my eyes. "That's enough. I swear, I'll tell your parents you snuck out last week to be with Trent."

"Oh, please don't. My mom will kill me."

I give her a smile. "I'm not a snitch. Use protection."

"We're not doin' it. We're just friends," she says with a laugh and removes her apron.

"Yeah, I know how that is," I say, the comment going over everyone's heads, thankfully.

"Hudson is here to get me," Emma says, standing carefully, one hand on her lower back.

"Are you feeling okay?" I ask.

"Just tired. The twins are heavy." She gives me a hug. "We sold out! Every single cookie on day one! Thank you."

"Tomorrow we'll triple the batch," I tell her.

"You're amazing. Lock up when you're done?"

"Of course."

Bethany grabs her backpack. "I'm gonna head to school."

"How many hours did you work this week while we were prepping?" I ask.

"Eighteen. I'm below my twenty-hour limit."

"Perfect. See you Monday?"

"Yep!" She waves and follows Emma out.

I watch them leave. Emma moves toward Hudson's truck, and Bethany strolls to her car, already on her phone.

The shop is quiet now. It's just me and the Christmas music and the smell of sugar.

I start cleaning up, boxing the leftover supplies, and wiping down counters. The rhythm is soothing, familiar. This, I can control.

As I walk into the kitchen to grab the broom, the bell over the front door jingles.

"We're sold out!" I holler, turning around. "Sorry, you'll have—"

A cold draft drifts over my skin, and the air changes when I meet Lucas Jolly's green eyes. After all this time, my body still recognizes him before my brain catches up.

He's taller and more muscular than I remember. Time has been annoyingly kind to him. A wool hat is pulled low on his head, and messy dark hair sticks out from underneath. His flannel shirt is open over a thermal that stretches across his chest. Stubble sprinkles across his chiseled jaw.

He looks like a lumberjack who'd rather chop me down than talk to me.

His eyes move over the bakery like he's assessing a problem he plans to solve with an axe.

I straighten my spine. "We're closed."

"Good thing I don't want cookies." His voice is rough and cold. He still doesn't look at me. Just scans around me like I'm part of the furniture.

"Then what do you want, Lucas?"

"I want to know why the hell you're here."

My jaw clenches. "Emma hired me."

"I know that. I'm asking why you took the fucking job." Now his eyes land on me and I nearly freeze in place. They're stormy green, wild as a West Texas sky right before it hails. "You had no problem leaving Merryville behind and pretending like nothing here exists. Why come back now?"

The words hit like a slap. "That's none of your damn business, is it?"

"It is when you're working on *my* family's property." He takes a step closer. "So, I'll ask again. Why are you here, Holiday?"

"Because I want to be. Oh, that makes you mad?" I'm being overly sarcastic. "Boo-hoo. Get over it, Jolly."

He narrows his cold eyes at me. "How'd Paris work out for you? How's your famous fiancé? Oh, wait."

I hate that he knows. Hate that everyone in this town knows my engagement fell apart. Small towns don't keep secrets.

"You can go fuck yourself," I snap.

"Trust me when I say I don't have to. Plenty of women are lined up."

I sarcastically clap my hands. "Good for you. Now, are you finished throwing a Jolly little tantrum? Because I'm not going *anywhere*."

"We'll see about that. You always run."

The air between us crackles. I want to throw something at him. Want to scream. Want to grab him by that stupid flannel and—

I don't dare to finish that thought.

"Get out," I say instead. "As much as you want to control everything, you don't get a say in what I do." I move toward the door, ready to physically remove him if I need to.

"Don't you dare touch me." He backs away like I've got the plague.

The rejection stings more than it should.

"Trust me, touching you is the last thing I'd ever want to do." The lie tastes bitter.

Because even now, even with all this anger boiling between us, I notice things I shouldn't. Like the way his thermal pulls tight across his shoulders. The veins in his hands. The sharp line of his jaw beneath that scruff.

I *hate* that I notice.

"Good. Keep it that way." He turns toward the door, then pauses. Looks back at me with an expression that's full of disgust. "Do us both a favor and stay out of my way this season."

"Gladly. I'd rather choke on candy canes."

"Wish you would."

I scoff as he walks out. The door slams and the bell crashes against it.

I stand there, frozen, watching him disappear into the crowd of customers. His stride is confident, cocky, and the asshole doesn't look back.

And the worst part? Some stupid, traitorous part of me wanted him to.

I lean against the counter and close my eyes.

Fifteen years since that summer after graduation. Since our secret nights together, since I left for culinary school, and he stopped answering my calls. Fifteen years, and he still looks at me like I'm the one who ruined everything.

Maybe I did. I was young and stupid.

I push off the counter and finish cleaning. The faster I'm done, the faster I can go home and pretend today didn't happen.

Merryville may sparkle like Christmas all year, but when I'm around Lucas Jolly, my surroundings go cold as ice. And this is just day one of the season.

CHAPTER 2

LUCAS

The first day of tree season is always hectic as hell.

By noon, the parking lot is packed with families, kids running between the rows of trees, and parents arguing over which one is perfect. The sound of chain saws fills the air, mixed with Christmas music blasting from speakers mounted around the property. This year, the snack stand started serving extra-large funnel cakes and large hot cocoas in red cups.

I'm in the back field with Jake, both of us cutting down precut stock to refill the tents up front. The physical work helps keep my mind busy. I love the sound of the saw roaring while wood chips fly. Sweat drips down my back, despite the fifty-degree weather.

But even this doesn't drown out my thoughts completely.

Holiday sold out this morning. Five hundred cookies in an hour. I heard my cousin Matteo mention it to one of the guys and noted the awe in his voice like she'd done something incredible. That's how everyone in Merryville has always treated Holiday, like she's special.

She's already making people remember why they love her so much. Reminding people why they want things they shouldn't have. Making them forget she's the kind of person who makes promises she doesn't keep.

"You good?" Jake asks during a water break, eyeing me like he knows something's up.

"Yeah. Why?"

"Because you've cut down ten trees in the time it took me to do five." He wipes his forehead with his sleeve. "What's going on?"

"Nothing. Just want to stay ahead of the rush."

"Right." He doesn't believe me. "This have anything to do with Holiday working at the cookie shop?"

I grip the chain saw tighter. "Absolutely not."

"Lucas—"

"Drop it, Jake."

He holds up his hands. "Okay. But you've been in a shit mood and it's pretty obvious why."

I don't respond. I just crank the chain saw again and get back to work.

But he's right. I am in a shit mood because she's here. She's running my sister-in-law's bakery, making cookies, smiling at customers, and acting like she belongs.

She doesn't belong anywhere close to me.

She left. She *chose* to leave. And now she's back like she didn't burn everything down on her way out.

"You wanna talk about it?" Jake asks when we load another batch of trees onto the trailer.

"Nothing to talk about. I'm fine."

"You're really not." Jake leans against the trailer. "Look, I don't know what happened between you two back in the day, but—"

"Then don't ask."

"Fair enough." He grabs his water bottle. "But whatever it is, you gotta find another way to deal with it. She's working here all season. You can't avoid her forever."

"Watch me."

Jake just shakes his head. "Claire and I are grabbing dinner tonight to chat about wedding stuff, if you want to join."

"Can't. Meeting Sammy for a drink."

"At Moonshiners?"

"Yeah."

"All right. Don't do anything stupid."

I flip him off, and he laughs before heading toward the main lot.

I stay in the back field until the sun starts to set, cutting trees until my arms ache and my head's finally quiet. By the time I head home to shower and change, I'm exhausted.

But it's the good kind. The kind that comes from honest work.

The kind that makes me forget, for a few hours, that Holiday Patterson exists and she's back in Merryville.

At eight, I drive to town to meet Sammy at Moonshiners.

The bar is packed, but I expected that. It's Friday night, the first weekend of tree season, and everyone in town is celebrating. Moonshiners is the only real bar in downtown Merryville, and it shows. The place is all dark wood, and Christmas lights are strung along the walls year-round. Garland wraps around the bar, wreaths hang in the windows, and there's a massive tree in the corner decorated with ornaments from local businesses. A neon sign behind the bar reads "Shine Bright" in red and green.

The live band is set up on a small stage in the back, playing covers of country songs. The dance floor is full of couples, and every table is occupied. The energy is high, and loud conversations mix with music and laughter. I find two empty stools at the end of the bar and order a Shiner.

"Long day?" the bartender asks. His name's Mike and he's been working here since I was old enough to drink.

"You have no idea," I tell him.

"First day was good?"

"Great. Busy as hell," I say, already feeling sore from the manual labor.

"That's what I like to hear." He slides my beer across the bar. "This one's on the house."

"Appreciate it," I say.

Sammy shows up twenty minutes later, grinning. "There's my favorite lumberjack."

"Shut the hell up," I say, finishing my first beer.

He slides onto the stool next to me and orders us a round. The bottles are set in front of us.

"How was day one?" he asks.

"Exhausting, but we broke last year's first day record. I couldn't believe it."

"I heard about the bakery selling out, too."

I take a long pull of my beer. "Yeah. Don't care about that."

Sammy laughs, but there's an edge to it. "Lucas. Come on. You both need to get over this thing between you two."

I signal Mike for another beer. "Nope. Don't have to tolerate her anymore."

"I'm still trying to figure out what the hell happened between you two." He leans forward. "I know something went down that Christmas when she came home from culinary school."

"Told you. She's a bitch. Don't want to be friends with liars. Your twin sister is a piece of shit. Glad you're not."

He studies me for a long moment, then sighs. "I wish we could go back to how things were when we were kids."

"Oh, that will never happen again," I say. "Don't count on it."

We drink in silence for a few minutes, watching the band. They're doing a decent cover of a George Strait song. My eyes scan across the room, and then I freeze.

Holiday's in a corner booth toward the back. And she's not alone.

Theo Williams is sitting across from her, leaning in close,

saying something that makes her laugh. Theo Williams was the star quarterback in high school and class president. The guy every girl wanted, including Holiday. I remember her talking about him back when we were teenagers. How excited she was when he asked her to prom.

She went with him instead of me.

And now, fifteen years later, here they are again.

She's wearing a black dress that shows cleavage. Her light brown hair is down, falling in soft waves over her shoulders. There's a gold necklace around her throat that catches the light every time she moves. She looks polished and expensive and like she doesn't belong in a small-town bar.

She looks like Paris. Like the life she chose over me.

And it makes me want to break something.

"Is that—" Sammy starts.

"Speak of the devil," I mutter, trying to ignore this.

"Wow. Didn't know they kept in touch," he says in a hushed tone. "Fuck that guy."

"She probably will."

Sammy gives me a look but doesn't comment. We both know Holiday's never single for long. She jumps from one relationship to the next, always looking for something better, never satisfied with what she has.

I try to focus on my drink, on the band, on anything but the corner booth and the way she laughs. But I can't.

Because she's home. In Merryville. Taking up space at my hangouts.

"Two shots of tequila," I tell Mike.

He pours them, and I slide one toward Sammy.

"Don't you gotta get up early?" Sammy asks.

"Yeah," I say, lifting the shot to my lips.

That's when Holiday's eyes finally find mine across the bar.

Our gazes lock. The music fades. The noise dims. It's just her looking at me and me looking at her.

That pretty smile on her face fades and her whole body tenses.

Good. I hope I ruin her entire night.

I take the shot, never breaking eye contact, making sure she knows exactly how I feel about her being here.

She is unwelcome and unwanted. A problem I want gone.

"You okay, man?" Sammy asks.

"Perfect."

I'm not. I'm a few beers and a shot in and watching Holiday squirm under my microscope.

A blonde appears at the bar next to me, flagging down Mike. She's pretty, in her midtwenties, and dressed like she's not from around here because she's not. As soon as the calendar flips to November, tourists come to Merryville. It's a magical holiday experience that a person can't get anywhere else in the world.

She glances over at me and smiles. "Oh, aren't you that guy from the tree farm?"

"Sure am," I say.

"I remember you." She orders a drink and turns to face me fully. "I'm Becca."

"Lucas Jolly." I shake her hand, but my eyes drift back to Holiday's booth.

"Jolly? Your family owns the farm?" Becca asks, scooting closer to me.

Holiday's zeroed in on me now, trying to pretend she's not, but I know better.

I give Becca my full attention. "What brings you to Merryville?"

"My sister used to follow Emma Manchester, well, Jolly now, on Instagram. The farm was on her bucket list." She takes a sip of her drink. "I think I just added something to mine."

"Mm," I say, holding back a smile.

I can practically feel the heat of Holiday's stare from across the bar.

"So, do you always hang out here on Friday nights?" Becca asks, playing with her hair.

"Sometimes." I smile at her.

Sammy clears his throat next to me. I ignore him.

Becca finishes her drink and glances toward the dance floor where couples are swaying to the band. "You want to dance?"

"You know how to two-step? This is Texas, darlin'."

"I'm a fast learner." Becca blushes as I stand, taking her hand and pulling her to the dance floor with me.

I can see Holiday in my peripheral vision. She's gripping her drink so tight her knuckles are white. She's not even pretending to listen to Theo anymore.

The band plays something slow. I put my hand on Becca's waist, and she moves closer, her arms looping around my neck. But I'm not looking at her.

I'm looking directly at Holiday. Our eyes lock across the dance floor, and I watch anger flash in her eyes. Watch her entire body go rigid.

I pull Becca closer, my hand sliding lower on her waist.

"You're a really good dancer," Becca says, her breath warm against my neck.

"Thanks." I barely hear her.

Becca leans in, saying something about the farm, about the trees, about how romantic it all is. I tilt my head down like I'm hanging on every word. Like whatever she's saying is the most fascinating thing I've ever heard.

Holiday's jaw clenches so tight I can see it from here.

I smile at Holiday and lean down to whisper in Becca's ear. "You having a good time?"

"The best," she says, giggling, her fingers playing with the back of my hair.

Holiday looks like she's having the *worst* time, which only makes me happy.

This is *perfect*.

She chose to come back here and invade my space. Now she's watching my every move like I'm the bother.

The song changes to something more upbeat. Becca keeps moving with me, clearly enjoying herself, oblivious to the silent war happening across the room.

I can see every microexpression on Holiday's face. Her nostrils flare, and she's biting the inside of her cheek. Theo's talking to her, but I know she hasn't heard a single word.

I spin Becca, pull her back in, and dip her.

The joy I feel seeing Holiday's scowl should be illegal.

After the second song, I lean down to Becca's ear. "I'll be right back. Gotta hit the restroom."

"Sure!" She touches my chest. "Hurry back."

"Won't be long."

I head toward the hallway where the bathrooms are, deliberately walking close to Holiday's table. I don't look at her or acknowledge her existence.

But I know she's watching. She always is. She's never been able to help herself.

The hallway is dimmer and quieter than the main bar. Christmas lights are strung along the walls, casting everything in a warm glow. I push open the bathroom door and suck in a deep breath, feeling the weird energy in the room.

What the hell am I doing?

I stare at my reflection. My jaw is tight. My eyes are hard. I look like I'm ready for a fight.

Maybe I am.

I'm about to head back out when the door slams open behind me.

Holiday storms in, locks the door, and stands in front of me, blocking the exit.

"Real fucking mature," she snaps.

I catch myself, smirking. "Wrong bathroom, *Peaches*."

She glares at me and time stands still.

"Don't call me that," she says between gritted teeth.

I straighten up, knowing I'm under her skin. "You got a problem?"

"You're trying to ruin my night."

"You don't know shit about me, Holiday, or what I'm trying to do. Don't pretend like you do." I cross my arms.

"Oh, I know you better than you think," she says, stepping closer.

"What's this about?" I lean back against the counter. "You jealous or something?"

"Jealous? I should warn the poor girl."

This makes me laugh. "I'm not the red flag. You are."

"Fuck you," she whispers.

"Actually, fuck *you*," I counter.

She shakes her head. "You started this. You kept looking at me—"

"It's a small bar, Holiday. Don't flatter yourself."

Her eyes flash with anger. "You're such an asshole."

"I'd rather be an asshole than be pathetic. Over a decade later, and you're still recycling old crushes." I laugh in her face, taking steps forward. She backs up, blocking the door, not letting me leave. "You've always been like this. Always wanting what you can't have. Always looking at me when you're with someone else."

Her breathing picks up. "I don't want you."

"No?" I let my nose brush against hers. "I remember you dating someone else and you trying to fuck me. What's changed?"

"Shut up," she seethes.

"Make me."

Her hands come up to my chest, fisting in my shirt, but she's not pushing me away. She's holding on. And I see that look in her eyes, the one that says she wants this.

I lean in, my mouth hovering over hers. We're so close I can feel her breath on my lips.

Her eyes flutter closed. Her mouth parts.

She's going to let me kiss her, and I move a little closer before pulling back. Sarcastic laughter falls out of my mouth.

Her eyes snap open with confusion, followed by fury.

"Proof you're pathetic," I say, still smirking. "You really thought I would kiss you?"

Anger takes over her face.

"You're a—"

"Asshole, right? Might want to get a better catchphrase. Asshole is getting boring." I step back. "So glad I'm not desperate."

"I'm not des—"

"Poor Theo. He's always been second best, hasn't he?"

She places her hands on her hips. "Get out of my way."

"Oh, now you want to run away. Typical. Thanks for proving my point." I reach for the door. "Go back to your date. Maybe if you focus hard enough, you can pretend it's not me you're thinking about."

"Go to hell, Lucas."

"Oh, I'm already there." I unlock the door and walk out, leaving her standing there alone.

My heart is racing, but I'm smiling because she desperately wanted it. She would've let me kiss her. And she knows I know.

Everything I said to her is true.

I head back to the bar wearing a cocky smirk. Becca's waiting for me, but I tell her I need to leave because I have work early in the morning.

She's disappointed but gives me her number. I take it, knowing I'll never call.

After I tell Sammy I'm leaving, I pay our tab. Holiday returns to her seat next to Theo. Her face is red. I catch her eye one more time and raise my half-full beer to her in a mock toast.

Holiday's eyes narrow.

"Shit, she looks pissed," Sammy says with his eyes wide.

"I'm sure she is," I tell him with a grin. "Gotta go."

I walk out into the cold November night and text Jake to

come pick me up because I drank too much. As I go to my truck to wait for him, I think about Holiday.

She's still the same girl who can't figure out what she wants. Still desperate for attention. Still looking for something she'll never find. And I *hate* her for it.

I hate that she came back.

Hate that she's working on my family's farm.

Hate how her blue eyes still sparkle for me.

I want her gone, and I'll do whatever it takes to make her leave.

Fuck Holiday Patterson.

CHAPTER 3

HOLIDAY

I wake up at three with my heart racing and my sheets twisted around my legs. My skin is too hot, my breathing too fast, and the dream is still clinging to me like smoke.

Lucas. Three days ago, in the bathroom at Moonshiners. But in the dream, he didn't pull away. He didn't laugh in my face and call me pathetic. Instead, his mouth crashed into mine. His hands were in my hair, pulling me closer, and when he whispered my name against my neck, it wasn't infused with hatred. It sounded like the way he used to say it—back when we were eighteen and stupid and I made promises I couldn't keep.

I throw the covers off and stumble to the bathroom, splashing cold water on my face. In the mirror, my cheeks are flushed, my pupils are dilated, and my lips are parted like I can still feel the ghost of a kiss that never happened.

"Get it together," I nearly growl at my reflection. That might've been three days ago, but I can't stop thinking about how close we were. How he smelled and how his hot breath felt against my skin. For one second—one horrible but perfect second—I thought he was actually going to kiss me.

And I would've let him.

Ugh! I shake my head.

I would've let him, and that makes me angrier than anything he said.

I dress, layering on clothes. I put on black leggings and an oversized candy cane striped sweater, then I pull my hair back in a braid. I need to be at the bakery by four if I want to triple my output. My parents are still asleep when I grab my keys and head out into the freezing predawn darkness.

The drive to the farm is short, but I keep the window cracked, letting the forty-degree air slap me awake. The sky is still black, stars scattered and sparkling like sugar crystals across velvet. My headlights cut through the darkness as I turn onto the long gravel driveway that leads to Jolly Christmas Tree Farm.

Even at this hour, the place is beautiful. Thousands of white lights are strung through the trees, twinkling like something out of a fairy tale. A giant inflatable Santa waves in the wind near the entrance. The main building—a massive log cabin that's used as a gift shop—sits in the center, decorated with wreaths and garland.

It looks magical…romantic, even, which only makes me want to be a big ole Scrooge. Because this is Lucas's world. His family's legacy. And I'm just the girl who came back when she had nowhere else to go. At least that's what he thinks.

I park in front of the cookie shop and unlock the door, flipping on lights as I enter. The space smells like yesterday's baking, and for a moment, I let myself breathe it in.

This, at least, I'm good at. And no one can deny that.

I brew a pot of coffee—the strong stuff—and pull out my notebook. Emma and I planned a rotating menu, different cookies each day so people keep coming back. Today it's snowmen and gingerbread reindeer.

I throw myself into work, mixing dough, rolling it out, and cutting shapes. The repetitive motions are soothing. Measure, mix, bake, cool, decorate. Over and over as my hands move on autopilot.

But I can't stop thinking about Lucas and how he looked at me on Friday night—like he hated me but couldn't stop staring. The way his body felt pressed against mine in that tiny bathroom haunts me. He leaned in so close I could taste his breath.

And then he laughed in my face, called me pathetic, and walked away like I was nothing.

My hands shake as I pipe icing onto a snowman cookie, and I have to stop, take a breath, and remind myself that I don't care. I don't care what Lucas Jolly thinks of me. I don't care that he still looks at me like he wants to ruin my life as much as I ruined his.

Truthfully, I didn't ruin shit. I left Merryville. People leave. That's what happens when you're eighteen and the world is bigger than a small town in Texas.

By the time Bethany arrives at seven, I've got a thousand snowmen cooling and another batch of gingerbread reindeer in the oven.

She's too cheerful for someone who has to work before school, bouncing through the door with her backpack and a box of decorations.

"Morning, Aunt Holiday!" She ties on her red and green apron, then studies me.

"You okay? You look…weird."

"Weird? Excuse me? Just focused."

"Right." She pulls garland and ornaments from the box. "We need to be shitting out Christmas spirit in here. We're on a tree farm!"

Before I can protest, she's stringing garland along the counter and hanging ornaments from the light fixtures. Then she pulls out several bunches of mistletoe.

"Absolutely not," I tell her.

"Come on! It's tradition."

"Bethany—"

"Already cleared it with Emma via text."

"She's on bed rest! Leave that woman alone."

"She said the bakery needs all the Christmas magic it can get." Bethany drags a chair over to hang mistletoe in the entryway. "Oh, I heard a rumor about you."

The icing bag explodes in my grip, spewing white frosting everywhere.

"What?"

"Small town, remember? People saw your car at Moonshiners on Friday. Who were you there with?" She grins. "Was Lucas there?"

"I'm not having this conversation with my sixteen-year-old niece."

"Was he?"

"Work on stocking the display case."

"Already on it!" she snaps.

At seven forty-five, the bell jingles. I tense, stupidly thinking it might be Lucas, but then I hear Sammy's voice and relax. He's wearing his firefighter uniform, a navy shirt and slacks, clearly about to start his shift.

"Want some coffee?" Bethany asks him.

"Please tell me it's the strong stuff," he says, pushing through the swinging door of the kitchen.

The look on his face tells me this isn't a social visit.

"What?" I ask, already defensive.

"What did you say to Lucas on Friday?"

"I knew it!" Bethany calls from the front.

I glare at my brother. "What are you talking about?"

"Don't play dumb. I know you two talked. What happened?"

"I told him to leave me alone."

"Holiday." His voice gets serious. It's the big brother voice he's used on me our whole lives since he's a minute older. "I'll tell you what I told him. This has to stop. He's been in a shit mood since you got back, and after going to Moonshiners, he's been worse than ever."

My stomach flips. "That's not my problem or my fault."

"You can't pretend like you don't care," he says.

"I don't. I really don't. I want him to leave me alone. It's that simple."

Bethany soaks up the entire conversation.

Sammy crosses his arms, looking so much like our dad in this moment, it's unnerving. "You're both acting like children, and I'm stuck in the middle. He's my best friend, you're my twin sister, and I don't want to have to choose anymore."

"No one's asking you to do that."

"Aren't you? Because I can't mention him without you shutting down, and I can't mention you without him losing his shit." He grabs a cookie from the cooling rack. "I just want things to be like they used to be. When we could all hang out without this...whatever this is."

I set down the piping bag and look at him.

He has no idea what he's asking for. No idea what happened that summer after graduation. What happened when I came home that Christmas.

"That can never happen, Sammy."

"Funny, that's the only thing you two can agree on," he says.

Bethany's eyes widen from the doorway, and I lower my voice. "Things changed. People changed."

"But you're still you, he's still him—"

"No." The word comes out harsher than I intend. "The three of us hanging out, laughing, and being friends are gone. It's been gone for years, and I'm sorry, but that's never coming back."

"Holiday—"

"I mean it. You can't fix this. He's an asshole, and I won't put up with his bullshit. He's not a kind person." I pick up the piping bag again and focus on the cookies because it's easier than looking at his face. "Keep us separate. It's better that way."

Sammy shakes his head, disappointment written all over his

face. "Fine. But you should know—being on this side of it is exhausting. And tree season just started."

He heads for the door, then pauses. "You think you have this under control. You don't."

After he leaves, I try to push his words away. But they stick—just like the memory of Lucas backing me against that bathroom door. Just like the dream I woke up from this morning.

The morning rush is crazier than it was over the weekend. By eleven, we're completely sold out. There was already a line of people waiting when I opened the doors at nine.

Bethany heads to school, and I spend the afternoon prepping for tomorrow. Mixing dough, cutting shapes, getting ahead. My back aches, my feet throb, but I push through. This is what I do. This is what I'm good at.

By the time the sun sets, I've prepped enough for two full days. My eyes are burning with exhaustion when I finally lock up and head to my car.

The parking lot is mostly empty with just my car in front of the bakery and Lucas's truck parked by the equipment shed near the gift shop. He's probably doing inventory or maintenance. He and his brothers take care of the endless jobs that keep a place like this running so smoothly. They're good at what they do.

I don't let myself think about how he used to text me when he was working late. How we'd sneak off to the barn and—

No. That was a lifetime ago.

I climb into my car and press the start button, but nothing happens.

"No, no, no." I try again.

I rest my forehead against the steering wheel, too exhausted to deal with this.

I could call my parents, but they're probably already in bed. Sammy, too. Everyone I know is settling in for the night because normal people don't work eighteen-hour days.

I glance at Lucas's truck and realize I'd rather walk the two miles home than ask him for help.

It's dark now, the temperature is dropping fast, and I'm wearing the wrong shoes for this, but I make my way across the parking lot. I'll manage because I always do.

I barely make it to the gravel driveway before I hear his truck rumble to life. Headlights flick on, and he drives past me without slowing down. Doesn't even look at me.

Good. I don't need his help anyway.

I keep walking, my breath fogging in the cold air. There's a trail that cuts behind his grandmother's house that I've taken a hundred times when we were teenagers. Back when we'd meet up to ride horses or sneak off to just be together. Back when he treated me like I mattered.

I turn on my phone's flashlight and keep walking, ignoring the way my feet already hurt, ignoring the cold seeping through my sweater.

Five minutes later, headlights appear in front of me.

His truck slows, and he rolls down the passenger window.

"What are you doing?" His voice is flat, annoyed.

"Walking home."

"Why?"

"I dunno. Thought I'd get some exercise after working eighteen hours. It's such a beautiful night." I keep walking, picking up my pace even though my legs are screaming.

He sighs. "Get in."

"No."

"Holiday—"

"Hell. No." I stop at his window, glaring at him through the open space. "No way I'm going to owe you one."

He gives me that fake, bitter laugh that's always pissed me off. "It's dark, you're exhausted, and you have to be back here in seven hours. Get in the truck."

"Not happening."

"You're being stubborn."

"And you're being an asshole. Nothing new."

"I'm gonna give you ten seconds, then I'm leaving your ass here." He starts counting. "Ten."

"You're so predictable," I snap.

"Nine. All you want to do is push my buttons."

"Eight," I say before he can. "And all you want to do is be rude."

He puts the truck in park and stares at me. "Get in. Last thing you need is to get sick. Who'd be your replacement? You're it. That's the last thing Emma needs."

The wind blows harder, tossing my hair across my face. A shiver runs through me.

"Fine. But know it's not because I want to, but because of Emma."

He rolls his eyes as I yank open the door and climb in. I'm hit by the smell of him. Pine and sawdust and that cologne he's always worn, the one that used to make me dizzy when we were pressed together in the dark.

He doesn't speak. Just drives back to the parking lot in silence.

The truck cab feels too small, and the air nearly chokes me. It's so thick. I stare out the window, hyperaware of every breath he takes, every shift of his hands on the wheel.

Being this close to him, remembering how it used to feel is pure torture.

He pulls up next to my car and gets out without a word, grabbing jumper cables from the back seat. I watch through the windshield as he pops both hoods, his movements efficient and familiar. He's helped people with dead batteries, fixed broken equipment, and kept this farm running.

He holds his palm open, and I hand him my key through the window. He climbs into my driver's seat, door open, and presses the start button. The engine struggles, then catches.

I get out of the truck and move toward him. "Thank you."

He doesn't respond. Doesn't even look at me as he slides out of my car. He unhooks the cables, drops my hood with more force than necessary, and walks back to his truck.

No acknowledgment. No *You're welcome.* Nothing.

He gets in, slams the door, and drives away without a single glance in my direction.

I stand there in the cold, watching his taillights disappear down the driveway.

How did we become this? Two people who can't even manage a conversation.

He helped me because he's not heartless enough to leave me stranded. But he won't give me even the smallest kindness of a response.

Before I left for culinary school, he would've followed me home to make sure I made it safely. He would've checked my battery connections, told me to get it looked at in the morning. He would've cared. Now we're just strangers who happen to work on the same property.

Actually, we're a step below strangers.

I don't know the man he's become.

I don't want to.

I climb into my car, crank the heat, and drive home.

The entire way, I think about his silence and how it feels heavier than any words he could've said.

Tomorrow, I'll be back at the farm before sunrise, and he'll probably already be there with his chain saw and his scowl. We'll continue this dance of avoiding each other until Christmas.

How will either of us survive the season?

By choice. By necessity. And by pretending that being near him doesn't still make my heart race the way it did when I was eighteen and stupid enough to believe we had a chance at forever.

CHAPTER 4

LUCAS

I'm standing outside the bakery an hour before it opens, and I can smell sugar seeping through the cracks. The scent pisses me off.

There was a time when Holiday and I planned to enter the annual Merryville cookie baking contest together. When we'd talk about sharing the trophy and taking turns keeping it at our houses. That was back when I believed we'd share a lot of things, before I learned her promises meant nothing.

Through the glass, Holiday places cookies in the display case like she's handling precious diamonds. Her brown hair is twisted into a messy bun. It's the way she used to wear it when we were teenagers. I used to reach up and tug it loose when we were alone in the barn.

I bury the memory down deep where it belongs.

The faint smell of cinnamon drifts in the cold morning air, mixing with fresh cut pine from the precut lot across the way. Frost clings to the windows and sparkles in the early sunlight. The whole scene looks like a damn Christmas card.

She smiles at something, probably herself, and I hate how she thinks she can waltz onto my family's farm like this. I told her to stay away from me. I will never, ever let her forget what she did.

Nine o'clock sharp, she flips the sign to Open and unlocks the door. "Silver Bells" plays from inside the shop. It's cheerful and bright, completely opposite of how I feel.

When she sees I'm first in line with twenty-five people behind me, her smile vanishes.

I love ruining her day as much as she's already ruined mine.

"What do you want, Lucas?" she asks through gritted teeth.

"Just in the mood for some sweets." I follow her inside, taking my time scanning the case. Peppermint bark brownies, butter cookies with icing, and sugar cookies shaped like Christmas trees. Behind her in the kitchen, I can see racks of more cookies cooling.

Bethany appears from the back, tying on her apron. "Lucas!" she says, actually excited to see me.

I give her a kind smile because it's not her fault her aunt sucks.

I shove my hands in my pockets. "I'll take everything."

"Excuse me?" Holiday's voice cracks.

"Every cookie. Every brownie. All of it. Whatever you have in the back, too." I pull out my card and tap it against the counter. "Ring it up."

Her face goes from confused to furious in three seconds flat. "You cannot be serious."

"Emma told me you get to leave when you sell out. I was serious when I said I want you gone." I smile, giving her the fake one I save just for her. "Start boxing it up, Peaches. Or should I call you HoHo?"

"Don't you dare call me either of those," she nearly growls.

The last one is the nickname I gave her when we were kids. The one I whispered against her neck in the dark. The one that used to make her laugh.

"Oh, it bothers you. Great, that's the only way I'll address you going forward."

The Christmas music switches to "Peace on Earth," and the irony isn't lost on me. There's no peace between us. There never will be.

"This is low, even for—"

"You refusing me service?"

Her jaw tightens so hard I think I can hear her teeth grinding. The muscles in her body tense.

The guy behind me groans. "Just ask for her number already. Damn."

"Lucas, hurry up," Janet Miller calls from six spots back.

Behind her, the line stretches out the door. I can already hear the complaints starting.

Holiday slams cookies into boxes, lids snapping shut like gunfire. Her movements are violent, angry. "Sorry, everyone. Lucas Jolly decided to selfishly buy everything."

"Everything?" Janet's face falls. "But I promised my book club I'd bring two dozen of your brownies—"

"Blame him. He bought everything." Holiday's voice is saccharine sweet, and her eyes throw deadly daggers at me. She smirks as the crowd behind me groans and glares. They look at me like I'm the villain.

But she's the bad guy. She always has been.

The grumbling gets louder and someone else mentions needing cookies for their kid's birthday party tomorrow.

"But," I say, raising my voice and turning to face the crowd, "I'm giving them away for free just for being on the farm today. Give me one second and we'll head to the picnic tables by the snack shack. There are plenty to go around. You can take as many as you want. My treat."

I turn back to Holiday. "How many did I buy?"

Her mouth is a tight line. "Twenty-five hundred."

That's more than I expected, but it makes the crowd erupt in cheers.

Holiday's face goes beet red, and I love this for her.

I lean in, speaking loud enough for her to hear. "Go away."

A VERY MERRY ENEMY

I can see dark flecks in her blue eyes.

"You wish," she says, rolling her eyes.

Twenty minutes later, every cookie is boxed. Guests help carry them outside.

Holiday stands behind the register, arms crossed, pissed. I haven't seen her this mad in a very long time.

"With your employee discount, it's two thousand, four hundred thirty-five dollars and sixty-three cents."

"That's it? Wow. Might have to do this every day of the season." I tap my card against the reader, not even flinching at the price. I've been working since I could drive, saved every penny. Money's one thing I have plenty of.

"Would you like a receipt?" she asks, voice unamused.

"Oh yes, please. Love a good tax write-off."

She rips the paper from the printer and tosses it at me. It floats through the air and I catch it before it hits the ground.

I chuckle. "Have a great day."

"Get. Out." Her voice is ice.

"Pleasure doing business with ya."

I help grab boxes of cookies and walk out. The door slams behind me hard enough to rattle the windows.

Outside, I place everything at the picnic tables near the snack shack. The giant inflatable Santa beside the gift shop waves in the wind like it approves of my plan.

Holiday stands at the bakery window, arms crossed over her chest.

A few people walk over to the bakery, see the Sold Out sign, and immediately start complaining.

I head inside the main gift shop, squeezing between customers browsing ornaments and wreaths. In the back office, I grab poster board from behind the door and a fat red marker from the top drawer.

I write Free Cookies in huge letters so no one misses out. I carry it outside and tape it to the picnic table. Within seconds, people swarm.

"Lucas, what's this?" Jerry Bradley asks as his kids snatch cookies from the boxes, comparing which ones taste better.

"Thought I'd spread some Christmas spirit today," I say, biting into one of Holiday's peppermint fudge brownies.

It's incredible. Chocolatey and sweet with the perfect texture. It's the kind of brownie that melts on your tongue. She's always been an incredible baker. But I make a face as if it tastes like reindeer shit and toss the rest in the trash.

I know she's watching, and that image will live rent-free in her head for weeks.

Today feels like a victory. I get to be the hero, handing out free cookies while she stews in her anger. As I move through the crowd, handing out boxes, I catch pieces of conversations.

"Who made these?"

"Holiday Patterson. She's back from Paris!"

"These are incredible. Where can I get more?"

"Right there at the cookie shop. The menu changes every day!"

"Holiday's a world-renowned pastry chef."

"We're coming back tomorrow. Early. Let's line up at seven."

My jaw clenches. By noon, there isn't a single crumb left. The quilting circle ladies walk past me, chirping about what a sweet man I am for promoting Holiday's pastries with so much passion.

I smile, but this is backfiring. I didn't do this to help her. I did this to piss her off.

My phone buzzes.

MATTEO

> Saw you gave away thousands of Holiday's cookies on Instagram! Are you two a thing, because if not...

LUCAS

> She's a red flag liar. But good luck with that. I did it for our customers. I don't give two fucks about her.

Another text comes in.

JAKE
> I just overheard someone say you were dating Holiday.

LUCAS
> HELL TO THE NO!!!!!!

I groan and glance at the bakery.

For the first time today, Holiday's not scowling. She's holding up a sign in the window, and I quickly read it.

Thanks for the free advertising, babe! Same time tomorrow? 🖤

The gossip gals of Merryville read the sign and immediately turn to me with smiles.

"Babe? Are you two dating?" Edna Parker asks. Now that she's retired, she's been hanging out at the farm with her sisters.

"Absolutely not," I snap.

Holiday blows me a kiss through the window.

For a second, I'm seventeen again. She's blowing me kisses across the lunchroom when no one's looking. Back when everything was simple. Back when I thought she might be mine.

Then I remember she's just trying to piss me off.

"Are you sure?" Edna presses. "You two used to be thick as thieves. You, her, and Sammy. We always thought you two would get married."

"We changed," I say through gritted teeth. "People change."

"That's a shame. You were good together."

I walk away before I say something I'll regret.

My jaw is clenched so tight it aches. I throw an extra chain saw and gas can in the back of a side-by-side, then drive to the back field to meet my cousins.

"Saw the pics of all those cookies," Dean says when I arrive. "Good on you for supporting Holiday. Guess you changed your mind?"

"No, I didn't. She can still fuck off."

"Yeah, now say it without that twinkle in your eye," Matteo adds, smirking.

I glare at him. "I can leave."

"Please don't," Dean says. "We're drowning back here."

I get to work, doing what I do best—cutting trees. The chain saw roars, drowning out my thoughts.

After I cut trees, I load them onto the lowboy trailer. We do this for over an hour, until my shoulders burn and my hands hurt even through work gloves.

By sunset, I'm exhausted. I make my evening rounds—checking that everyone has what they need, the equipment is stowed, and the gates are locked.

Then I notice her car still parked in front of the bakery. For a second, I wait to make sure it actually starts this time, and I won't need to save her ass again.

As if I summoned her, Holiday exits with boxes stacked in her arms. She's balancing them against her hip, nudging the door shut with her elbow. Her hair has come completely loose from the bun, falling in messy waves around her face.

Thankfully, she doesn't notice me standing by my truck.

I should look away. Should get in my truck, drive home, and stop letting her get under my skin.

But I don't.

I watch as she nearly drops a box, muttering something under her breath. The trunk won't open at first, and she has to set everything down and fumble with it.

She looks tired and frustrated.

Human.

Finally, she gets the trunk loaded and climbs into her car without looking back.

The cold settles into my bones. I slide into my truck and

crank the heat, sitting there as her taillights disappear down the driveway.

I really can't believe she's staying through the season. Or that I spent over two thousand four hundred dollars on cookies just to piss her off.

Holiday will lose this game.

Not me.

Not ever again.

But as I drive home, I can still taste that fudge brownie on my tongue. And I hate that it was the best damn pastry I've ever had.

CHAPTER 5

✻

HOLIDAY

I glance up at the candy cane clock on the wall and see that it's just past six in the morning. I've been at the bakery for two hours already, and I'm debating whether cookies can be used as weapons. Especially if Lucas tries to come in here and buy everything to ruin my day again.

My feet ache, my back is screaming, and I'm only halfway through prepping today's menu. When I told Emma I'd manage the bakery while she was on maternity leave, I knew that meant working seven and a half weeks straight without a day off.

Being busy is what I need, what I came back for. This job keeps my mind off Paris, off my failed engagement, and off the disaster my life became.

Last night, I barely slept because I couldn't stop thinking about how much I want to murder Lucas Jolly. I turn the Christmas music up and sing along like it's a cry for help. Mom used to say singing soothes the soul.

Today, I have two of Lucas's cousins helping me—Bella and Wendy. They're both in their midtwenties and work around the farm when needed. Bella is opening her own coffee shop and bookstore in town soon but has extra time to help Emma this season. I used to babysit the Jolly cousins when I was a teenager for extra money. Once the display case is full, I wipe my hands on my apron. Today, I'm prepared for the Great Cookie Massacre of Merryville, Round Two.

I grab a peppermint pinwheel from the cooling rack and bite into it. It burns my tongue, and I mutter swear words that would've gotten my mouth washed out with soap as a kid.

They're perfect and I know they'll fly out of here.

Hopefully not as fast as Lucas buying out my entire stock and handing out cookies like a sexy Santa Claus in designer denim.

I groan. The whole town won't shut up about it. Pictures were posted on the community Facebook page and the comments were all about how cute we are. Some said his stunt was romantic.

It wasn't. It was calculated and cruel. And the fact that it backfired and gave me free advertising doesn't change that he did it to piss me off. It worked.

He may have won yesterday's battle, but I will win the war this season.

My eyes sting from lack of sleep. My hair is still in whatever messy twist I threw it into this morning, and I haven't even looked in a mirror.

I walk to the front and add cookies to the case. I glance at the counter, replaying how Lucas leaned against it like he owned the place. I remember that cocky smirk when he said he'd buy everything. The way he called me Peaches and HoHo, knowing those nicknames would get under my skin.

I don't need a reminder of our past.

Ugh. Lucas Jolly can go straight to hell.

I scrub a mixing bowl harder than necessary, trying to focus on what's next on my to-do list.

Lucas isn't part of my life anymore. He's not even a friend. And after the stunt he pulled yesterday, I'm more convinced than ever that keeping him at a distance is the only way to survive this season. Or he might get his wish and really run me off.

The bell above the door jingles. I glance at the clock. Bella and Wendy aren't due for another twenty minutes.

"Coming!" I call out.

"It's just me!" Emma's voice, which is impossible because she's on bed rest.

I rush to the front, flour flying off my apron. It's not Emma, but her voice coming from Hudson's phone, held up for FaceTime.

"You could've just called me directly," I tell her, giving Hudson a smile. He's six years older than me, the oldest Jolly brother. He used to be the grumpiest, but it's clear Lucas has taken over that title.

"We were already chatting, so it was easier to just make Hudson walk over." Emma's propped up on approximately twelve pillows. "I want to be there."

"Let me show you what I made this morning." Hudson hands me his phone and follows me to the back. "This is what I have so far."

I pan the camera across racks of cooling cookies and the trays ready for the oven.

"That's way too much," Emma protests.

"I'm in charge," I remind her.

"You are, and I know you're completely capable of selling every single one," she says. "I miss being there. Miss the smell of baking cookies. Miss eating them fresh out of the oven."

I grab a box and load it with still-warm cookies. "Sending these home with Hudson."

"Speaking of..." Hudson clears his throat. "I should do that before Emma decides she needs to inspect the tree lot, too."

"I heard that!" Emma says. "But fine. Holiday, you're doing amazing. Text me if you need anything."

"You know I won't."

She groans. "I know. But I can make phone calls and order supplies."

I laugh. "Thank you. Now rest. See you soon. Enjoy those cookies."

Hudson takes his phone and the box just as the bell rings again.

"Morning!" Bella chirps, way too cheerful for this early in the day. She's wearing a Jolly Christmas Tree Farm sweatshirt, and her hair is in a high ponytail.

I open the kitchen door for her. "Bella!"

"I go by B now."

"I'm not calling you that. You'll always be my little Bella-boo."

"I'm twenty-four now. Soon to be twenty-five." She rolls her eyes.

Hudson barely holds back his laugh as he leaves. "Bella-boo. Using that from now on."

Bella groans.

Wendy steps inside and slides an apron on. They both look just like all the other Jolly women, with dark hair and bright green eyes. They've both already tied on their aprons.

"Smells incredible in here," Wendy says.

I trained them both last month on bakery basics, since Bethany can't work more than twenty hours a week. Their little sister, Bristol, moved away for college or she would be here, too.

"Thanks for helping," I offer. "Very appreciated."

"Looking forward to it," Bella says. "I'm doin' recon for my coffee shop and bookstore."

I grin. "I'll invent special recipes for you."

Her eyes widen. "Really?"

"Of course. I love creating new things," I tell her, and she's instantly giddy.

As Wendy arranges cookies in the display case, Bella keeps sneaking glances at me.

"What?" I finally ask.

"Nothing," she says.

"Bella."

Wendy snorts. "She's been dying to ask you about Lucas since we got in the car."

"Seriously!" Bella scolds. "I told you to keep your mouth shut."

"What about Lucas?" I ask, my eyes narrowing.

Bella arranges chocolate peppermint cookies with intense focus. "The whole cookie thing yesterday. Everyone's talking about it."

"Of course they are." I grab more trays from the kitchen, slamming them down harder than necessary. "It's Merryville. People around here have nothing better to do than make up stories."

"It's just—" Bella exchanges a look with Wendy. "Lucas usually doesn't do grand gestures. That's not his style."

I laugh and it comes out bitter. "Trust me when I say, it wasn't a grand gesture. It was him being a vindictive asshole. He did it to hurt me, and everyone who thinks it's romantic is delusional."

"That's what I said!" Wendy pipes up. "But it is kinda romantic."

"It's not." I wipe down the counter with more force than needed. "He spent twenty-four hundred dollars just to piss me off. That's psychological warfare."

Not to mention, he chewed up my fudge brownie and then spit it out like there was something wrong with it. Dickhead!

"Potato, po-tah-to." Bella grins, clearly not taking me seriously. "Lucas buying out an entire bakery is pretty dramatic for someone who claims to hate you. That's a lot of money."

I stop wiping and look at her. "He does hate me. And the feeling is more than mutual. So everyone needs to stop shipping us like we're kids again. We're not."

"Does he hate you, though?" Bella pushes. "Because my

cousin doesn't have a hateful bone in his body. He's one of the sweetest guys I know."

Sarcastic laughter falls from my lips. "You clearly don't know him like I do. I deal with the worst versions of his personality. And he's made it very clear he wants me gone. Wanted me gone the moment I arrived."

"Not convinced." Bella pauses, and I can tell she's debating whether to say what's coming next. "Lucas hasn't dated anyone seriously since your engagement was announced."

My hand stills on the counter. "What?"

"It's true," Wendy confirms. "Half the women in Merryville have tried. He goes out with them for a few weeks, then dumps them. Mrs. Harold's daughter. That teacher from the elementary school. The new veterinarian threw herself at him last Christmas."

"Once news spread about you, he cycled through women like he was searching for something, then eventually gave up," Bella adds. "The family jokes that he's now married to the tree farm. This is his escape."

That's the real reason he hates me being here.

I force myself to focus on my task at hand, to keep my expression neutral. "Some people are better off being single."

My mind is racing. Why can't Lucas commit to anyone? Unless…

No. I'm not doing this. I'm not reading into it.

"Yeah. You know…" Bella leans against the counter. "It's like he's been waiting for something. Or someone."

"He needs a miracle," I snap, harsher than I mean to.

"I'm just saying, you're both sing—"

"Lucas and I will never be a thing. He literally hates me. Did you miss the part where he called me pathetic? Told me I was desperate? After everything I've been through. That's not the behavior of a man who's waiting for me. Putting us together was super cute when Lucas and I were teenagers. It's not anymore."

"Did you ever like him?" Wendy asks softly.

"No," I lie, my throat tight. "Conversation over. No more talking about him. Seriously. It puts me in a bad mood."

I grab tea lights from storage and place them around the bakery, hoping to brighten the mood. The morning is overcast, with gray clouds hanging low.

Bella looks like she's going to say something, but Wendy touches her arm. I pretend not to see because this conversation needs to end before I lose my cool. If they all saw how he treated and spoke to me, they'd realize we're dancing in hell together.

The bell above the door jingles.

"Positions, everyone," I announce, forcing brightness into my voice. "Let's sell some cookies."

As the morning rush begins, Bella's words circle in my head like vultures.

Lucas hasn't dated anyone seriously since your engagement was announced.

It doesn't mean anything. It can't.

He probably just hasn't found someone who's worth his time. He was always very picky when it came to women. Or maybe he really is married to the farm. Or maybe, and this is most likely, he's been too busy being an asshole and scaring everyone away.

"You good?" Wendy asks when there's a lull before the lunch rush.

"Yeah," I say, rearranging cookies. "I'm perfect."

But I'm not. Because now I'm angry at Bella for planting that seed about Lucas's love life. I'm angry at Lucas for just existing. Not to mention, I'm upset at myself for even caring whether he's dated or not.

None of it matters.

Not when he looks at me and calls me pathetic. He meant it with every part of his being. I saw it in his eyes.

Whatever we had is dead and buried and rotting.

And it has to stay that way.

Crossing the line with him ruined our friendship. I knew it would. If I could go back in time, I'd undo it all. I'd erase every memory of that summer to have him back. It's almost funny how every life regret I have includes him.

By the time we've sold out, I have flour in places flour should never be. But the register is full and that's all that matters.

"I'm never eating another cookie again," Wendy groans, wiping down the fingerprints on the windows.

"You said that last time we worked at the shop," Bella reminds her.

"Today, I mean it. My stomach hurts from eating so much sugar," she says.

I grab the broom and start sweeping, pushing crumbs toward the door with aggressive strokes. Through the window, Christmas lights on the tree lot are twinkling to life.

And then I see him.

Lucas is carrying a massive fir over his shoulder like it weighs nothing, muscles flexing beneath his red and black flannel. His jeans are worn and dusted with dirty work boots crunching through gravel.

He's smiling at the young couple following him. He gives them that easy, charming smile I always adored. The one that shows his little dimple.

I hate that I notice. Hate that my eyes track his movements across the lot. Hate that some traitorous part of my brain registers how good he looks.

"Busted."

I jump, nearly dropping the broom. Bella's standing in the kitchen doorway, arms crossed, smirking.

"I wasn't—"

"You were totally staring." She joins me at the window.

"I was not," I snap. "Just looking at the gift shop."

"Uh-huh. And that's why you were biting your lip?"

"I wasn't biting my—" I stop myself. "I'm not going to argue."

"Holiday." Her voice lowers. "You can admit he's attractive. It's not a crime. Everyone knows Lucas is hot. All of my friends tried to get with him. I've heard every disgusting thing a person could say about my cousin."

I sweep harder, the bristles scraping against the floor. "His attractiveness is irrelevant. His personality makes him ugly as fuck."

"He watches you, too." She pauses. "I caught him."

My head snaps up. "What?"

"When you're not looking. I've seen him standing out there, staring at the bakery." She shrugs. "Dean had to call his name three times yesterday to get his attention."

Something twists in my chest, something I have to ignore.

"He's probably just making sure I don't burn the place down," I say, emotionless. "Or planning his next move to piss me off."

"Or maybe he has a thing—"

"Whatever you're about to say, don't. Lucas made it very clear how he feels about me on Friday night. And yesterday. And every single day since I got back. So, I don't care if he watches the bakery. I don't care if he hasn't dated anyone. None of it matters."

Before she can respond, Wendy pokes her head out. "I'm done! Same time tomorrow?"

"Yeah. Thanks for today. You kicked ass."

"We made bank in tips," Bella says with a grin, deciding to drop it. "People are generous when they think they're part of a love story."

Never mind.

"I'm going to kick your ass," I say. "This little matchmaker thing you're trying to do won't work."

"If you say so." She grabs her coat and gives me an evil smirk. "See you tomorrow, HoHo."

The bell jingles as they leave, and then I'm alone with the half-swept floor and my thoughts.

Outside, Lucas is helping another family now, hoisting a little girl onto his shoulders so she can touch the top of a seven-foot tree. She squeals with delight, and he laughs. It's a real one, and it floats through the cold air.

He watches you, too.

I grip the broom handle tighter, my knuckles going white.

Of course, he watches the bakery, so he can figure out his next stunt to humiliate me. Or maybe watching me struggle or squirm gets him off. Whatever his reason, it's not romantic. It's not sweet. It's Lucas who's determined to make my life miserable. He'll do it, too.

We both know he's capable.

I force myself to look away and finish with the floor.

Seven and a half more weeks of his cousins trying to play matchmaker. Of the town gossiping about us. Of him finding new ways to get under my skin.

But what Lucas doesn't realize is that I'm no longer that timid teenager he knew so well.

I'm stronger and take less shit.

I can handle it. I survived falling apart in Paris. I survived my engagement ending. I survived living in my own personal hell. And I can survive Lucas Jolly and his petty little games.

When this season is over, I might leave Merryville for good. No looking back. No second thoughts. No letting anyone—especially not Lucas—make me question that decision.

I've applied at different bakeries in New York. Emma will give me a reference, and with her connections, I'm a shoo-in.

He'll get exactly what he wants.

And I'll try my best to forget every memory I made with him while surviving the season.

It's as simple as that.

I grab my coat and purse, lock up the bakery, and head to my car without looking back at the tree lot. I don't check to see if he's still out there, not wanting to give him the satisfaction of knowing I noticed him, too. He's probably zeroed in on me right fucking now.

I shake my head, annoyed.

Tomorrow, I'll bake twice as many cookies. I'll smile at customers. I'll ignore every comment about Lucas and me. I'll prove to this entire town—and to him—that I don't care because I don't.

I really, really don't. And hopefully, if I keep telling myself that, I'll eventually convince myself, too.

CHAPTER 6

LUCAS

I've been up since four thirty, which is nothing new. What is new is spending the entire morning trying to convince myself that the bakery and the stubborn woman inside it don't exist.

It's not fucking working.

I hoist another Fraser fir onto the tractor bed, the scent of pine sharp in the cold November air. My breath comes out in clouds, and my hands are numb even though I'm wearing leather gloves. The physical burn feels good, much better than thinking about her.

Each day, I've worked myself to the bone.

By eight, the farm's crawling with families. Kids run around in puffy coats, racing between tree rows while parents sip hot chocolate from our snack shack. A group of teenagers pose for Instagram photos in front of the giant nutcracker statue near the entrance. Christmas music plays from speakers hidden in the trees. Right now, it's "Rockin' Around the Christmas Tree" and many are singing along.

Being on Jolly Christmas Tree Farm isn't just about the trees anymore. It's an entire experience. Photo ops, food trucks on weekends, a petting zoo with reindeer. This year, Emma's bakery is the crown jewel.

The farm was my escape. Now it's become my personal hell.

"You planning to load that tree or just strangle it?" Dean asks, walking up with a clipboard.

I realize I've been gripping the trunk hard enough to leave imprints in my gloves. "Obviously loading it."

"Could've fooled me." He marks something off his list. "You're so convincing."

He glances toward the bakery—its windows glowing warm against the gray morning, garland framing the glass, and a Sold Out sign already hanging on the door even though it's only ten a.m. "Wow, Holiday sold out again."

My jaw tightens. "Good for her."

"Already doubled Emma's projected revenue for the season."

"Great."

Dean studies me for a long moment. "You know, for someone who claims to hate Holiday Patterson, you sure do pay a lot of attention."

"Yeah? It's because I promised Emma I'd keep an eye on things."

"Right. And we know how you like to keep your promises."

I exhale.

"Noticed you nearly walked into a golf cart yesterday when Holiday came out to help load cookies into Mrs. Appleton's car."

"Mind your own damn business," I tell him. "Don't you have actual work to do?"

"I do. But watching you be miserable is *way* more entertaining." He claps me on the shoulder. "For what it's worth? She's hot and I'd do her."

My jaw clenches, and he bursts into laughter. He sees me, but says nothing, just walks away.

The rest of the morning drags by. I throw myself into work —hauling trees, running the netting machine, helping a family tie a ten-footer to a minivan while the kids argue about who's putting the star on top of the tree.

Today I've had too much time to think, and that always leads to scowling at the bakery.

I've seen too many glimpses of her through those windows, laughing with Bella and Wendy. She's wearing a red apron today, and her hair piled on top of her head in that messy way I like.

I turn away and nearly crash into a customer.

"Lucas Jolly!" Mrs. Blankenship beams at me, her arms full of shopping bags from the gift shop. "I heard the wonderful news!"

Something cold settles in my stomach. "What's that?"

"About you and Holiday. My quilting club was just saying how we always knew you two would end up together."

"We're not—"

"Don't be modest. You buying all those cookies to support her is the most romantic thing I've heard in years." She pats my arm. "My granddaughter's been asking you out for months, but I told her you're with Holiday."

"Mrs. Blankenship, we're not dating—"

"You don't have to be shy about it. The whole town's rooting for you." She winks and walks away before I can correct her.

The *whole* town. That sounds like an exaggeration.

My phone buzzes, and I pull it out and see a notification from Sammy.

Convenient.

> **SAMMY**
> Why are you and my sister the talk of the town?

> **LUCAS**
> I have no fucking idea.

> **SAMMY**
> Why would you spend $2,400 on cookies? Had a change of heart?

LUCAS
Nope. I did it to piss her off.

SAMMY
Enjoy your bad karma.

I want to throw my phone into the wood chipper.

The rest of the afternoon, I hear some version of the Lucas-and-Holiday-are-finally-together story from at least twenty people. The cashier at the gift shop gives me a knowing smile. Customers congratulate me. One guy actually shakes my hand because he's addicted to her cookies.

Bella corners me by the wrapping station with a grin that makes me want to disappear into the forest and never return. "So, when are you going to make it official?"

"Don't antagonize me."

"Don't do dumb shit," she tells me. "It's almost like you like her."

"Fuck that," I mutter under my breath as I smile at customers. "I want her gone."

"I don't believe you." She crosses her arms, and luckily, I'm pulled away by Hudson. He doesn't say shit about it, which I appreciate. Hudson is quiet; he only speaks when he needs to. It's not an awkward silence, though.

By five o'clock, I'm exhausted. After I finish stacking firewood by the gift shop, my phone rings.

Mawmaw's name lights up the screen.

"Hey Mawmaw," I answer.

"Lucas, honey, I need a favor." My grandmother's voice is sweet, almost too sweet. "Could you come by after work? I need wood carried inside. Another cold front is coming tonight, and my back's acting up."

I glance up at the darkening sky. Temperatures are already

dropping. "I can finish up here and then come over if you want."

"Oh, that would be perfect. About an hour? I'll have dinner waiting."

Free dinner and helping my grandmother? Easy choice. Plus, an evening with just me and Mawmaw sounds perfect with no drama.

"I'll be there."

"Love you. See you soon."

The last forty-five minutes drag by. When I finally clock out, the bakery's dark—Holiday's car is already gone. I refuse to acknowledge the twist of disappointment in my chest.

I drive past Hudson's place—his Christmas lights are up, blinking red and white. When I drive by my own place, it looks dark and empty. Then I pull up to Mawmaw's cabin that's already decked out, too. Her manger scene is in the front yard, and when I pass baby Jesus, I laugh, seeing it's still that old Chucky doll I had, wrapped in a blanket.

Her log cabin sits on ten acres at the edge of the farm property. There's a wraparound porch and flower boxes that bloom year-round, thanks to her borderline magical gardening skills. Smoke curls from the chimney, and every window glows with warmth. This is home.

I grab my leather gloves and take the porch steps. The door swings open before I can knock.

"Come in, come in!" Mawmaw ushers me inside.

The smell hits me first. Chocolate chip cookies. Fresh from the oven.

She's wearing her favorite apron, which has "Jolly Good Times" embroidered across the front in gold thread.

"Let me check your wood situation," I say, leaning down to hug her. I head to the living room to assess the woodpile.

It's already stacked perfectly and recently.

My brows furrow as I walk back to the kitchen. "Mawmaw—"

"Sit. Jake stopped by."

I hear that familiar tone that makes goose bumps trail over my arm. It's the same one she used when I was seventeen and tried to sneak out to meet Holiday. The one that means I'm in trouble but don't know how bad it will be yet.

I do exactly as all five feet, two inches of her says.

Mawmaw places a bowl of chicken and dumplings in front of me. She pulled out the fancy china with the gold rim. She hands me one of her cloth napkins that has lace around the edge. This is the meal she makes when she has bad news or wants something.

"Shit," I whisper under my breath.

"Eat," she commands, sitting across from me with her own bowl.

The dumplings are perfect. They're fluffy, savory, and exactly how I remember from my childhood. Nostalgia wraps around me like a warm blanket as dread settles in my stomach.

Mawmaw watches me with those bright green Jolly eyes that miss nothing. The same eyes that always caught me doing stupid shit.

"How's the farm?" she asks casually.

"Busy. Good numbers this year."

"Your brothers?"

"Hudson's obsessed with Emma. Jake's wedding planning with Claire. Nothing has changed."

"You have." She blows on a spoonful of broth.

There's something in her tone. She knows. She's heard.

"How?"

She takes her bite, chews slowly. "You've been extra grumpy. Short with customers. Walking around like a thundercloud ready to strike. Someone at the quilting club called it big balls syndrome."

I nearly choke on a dumpling. I'm not sure Mawmaw could do the Heimlich on me.

She takes another bite. "That has nothing to do with Holiday Patterson being back, right?"

My spoon stops halfway to my mouth. "Mawmaw—"

"Don't you dare *Mawmaw* me. I've known that girl since she was in diapers. Babysat all of you together more times than I can count."

She narrows her eyes at me.

"I know she left for culinary school. I know you've been angry at her for a long time." She sets down her spoon.

"I'm not required to tolerate anyone," I say. "Ever."

"People change, Lucas. You both were eighteen."

I've never told anyone the full story. Not even Sammy. "She hasn't changed. She's still the selfish, insecure girl she was fifteen years ago."

"Where are your manners?"

"It's the truth. I won't sugarcoat a turd for her or you." I try to stay calm. "Now, can we pretty please not do this?"

"We can after you answer this one question for me." She stands, pulls the cookies from the cooling rack, and arranges them on a plate between us. They're my favorite and she knows it. That only makes me dread what's coming next.

"The Merryville Christmas cookie contest," she says. "It doesn't have a Jolly entry this year."

"Then you should enter."

"Can't. My arthritis is acting up. Can't roll dough like I used to."

I grab a cookie and bite into it. It's still warm. "What about Jake and Claire?"

"They're too busy with wedding planning."

"Bella and Wendy?"

"Please, you know those girls can't cook." Mawmaw sits back down, folding her hands on the table. "I signed you up."

The cookie turns to sawdust in my mouth. "Excuse me?"

"You're entered."

Anger floods through me. "Mawmaw, I don't have time. Jake

is busy with his wedding, and Hudson is occupied with Emma. It all falls back on me, you know that."

"I know. Dean and Matteo have agreed to pick up the slack. And this year is partners only."

No.

"Who did you sign me up with?" I ask, nostrils flaring.

"Well, you see…"

"Mawmaw!"

"You'll be working with Holiday," she says, then smiles.

Her name lands like a physical blow.

I stare at her. "You didn't."

"I did. Paid the two-hundred-fifty-dollar entry fee this morning. Nonrefundable."

"From your Christmas fund?"

"Yes. And I'd do it again." She takes a cookie for herself. "The Jolly family has won that contest for twenty years running. Hudson and Emma won last year. Our family should keep that title."

"I can't."

"Holiday can win." She waves the cookie dismissively. "She's the best baker in the state. You're a Jolly. It's perfect."

"We can't even speak to each other without fighting."

"Then figure it out." She's direct.

"I can't work with her. I can't be in the same room as her without wanting to—"

"Without wanting to what?" Her eyes narrow knowingly.

I stand up, the chair scraping against the floor. "This is manipulative."

"I prefer the term *strategic*." She stands, too, and somehow, she seems ten feet tall. "You're going to partner with Holiday. You're going to bake delicious cookies. And you're going to win."

"No, I'm not."

"Yes, you are."

"I refuse."

"Lucas James Jolly." The full name means I'm definitely in trouble. "I raised you better than to be a quitter."

"This isn't about quitting—"

I'm growing more frustrated with every passing second.

"It's not?" She crosses her arms. "You've spent nearly two decades avoiding that girl. Running from whatever happened between you is quitting. It's time to face it."

"There's nothing to face."

"Then baking a damn cookie should be easy." She walks to the door and opens it, allowing the cold air to rush in. "Contest is on December fourteenth. Two weeks after Thanksgiving. You'll need to practice. You can't use the family gingerbread recipe because Hudson and Emma used it last year. You need something new. Innovative. Delicious. The competition will be intense. Now, go get 'em, tiger."

"Mawmaw. I'm *not* doing this."

"You are. Because I said so." She smiles. It's sweet and deadly.

"You can't—"

"I can and I did. Now go home. Get some rest. You look terrible."

She practically pushes me out the door. I stand on her porch, cookies and dumplings sitting like lead in my stomach.

"Oh, and Lucas?" She opens the door to go back inside.

I turn to look at her.

"The prize is five thousand dollars this year. Holiday can keep the money. You keep the trophy. Everybody wins."

She closes the door before I can argue.

I walk to my pickup, shocked and ready to crash the fuck out.

After I get in my truck, I sit there gripping the steering wheel. Through Mawmaw's window, I can see her dancing around the kitchen like she didn't just detonate my life.

Partnering with Holiday in a high-stakes baking competition sounds awful. No way she's agreed to it and that's what I'm holding on to. After what I've put her through, she'll say no.

I smile like the Grinch who just stole Christmas.

Spending hours alone with her is too risky. I won't be able to hold my tongue. I would make it awful for her because I want her to quit and show everyone, including my grandmother, who she really is.

I pull out my phone to text her—to warn her, to argue, to do something. But I've had her number blocked for fifteen years.

I don't even know what I would say.

Hey, my grandmother signed us up for a couples baking contest. Quit and go away.

I unblock her, knowing she kept the same number she's always had, then shove my phone into my coat pocket.

This is a nightmare, and I have no idea how to wake up from it.

I live a few minutes away from Mawmaw, so my drive home is short. I try very hard not to think about Holiday's face when she finds out. There is no way I will be forced to stand in the same kitchen with her. No way I'd survive this without completely losing my mind.

The answer is no. But I'll make her quit first, showing everyone she can't commit to anything.

CHAPTER 7

❄

HOLIDAY

The next morning starts like any other, except I actually got some sleep. No dreams about Lucas, no tossing and turning. I experienced blissful unconsciousness until my alarm screamed for me to get the heck up at four.

Small victories.

I'm in the bakery kitchen by five, pulling prepped dough from the fridge and arranging baking sheets. The rhythm is soothing. By seven, I've got three hundred gingerbread stars cooling and another batch of peppermint bark cookies in the oven.

My phone buzzes in my apron pocket.

> **EMMA**
> Congrats! Saw the news first thing this morning. So excited for you!

My brows furrow. What news?

> **HOLIDAY**
> Um…I think you texted the wrong person.

> **EMMA**
> No, I didn't! Check the town Facebook page.

A second later, she sends a screenshot. I make it bigger and my blood runs cold.

It's a post on the Merryville Community page with photos of me and Lucas side by side.

Welcome to our newest Cookie Contest team: Holiday Patterson & Lucas Jolly! Can't wait to see what magic these two create together! 🎄

I stare at the screen. My heart pounds so hard I can feel it in my throat.

> **HOLIDAY**
> EXCUSE ME? I did not sign up for this.

> **EMMA**
> What? There was a whole packet that had to be filled out to enter, plus a $250 entry fee.

My hands shake as I type.

> **HOLIDAY**
> NO! Who would do this without asking? Lucas?

> **EMMA**
> It would've had to have been him. Did you see the prize this year is $5,000?

I freeze.

$5,000.

That money could change everything. It could get me out of my parents' house and give me a cushion while I wait to hear back from the NYC bakeries. That's enough money to buy me time to figure out what the hell I'm doing with my life.

But working with Lucas for five weeks? Absolutely impossible.

> **HOLIDAY**
> I'm going to City Hall after work to remove my name.

I set my phone down before I throw it across the kitchen.

Who would sign me up for this? And why would they pair me with Lucas of all people?

I text Sammy.

> **HOLIDAY**
> Did you sign me up for a cookie baking contest with that monster?

> **SAMMY**
> Why would I do that?

> **HOLIDAY**
> For a dumb joke?

I send him the screenshot.

> **SAMMY**
> HOT DAMN! That wasn't me. But you should do it. You'd win.

> **HOLIDAY**
> I'm not doing it.

> **SAMMY**
> Why not? Scared you can't handle working with Lucas? You know he'll be banking on you to quit. That's exactly what he wants.

> **HOLIDAY**
> I don't care. I left all my fucks in Paris.

I'm not scared. I know that Lucas and I can't be in the same room for five minutes without wanting to kill each other. But then again, for five thousand dollars, I can almost handle anything.

Maybe he'll quit, then I can find another partner to stand in. I really want to figure out who did this and get both our names removed before this becomes an even bigger disaster.

I yank off my apron and storm outside.

The farm is already busy, and cars are stacked as far as I can see in the loading area. Music plays, and children are laughing in the distance. Normally, I'd appreciate the festive atmosphere. Today, it just pisses me off.

I spot Jake unloading trees from a flatbed trailer.

"Where's Lucas?" My voice comes out harsher than I mean, and I feel bad. He's the nicest guy.

Jake blinks up at me. "Uh, I think he's helping a family with their first tree cut. Down that path." He points. "Everything okay?"

"I'm sorry for being short with you," I say, already walking away.

The path feels longer than it should, giving me too much time to think about Bella saying Lucas hasn't dated anyone seriously since I got engaged. Too much time to wonder why that information won't leave my head.

I find him crouched down, showing a little kid how to hold a handsaw safely. He's patient, smiling, and his voice is warm as he explains. The kid's dad laughs at something Lucas says. For a brief moment, I see the guy I was friends with.

But when our eyes meet across the clearing, his smile vanishes. His expression goes blank.

He says something to the family, hands over the saw, then walks toward me with an attitude.

I force myself to stand my ground even though every instinct screams to turn around.

"Holiday—"

"Why did you sign me up for that contest?" I cut him off. "What kind of sick game is this?"

His eyebrows shoot up. "You think *I* would do that? You're the last person on this planet I want to see. Why would I volunteer to be around you? That's modern-day torture."

"Who did it?"

He crosses his arms. "Just quit."

"No." I let out a harsh laugh. "You quit."

"Stop playing games. You don't want to do it, so why don't you march your sassy little ass down to the chamber and remove your name from the list?"

"Actually, I will," I tell him. "You're right. I'll find someone else to partner with me. I advise you to do the same."

We stare at each other. The air between us crackles with tension.

"You can't do that," he says.

"Actually, I can do whatever the fuck I want," I tell him.

"You're impossible," he says as I turn to walk away. "Mawmaw signed us up."

I turn back to him. "Why would she do that? You know what? I'm not doing this. Not here."

I storm toward the bakery. Lucas's boots crunch on the gravel behind me.

"Holiday—"

"Leave me alone!"

I reach the bakery and yank the door open. He catches it before I can slam it in his face.

"Get out," I snap.

"Not until we finish this conversation."

He steps inside. The bell jingles cheerfully. It's completely opposite from the rage radiating off both of us.

"There's nothing to finish."

"You either quit or you bake with me."

"You don't get to make the rules, Lucas." I scoff. "You know that if I bake against you, I'll destroy you. You need me, don't you?"

"No. I don't fucking need you." His voice rises. "You really think I want to spend the next five weeks trapped in a kitchen with you?"

We're standing too close. Close enough that I can see his chest rising and falling rapidly. Close enough to notice the exhaustion in his eyes. I hate that I notice.

"Why do you hate me so much?" The question escapes before I can stop it.

Something dangerous flashes in his eyes. "You really want to know?"

"Yes."

"Because you're selfish. You make promises you don't keep. You leave when things get hard." He takes a step closer. "You came back here because your perfect life in Paris fell apart, and now you're slumming it in Merryville until you find your next escape. That's why I can't allow you back into my life, and I'd very much prefer if you just went ahead and fucked straight off."

Each word is a knife.

"You don't know anything about why I came back."

"Sure, I do. I know your very public engagement ended, and your fancy culinary career hit a brick wall. So, you ran back home to lick your wounds, where everyone compliments you. When you've had enough, you'll run away." He leans in. "Just like you always do."

"I didn't run—"

"You left for culinary school and never looked back. Moved on in three months." His voice is cold as ice. "Forgive me if I don't trust a single word out of your mouth."

"That's what this is about? We never discussed being exclusive! You told me to live my life! One picture is posted of me and a guy on the internet and you ghost me!" My throat burns.

"You were on his fucking lap!" he yells.

"I'm doing this contest without you. Tell Mawmaw yourself."

"Already planning to."

"Good."

"*Great.*"

We glare at each other.

"Now get out of my bakery," I say.

"Gladly."

"Why do you always do that? Have to have the last word. It's annoying. You're annoying," I mutter.

He turns toward the door, and his phone rings.

He pulls it out, glances at the screen. "It's Mawmaw."

"Don't answer it."

Lucas rolls his eyes at me. "You don't get to tell me what to do, *Peaches*."

"Stop with that."

He answers, putting it on speaker.

"Honey!" Mawmaw's voice fills the bakery, sweet and cheerful. "Did you tell Holiday about the contest?"

Lucas and I exchange looks.

"Yep," he says. "She said she'll do it, but she won't work with me. Only against me."

"What?" Mawmaw sounds disappointed, and I glare at Lucas.

"I told you she's stubborn and selfish. And only thinks about herself. Sorry, Mawmaw, I know you had your heart set on us winning this for you," he says, really playing it up.

I hate you, I mouth, and it breaks my heart to hear his grandmother's disappointed voice.

"Now, hold on just a minute," Mawmaw says, her voice shifting. "Where are you right now?"

"Funny you should ask," he says through gritted teeth. "I'm at the bakery."

"With Holiday? Let me speak to her," Mawmaw says.

I shake my head.

"Oh, you're on speakerphone and she heard the entire conversation, so go ahead," he says, giving me a shit-eating grin.

"Honey, can you explain to me why you won't work with my grandson?"

I sarcastically laugh. "Because he's impossible. He *hates* me. He's mean, and he says horrible things. We can't be in the same room without fighting."

"That's not true," Mawmaw says sweetly. "You're in the same room right now."

"And we're fighting," Lucas points out.

"I'm sure it's just normal bickering," she offers. "There's a difference. Now listen, both of you. I already paid the two-hundred-and-fifty-dollar entry fee from my Christmas fund."

Lucas grits his teeth. "Mawmaw—"

"That was money I was going to use for gifts. But I thought keeping our family's twenty-year winning streak was more important."

Guilt slams into me. Twenty years?

"The rules changed this year," she continues. "Teams only. No solo entries. If one of you withdraws from the team, neither of you can reenter with another contestant. That's so no one can cheat. So, either you work together and win, or you both lose."

"That's not—" I start.

"That's the rules," Mawmaw singsongs.

Lucas and I stare at each other in horror.

"I guess you'll both be quick and let me down easy," Mawmaw says, her voice taking on that steel-beneath-sugar tone.

The silence is deafening.

"I really had my heart set on this. Everyone was so excited to see you both working together after Lucas supported you so openly and bought all those cookies."

Lucas looks like he wants to murder someone. Possibly me. Possibly his grandmother.

"We're not doing the contest," he says flatly.

Silence.

"Lucas James Jolly." She only says that when he's in trouble.

He closes his eyes.

"Your parents raised you better than this."

"This isn't about—"

"Twenty years, Lucas. Twenty years our family has won. Your brothers won. And now it's your turn." Her voice cracks slightly. "This is the last thing I'll ever ask of you."

"Don't pull the guilt card, Mawmaw," Lucas mutters. "I see what you're doing."

"I'm stating facts." She pauses.

"I'm leaving it up to Holiday," Lucas says, smirking.

My mouth falls open.

"Holiday! Honey, please do this for me."

He completely trapped me. We both know it.

"Go ahead, Holiday. Tell her you can't commit," he mutters.

I want to say no. Want to tell her I can't spend five weeks working with someone who looks at me like I'm the worst mistake he ever made.

"Pretty please with sugar on top?" she begs.

"One baking session," I force out. "That's all I'm agreeing to."

Lucas rolls his eyes. "Stubborn."

"Thank you!" Mawmaw says and hangs up before either of us can respond.

Lucas and I stand there, staring at his phone like it's a bomb that just went off.

"This is a fucking nightmare," he finally says.

"Agreed."

"I'm going to make baking with me so unbearable you'll quit."

My spine straightens. "Good luck with that. I think I'd rather torture you for the next five weeks. Mawmaw would be so disappointed if her perfect little grandson couldn't handle his stinky-ass attitude."

He grins. "Everyone has a breaking point."

I cross my arms. "Try me, Jolly."

His eyes flash with something dangerous. "You're going to hate your life."

"Ah, well. Nothing new there."

He walks to the door, pauses with his hand on the handle. Turns back to look at me. "Can't wait for you to leave."

I laugh in his face.

His voice drops. "I meant what I said about you being selfish. Don't expect me to be nice just because Mawmaw wants us to pretend like we're friends."

"I don't expect anything from you, Lucas. Just your impossible attitude."

For a second, something like pain flashes across his face, then it's replaced by cold hatred.

"Good. Then we understand each other."

He leaves. The door closes with a soft click.

I stand there, shaking with anger as the timer goes off.

I return to the kitchen, check my pecan cookies. They're perfectly golden, not a single one burned. I take them off the tray, and my hands are shaking.

Lucas is right about everyone having a breaking point, and I just hope he never finds mine. He will try, though.

This cannot be happening.

CHAPTER 8

❄

LUCAS

I pull up to the bakery at six thirty, a full thirty minutes late on purpose.

If Holiday wants to work with me, she can learn right now that I don't follow her rules. The bakery lights glow golden against the darkening sky. Through the window, I can see her moving around inside, already prepping like the overachiever she's always been.

I sit in my truck for another five minutes, just to make a point.

My phone buzzes, and it's Holiday, which is a surprise. I unblocked her number a few days ago so we could chat about when we'd bake.

> **HOLIDAY**
> Hurry up.

> **LUCAS**
> On my way. Relax.

> **HOLIDAY**
> You're purposely wasting my time.

A VERY MERRY ENEMY

LUCAS

And?

I pocket my phone and climb out. The November air is cold enough that my breath fogs. Christmas lights twinkle on the trees across the lot, and somewhere by the gift shop, Bing Crosby croons from the outdoor speakers.

I push open the bakery door. The bell jingles, and Holiday looks up from the kitchen in the back where she's arranging ingredients.

She's wearing jeans and an old Merryville High sweatshirt, the same one from our senior year. Her hair is pulled back in a ponytail, no makeup. She's even tied her apron the same way she always did—loose knot at the back, strings wrapped tightly around her waist. I watched her tie that knot a thousand times when we worked together at the county fair booth. When she'd lean against me while we waited for the next customer, smelling like cinnamon and sugar.

The memory hits me like a physical blow.

I hate that seeing her like this makes something tighten in my chest.

"You're disrespectfully late," she says.

"Great. That's the level I was hoping for." I shrug off my jacket and toss it on a stool. "Let's get this over with."

Her eyes roll. "Wow. Love the attitude."

"You want me to pretend I'm happy to be here?" I give her a sarcastic smile, then move to the counter, deliberately invading her space.

I scan the ingredients she's laid out. Flour, sugar, butter, eggs, vanilla extract, and chocolate chips. Basic. Safe.

"Chocolate chip cookies?"

"I was thinking we'd start with something classic. Test our combined skills on something simple—"

"I think the fuck not."

She blinks. "Excuse me?"

"We're not doing a boring chocolate chip cookie. We don't have time to waste, Holiday. Let's start with something that stands out and build from there." I lean against the counter. "You've been gone a long time."

Her eyes flash. "I competed professionally in Paris. I think I know what wins baking competitions worldwide."

"This isn't some fancy European competition where judges care about technique and presentation." I cross my arms. "This is Merryville. Not sure you can relate."

Her face goes white, then red. "Don't you dare."

"Want to talk about the engagement you couldn't commit to? Seems relevant. Just proves my point that you have commitment issues."

"You're an asshole."

"So predictable. Something gets hard, you run. How long did that engagement last, anyway? Three years? Right on time. That's when you start getting bored and need something more exciting in your relationships." I shake my head. "That's what we call a cycle."

"You don't want to talk about this."

"After all this time, you're still a red flag."

She grabs a bag of flour and slams it on the counter so hard, a cloud of white explodes everywhere. It coats her sweatshirt, dusts her hair, and settles on both of us like snow.

"Red is still your favorite color," she says, unamused.

I cough, waving flour out of my face. "Real mature, HoHo."

"Stop bringing up my personal life like you have any right to know about it."

"It's hard when we're forced together and—"

"We were forced together by your manipulative grandmother. That doesn't give you the right to throw my failed engagement in my face. There, I said it. You're right. Is that what you want?"

I brush flour off my flannel. "Did you call it off, or did he? That's the answer I couldn't ever get out of anyone."

Her hands curl into fists. "None of your damn business."

"I'll eventually find out." I move closer. "Bet it was you."

"Don't you even," she snaps with venom in her voice. "Why haven't you dated anyone in a few years? What's your excuse?"

I freeze. "That's different."

"Heard you started cycling through women when you learned I got engaged."

"I absolutely did no—"

"No?" She steps forward, closing the distance between us. "Small town, remember? You may know details about me, but trust me, I've heard so much about you, too. Grow up, Lucas."

The silence stretches.

"You know what," I finally say, my voice rough. "You don't get to act like I'm the bad guy for protecting myself."

"Protecting yourself? You ghosted me, Lucas. You owed me an explanation."

"I told you if you started dating someone else, I'd know you were done."

The air between us crackles with years of unresolved hurt.

I take a step closer. "Then you used me as your fuck toy when you came home for the holidays."

"And? You enjoyed fucking me, knowing I was with someone else. You knew I was weak for you, and you never once told me no. Actually, I recall us promising to secretly spend every Christmas together." She blinks at me, not giving a damn. "Maybe I should tell everyone the truth."

"You're so damn dense. Even now."

She backs away from that conversation. It's clear she's not ready to discuss it yet.

"I think we should make a sea salt caramel chocolate chip cookie. Elevated but familiar," I say, needing to change the topic so we can be done and leave.

She opens her mouth to argue, then closes it. "I'm in charge of presentation and technique."

"And I'm in charge of—"

"This isn't your area of expertise. Remember, you're here because you want to be," she says.

"Maybe," I say, moving closer, backing her against the counter, "you could quit. Make this easier for everyone."

Her chin lifts as her back touches the surface. "Won't be me who quits."

"We'll see about that."

"Is that a threat?"

"It's a promise. You won't be able to handle me for five weeks."

Something flashes in her eyes—pure anger. "You'll have to do more than showing up late and trying to use my past against me."

She steps forward, closing the distance. We're toe to toe now, and I can smell vanilla and sugar on her skin. The same scent she wore when we were teenagers.

"I plan on making this a living hell for you, too."

The words hang between us. "It already is," I say through gritted teeth.

"Love to hear it."

The music shifts to "I'll Be Home for Christmas." At one point in our lives, it was our song. The one we used to dance to outside my truck on a back lot away from everything, her head on my shoulder, both of us pretending we had forever.

When she hears it, her eyes soften, but she turns the music off.

"Jerk," she mutters, turning away.

I let it slide. Mostly because she's right.

Holiday starts measuring flour and aggressively slams it into a mixing bowl. Another cloud explodes over the counter, coating us both again.

"You're making a mess."

"Not like you're going to clean it up."

"You're right about that."

She spins around, wooden spoon in hand like a weapon. "Do you want to do this? Because I can walk out right now."

"Please do. Save us both the trouble," I say, lifting my hand toward the door. "I'll lock up."

"No." She jabs the spoon toward me. "I need this money, and I'm going to earn it. With or without your cooperation. You can stand there and look pretty for all I care."

"What do you need five thousand dollars for? Plane ticket back to Paris?"

Her nostrils flare. "Again, that's none of your business."

"What makes you desperate enough to put up with me for five weeks?"

Something flickers across her face, and she exhales. "New York."

"What?"

"The money would cover moving expenses and first month's rent." She says it like she's confessing something. "I need to win this. Then I can grant you your wish and disappear like you've wanted since I returned."

"Yes!" I do a mock celebration. "Thank you!"

New York. I knew she was already planning her escape.

"Must be real nice," I say, my voice without any emotion. "Always going somewhere else. Some new city where you don't have to deal with your past."

"That's not—"

"Save it." I move to the stove, start pulling out pots for the caramel. "Let's just get this over with."

The silence is tense. Holiday cracks eggs with more force than necessary. One splatters, and pieces of the shell fall into the bowl.

"You gonna fish that out?"

"Lucas, I swear to—"

"What?"

"You're not helping. You're hovering and criticizing and giving me attitude. You're worse than first-year culinary students. You wouldn't last five minutes baking for real." She fishes out the shell with her finger, flinging it into the trash. "But if you're going to be here, at least be useful."

"Fine. What do you want me to do?"

"Make the caramel. And don't burn it."

I bite back a comment and focus on the task. Sugar, water, butter. I've watched Mawmaw make this a hundred times.

The mixture starts bubbling, turning from clear to amber. I stir it, noticing the color darkening.

"Stir it more and turn the heat down," Holiday says from behind me. She's so close I can feel her breath on my neck. "It's going to burn."

"I know what I'm doing," I snap.

"Really? Because it's already too dark."

The smell hits us both at the same time. Bitter.

"Shit." I yank the pan off the heat, but it's too late. The caramel is ruined.

"Told you," Holiday says, but there's no smugness. Just exhaustion.

I dump it in the trash and grab a clean pot to start over. This time, Holiday stands next to me, close enough that our elbows bump.

"Slow and steady," she says, turning the heat down.

Her hand closes over mine on the wooden spoon, guiding my movement. Her fingers are warm, and for a second, I remember what it felt like when she used to touch me like this. When we'd bake together at Mawmaw's house, her teaching me how to fold dough, both of us laughing when I'd mess it up.

Natural. Like we fit together.

She realizes how close she is and jerks her hand away like she's been burned.

"You've got it," she says, her voice strained. "Just like that."

I don't respond. Can't. Because my skin is still tingling where she touched me, and I hate it. Hate that my body remembers even when my mind is screaming to forget.

The caramel turns out perfect, and I pull it off the heat.

"Much better," Holiday says.

We work in silence, both trying to ignore how small this kitchen is. Every movement brings us closer together. In this short amount of time, we've developed a careful dance of not touching, not looking, not acknowledging the charged air.

Holiday portions out the cookie dough while I prep the caramel drizzle. Our hands keep almost touching when we both reach for something—the spatula, the salt, the baking sheets—and every time, we jerk away.

"Roll them bigger," I say.

"They're the right size," she throws back.

"They're too small. We need to make an impression."

"Lucas, I've been doing this for—"

"Size fucking matters, okay?"

She glares but rolls the next one bigger. Slams it onto the baking sheet hard enough that it flattens too much.

"Now you're just being a brat," I say.

I grab the dough and start rolling it into a ball.

Holiday snatches it from my hands. "You're being a bitch," I continue.

"You're being too critical!" she throws back.

"Maybe if you actually listened—"

"I'm the professional here! You're just—" She stops, breathing hard.

"Just what?"

"Just someone who can't let go of the past long enough to see what's right in front of him."

Her words are a stab to the heart.

Before I can respond, a knock on the window makes us both jump.

Hudson stands outside, waving. Grinning. He points at his phone, and mine buzzes with a text.

. . .

HUDSON
You two look like you're having fun.

LUCAS
Go away.

HUDSON
Do you need a referee?

LUCAS
Worry about yourself.

HUDSON
How about you keep it down? Pretty sure the whole farm can hear you fighting.

He looks up at me and grins, then goes back to typing.

HUDSON
We're about to go to the snack shack and make popcorn.

I immediately send him a middle finger emoji.

I glance at Holiday, who's glaring at Hudson through the window. She flips him off. Hudson laughs and sends me another text.

HUDSON
You're both so much alike it's scary.

He walks away, but not before giving me a look that says we'll talk about this later.

"Your family is nosy," Holiday mutters.

"You used to love my family."

"Oh, I still love them. But you? Absolutely fucking not."

We finish rolling the cookies in hostile silence. She slides two trays into the oven, sets the timer, and we wait.

Holiday leans against the counter on one side. I mirror her position on the other, maximizing the distance in this limited space.

"We can't keep fighting like this," I say.

"What do you expect from me, Lucas?" She pushes off the counter. "To say I'm sorry for leaving? That I regret Paris? That I should've stayed in Merryville and lived the small-town life?" Her voice rises with each sentence.

"Yes," I say, my voice low.

"I'm not sorry. I needed to leave. I needed to see what else was out there. And if that makes me selfish, then fine. I'm selfish."

The confession hangs between us. Too raw.

Holiday stares at me, her eyes wide. "Lucas—"

"Finally, the truth." I give her a slow applause.

The timer goes off.

Saved by the bell. Literally.

Holiday pulls the cookies out, and I can tell something's wrong. The edges are dark brown, almost burnt, while the centers are still pale and underbaked.

"What the hell?" Holiday stares at them.

"The oven was too hot. Did you bake them at three fifty?"

"I baked them at three seventy-five. I know this oven. I've been using it for two weeks." Her face falls because she knows I'm right.

"We just ruined an entire batch."

"We?" She spins around. "You're the one who insisted on making them bigger!"

"Yeah? Well, you're the expert!" I use air quotes with the last word.

We're yelling now, both red-faced and furious. The burnt cookies sit between us, evidence of our failure.

"And you're the one who keeps questioning everything I do! If you'd just let me work—"

"If you'd listen to someone who actually knows—"

"You don't know anything! You just think you do because your family wins every year!"

"And you think you know everything because you went to Paris!" The words explode out of me. "Newsflash, Holiday, but you failed there, too. That's why you're back here, working in a small-town bakery instead of some fancy Michelin-star restaurant. That's why you need the contest money to run away again. Because you couldn't make this work, either."

The words are cruel, meant to hurt her.

And they do. Her face goes white, then turns red after a few seconds. Her hands curl into fists, and for a minute, I think she might actually knock me the fuck out. I'd deserve it.

"You want to know why I left Paris?" Her voice shakes. "Because I was engaged to a man who controlled every aspect of my life. Who told me when to work, what to cook, who to talk to, and what to wear. He made me feel like I was never good enough, never talented enough, never enough, period."

She steps closer, and there are tears in her eyes now, but her voice is steel.

"And you know what the worst part is? The way you're acting reminds me of him. He also tried to make me feel like I was abandoning him, betraying him, choosing my dreams over him. It's funny that when some people can't get what they want from you anymore, they say you're the selfish one, when maybe they are."

She's breathing hard now, and so am I.

"So yeah, Lucas. I failed at being engaged. I failed at a lot of things. But at least I can also say I tried. At least I took the risk instead of hiding and pretending the world doesn't exist beyond the tree line of the farm."

The silence that follows is deafening.

I can't breathe or think. Her words ricochet through my head like bullets.

The way you're acting reminds me of him.

He treated her like he hated her. The thought makes my jaw clench tight.

"Now leave," she says, her voice breaking. "I can't do this."

"Holiday—"

"No. I need you to leave. Right now. Before I say something I'll regret."

I should argue and defend myself. Should explain that I never meant to make her feel that way.

But I can't. Because some part of me knows she's right.

"Glad to be done," I say. I pause at the door, my hand on the handle. "I meant what I said about breaking you. I will keep trying until you quit this competition or leave town. Hopefully both."

I walk out before she can respond.

The November air hits me like a freight train. I suck in a breath, trying to clear my head, but all I can smell is burnt sugar and vanilla and remember the feel of her hand on mine.

I climb into my truck and sit there, hands gripping the steering wheel. My heart is racing. My chest feels tight. And I can't shake her words.

She was engaged to a man who made her feel like she was never enough.

Did I do that to her? I never wanted her to choose between me and her dreams. But I guess she did in the end.

Through the bakery window, I can see Holiday. She's standing in the middle of the kitchen, and her shoulders are shaking.

She's crying.

Because of me.

I should apologize. I should tell her I didn't mean it, that I was hurt and angry and lashing out.

But I don't. Because seeing her cry just makes me angrier—angrier at myself for being the asshole, angrier at her for making me feel guilty, angrier that after all these years she can still get to me like this.

A few minutes later, after she's finished cleaning up, my phone buzzes.

HOLIDAY

> I'm not quitting this competition or leaving town right away. You better get used to seeing my face during the holidays.

I stare at the text. Even after everything, she's not backing down.

LUCAS

> See you next week, Peaches.

HOLIDAY

> Call me that again and I'm poisoning you.

LUCAS

> Great. Can you do that soon? Put me out of my misery. 😊

I love the smiley at the end. It's a nice touch.

I start the truck, but before I flick on the lights, Holiday walks out of the bakery. She gets in her car and just sits there.

I watch as she leans forward, pressing her forehead against the steering wheel.

All this time, I've been so focused on my own anger; I never considered that maybe she's actually struggling.

She starts her car, and the engine rumbles to life, but she doesn't move. Holiday just sits there like she's gathering the strength to drive home.

I should leave. Should get out of here before she sees me watching her.

But I can't make myself move.

Finally, Holiday lifts her head and wipes her eyes. She puts the car in reverse and pulls away.

I wait until her taillights disappear down the drive before I follow.

The whole way home, all I can think about is her hand on mine. How natural it felt before we both remembered we hate each other.

I spent fifteen years trying to forget Holiday Patterson.

Five weeks of this, and I'm either going to break her or break myself trying.

And I can't decide which one pisses me off more.

CHAPTER 9

❄

HOLIDAY

I've barely slept all week.

Every time I've closed my eyes, I see the look on Lucas's face when I told him he reminded me of my ex-fiancé.

The way you're acting reminds me of him.

The words echo in my head on repeat.

I said them, hoping he'd understand what I went through, even if the words were cruel. As I lie in bed at four in the morning, staring up at the glow-in-the-dark stars Lucas helped me put up when we were sixteen, I think about my words. He needed to hear them, even if they were the ugly truth.

My phone sits on the nightstand. There are no texts from Lucas. Not that I expected any. He may have unblocked my number so we could discuss our baking sessions, but he hasn't gone out of his way to reach out to me. He won't.

I drag myself out of bed and into the shower, letting the hot water wake me up. By five, I'm dressed and driving to the bakery, the mid-November air biting at my skin. I can't believe it's already Saturday.

The week has passed by in a blur of sold-out cookie trays and curious customers trying to get details about the new romance in Merryville.

Monday, I saw Lucas's truck in the parking lot when I arrived. My stomach did a stupid flip, but he was nowhere near the bakery. It was hard to focus on my work. Tuesday, he walked past the bakery windows twice. Both times, our eyes met through the windows. I didn't look away first; he always did. Wednesday, Bella asked if everything was okay between us because she could feel the tension. Thursday, I caught him watching me from across the parking lot while I loaded cookies into a customer's car. When I looked up and met his eyes, he didn't turn away. We stared at each other for a long moment before I broke contact and walked back into the bakery. Friday, I didn't see him at all. The bakery was slammed with pre-Thanksgiving orders, and I didn't have time to think about anything.

This morning, I'm exhausted but determined. We need to discuss our presentation for the contest and work on other recipes. We're running out of time. We have exactly one month and haven't made a batch of edible cookies. That's a fact.

The bakery is chaotic. We sell twenty-five hundred cookies by two o'clock, which is a new record. Bella and Wendy handle cleanup while I prep dough for tomorrow's batches. Pre-prepping and the two extra ovens Emma had delivered a few days ago have made us more efficient. We can now bake twenty-five percent more cookies.

"You should go home and rest," Bella tells me around four. "You've been here nearly twelve hours."

"I'm fine. I'm baking tonight with Lucas anyway."

"Go home and take a nap beforehand," she says. "Two hours will do you some good."

"I doubt I'll sleep," I tell her, knowing I won't.

"Then rest with your eyes closed," she says. "You can't keep going at a hundred miles an hour. We're not halfway through the season yet."

"I know. Thank you," I say. My feet pound as I drag myself to my car. The two-mile drive goes fast, and I pull up to my parents' place. As soon as I take the stairs to my bedroom, my phone vibrates with a text.

I walk into my room and sit on the edge of my bed.

> **LUCAS**
> Still good for 6?

> **HOLIDAY**
> Yep.

> **LUCAS**
> Meet me at my house tonight to bake. Too many wandering eyes at the farm.

> **HOLIDAY**
> Not a good idea.

> **LUCAS**
> Then fuck off. I'm not baking at the shop.

It's short and to the point. Nothing like the texts we used to send each other.

I set an alarm on my phone and somehow drift to sleep.

It feels like only minutes pass, but really, an hour and a half goes by. I drag myself out of bed and change into some comfy jeans that make my ass look awesome and a soft sweater.

At five fifty, I head to Lucas's place. I could drive there with my eyes closed. I make my way to the farm and turn off onto the gravel loop where all the Jolly family houses sit. I pass Hudson's place first, and it's all lit up, then turn onto Lucas's long driveway. My headlights illuminate his two-story home, which sits at the back of the property, exactly where he told me it would go.

Each of the brothers inherited land as a part of their legacy.

They each built their forever homes on the same loop where their parents and grandmother live.

I park next to his truck and walk up the porch steps. The house is hardly decorated, with a lone garland wreath on the front door. Icicle lights partially hang from the eaves, like he gave up halfway through.

Before I lift my hand to knock, the swing door opens.

Lucas is wearing jeans that hang low on his hips and a heather gray T-shirt that's been worn soft. It stretches across his torso, accentuating his chest and arms. That's when I realize he has tattoos on his arms. His hair is slightly damp, and he smells like he just showered. There's a shadow of stubble on his jaw, and he looks tired but good. Too good.

My mouth falls open, and I quickly close it. This is the first time I've seen him in normal clothes. No long-sleeved flannels or hoodies.

"Hey," he says, unamused.

"Uh, hey."

We stand there for a second too long, and I can feel the tension from last week still hanging between us.

"Come in," he finally says, stepping aside.

I walk past him and stop in the entryway.

The open floor plan, with vaulted ceilings and exposed beams, is exactly how he once described it to me. A stone fireplace is the showpiece of the living room with a thick wooden mantel that's been stained dark. The kitchen has tons of counter space, an island with barstools, and professional-grade appliances.

"Wow," I say, moving forward, noticing the windows overlooking the woods. "This is a dream kitchen."

"I know," he says.

"This house is exactly like we talked about. The layout, the windows, even the fireplace." I turn to look at him. "You made it happen."

Something flickers across his face. "Almost."

The words hang between us, weighted with everything we're not saying.

He follows me farther into the kitchen, breaking the moment. "You want a tour?"

"Yeah. I'd like that."

He shows me around the first floor—the living room with built-in bookshelves, filled with thrillers and books about tree cultivation. His office has a large oak desk that faces the windows. The half bath has the subway tiles he'd always loved. I follow behind him as he leads the way upstairs, and I try not to stare at the muscles that cascade down his back.

He shows me all three bedrooms, along with the suite that has a king-size bed and vaulted ceilings. He even has a gas fireplace up here. There's a gigantic walk-in closet and a bathroom with a big shower and a deep tub.

"You have a lot of space," I mutter.

"Built it for a future that didn't happen." He shrugs, but I can see the tension in his shoulders. "Anyway, this is it. We should get started."

Back in the kitchen, he removes ingredients from his pantry that's tucked away in the corner. The tension is noticeable, but it isn't unbearable.

I wash my hands at the farmhouse sink, a style I always loved. It's not lost on me that this is *my* dream kitchen, not his. "I read the contest rules. We have to bake at the Christmas Festival contest area, and each team will have its own oven, sink, and prep area. It all has to be done in front of the judges. We have to bake fifty cookies without rushing. I think three hours is plenty of time."

"Good."

"I was thinking we could try a different cookie. What family recipes do you have memorized?" I ask.

"Gingerbread, which we can't use because Emma and Hudson used it last year to win. And my favorite of Mawmaw's, a chunky chocolate chip with pecans."

"Make the dough for the chocolate chip pecan ones. I have an idea."

His brows furrow, but he doesn't argue. Lucas seems indifferent today.

We fall into our rhythm. He measures flour and sugar while I melt chocolate in a double boiler. The kitchen is smaller with him in it, which means we keep bumping into each other. His arm brushes mine when he reaches for the vanilla. My hip bumps his when I move over to his stand mixer.

"Sorry," I say after the third collision.

He ignores me.

We work in silence, mixing the two separate doughs—my fudge cookie base and his chocolate chip with pecans. His movements are confident. Out of everyone in Merryville, he's actually the best baking partner for me because he pushes me to be better.

I watch him fold chocolate chips gently, and I'm impressed. It makes me think about all those summers we used to bake together just for fun.

He glances at me, and there's almost a smile. I wonder if he thinks about those times, too. Probably not.

Once our doughs are ready, Lucas plops them down on the tray. I scoop some of my fudge dough and place it in the middle of his cookies and place them on the baking sheet in neat rows.

Our hands keep almost touching, but neither of us jerks away quite as fast anymore.

"Remember when we tried to make snickerdoodles at Mawmaw's and you forgot the cream of tartar?" I ask.

"That was *you* who forgot it."

"For some reason, I remember it definitely being you."

We're lost in our thoughts for a few seconds.

He shakes his head, but he's almost smiling. "You've always been impossible."

"Oh, big same."

We slide the trays into the oven, and I set the timer. Lucas leans against the counter, tattooed arms crossed, watching me.

"What?" I ask.

"Nothing. You're the one staring."

"Um. It takes two to stare. I just didn't realize you were tatted up like…"

His brows raise, and he smirks as he lifts his shirt. Abs for days and more tattoos.

"How many do you have?"

"Lost count," he says and clears his throat, looking away.

The timer ticks in the silence between us.

"You want a drink?" Lucas asks. "I've got whiskey."

I should say no. Alcohol and Lucas, and this house and old memories sound like a recipe for disaster.

"Yeah. Sure," I say, not caring.

He pulls out a bottle that looks expensive. He pours two glasses and slides one across the counter to me.

The whiskey burns down my throat in the best way.

"Damn, that's good," I say, needing it to work.

He shoots the whole glass down and then fills it again.

The timer goes off, and Lucas grabs oven mitts to pull out the trays. The cookies are perfect—golden brown, the fudge centers just visible where they cracked slightly during baking.

"These look incredible," Lucas says, leaning in close to inspect them.

"Hope they taste good."

We keep drinking while waiting for them to cool. Lucas pours us both another round without asking.

"You trying to get me drunk, Jolly?" I ask.

"Maybe." His eyes meet mine, and there's something there—a challenge, a question. "Or maybe I just need to take the edge off."

"Edge off what?"

"My personal hell." He takes another drink.

I study him, wanting to say something, but let it slide. I break one of the cookies in half and take a bite.

The crispy chocolate chip exterior gives way to the rich, gooey fudge center. It's perfect.

"Holy shit," I say around the bite. The texture is crispy and soft, a delicious combination.

"Are they good?"

I hold out the other half. "Try it for yourself."

He takes it from me, our fingers brushing for just a second longer than necessary. He bites into it, and I watch his expression change.

"Damn," he mutters.

"Right?"

"This tastes incredible." He looks at me, tilting his head. "How did you know to do that?"

"Instinct. Years of training. Being better than you." I grin. "Take your pick."

"All of the above, apparently." He pours us both another drink. "We're actually going to win this thing."

"You sound surprised."

"I'm not. You're annoyingly good at everything you do."

"Is that a compliment?"

"It's a fact." He leans against the counter, those tattooed arms on full display. There's an edge to his voice, but it's not entirely hostile. It's something else.

"For someone who claims he can't bake with measuring cups, you did a good job. Great dough."

"I used to bake a lot with this girl I knew. She taught me all the basics," he says.

"Yeah?" I ask, thinking about old times. "What happened to her?"

"She disappeared." His eyes meet mine, and my face heats.

I don't want to get hung up on that, so don't respond.

We work in silence as we clean up our mess, but it's less tense now. The whiskey loosens up both of us.

"Remember when we made those gingerbread cookies that got us detention?" I ask.

"The dick cookies? Yeah, Mawmaw still brings that up sometimes." He smiles. "Six inchers. Can't believe you even added—"

"Don't finish that sentence."

"—veins."

I'm laughing. "They tasted great, though."

"It was the best week of detention ever," he says. "We got to fuck off the entire week."

"Remember how you used to draw tiny dicks randomly in my notebooks?"

"Payback." He's laughing now, and I forgot what his real laugh sounds like. Not the polite chuckle, but the genuine one that makes his eyes crinkle. It feels like we're just two old friends reminiscing. If only…

The laughter fades, and I realize we're standing close. Really close.

His eyes drop to my mouth, then back up.

"Holiday," he says, his voice a growl.

"Yeah?"

"Don't."

I look up at him, studying those green eyes that have haunted me since we were kids. And I close the distance between our mouths. Slowly, I move in, our lips just inches apart. My eyes close as I gently slide my lips against his.

He goes completely still, but I feel his sharp intake of breath. His lips are soft against mine, but frozen, not moving, not responding, not kissing me back. Lucas's whole body tenses like every muscle is locked. His fingers press harder into the counter behind me. Then I feel him lean forward, his body betraying what his lips won't admit. His breathing changes, becoming ragged and heavy. I feel the exhale against my mouth, warm and shaky. But his lips stay still. A wall I can't break through.

I pull back, and his eyes open.

He gives me a shit-eating grin.

"What exactly did you think would happen?" He sounds amused.

My face burns hotter.

"Go ahead. Tell me." He's still close, and he rests his hand on my hip. "You thought you'd kiss me and I'd what? Just fall at your feet and worship you?"

"Hoped," I say, not giving a fuck.

His eyes drag down to my mouth and focus on it. "You want me so badly you can barely stand it."

My breath catches because he's right, and we both know it.

"And you know what's really funny?" He leans in closer, his lips almost touching mine. "Part of me wanted to kiss you back just to fuck with you. But I'm not playing games." He gestures between us. "This can't happen."

"I need to go." I take a step away, needing distance, feeling stupid as hell.

"Yeah. Probably a good idea." He steps back, finally giving me space. "Where are your keys?"

I pull them out of my pocket to show him and he snatches them from my hand.

"You're not going anywhere," he says.

"Give me my keys, Lucas."

"Fuck no."

"I'm fine—"

"You've had four glasses of whiskey. You're *not* fine." He heads for the stairs. "Come on."

"I can call Sammy—"

"At nine? So he can drive over here and ask why you're trashed at my house? No fuckin' thanks." He looks back at me. "You're staying. Now, you can follow me, or I'm throwing you over my shoulder and carrying you."

"Please. You wouldn—"

A second later, Lucas is lifting me just as he said, like I weigh nothing. "You can't just do that!"

"Stop me," he says, basically slinging me over his shoulder, holding my thighs. My face is still burning from the non-kiss, his smirk, from all of it.

Once we're in his bedroom, he sets me down on the edge of the mattress, then clicks on the lamp. "I'll be downstairs sleeping on the couch."

He's almost to the door when I blurt it out. "Stay."

He stops, but he doesn't turn around.

"Holiday—"

"Please. I don't want to sleep in this big room and house by myself."

He's quiet for a long moment.

"Promise you'll keep your ass on your side of the mattress," he says. "If you cross it once, I'm out."

"Okay."

"I mean it."

"I'll behave!" I promise.

He moves to the opposite side of the bed. We lie down fully clothed with plenty of distance between us.

The silence stretches on, and I can hear him breathing.

Several minutes pass, and the world is spinning from the whiskey.

I feel the bed shift. His strong arm wraps around my waist, pulling me back against his chest. His face buries in my hair, and I feel him inhale deeply. It's a long, slow breath like he's trying to memorize the scent of me.

My hand finds his where it rests against my stomach, and our fingers tangle together. He pulls me closer, his leg hooking over mine. His thumb traces small circles on my stomach, and my fingers tighten around his. Neither of us speaks or says a single word.

Lucas Jolly's arms wrap around me, holding me, and when I close my eyes to go to sleep, I let myself believe that maybe everything will be okay.

CHAPTER 10

LUCAS

I wake up at four, holding Holiday Patterson like she's going to slip through my fingers.

Her face is buried in my chest; her arm is slung across my ribs. Her breath is warm against my collarbone. I stay perfectly still, feeling every spot where our bodies connect. Her other hand rests on my stomach, and I memorize all of it like a fucking idiot because this is the closest I'll ever get to having her again.

I am so fucked.

My head pounds from the whiskey. My mouth tastes like ass. My body aches from sleeping in jeans. Not to mention, the memory of her kissing me keeps playing on repeat. Her lips were soft and desperate. I didn't kiss her back even though every cell in my body screamed at me to give in.

I have to get out of this bed before I do something stupid.

I slowly slide away from her. She makes a small whimper but doesn't wake, just curls into the warm spot I left behind. That contented sigh nearly breaks me.

When I'm finally free, I watch her sleep. She's curled up, her brown hair spread across the candy cane striped pillowcase like she belongs here.

She looks peaceful. Soft. Mine.

Except she's not. She never was and never will be.

I quietly change my clothes and place her keys on the bedside table next to the lamp, then get the hell out before I talk myself into climbing back in bed with her.

My truck is freezing; the windshield is covered in ice. I crank the engine and blast the heat, shivering while it warms up.

I drive to the farm even though my shift doesn't start until six, taking the curves slowly through the mist. Fog rolls over the gravel road.

I park near the barn and squeeze my eyes tight.

Holiday kissed me, and I felt it everywhere. All I wanted was to grab her face and kiss her back until neither of us could breathe.

I didn't because I can't open the door I spent over a decade nailing shut. It leads to hoping and wanting and getting destroyed when she gets bored. When she misses Paris. When she moves to New York. When her celebrity chef ex decides he wants her back.

Dominic Laurent.

Just his name makes my jaw clench. He's everything I'm not. Sophisticated. Famous. Someone who could give her the world instead of a Christmas tree farm in the middle of nowhere.

My phone sits on the passenger seat. I stare at it for a full minute before I pick it up.

HOLIDAY
About last night.

Fuck.

LUCAS
Forget it.

HOLIDAY
We should probably talk.

LUCAS
Nothing to talk about.

HOLIDAY
But you held me.

My hands tighten on the phone.

LUCAS
Don't read into it. Meant nothing.

HOLIDAY
You're impossible.

I want to tell her it meant everything. I should apologize for being an asshole.

Instead, I lock my phone and toss it back on the seat.

I get out and slam the door so hard it echoes across the empty lot.

The barn smells like hay, motor oil, and wood shavings. It's dark and cold, and I flip on the overhead lights. They flicker before coming on fully.

Extra Christmas decorations are stacked in the corner. There are boxes of lights, garland, and ornaments. They're mocking me with their cheerfulness.

I climb to the hayloft and start throwing bales down to bring to the horse barn. Each bale weighs around sixty pounds and drops with a loud thump. Once I'm done with the hay, I move to the firewood. We sell tons of cords during winter, and I start restacking the bundles of logs, tossing them harder than necessary.

One slips from my grip and crashes to the ground, splitting open.

"Fuck," I whisper. Everything I touch breaks.

By the time Jake shows up around seven, I've reorganized half the barn and I'm soaked with sweat.

"Morning," Jake says, too cheerfully. He's carrying two coffees from the gift shop. "Brought you—"

"Don't need it."

He stops. "You want to tell me what's going on?"

"Nothing."

"Lucas, you've almost done all your tasks. The sun is barely up."

"Maybe I just wanted to get ahead so I can leave early."

"Or maybe something happened with Holiday last night." He sets both coffees down and crosses his arms. "I saw her car at your place. What happened?"

"We baked cookies. We drank too much. She crashed at my place. End of story."

"And?"

"That's it."

"You're so full of shit."

"Drop it."

"Lucas—"

"Jake! I said to fucking drop it!" My voice echoes through the barn.

He doesn't react to my outburst. Instead, he takes a step closer. "You know what your problem is? You're so busy protecting yourself that you're gonna let her slip away again. And this time, you won't have anyone to blame but yourself."

"I don't know what you're talking about."

"Yes, you do. She came back, Lucas. She didn't have to."

"Because she had nowhere else to go."

"Keep telling yourself that." He heads for the door. "You're gonna fuck this up."

He leaves.

I stand there alone, breathing hard.

I hate that Holiday kissed me. That I wanted to kiss her back so badly it hurt. I hate that holding her felt like home. I hate that I told her it meant nothing when it meant everything.

The morning drags on. By nine, families are everywhere. Parents sip hot chocolate, the smell of cinnamon and chocolate mixing with pine and wood smoke. Christmas music plays through outdoor speakers. Some cheerful bullshit about sleigh bells and snow.

I force myself to smile at customers, but it doesn't help my mood.

The hangover gets worse, and my head pounds. The bright sunlight makes my eyes hurt. I forget to eat breakfast.

Around eleven thirty, Hudson shows up with Colby.

"Uncle Lucas!" Colby runs over and hugs my legs. He just started kindergarten this year.

"Hey, buddy." I ruffle his hair.

"We're getting hot chocolate! Then we're going to see Aunt Holiday and get more cookies!"

The name hits me like a punch. "She's not your aunt, Colby."

"Yes, she is!"

Hudson squeezes my shoulder hard. "Leave him alone."

He crouches to Colby's level. "Go get in line. I'll meet you there."

Colby runs off, laughing.

Hudson straightens up and stares at me. "Get your shit together, Lucas."

"I'm trying."

"Try harder." He walks away, shaking his head.

I avoid looking toward the bakery.

Around noon, she walks out with Bella, carrying boxes to a

customer's car. Holiday's wearing tight jeans and a red hoodie. Her hair is in a high ponytail. She looks rested, happy even, like last night didn't wreck her the way it wrecked me.

Then she glances toward me.

Our eyes meet across the parking lot.

For a second, neither of us moves. We just stare at each other.

I'm the one who turns and walks away.

I get lost in work. I help families find trees and load them onto cars. Pine sap sticks to my hands.

Every time I turn around, I catch a glimpse of red across the parking lot. Her laugh carrying on the wind. I keep thinking about that sigh she made in her sleep.

This is killing me.

By two, the hangover drags me under. Dean catches me leaning against someone's car, eyes closed.

"You okay, man?"

"Tired."

"You look like you're gonna pass out." He pulls a granola bar from his pocket. "Eat this. And drink some water."

He shoves it in my hand and walks away.

I force myself to eat it even though it tastes like sawdust.

Around three, I'm in the barn when I see her through the window walking to her car.

My body moves before my brain catches up.

I walk out of the barn, toward her. I'm halfway there when I stop dead in my tracks.

What the fuck am I doing?

She hasn't seen me yet because she's too busy searching through her purse.

I could close the distance and give her an apology.

I stand there frozen, twenty yards away.

She finds her keys and unlocks her car.

Then she looks up and sees me standing in the middle of the parking lot.

A VERY MERRY ENEMY

For a moment, neither of us moves.

The air between us sizzles with everything that will be left unsaid.

She gets in her car and drives away.

The rest of the afternoon blurs together. More customers. More trees. More pretending.

I mess up an order. Drop a saw. Forget to tie down a tree properly, but Dean catches it just in time.

"You should go home," he tells me around four thirty. "Before you hurt yourself or someone else."

I don't argue, but don't leave.

By five, the exhaustion has taken over, so I find Jake and tell him I'm leaving.

"Get some rest. Show up tomorrow with a different attitude."

"Yeah."

I drive home to my empty house.

The second I walk in, I go straight upstairs. The bed is unmade. The pillow she used still has the indent from her head. I can still smell her skin on the sheets.

Panic rises in my chest.

I strip everything and throw it into the washing machine on the hottest setting, like I can wash her away.

I should shower because I have sweat dried on my skin. I should eat because my stomach is empty. I don't.

Instead, I walk to the kitchen and see the box of cookies we made last night still on the counter.

I pick up the container and take one out, then bite into it.

Even today, it's incredible. The crispy exterior and the gooey fudge center are a perfect combination.

Better than anything that French asshole ever made, I bet. The thought hits me with bitter satisfaction. This is ours—mine and Holiday's—and it pisses me off that even now, even hating her, we still create magic together.

This recipe is a winner and it could actually win the contest.

That devastates me because I know what she'll do with the money. I know that she's planning her escape.

We created something perfect, and I'm destroying us in the process.

I set the container down and walk to the living room. I sit on the couch, looking around the house I built for a family I may never have.

For her.

Always for her.

My phone buzzes on the coffee table.

I pick it up and read the calendar notification.

Baking contest meeting
Wednesday, 6pm at the Community Center.
Mandatory for all contestants.

That's the next time I'll be around her. I'll sit in the same room with her and we'll act like a team.

I lean my head back on the couch, closing my eyes.

The house is silent except for the washing machine.

My body aches. My chest feels hollow. I'm still covered in the day's work—dirt, sweat, and pine sap—but I'm too exhausted to care.

I just sit in the dark with Holiday on my mind, wishing I could erase her.

It's going to be a long week.

CHAPTER 11

❄

HOLIDAY

Three days ago, I woke up in Lucas Jolly's bed, and the world hasn't felt right since.

The sheets were ice-cold when I reached for him. He'd slipped out like a thief in the night and left my keys on the nightstand.

I stared at his ceiling, at the exposed beams he described when we were eighteen, while still wearing my rumpled clothes from the night before. My lips still tingled from the kiss he didn't return. My body still remembered being wrapped in his arms all night with his face buried in my hair. Our fingers tangled together like we'd never let go.

Then he left in the morning and has since pretended like it didn't happen.

The humiliation burns worse than any hangover.

I've barely survived.

By this afternoon, I'm falling apart, knowing tonight we both have to be at the contest kickoff meeting. We've not spoken, not texted, just exchanged stolen glances. I've forgotten to eat, my hands shake, and my jeans slide down my hips even though I tightened my belt to a smaller hole. I'm running on spite and too much coffee. When I catch my reflection in the bakery windows, I barely recognize the hollow-eyed girl staring back.

Around three, I see him through the front windows talking to Jake. Even from here, I can see the exhaustion in the set of his shoulders, the way he runs his hand through his messy hair like he does when he's stressed.

I hope he's as miserable as I am.

At four, Jake walks into the bakery carrying a cream-colored envelope embossed with gold.

"Claire and I realized you weren't on the guest list for the wedding and wanted to give you a hand-delivered invitation." He slides it across the counter. "Saturday after Thanksgiving. I hope you can be there."

That's ten days away.

"I don't want to impose," I tell him.

"Never, you're basically family," he tells me. "Please say yes."

"Of course," I say.

"Thank you."

When he walks out, I open the envelope and pull out the invitation that's written in an elegant script.

Jake Jolly & Claire Manchester request the honor of your presence...

I scan over the details. Ceremony at six. Reception following. Live band. Open bar. Dancing.

The invitation feels like it weighs ten pounds in my hands.

I think about Claire, who looks at Jake like he hung the moon. She gets to start forever without any of the baggage or mistakes I'm drowning in. My engagement lasted three years and ended in ashes. Some people get their happily ever after. The rest of us get a lifetime of regret.

Bella told me Lucas is Jake's best man; that means there will be a speech. I'll have to watch him talk about love and forever as I stand on the sidelines.

My phone buzzes with a reminder about the kickoff meeting for the baking contest that's later.

It will be the first time I've been close enough to Lucas to speak to him since Saturday night. I'm already dreading it. But then again, I can do hard things.

I arrive at the community center early, hoping to find a seat in the front to avoid him.

The building is decorated like a Christmas wonderland with lights wrapped around every column, a massive tree in the lobby with ornaments made by local school kids, and twinkling lights strung across the ceiling. The air smells like funnel cakes from the annual winter festival that's happening right now in the town square. Classic holiday music drifts from speakers. Tourists fill the sidewalks, many taking photos, enchanted by the magic of Merryville.

Inside the community room, excitement buzzes. As a contestant, I have to find my name on the list and discover that Mawmaw named us Team Jolly Holiday. It makes me smile as I scribble my signature in the currently empty box.

Most are treating this like the fun small-town tradition it is. Not me. This is my ticket out of here. No one wants me here anyway.

I find a seat a few rows from the front and check my phone. My hands shake and I press them against my thighs. My nerves are getting the best of me, but I stay focused on the front podium, hoping this goes by quickly.

People trickle in. Edna sits behind me with her sisters, Melinda and Brenda.

Edna leans forward. "Not really fair that you entered this contest."

I laugh. "Scared?"

"Honey, everyone who saw your name on that list is intimidated. Heard a few people dropped out because of you."

I turn and look at her. "Why?"

"Because let's get real, you can out bake them in your sleep."

"Oh, stop gassing me up," I tell her.

"Now you're being humble."

The Waverly family takes seats near the front. My parents arrive with Sammy, who stands by the back door with one of his firefighter friends. Mawmaw enters and speaks to every single person on her way to the front. She comes to me, and I stand to give her a hug.

"Doin' good?"

"Yes, ma'am," I say as she glows with Christmas cheer.

Mom catches my eye and gives me a thumbs-up.

At 5:57, someone drops into the seat beside me. I don't even have to glance over to know it's Lucas. Freshly showered. Smelling like my past.

My heart stutters and stops.

He doesn't look at me or speak, just sits close enough for me to feel his body warmth. Our legs touch and it drives me absolutely wild. He's doing this on purpose.

Heat spreads through my body like wildfire. I'm hyperaware of how damn close he is. Every nerve ending screaming. After three days of nothing, this feels monumental.

Is he doing this for show? For Mawmaw?

He still hasn't looked at me or acknowledged me at all. I keep my eyes focused forward, but my breathing grows shallow.

Exhaustion, my recent lack of food, and the constant anxiety all crash over me at once. Black spots dance at the edges of my vision, and I close my eyes, then rub my temple.

"Are you okay?" he asks.

"Don't talk to me."

"There's my winning team!" Mawmaw's voice rings out when she sees Lucas next to me.

Everyone turns to look at us. The tension is thick enough to choke on.

People smile and whisper. Someone giggles. Edna Parker and her sisters lean in, clearly delighted by this development.

Lucas shifts and wraps his arm around the back of my chair. My breath catches. The weight of his arm is so close to my shoulders that I can feel the heat radiating from it. Every instinct screams to lean back into him, to let myself have this, but I force myself to stay in place. Pretending this doesn't affect me.

The room fills with the scent of hot chocolate and cookies from the refreshment table. Outside the windows, I see Main Street is lit up with thousands of lights—the lampposts wrapped in red ribbon, storefronts glowing, and couples strolling hand in hand through Merryville.

This town lives and breathes Christmas, but right now, I'm suffocating in it.

At six fifteen, Mayor Thompson takes the podium.

"Good evening, everyone! Welcome to our annual Merryville Christmas cookie contest orientation!"

Applause erupts, and when I turn to look behind me, the room is full. People are standing around the perimeter of the huge room.

"We've had many teams register this year. A total of thirty-seven. This contest is a Merryville tradition, and we've had more tourists visit the town this year than ever before. Word about Merryville is spreading, and we're so excited about that." He grins. "Your cookies will be judged during the festival on December fourteenth, right in the town square, in front of hundreds of visitors. This is your chance to have your favorite cookie recipe shine and be inducted into the hall of fame!"

My stomach twists. Hundreds of people will watch us compete. Hundreds of people will see me fail or succeed.

The mayor walks through the rules: fifty identical cookies, baked on-site, in front of judges and festival-goers, three hours total. All ingredients are provided by contestants. Presentation, taste, and creativity are scored.

"The winning team receives five thousand dollars and the

Merryville Champion Cookie Trophy, not to mention, you'll be memorialized in the hall of fame. Many of you know the Jolly family has kept the title for twenty years running."

More applause as people glance at Lucas and me.

The pressure feels too much. I can barely breathe under the weight of it. I think I'm on the verge of a panic attack. I count to ten, try to steady my breathing, because I need control.

"Now," Mayor Thompson says, practically shaking with excitement, "let's have Santa announce the judges."

Lucas's dad moves to the front of the room, jingling with every step. He lets out a big *ho, ho, ho* before thanking everyone for being here. His dad shoots me a wink, and I smile.

"Now, let's get on with who will be helping Santa this season with this contest."

The screen lights up with five professional headshots.

"First, we have Patty Morrison—food critic for *Texas Monthly* and this year's James Beard Award winner."

A woman with kind eyes and silver hair stands from a chair in the front and waves. Everyone gives a polite applause.

"Second, Chef Marcus Williams—owner of Williams Steakhouse in Austin. He's been featured in *Bon Appétit*'s Top 50."

He stands and nods. The crowd grows more enthusiastic.

"Third, Chef Mary Carter—award-winning pastry chef and author of *Southern Sweets and Treats* and *Preparing the Perfect Cookie*."

A woman in her sixties with a warm smile appears. I have her cookbooks and am shocked the mayor was able to get so many professionals to judge this contest.

"Fourth, Chef Thomas Reeves—last year's Texas Baking Champion and owner of Confetti Cupcakes in Houston."

A young guy with tattoo sleeves appears. He can't be any older than twenty-five.

My hands are ice-cold, despite the warm room.

"Mayor Thompson will announce the final judge," Lucas's dad says.

But I notice the chair is empty by the others.

Seconds later, the lights slightly dim in the room and the projector comes on.

Mayor Thompson takes the microphone. "And for our final judge, we pulled out all the stops. I am beyond honored to introduce Chef Dominic Laurent—world-renowned pastry chef, owner of three Michelin-starred restaurants, and star of the Netflix series *The Pretty Plate*."

The room explodes with excitement.

But I've stopped breathing.

I might actually throw up.

Dominic's face fills the screen with his chiseled jawline, dark hair perfectly styled, and those calculating honey-brown eyes that used to make me feel special.

Ice floods my veins, and my vision blurs.

Beside me, Lucas freezes.

"Chef Laurent has graciously agreed to join us via video," Mayor Thompson announces. "Chef?"

Dominic sits in his New York office with the black-and-white photographs behind him, and the industrial shelving where every detail is as controlled and perfect as he is.

"Bonsoir, everyone." That thick French accent is performative. "I'm delighted to be a part of this charming southern tradition. Texas baking has heart and authenticity. I'm very much looking forward to experiencing Merryville's *famous* Christmas hospitality. I've heard so much about it."

The way he says *charming* and *hospitality* makes my skin crawl. He's heard me talk about it.

"I should mention something that makes this competition particularly meaningful to me." He leans forward and gives one of those sexy smirks I used to adore. "I've learned my former fiancée is competing."

The room goes silent, and every head whips toward me, even though he didn't say my name.

Heat floods my face as my hands ball into fists. The walls close in. I can feel every eye on me—judging, pitying, and considering.

Someone mutters "oh shit" under their breath.

Mawmaw's expression is unreadable, but there's something in her eyes that I can't quite place.

Lucas's entire body tenses beside me.

Dominic smiles, warm to everyone watching, but poisonous to me. "But let me assure you all, I take judging this competition very seriously. Every entry will be evaluated fairly and objectively. I'm here to celebrate exceptional baking, regardless of who created it."

Lies. All lies.

"In fact," he continues, and dread pools in my stomach, "I'm planning to arrive in Merryville early—next week, actually. I thought it would be wonderful to connect with the town and experience your famous Christmas Festival firsthand." His eyes seem to bore through the camera directly into me. "And of course, I'm hoping to spend some time with Holiday and catch up properly. We have so much to discuss."

No. Nope.

Edna and her sisters erupt in excited whispers. This is the kind of drama they live for.

"Holiday and I built something extraordinary together in Paris. But I won't bore you with details—I'm just thrilled to see what she creates."

The room spins, and I think I'm going to be sick. I can feel it.

I hold on, swallowing down the saliva that pools in my mouth.

"I'm very much looking forward to seeing what Holiday creates for this competition," Dominic continues smoothly. "She trained under me for three years. I know exactly what she's capable of when she's working with the right *partner*. But let's be real, she only needs herself. Can't wait to see you all and hope to experience the magic of Merryville."

The emphasis on *partner* is deliberate and threatening.

The room erupts in whispers and a seemingly collective "Aw."

"Her ex wants her back!" someone says.

"This is so romantic!" exclaims another person.

My throat closes. I can't get enough air.

"Good luck to all the contestants," Dominic continues with that rehearsed smile.

The screen goes dark, and the room explodes with noise.

I can't breathe or think. The room is too loud, too bright, too full of eyes staring at me, whispering about me, and speculation about what I'll choose.

I stand to leave, trying to avoid everyone's conversations about me. I walk out of the room.

"Holiday—" My mom reaches for me with worry etched on her face.

"I need air." My voice cracks.

I shove through the crowd toward the exit, stumbling over someone's feet.

I make it outside, and the cold air slaps my face. I stumble to the side of the building as I start dry heaving. Nothing comes up.

I feel Lucas's hand on my back, hesitant at first, then more firm. Steadying me.

"Breathe," he says quietly.

I want to shove him away, but his hand is the only thing keeping me grounded.

Dominic is coming here. Next week. And he won't make this easy for me.

The realization crashes over me that he probably pulled whatever strings necessary to get on that panel once my name was posted online as a contestant.

This is exactly the types of games he likes to play, and he loves an audience.

"Holiday," Lucas says beside me.

"Please," I tell him, trying to throw up. "Leave me alone."

"No." He's standing there with his hands clenched into fists and every muscle tense with rage.

"I can't do this." My voice breaks. "I have to quit, Lucas."

"Absolutely not," Lucas says, his jaw locking in place.

I try to move past him to go to my car. He grabs my hand, pulling me to him. "I can't."

He lifts my chin. "The Holiday I know isn't a fucking quitter."

"You don't know me anymore, Lucas. Let me go."

He shakes his head. "Not happening, Peaches."

"Stop calling me that," I say.

"Not a chance, HoHo." His smile is small, almost sad. "Someone has to remind you who you are because you seem to have forgotten." He's closer now, so close, I can see the gold flecks in his eyes. "We're doing this. We'll make sure our cookies are so damn good he has no choice but to judge fairly. Make him eat his words. We make him watch you succeed without him."

"I don't have the energy to fight you both."

His stare is unwavering. "Giving up isn't an option."

"Okay."

He's looking at me like he can see straight through to my soul. "Prove to him and everyone else that you don't need him. That you never did."

Then he turns and starts to walk away, leaving me gasping against the wall.

"So now you want to bake with me?" I ask.

He laughs. "Shut up."

I stand in the cold, watching the whole town glow.

A shiver runs over me, so I walk to my car and get inside.

A VERY MERRY ENEMY

I lean my head against the steering wheel, squeezing my eyes shut, trying to steady my breathing.

Dominic will be here next week, and I know he's going to try to take me away from the one place I've ever really belonged.

And Lucas is standing beside me, ready to fight for this.

I drive home in a daze and go upstairs to crash in my bed.

My phone vibrates, and I pull it from my pocket.

LUCAS
I'm worried about you.

HOLIDAY
Don't be.

LUCAS
Too bad. Deal with it.

HOLIDAY
I'll be fine.

LUCAS
You will, but right now, you're not.

He genuinely cares, and that wraps around me like a promise, like a memory, like everything we used to be.

I slide out of my clothes and shower until my skin turns red. Afterward, I collapse into bed, but I don't fall asleep.

In less than four weeks, I have to stand in front of hundreds of people and bake beside Lucas while Dominic watches, while Dominic tries to prove I belong to him, and while the whole town watches to see what move I make.

The love triangle rumors have already started.

My phone glows on the nightstand. I reach over to read the text.

LUCAS
Night, HoHo.

I stare at it until my vision blurs. Then I press the phone to my chest and let myself cry for everything we lost, for everything we might still lose, and for the impossible situation I've been put in.

When I open my eyes, I focus on the glow-in-the-dark stars until they blur to nothing.

And for the first time since I came back home, I think about staying instead of leaving. I dream about Christmas lights and cookies and a town that feels like home. I dream about choosing him, choosing us, choosing to fight for something instead of running away.

When I wake up, I can't remember the details.

But the feeling lingers.

I think it's hope. Or maybe it's delusion.

CHAPTER 12

❄

LUCAS

I wake up at five and can't fall back asleep.

Every time I close my eyes, I replay the look on her face when Dominic appeared on that screen. I'll never forget how the color drained from her cheeks or how she ran outside and dry heaved against the building while most of the town was inside finishing the kickoff meeting.

I followed her without thinking. Heads turned and watched me leave. I can only imagine the rumors that have started. Watching her fall apart broke something in me. For the first time since she came back, I stopped wanting to push her away. I won't let her quit. Not anymore.

I won't let that bastard win. I can't.

Seeing her so vulnerable reminded me of who we both used to be.

I suck in a deep breath, knowing her ex is coming to Merryville in one week, the same day as Jake and Claire's wedding.

Instead of staying awake behind my eyes for the next hour, I get up and head to the farm early.

By six, I've reorganized the entire equipment shed, sharpened every chain saw blade, and checked oil levels on machines that don't need to be serviced. Keeping my hands busy usually makes my brain shut up, but this time it doesn't work.

Actually, it hasn't happened since Holiday arrived.

At six thirty, Dean arrives and takes a look around the barn.

"You've been here a while," he says with a low whistle.

"Couldn't sleep. Thought I'd get started early on our list."

"Good job." He nods, moving closer to me. "Saw the Facebook posts about last night. About the contest and the judges."

Of course he did. The entire town saw. But that was expected, considering Holiday's ex is a celebrity chef. She dated the French equivalent of Gordon Ramsay.

Dean's quiet for another minute, then he clears his throat. "For what it's worth, I've seen the way she looks at you."

I don't know what to say to that. "This has nothing to do with me."

"So, this isn't about you trying to get with Holiday and her famous ex coming to steal her back?" He scoffs. "Could've fooled me."

Dean grabs his gear and heads out, chuckling, because there is nothing I can say to that. I'm just thankful he leaves me the fuck alone with my thoughts.

Five minutes later, I walk to the edge of the barn, seeing Holiday's car at the bakery. I must've been too focused to notice when she arrived this morning.

Just as I exhale, my phone vibrates in my pocket.

HOLIDAY
You at the farm yet?

LUCAS
Yep.

It's like she knew I was thinking about her.

> **HOLIDAY**
> Can you come to the bakery? Need to talk about our next baking session.

The first time we worked together, we burned cookies, and she told me I reminded her of her ex. The second time, she kissed me, and I didn't kiss her back, but then held her all night, leaving before she woke up. Tomorrow, we have to figure out how to bake together without wasting any more time. The stakes have been raised.

> **LUCAS**
> When?

> **HOLIDAY**
> Now? I prepped for this morning yesterday, so I just need to bake. I can chat while I do that.

I look at the chain saws I'm supposed to deliver to the back lot. My heart races as I type out my message.

> **LUCAS**
> On my way.

I head toward the bakery like a man on a mission.

When I push the door open, the bell jingles cheerfully, like it has all season.

In the kitchen, Holiday's placing cookies on a sheet. She's

wearing jeans and a Grinch sweatshirt, and her hair is pulled into a high ponytail. And she's wearing her red lipstick.

I'm staring, not able to help it. Holiday looks up and waves me to the back. We haven't been face-to-face since last night when I told her she wasn't a quitter.

"Hey," she says.

"Hey. Mornin'."

The energy buzzes between us, but it's different than it's been, more charged, and I want to figure out what that means.

She twists her hands together. "So. I was thinking we could get together and bake tomorrow night."

"Sure."

"We need to create a showstopping cookie." She smiles but it doesn't reach her eyes. "Since we're running out of time before—"

"He gets here."

She nods. "Yeah."

"You upset about this?" I shove my hands in my pockets.

Our gazes lock, like she's not used to people asking her how she feels about things anymore.

"Very much so. You?"

"Oh, I'm fucking *pissed*," I admit.

Agreeing on anything is new for us.

She takes a breath. "Lucas, about last night…"

"We don't need to discuss it."

Her brows crease. "Do you really want to do this with me?"

"I'm *not* quitting." I know it's not what she's asking, but it's the best answer I can give right now. Every damn day, she prepares a new menu that has sold out without any problems. "There is no other person I'd rather have as my partner," I add, not wanting to be a complete asshole to her today. "We always said we'd participate in this contest."

She chuckles. "I'd forgotten about that. Wait, do you think that's why Mawmaw signed us up?"

"I can't even begin to try to read that woman's mind," I admit. "Mawmaw does things for her own reasons."

Holiday smiles, removes the cookies from the ovens, and places the next batches inside. "True. Okay then, we'll meet tomorrow night at six."

"At my place," I say.

She tilts her head and makes a face. "Absolutely not."

"Why? Afraid you might end up in my bed again?"

The ghost of a smile plays on her lips. "Don't make me kick you out of here."

I notice how her eyes trail down to my mouth. "Try me."

She groans. "Fine. Your place. But only because I don't have the time or energy to argue about it. But you're going to behave yourself."

A scoff releases from me. "Me? Behave myself? *Puh-lease.* You need to behave yourself. *You* kissed *me.* Per usual."

"And you've been the perfect gentleman," she says, rolling her eyes. "Doesn't matter. We have to create the best damn cookie Dominic's ever tasted so he cries himself to sleep wishing he knew the exact recipe."

"Yeah, I hope he fucking chokes on it," I mutter.

She's almost smiling now. "No, because then I'd have to save him."

The tension breaks just enough for me to breathe again.

"I should get back," I say.

"Yeah. You *are* distracting."

But neither of us moves.

The early morning sun slices through the windows of the bakery. It's like we're trying to memorize this moment before everything changes. For better or worse.

I turn to leave, and she says my name. When I glance back at her, she's biting the inside of her cheek. "I'm thankful you came last night. To the meeting. That you followed me outside."

My chest tightens. "I wasn't going to let you be there alone."

"Everyone saw what you did. There will be rumo—"

"I don't give a flying fuck, Peaches. There will *always* be rumors about us."

The silence streams between us. Her blue eyes get shiny but she blinks it away. I notice the way her hands shake, and she tucks them in her apron pockets. "See you tomorrow night."

"Tomorrow."

I walk out before I do something stupid like pull her into my arms and devour her lips. Wish I knew why this feels like the beginning of goodbye, like something or someone is going to pull her away from me.

I don't know if I can let that happen again.

After I leave the cookie shop, I stand in front of it, feeling electricity flowing in my veins. That always happens when we're close.

For the rest of the day, I cut trees on autopilot. I smile and make small talk about decorating trees. I catch glimpses of Holiday in the window, and this time her smile doesn't fade when she sees me.

Midafternoon, my phone buzzes, and I pull it out to see a text.

> **MAWMAW**
> Family dinner Sunday. You're coming. Not optional.

Great. Nothing like mandatory family time when my life is imploding.

> **LUCAS**
> Can't. Busy.

> **MAWMAW**
> With what?

> **LUCAS**
> Farm things.

> **MAWMAW**
> Lucas James Jolly. 5 o'clock on Sunday. Bring Holiday.

I stare at that text.

> **LUCAS**
> Why would I do that?

> **MAWMAW**
> Because I want to feed you both and talk about strategy to win this contest, considering her ex is a judge.

> **LUCAS**
> I'm not asking her to join us. She's dealing with enough stress.

> **MAWMAW**
> Then I will.

> **LUCAS**
> Mawmaw! Don't. This is ridiculous.

But she's already stopped responding.
Fuck.
Five minutes later, Holiday texts me.

> **HOLIDAY**
> Your grandmother just invited me to dinner on Sunday. Did you know about this?

> **LUCAS**
> Just found out.

> **HOLIDAY**
> Do I have to go?

> **LUCAS**
> No, but she'll be disappointed and you'll have to hear it until the end of time.

> **LUCAS**
> Your choice though.

> **HOLIDAY**
> UGH!

> **LUCAS**
> Sorry. I don't make the rules.

> **HOLIDAY**
> Mawmaw does, apparently.

Three dots appear and disappear about six times.

> **HOLIDAY**
> You owe me.

> **LUCAS**
> How do I owe YOU? I don't want to go either.

> **HOLIDAY**
> Okay, but it's your family.

She has a point.

> **LUCAS**
> Fine. You've been granted one IOU.

> **HOLIDAY**
> Thank you very much. I will cash in.

> **LUCAS**
> Make it good.

I can't begin to imagine what she'll ask of me. We used to exchange IOUs like they were currency. In a way, they are.

As soon as the sun sets, I go home.

My house is cold and empty, per usual. I turn up the heat and stand in the kitchen, staring at the container of cookies we made last Saturday. I haven't been able to toss them out because it seems like a waste.

I grab one and bite into it, and it's unsurprisingly still good, even almost a week later. But she's determined to do better, and I get it.

I almost feel sorry for Dominic because when Holiday gets a chip on her shoulder, she's dangerous. Unstoppable. She'll run circles around him with a smile on her face.

I finish eating the cookie and wipe down the counter, knowing Holiday will be here again, baking in the kitchen that was built for her. It was odd seeing her as I'd always imagined.

I pull my phone from my pocket.

> **LUCAS**
> Tomorrow night. Don't be late.

Her response comes immediately.

HOLIDAY
> I'm going to be annoyingly late.

I chuckle, knowing she won't. Holiday is the kind of girl who arrives early and waits. Maybe she's changed, though.

I go upstairs and change out of my work clothes when I hear knocking on the front door. I pause, pulling a clean T-shirt on, and then I hear it again. It's loud and persistent, the kind of knock that says *Hurry the fuck up*.

I jog downstairs and see Sammy's truck in my driveway. I open the door, and he's standing there with a six-pack of beer, wearing a look I recognize but don't like. It's the same one he had senior year when Theo Williams made Holiday cry at prom.

"We need to talk," Sammy says.

I step aside, letting him in. "Everything okay?"

He enters my living room and sets the beer on the coffee table, then looks around.

"You don't have a fire goin'? It's cold as hell in here, Lucas." He's already moving toward the fireplace.

"I got it," I tell him, grabbing logs from the stack and arranging them. Seconds later, flames lick the wood, filling the room with that smoky smell that means winter's arrived.

He cracks open two beers, hands me one, and drops onto my couch.

"So," he says. "Dominic fucking Laurent."

I take a long drink, following his lead. "Yeah."

"That piece of shit is coming here."

"Next week."

"He's going to try to win back my sister." Sammy's jaw tightens. "Which is why I'm here."

I sit in the chair next to the couch and glare at him. "Only one part of that is my business. Your sister does whatever and whomever she wants."

"That *cannot* happen." He leans forward, and his blue eyes narrow. "I need to tell you some things that she won't tell you because she's ashamed. Things I only know because Mom dragged it out of her last Christmas when she canceled coming home again. Keep it to yourself."

My stomach knots. "I don't need——"

"Yes, you fucking do." Sammy takes a drink, and his jaw clenches tight. "Holiday met Dominic her final year at culinary school. He was guest teaching a pastry course, and she was starstruck because this famous chef with connections was paying attention to her."

The fire crackles. I say nothing, not wanting to hear about their love story.

"Years later, after she interned at a few elite bakeries, he offered her a job in Paris. They immediately started dating. He told her she was talented, special, and that he could take her far." Sammy's voice hardens. "Within six months, she'd moved into his condo. Within a year, she was managing his bakery. He took credit for her hard work."

My heart races, and the beat pounds in my ears. "How?"

"Every recipe *she* developed, every technique *she* perfected, he put his shitty name on it and told her that's how the industry works. That she was learning from the best and should be grateful, and they were getting married, so it was something they could share."

My hands tighten around the beer bottle.

"Oh, it got so much worse," he says, kicking his feet up on my coffee table.

"I can't fucking listen to this unless you want me to fly to Paris and John Wick him."

"This isn't a joke," he says.

"I'm not joking." The more I think about that scum taking credit for Holiday's cookies, the angrier I grow.

"He controlled what she wore to events. How much she weighed. Who she could be friends with. Everything she posted on social media had to be approved." Sammy's voice drops. "He told her she was too small-town. Too unsophisticated. And she believed he held her professional career in the palm of his hand. Without a reference, years of experience were wasted."

The words land like punches.

"He trapped her," I say.

"Yes," he whispers, staring at the fire.

I breathe out hard, but it's ragged.

"She escaped Paris, knowing she would lose her entire career."

My blood runs cold. "Did he hurt her?"

"Mentally." Sammy's knuckles are white around his beer. "Mom confronted her, and Holiday eventually broke down and admitted everything. He isolated her and made her doubt herself. It took years, but he had her convinced she was nothing without him and never would be."

I can't breathe.

"When she returned, Dominic wouldn't stop calling her. He'd send letters, telling her how much he loved her. When that didn't work, he tried to ruin her professional reputation. Called her ungrateful, selfish, talentless, and made sure she was a nobody. He caused a lot of anxiety attacks."

"She left him, knowing she'd lose it all," I whisper.

Sammy meets my eyes. "Yes. His connections run deep. Every door she knocked on, he'd already closed and locked it. She's applied to bakeries in all the major cities. She hasn't received one call in spite of having over a decade of experience. He knew she'd keep going, and whoever hired her would be his new competition."

As I stare at the fire, anger surrounds me. A few minutes pass, and then Sammy speaks up again.

"He's not here to judge cookies." Sammy leans back. "He wants her back. He needs her to return to Paris. Holiday working for Emma is dangerous for him."

The fire pops. A log shifts.

"Should we quit this competition?" I ask Sammy, not wanting this to cause Holiday any unnecessary stress, especially if this man was mentally abusive. "If you think we shouldn't do it, I'll go down to city hall tomorrow and withdraw, which will pull her out, too."

"No." He points at me. "Holiday needs to prove to everyone she doesn't need him and she never did. She's been running Emma's bakery for three weeks, and it's currently the most successful thing on the farm."

"I'm aware."

"Are you? Because from where I've been sitting, you've been doing nothing but pushing her away and treating her like shit. She needs someone to believe in her. I'm her twin brother. I love her. But I can't be what she needs right now." Sammy walks to the fire and stares into it. "You can, though. You always could."

"Please, don't—"

"Before she left for culinary school, you two had something special. Then everything got fucked up." He turns to look at me. "I watched you guys fall in love. Watched you sneak around, thinking no one knew. Watched *you* fall apart."

I don't deny it. I can't.

"She made mistakes. But that's not what matters now. The past is in the fucking past, isn't it?" He crosses back to the couch, sits down. "Dominic is coming here, and you have a choice to make."

"It's never been my decision," I say, nostrils flaring.

"Don't let him manipulate his way back into her life. You can't fucking let him whisk her back to Paris or New York or wherever the hell he wants to take her and watch her disappear into his dark web again." Sammy's eyes are stern. "Fight for her, show everyone who she belongs to. She doesn't need his validation or his name or his fucking Michelin stars. But she needs you."

My heart pounds. "You have no idea what you're talking about."

"Deny it all you want. That contest isn't about a trophy anymore, Lucas. It's about proving a point." He moves back to the couch and leans his head back on the cushion. "Don't be a pussy. This is your last chance."

"Well, this conversation wasn't on my bingo card for today," I say, chugging the beer and grabbing another one.

Sammy does the same while the fire crackles. The bottles are leaving rings of condensation on my coffee table.

I lick my lips, replaying every conversation Holiday and I have had. "The first night we baked, she told me I reminded her of him."

Sammy's head snaps toward me. "What?"

"We fought, and I said some shit I shouldn't have. She told me the way I was acting reminded her of her ex." The memory carries a late punch. "How he made her feel like she was never good enough."

Sammy shakes his head. "What did you say?"

"Nothing. I left." I stare at my beer. "Been trying not to be that guy ever since."

"You're not that guy."

"How do you know? What if I am? What if I can't do any better than him?"

"You're sitting here, gutted that you hurt her. Dominic never gave a shit about her." Sammy's voice softens. "You loved her. You never stopped. You were broken. It's different."

I don't confirm or deny it. Don't need to. He already knows.

"When Dominic shows up next week, you look him in the eye and show him exactly who Holiday Patterson should be with. And if you break her heart, I'll kick your ass."

"Thanks, bestie," I say, chugging my beer. "I'd deserve it."

"You two are both stubborn and honestly deserve one

another." Sammy heads for the door. "Now win this shit. Please. Not for the money. Not for the trophy. But because fuck Dominic Laurent."

I follow him to the door.

He stops on the porch, turns back. "One more thing."

"Yeah?"

"Did you know she still has those glow-in-the-dark stars you put up in her room when we were sixteen? She never took them down." He gives me a small smile and leaves.

I stand in the doorway, watching his taillights disappear down my driveway.

The cold air bites at my skin, but I don't move.

Holiday still has those stars. She always hated sleeping in the dark alone, something she never grew out of. Sometimes, when she'd text me that she couldn't sleep, I'd sneak in through her window and hold her until she drifted off to dreamland. We wished upon the stars together, and then I put them up there so her eyes could focus on something else instead of the darkness.

Countless nights, we'd lie under the neon green stars and make wishes about her dreams of owning a bakery, me expanding the farm, and us being together.

Knowing she's still sleeping under them does something to me.

I go back inside and sit on the couch. I grab another beer, crack it open, and watch the roaring fire.

Sammy's right.

This isn't about the trophy anymore or keeping Mawmaw's winning streak alive. It's not about the money. This contest is about proving to Holiday that she's always had everything she's ever needed.

Guilt washes over me, and I pull out my phone to text her.

LUCAS
You're right. I am an asshole.

. . .

The dots appear for a long time before she finally responds.

HOLIDAY
> Always have been, always will be. 🙂

The smiley face doesn't erase the awful things I've said to her. Knowing this information changes so much for me. My heart aches for her, and I barely understand what she went through. But it's more than e-fucking-nough.

All Holiday has ever wanted is to be loved by someone who loves her just as much. Fifteen years ago, I couldn't tell her she was the love of my life. If I had, would things be different?

I set my phone down and watch the fire until it burns low.

Some women never leave situations like that. My strong girl did, and she came right back to me, where she's always belonged.

CHAPTER 13

HOLIDAY

My phone won't stop buzzing.

I crack one eye open and see seventeen missed calls from my big sister Tricia. She runs a taco truck with her best friend in downtown Merryville and works seventy-hour weeks to support herself and Bethany after her divorce last year. We've barely talked in the past three weeks, even though we live seven minutes away from one another. I guess that's the reality of being an adult these days.

Between her food truck hours and my bakery schedule, we've been like ships passing in the night, exchanging quick texts about Bethany's work schedule and not much of anything else. I've had nothing exciting to share, and I refuse to complain about my life when she's been through so much. Instead of dragging each other down, we just don't.

Before I can text her, she's FaceTiming me.

"Have you seen it?" she says in a whisper, her blue eyes soft. Her face is too close to the camera, and she looks exhausted, with dark circles under her eyes that match mine.

I sit up and turn on the bedside lamp, seeing it's just after four. I look like a hot fucking mess and try to smooth my hair down. "Seen what?"

"The Instagram post. *People* magazine. You're trending, Holiday. Like, actually trending. I should warn you, though. You're not going to like why."

My stomach drops as she flips the camera to show me her laptop screen. There's a photo of Dominic from Wednesday night's cookie contest meeting, looking polished and perfect in his expensive sweater, wearing a million-dollar smile.

The headline reads:

Michelin-Starred Chef Dominic Laurent to Judge Small-Town Baking Contest Where His Ex-fiancée is Competing. Is This a Second Chance at Love?

"I have to go." I hang up before she can ask me any questions.

It's too early for this.

My hands shake as I google my name. Seventeen articles pop up: TMZ, Food & Wine, and Bon Appétit. Basically, every food publication I've ever dreamed of being featured in, and they're writing about my failed engagement instead of my incredible holiday baking skills.

My brows furrow. "Fuck him. He did this on purpose."

I'm sure this was part of his sabotage plan.

The headlines eventually blur together into keywords—celebrity chef, small-town baker, second chances, holiday romance. They've turned my life into a Hallmark movie plot. *Ugh!*

I cannot be the main character in that type of scenario. I nearly burst into tears thinking about this, because it's a living nightmare.

How!? How did I end up here, and I'm still somehow running from this man?

Dominic did tell me he'd *never* let me go. I shudder thinking about that night when he was so upset. He tossed a crystal wineglass against the wall because he was so frustrated that I wanted to see my family for the holidays last year. I ended up canceling my trip. That was the second time I stayed when I knew I needed to end it.

The third time, well, I'm currently living it.

My phone explodes with notifications. My Instagram followers jump by thousands each time I refresh. There are hundreds of comments on posts of Dominic and me from three years ago that I'd forgotten existed. There are DMs from people I haven't spoken to since culinary school, asking if Dominic really wants me back.

Of course he does.

He's always needed me, but what we had wasn't love. It was convenience, a business decision that came with sexual favors and fancy dinners. We looked great together, seemed to work together flawlessly, but it was all a lie. Isolation will do that to a person.

When I see a text from an unknown number, my heart races.

> **UNKNOWN**
>
> Holiday, I'm so sorry for how things ended between us. I miss you terribly. I made mistakes, but I've changed. I hope we can talk when I arrive. I want to make things right. You deserve that. We deserve that.

I stare at the words until they blur, then I program the stupid ass's name into my phone. *Dominic.*

The old Holiday, the one who spent years in Paris trying to be perfect enough for him, would have read this and run back. I would've believed him when he said he changed. But I'm not that Holiday anymore.

Once my blinders were off, I couldn't unsee the ugly, competitive, toxic person he was. Dominic wanted to dull my shine so I would never be his competition. He saw in me what I didn't see in myself and wanted to make sure I never recognized my talent.

When I overheard him speak about my pastries like they were his masterpieces, I woke up. I refused to die in his shadow as he took the credit and kept the crown. He's not creative, he's conniving. Stupid me almost married him.

There are a million things I want to say to Dominic, but instead, I block the number. Somehow, I force myself out of bed, more pissed off at the world than I should be for how early it is. He'd barely crossed my mind until now.

Merryville is my sanctuary, my home, the one place where I know exactly who I am. My hometown is a place where Dominic can never erase me. My talent speaks for itself. No one here gives a fuck about him. Not even me.

I shower, throw on jeans and a candy cane sweatshirt, then grab my sparkly green gloves, hoping they'll brighten my mood. It's the small things in life.

Bella and Wendy are already waiting by the bakery door when I arrive. Their expressions are neutral, and they treat me like I'm an if-you-break-it-you-buy-it vase in an antique store.

"We saw the articles," Bella blurts. I knew she'd spit it out before I unlocked the door because she can't help herself. She was like that when I'd babysit her. Bella would literally tell on herself before I found out she and Wendy did something they shouldn't have.

"I expected as much." I unlock the door and gently push it open for them. "Nothing I can do about it. There will always be rumors about me," I say, remembering what Lucas said.

He was right.

I can do hard things.

Dominic may have smeared my name and spread rumors about me to our colleagues, but knowing he never loved me somehow hurt worse. I was both the beauty and the brains in his bakery. He just had balls in a business where men and money still rule.

"What someone thinks about you isn't your problem. It's theirs," Bella says with a shrug.

"You're right."

The three of us fall into our routine, and I lose myself in the familiar rhythm that comes with baking. My hands know what to do even when my mind is playing Dominic's text on repeat, wondering what the hell I'm supposed to do when he shows up next week. He's charming when he wants to be and he's gorgeous. I turn the holiday music up to drown it all out.

Bella eventually clears her throat. "When are you baking with Lucas again?"

I think about tonight and keep a straight face, not wanting to show any excitement.

Wendy gasps. "Did you just almost smile about that?"

Guess I failed.

The two girls scream and jump around.

"You two better stop!" I warn, throwing a wad of dough at them.

Bella catches it, then takes a bite.

"Oh my. Do *not* eat raw dough. Seriously." I point my finger at her like she's six years old again with dog food in her mouth.

Her eyes go wide as she playfully grins.

"It's not always the raw eggs you have to worry about, but the flour. I'll spare you the details, but unless you want the possibility of getting E. coli or salmonella, don't swallow."

Bella spits wet dough onto the floor, then washes her mouth out in the handwashing sink. "Why didn't anyone tell me that before I took this job? Do you have any idea how much raw cookie dough I've consumed in the past week alone?"

"You're lucky," I tell her, happy for a conversation change. "Need to make you a shirt that says, 'Risking It All for Raw Cookie Dough.'"

She bursts into laughter. "For real."

As soon as we unlock the door, we're thrown into a rush. But every customer has the same curious look when their eyes meet mine. It's different from before. I glance out the window and see the line is winding down the sidewalk, but I don't know how far back it goes.

I swallow hard.

"Take this, Bella," I say, handing her the tongs in my hand, along with a box.

I move outside, and my eyes widen. There are at least one hundred people waiting for my cookies. When the crowd cheers for me like I'm some sort of celebrity, my face goes bright red.

Word quickly spread around town, and I'd bet anything people came here for a glimpse of the drama. But I smile, knowing every single person in this line will fall in love with my desserts.

I walk inside, knowing I won't have enough cookies for everyone unless I start a buying limit. This isn't something I'd planned to do until next month. But at the speed and quantities Bella is boxing dozens, there is no way we'll make it through half the waiting customers. I do some quick math and shove my shaky hands into my pockets, coming up with a solution. I smile, knowing it's my decision. One I get to make without permission from anyone.

"Hi! Good morning, everyone. Due to the overwhelming number of customers outside, I'm going to limit sales to one dozen max," I announce.

Suddenly, a guy in line loses his entire shit. "What the fuck? That's not fair! We've been waiting in line since seven!"

I move from behind the counter, closer to him, so I won't have to raise my voice. "Sir, I know you're really upset, and I will happily let—"

"Upset? Upset!? You have no fuck—"

Moments later, the man is being dragged out by the back of his shirt, and that's when I see Lucas. Customers move out of the way, allowing him access to the door. I steal glances out the window.

Lucas places his hand on the guy's shoulder and keeps his voice low and controlled. Lucas says something, then points to the Jolly that's embroidered into his jacket. A moment later, Lucas nods toward the exit, and I know he's kicking him off the farm.

Lucas returns and I stare at him. Dominic never took up for me when I was being yelled at. He let me be his scapegoat for irate customers.

"Now, does anyone else want to be rude? It's the ho-ho-holidays. We can do better than that guy. I won't tolerate disrespectful behavior anywhere on the farm. Understood?" He looks around the room, giving them a cheeky smile. It's boyish, cute, and kind. And real. I see his dimple. Then his eyes land on mine and time freezes. "Have a good day."

"You too." My voice cracks, and I'm in shock. I swallow hard. When Lucas leaves, it's dead quiet inside the bakery, and I can feel the vibe is off.

"I'm so sorry that happened, everyone. If anyone else is especially upset, please let me know. I'll happily let everyone inside this building who can hear my voice get more than one dozen just because. I'm not prepared for the line today, which is my fault. Tomorrow, I'll give each of you a free dozen if you come back."

"Deal!" someone screams from the doorway, and another person laughs.

"We're patient. We'd rather have a dozen cookies than none," another woman tells me. "We heard your cookies were better than anything in the fancy bakery you worked at in Paris."

"You did?" I ask. "Who said that?"

"Someone outside." They shrug.

Like that narrows it down.

"Wow. Well, thank you all so much for understanding.

Seriously, thank you," I say. "Give everyone half off, up to and including the lady in the red sweater," I tell Wendy, loud enough for them all to hear.

Bella and Wendy look at me with heart emojis in their eyes.

"Lucas to the rescue. That was interesting," Bella whispers.

"So broody," Wendy adds, waggling her brows.

"Hush," I say with a laugh, but they're right. It was hot. I have to admit that.

Between customers, I keep catching glimpses of Lucas through the bakery windows. At one point, he's loading trees onto a minivan and lifts one of those massive trees like it weighs absolutely nothing. Every single time I glance up, he's already looking at me and shaking his head.

I can't do this with him.

Not with Dominic coming to town.

Not with how things have gone so far.

Lucas has boundaries, and I can't plow over them. Even if I want to.

We sell out by twelve o'clock, which is a massive problem because I'm going to have to somehow triple production or start baking throughout the day. We had over two hundred customers and still had to send more than one hundred away. They were blocking the sidewalk, and eventually Lucas had to move the line.

My back aches, my feet throb, and I smell like I bathed in butter and sugar.

We prep as much as we can for the next few days until we have no more room in the fridges. I send Emma a quick text.

I snap a picture of all the prep we did for tomorrow, and every rack is full in the industrial-sized refrigerators we have now.

A VERY MERRY ENEMY

> **HOLIDAY**
> We sold 3000 cookies in three hours with a limit of one dozen per customer. The line was wrapped around the block.

> **EMMA**
> Is this the sensation you were talking about?

> **HOLIDAY**
> This is just the beginning.

> **EMMA**
> The magic of Merryville! Thank you so much. You should be proud. Like I said before, you're a pastry godsend.

> **HOLIDAY**
> You're the best boss I've ever had.

It's not a lie. I've worked for some shitty bakery owners.

> **EMMA**
> You're the boss here. I'm along for the ride with you. Without your help, they'd have gotten gingerbread and chocolate chip cookies every day.

> **HOLIDAY**
> I'm just living my dream. Working in a cookie shop at one of the happiest places on earth. I feel lucky.

> **EMMA**
> I do too. Thank you for everything.

> **HOLIDAY**
> How are you feeling?

EMMA
Spoiled. 😊

Hudson is such a good guy. Honestly, all the Jolly men are perfect gentlemen and love their women fiercely.

I drive home and shower until the water runs cold. I get dressed in black leggings and a hoodie, leaving my hair in a messy bun. I don't look like I'm trying to impress him, which is great. That's the very last thing I want Lucas to think.

The drive to his house feels both too long and too short. The sun has already set when I pull up next to his truck in the driveway. Smoke curls from the chimney, and every window glows warm.

I force myself out of the car and tuck my hands inside my pockets as I walk toward his house. The porch steps creak under my weight, and as I'm raising my hand to knock, the door swings open.

Lucas stands there with jeans low on his hips, and he has on a dark gray T-shirt that looks like it wants to be ripped straight off him. His eyes look impossibly bright tonight. His dark hair is messy and damp. He showered for me.

"You're actually on time," he says sarcastically, in mock surprise.

"Don't get used to it *ever* happening again. Next time, I'm going to purposely be an hour late."

"Pfft. Your obsessive need to be on time won't ever fucking allow it. Even after all this time. Guess some things don't change, do they?" The corner of his mouth twitches as he steps aside. I notice how his eyes trail up to my hair as I walk past him.

A buttery garlic aroma makes my mouth water as I enter.

"What is that amazing smell?" I ask.

He closes the door. "Our dinner."

"Our?"

"*We* have to eat something, don't we? Might as well do that before we bake," he says as I move into the kitchen. "Unless you already ate."

"I haven't," I mutter, noticing the wineglasses on the counter. One already has dark liquid in it. Lucas moves to the stove and stirs something.

"You cooked for me?" I ask, truly honored.

"Don't sound so shocked about it."

I pour a glass, spinning it around and taking a sip. The flavor touches my palate, and Lucas pulls two plates from the cabinet. I take in the small details of the house that I overlooked before, like the seat in the window that overlooks the woods. It's a perfect reading nook.

He built everything the way we'd talked about.

I move farther into the kitchen as he plates our food.

"Lucas," I say, but my voice comes out strangled.

"Relax. It's just dinner." But he won't meet my eyes.

"Yeah? Who else have you cooked dinner for here?" I ask, lifting the glass to my lips and taking two big gulps.

He sets both plates at the breakfast nook. "Just you."

I force myself to look away from him as he sits in front of me, and I slide onto the stool. "Chicken piccata with roasted veggies."

"Yeah, like I said, this girl I used to be friends with taught me some things."

I laugh. "The one who disappeared?"

"Yeah," he says, handing me a fork and napkin. "But I think she might come back."

"Really? Should I be worried?"

He smirks. "Probably. She had a thing for me. Rumor has it she still does."

My cheeks heat, and I know my face is red as I cut into the chicken. No way I can respond to that, but luckily, the first bite is perfect. It's tender, lemony, and buttery, exactly how we'd practiced.

"Wow," I say. "That girl must've been one hell of a cook."

"Still is." He's watching me.

I can't help but smile. "We made this so long ago."

"I memorized every recipe we made by heart," he says, and heat rushes through me.

The intensity of his stare is impossible to avoid.

"Figured you deserved something better than frozen pizza or grilled cheese," he says.

I snort. "Guess I really haven't changed that much."

"About today." His jaw tightens. "Sorry I stepped in like that. I know you had it under control, but I lost my shit seeing him hollering at you."

"Thank you for caring." I take a sip of wine. "Where'd you even come from? One second, he was yelling, and the next, you were basically throwing him outside."

"I did not *throw* him. I pulled him. Nobody talks to you like that. Ever. I don't care what you did or didn't do. It's about respect." He says it like it's a cardinal rule.

Heat creeps up my neck. "You didn't have to defend me."

"I don't have to do a lot of things." His eyes meet mine. "I choose to. But isn't that what life is all about? Choices?"

"Yeah, I guess it is," I say.

We eat in comfortable silence for a few minutes. The only sounds are forks scraping against glass plates and the fire crackling in the other room. I'm hyperaware of how shallow his breaths are and how his tattoos creep up his arms. I also notice how his eyes soften at the edges when he looks at me.

"Thank you for this," I say as we finish eating. "I don't remember the last time a man cooked for me."

"That's sad as fuck, Holiday." He stands and takes our empty plates to the sink.

"I know," I tell him.

"This is the bare minimum that friends do for one another. You deserve better than that bullshit. Okay?"

I nod. "I don't know what I deserve anymore."

"You deserve to be happy," he simply says.

"Not sure I know what that is, either." I laugh sarcastically.

"You will," he says. "Ready to bake?"

"Yes, drill sergeant," I say, breathing out of my nose as he quickly cleans up after dinner.

"I'll pull the ingredients," I tell him.

"Go for it. Everything is in the pantry or fridge." He tilts his chin toward the door.

I place my hands on my hips, doing a quick scan of what I've pulled.

"Let's make some magic," he says, shooting me a wink.

My heart palpitates.

And for the first time since I returned home, I actually believe we can.

CHAPTER 14

LUCAS

I've been trying not to think about what Sammy told me, but with Holiday right in front of me, it's hard. Every time I look at her, I think about how that piece of shit controlled and isolated her from everyone who ever loved her. There is a special place in hell for him.

The thought makes me want to put my fist through a wall, but I can't tell her I know. I think that would make everything worse, considering she's still working through the end of that relationship. I know Holiday and know she pulls away when things get too awkward. That's the last thing either of us needs right now when we've barely started to find our way back to something I've tried to forget.

I'll watch and protect her. If anyone tries to get close enough to hurt her again, they'll have to go through me first.

This morning, when that asshole started yelling at her in the bakery, I dropped the tree I was carrying and stormed through that door in seconds. I could hear him cursing in front of kids and families.

Not sure I'll ever forget the look on his face when I dragged him outside and explained who the fuck I was. I banned him from the property. The look on Holiday's face made everything worth it.

Now she's standing in my kitchen with her hands tucked into her hoodie pocket, studying the ingredients like she's doing calculations in her head. Her hair is up in that messy bun I like, but it's intentional, not a chaotic disaster. This is exactly how I like to see her, relaxed and being herself. Not trying to impress. She showered before coming over, and the smell of her soap makes me want to lean in closer every time she moves past me.

"Okay," she finally says. "So, we tried other recipes before, and they were good, but I think we can do better."

"You always think you can do better."

"I usually can," she says and pauses. "But not with everything."

"You're damn right about that," I say, reading between the lines.

It does something to my chest that I'm not ready to feel. I don't say anything else, because it's best if I don't. Right now, Holiday needs a friend, someone to keep her ass honest and not let her forget who the hell she is.

She continues. "Hmm. What if we tried something like a shortbread with a chocolate fudge and pecan top? A decadent cookie bar."

I lean against the counter. "Sounds complicated."

"It's not. It'll just take multiple steps that will need to be timed perfectly. It's also layered, which is impressive, and possible in three hours." She moves to the sink to wash her hands. "A wise person once told me to trust the process."

I used to tell her that all the time.

She pauses and looks over her shoulder at me. Her baby blues catch the light from the overhead, and they're shining a little brighter than they were when she arrived.

"The good ole days," I say, reminiscing. "When my biggest concern was getting ungrounded so I could hang out with you at the fair."

"I'd trade anything to go back." Something vulnerable flashes in her expression and it makes me want to move to her. It takes all my effort to stay right where I am.

If I had a time machine, I'd do things differently, that's for damn sure.

"Well." Holiday dries her hands on a dish towel and quickly wipes down the counter. I grab two mixing bowls and measuring cups.

"Let's start with the shortbread dough," Holiday says, preheating the oven.

She calls out directions so I can follow along. I'm shocked when she says it's only butter, sugar, and flour with salt.

"Gradually add the flour. Don't dump it all in at once," she instructs. "We're not going to overwork the dough. Got it?"

"Understood," I say, knowing how good a teacher she is. I almost feel sorry for her former employees, because I know how hard it is to lose her. When it looks crumbly like hers, I stop mixing.

Holiday takes the dough out of her bowl and plops it on the counter. We stand side by side, combining our mixtures into one big ball. I can't help but watch her hands work it.

"Rolling pin?" she asks.

I bend down on one knee and reach to the back of the cabinet directly below me. I look up at her, and she swallows hard. The air crackles with the knowledge that I would've married her. I let the moment grow uncomfortable for her because she needs to sit in that feeling.

I slowly stand and hand it to her.

"We're going to flatten it out," she says. "I need two baking pans. The largest ones you have."

The soft sound of our breaths mixing as we make magic in the kitchen is something I haven't heard in a long time. It reminds me of being seventeen and having sleepovers at Mawmaw's so we could bake cookies at midnight. Holiday would invent recipes. Sometimes they'd turn out great, other times they wouldn't. It was trial-and-error baking, something we bonded over.

"So," I say as she places the sweet dough in the bottom of two pans. "Three thousand cookies in three hours today."

She groans as she grabs a fork, stabbing the top of the shortbread. "Please don't remind me."

"That's unheard of, Holiday. You're going to burn out trying to keep up with that."

"What else do I have to do this season?" She sighs. "It's the only thing that keeps my mind busy, and right now, I need that distraction."

"Okay, but it's not healthy to work yourself to death," I offer.

She tilts her head at me. "You're one to talk. You're at the farm more than me."

I suck in a breath, realizing she noticed.

"Some of us still have to prove ourselves around here. I'm not a Jolly who's automatically loved because of the namesake," she says. "You have it easy, Lucas."

I can't deny that my life is easier than most. It doesn't mean I work less hard, but there are privileges when your dad is Santa and your family owns the only tree farm in a hundred-mile radius.

"I just want as many people as possible to eat my cookies this season. I don't care what it takes."

"Let me help you," I offer, understanding this is personal for her.

"You want to help me?" she asks. "Come on, Lucas. Like you have time for that."

When the oven is at temperature, Holiday places the pans inside, then sets a timer for twenty minutes.

I lean against the counter, crossing my arms over my chest. Her gaze trails over my arms.

"It would be good practice."

"Lucas, you don't have to—"

"I want to." The sweet smell of cookies baking fills the kitchen. "Might as well practice as much as possible."

"You're already working sixteen-hour shifts, how will that work?" she asks with brows lifted.

"I stick around until you leave, Peaches," I admit. "My shift ends at three every day. I worked hard for my cushy schedule."

She gives me a look. "Why would you do that?"

"I'm not leaving you on the farm alone," I say.

A smile touches her lips. "But you *hate* me."

I playfully roll my eyes. "Yep. Imagine what it would be like if it were love."

This makes her chuckle. "Helping me prep isn't the same as practicing for the contest."

"We need to relearn how to work together in the kitchen again." I look at her directly. "Plus, I'm lonely as fuck. My brothers moved on with their lives. Sammy's been busy as hell with work. What else do I have going on? This is pretty much it."

The admission hangs between us. I haven't shared that with anyone because who wants to hear about me coming home to an empty house I built for a future that never happened. It feels safe to be honest with her.

"I've been lonely, too," she tells me. "It's really weird being back. I feel like I'm stuck between two different versions of myself."

"Yeah, that girl who went to Paris, I don't like her very much."

She sarcastically laughs. "Me either. I don't know who that person was."

I hold her gaze, knowing the person I fell in love with is still in there somewhere, fighting to be released from that prison.

While the cookies finish baking, I add more wood to the fire.

Eventually, the oven dings and Holiday removes the pans, setting them onto cork rounds on the counter. "While it cools, we'll make the fudge. We'll pour it on top and let it chill in the fridge until the timer runs out, then serve it."

My mouth falls open. "You're so talented."

"Oh, stop," she says, tucking her lips into her mouth. "You give me too much credit."

I stand to the side, watching Holiday make the fudge. A strand of hair has escaped her bun and curls against her neck. I want to reach out and tuck the loose strands behind her ear. But then again, I've wanted a lot of things when it comes to Holiday.

She works with absolute confidence as she pours pecans into the mixture, then scoops it on top of the shortbread. She does a swirl design on the top that makes it look fancy.

Seconds later, she's reorganizing my fridge so she can place it inside to cool the fudge topping. Once she shuts the doors, she turns to me. "Now we wait an hour."

"Impressive," I tell her.

"Can we sit by the fire?" she asks, swiping her wineglass from the counter and filling it.

"Of course." I fill my glass, too, then place my hand on her lower back before immediately pulling away. Some habits die hard.

I've tried to forget what it felt like to have her hips pressed against mine. We spent so many summer nights in the bed of my truck, sneaking around like no one knew. I'll never forget how the late afternoon sun made her skin glow. It feels like a dream now.

Focus, Jolly.

We move into the living room and settle on opposite ends of the couch. The fire crackles and pops. She tucks her feet under her and wraps both hands around her wineglass.

"Can I ask you something?" she says after a moment.

"You just did."

She huffs. "Why did you throw out my peppermint fudge brownie?"

I nearly choke on the wine I was drinking. "Ah. I was almost convinced you didn't see that."

"If it tastes bad, I kinda need to know becau—"

"It was *perfect*. I was fucking with you." I try to hold back a smile but fail.

"*Asshole!*"

I shrug. "I do what I can to live rent-free in that pretty little head of yours."

"And you continue to prove my point." Holiday smiles, like she's committing this to memory.

I know I am.

Her shoulders relax, and she leans against the cushion. Neither of us says anything else; the truth is, I don't know where to start. So instead, I watch the firelight play across her face, wondering what she's thinking.

Eventually, she speaks. She always speaks first when the silence lingers too long between us. "This is what we used to wish for. Baking because we can. Being able to hang out with no curfew."

"Yeah," I say, sipping my wine.

"Do you think I'm romanticizing it?" She looks at me. "Everything I wanted in life felt like it was possible."

The way she's looking at me right now makes it hard to breathe. Like maybe she's remembering the same things I am. The same nights. The same promises.

"It still is," I encourage her.

"Everything?" She studies my face, and by her expression, I know what she's asking. *Us.* Do we have a chance?

The timer on the oven goes off. Saved by the bell.

She moves to the kitchen, and I follow behind her. It's hard for me to predict our future when I've been so damn wrong before.

Holiday grabs a knife and carefully cuts the cookie bar into fat squares. She places a slice on a plate and scoots it toward me.

"Shall we?" she asks.

"Together," I tell her, slicing it in half.

Crumbs fall to the ground as we pick each of our halves up.

"On the count of three," she says.

We tap the pastry like we're toasting with wineglasses, then take a bite.

"It's missing something. It needs sea salt on top," I tell her. "To counteract the richness."

Her eyes widen. "Yes, I think you're right. Do you have some?"

"Yeah." After we sprinkle the salt on top of another piece and halve it, we pop it into our mouths.

She moans. This is fucking torture.

"It needed that," I say. "Perfect cookie bar."

Holiday reaches for the salt and somehow knocks the box over. It tips to the side and crashes to the floor, spilling everywhere.

"Shit," she says.

I chuckle, and we kneel at the same time to pick it up. Leaning forward, I pinch some salt and throw it over her shoulder. She does the same for me.

"No bad luck for either of us," I say. It's one of Mawmaw's rules. Salt gets spilled, salt over the shoulder.

We stand, and we're close enough that I can see her pulse jumping in her throat. Close enough to smell her shampoo. Close enough that if I just leaned forward—

"Lucas," she whispers.

"Yeah?"

She doesn't finish what she was going to say, but neither of us moves.

Another second passes. Two. Three. An eternity could slip away right now and I'd welcome it.

Her phone buzzes, pulling her attention away, and the moment is lost.

"It was just Sammy checking in."

I sprinkle salt on the tray of bars and take another square. It's so fucking good, it makes me moan.

Holiday turns red.

Every instinct is screaming at me to close this distance and finally taste her lips again after fifteen years. But I can't.

"I should sweep up this mess." It gives me an opportunity to break away from her.

"Sorry about that," she tells me. "Also, the salt is a perfect touch."

"We should make some of these for Mawmaw to try on Sunday."

"Yeah." Holiday chuckles. "These won't last until then."

"No chance. I think it's the one. This recipe has everything. Tastes like the holidays."

She cuts herself another slice. "Yeah, they're damn good."

"I think I could eat this whole pan myself."

"Feel free," she says, adding dishes to the sink. She yawns and I notice how tired she looks.

"I've got it. Seriously. You should go home and get some rest. You'll need it."

She yawns again. "Are you sure?"

"Yes," I confirm, moving her toward the door.

"Thanks." She reaches for the knob. "For tonight. For everything."

"You don't have to thank me."

"I know. I want to," she tells me.

I open the door and cool air rushes in with a whisper.

"Good night."

"Night, Peaches."

She shakes her head as she takes the steps off the porch. I lean against the door as she turns and looks back at me. I pop my brows at her, and she smiles while climbing into her car.

I don't go inside until her taillights fade away.

What the hell am I doing?

I thought I was over her, that I could do this, but tonight proved I'm a liar.

I'm not over Holiday Patterson. I never was. And she looked at me like maybe she feels it, too.

Yeah, I'm completely fucked.

CHAPTER 15

❄

HOLIDAY

By one o'clock, we sold four thousand cookies. It's impossible to bake more than that with the equipment, employees, and space I have. I knew I'd hit this number eventually, but I thought it would be in mid-December when the holiday rush peaked. Not before Thanksgiving.

I stand in the middle of the bakery and let it sink in that I underestimated myself. Again. Somehow, I planned for less, expected less, because some part of me still believes I'm not good enough.

Dominic's voice echoes in my head. *You were nothing before me. You needed me.*

I shake it off and turn to my staff. Bella and Wendy are both dead on their feet, and Bethany looks ready to collapse. Last night, I slept like a baby and actually feel rested today.

"Okay," I announce, clapping my hands together. "You three are done for the day."

Bella looks up from wiping down the counter, flour dusted in her dark hair. "But we still need to prep for tomorrow."

"I've actually got it covered."

"You can't do it alone. It's going to take hours," Wendy says.

"I won't be alone," I say, moving to the kitchen.

The three of them freeze and glare at me.

"You have help?" Wendy's eyebrows shoot up. "Who?"

"Tell us!" Bella moves closer, eyes narrowed.

"Does it matter?"

"Yes!" all three of them say together.

I sigh and untie my apron. "Lucas."

They scream with excitement.

"I knew it!" Bethany shouts, jumping up and down and nearly knocking over the decorations on the counter.

"You're baking together again!" Bella clutches her chest like she might faint.

Bethany grins. "Aunt Holiday, that's so romantic."

"It's not romantic. He offered to help so we could get used to working together for the contest. That's it. Now, time for y'all to go home before I change my mind." I shoo them toward the door.

"But we want to see—" Bella starts.

"Out. Now."

They gather their things, but they're giddy. Bethany hugs me. Bella and Wendy are already whispering and giggling as they head across the parking lot toward the gift shop.

I look around, taking in the bakery. The Christmas lights strung along the exposed beams are twinkling in the afternoon sun, and the massive tree in the corner that Hudson and Emma decorated with Colby catches the light and sparkles with silver and gold ornaments.

When I think about Lucas, my stomach does a nervous flip that I refuse to acknowledge. I redo my ponytail, pulling it high and tight, then immediately let it down. I go with a low messy bun that's effortless as I clean until the bakery is spotless.

Five minutes before three, I hear the low rumble of an engine that makes my pulse kick up. I hate myself a little for it.

Lucas is tolerating me because he has to. We're two people making cookie dough together. That's it.

I glance out the window, watching him. He's in his jeans,

wearing layers, with a scarf wrapped around his neck. The black beanie does something to me.

Lucas tries the door, but it's locked. I rush to open the door, and when he steps inside, I can smell his cologne. Cold November air rushes in with him. When I look up into his green eyes, my stomach flips with anticipation.

"Hi." His voice is rough.

"Hey. You're on time."

"Thought I'd spare you today," he says, locking the door behind him.

As we're standing beside one another, the bakery feels like it shrinks in size. It grows more intimate as Bing Crosby croons "White Christmas."

The afternoon light streams through the windows, giving everything a golden glow.

"You've got pine needles stuck to you," I say, plucking them off his shoulder.

He removes his beanie and runs his hand through his dark hair.

"This is really awkward," I tell him, moving back to the prep area.

"Yeah," he agrees, shrugging off his jacket and scarf. He hangs everything on the coat rack by the door. "How do we get past that?"

I shrug. "Have sex?"

His jaw clenches. "Not happening."

"I was joking!" I tell him.

"Right," he says. "You can't handle this, HoHo."

I scoff, but as my eyes slide over him, I think he might be right.

"Anyway. Guess we should get started?"

He smirks, like he can read my mind. "Let's."

He pushes off the counter and moves to the sink to wash his hands.

After he dries them, he stands beside me. Having him so

close is making me hella nervous. I take a step away from him. "This is my personal bubble."

"Wait a damn minute." Lucas gives me a smirk, and I glance away from him. "Am I getting to you?"

"Absolutely not." I set our ingredients out as "The Christmas Song" plays.

He returns to my space. "You're lying. Wow, Holiday. After all this time, I'm still front and center in your fantasies."

"You wish," I whisper.

A playful laugh releases from him. "If it's not true, deny it."

I turn to him, getting ready to rip him a new one.

But he's smiling like he's the Grinch who stole Christmas. Lucas leans in and whispers, his hot breath on my ear. "I'm not going to fuck you, HoHo. So get those thoughts out of your dirty mind."

Heat creeps up my neck as he pulls away.

We work in comfortable silence, and he wears a cocky smirk the whole time. The afternoon light shifts lower, making the Christmas lights overhead seem brighter.

"You still do that," Lucas says without looking up from adding eggs to the mixer.

"Do what?"

"Hum when you bake," he says.

I stop mid-scoop, not realizing I was doing it. "You noticed?"

"I notice everything about you. All your little quirks and habits," he says nonchalantly, like we're talking about the weather.

The words shouldn't make my heart race, but they do.

"You shouldn't say things like that," I tell him.

"I won't keep shit to myself to make you comfortable anymore. It got me nowhere before."

I don't know what to say to that, so I focus on measuring vanilla extract just to have something to do with my hands.

We move around each other like a dance we both still

remember the steps to. Every time our hands brush, reaching for the same bowl, every time he leans in close to check my measurements, I feel it. That pull. That heat. The thing that never really went away, no matter how many years or miles were between us.

"So," he says as we start on the chocolate chip dough. "You ready for tomorrow?"

"Dinner at Mawmaw's while your entire family stares at us? Absolutely not."

"It won't be that bad." He adds chocolate chips to the mixer. "The food will be good and Mawmaw will love the cookie bars."

"I've been thinking about a name for them," I admit.

"Yeah?"

"The One," I mutter. "I think it's fitting. And it's something people search their whole lives to find."

"The One," he whispers. "I like it."

We start making snickerdoodle and sugar cookie dough.

As I'm measuring cinnamon, Lucas reaches up to grab a sheet pan from the top shelf above me. He could've asked me to move, should've asked me to move. Instead, he steps up behind me and reaches over my head. His chest presses against my back as one hand steadies himself on my hip.

I can feel the heat radiating off him as his warm breath brushes against my neck. Every place our bodies touch is on fire, like he's branding me with the mark of him.

My heart is pounding so hard I'm sure he can feel it.

"Sorry," he says.

"No, you're not." My voice comes out barely above a whisper.

"You're right. I'm not." He doesn't step back right away. His hand is still resting on my hip. His thumb brushes against the strip of skin where my thermal has ridden up. That one touch sends sparks straight through my entire body.

I turn to face him, studying his intense green eyes, wishing I knew what was sprinting through his mind. His lips are parted like he wants to say something but can't find the words.

For a heartbeat, neither of us moves. Neither of us breathes.

We don't talk about those charged moments after they happen.

We both go back to work pretending like it's nothing, but my hands are shaking with nerves as I portion out the last batch of dough.

I notice he seems distracted, too.

By the time we finish, the fridge is packed. I feel good about tomorrow, and with Lucas's help, we're set up for success.

"I think that's everything." I double-check my list. "We make a good team."

"Yeah." He licks his lips as he stares at my mouth. "We do."

"Stop," I whisper.

"Stop what?" he asks.

"Looking at me like that," I say.

"The way I always look at you? Come on, Holiday."

I start to wipe down the counter, but he takes the towel from my hands.

"Sit."

The commanding tone does something to my insides, but I do exactly what he says. Lucas cleans the bakery, wiping surfaces, washing dishes, even straightening the Christmas garland that's been crooked all day.

When he's done, he flicks off the overhead lights, leaving nothing but the Christmas ones lit.

He grabs his jacket. "Don't forget about dinner at five. I'll pick you up."

"I can drive myself."

"I'll be there at four thirty." He pulls on his jacket and puts his scarf on. "Wear something comfortable. Mawmaw cranks the heat up like she's trying to recreate the surface of the sun."

I laugh. "Still?"

"Yep." He walks to the door and pauses with his hand on the handle. "Thanks for this."

"Thank you."

"That's what partners are for, right?"

He steps out into the cold, and I watch him walk to his truck. Before he gets inside, he looks back at me, watching him. I see a small smile play on his lips, and that shouldn't please me as much as it does.

I lock up, then head to my car with my mind racing. I can't stop thinking about the way he looked at me tonight or how his hand naturally rested on my hip.

I like having Lucas around. He makes me feel capable and strong. But I have to stop reacting to his voice, his touch, and his presence.

Honestly, I thought this crush of mine would've faded. Guess not.

And in seven days, Dominic is going to show up and try to take all of this away from me. He'll try to make me doubt myself, doubt Lucas, and everything in between.

But as I drive home, Lucas's words echo in my head—*I notice everything about you.*

For a brief moment, I let myself believe things will work out and that maybe I'm strong enough to handle whatever comes next. Even if this is the calm before the storm.

CHAPTER 16

LUCAS

It's a brand-new day of me trying to not lose my fucking mind as she bites her bottom lip.

Holiday's been doing it for the past ten minutes while she measures ingredients for the cookie bars we're bringing to Mawmaw's tonight. She has no idea what she does to me, and I can't focus on anything except the way her teeth catch her bottom lip and—

Focus.

I've been playing this game with her all week. Watching her and noticing things I shouldn't is at the top of my list. It's hard to ignore how she hums when she's happy or the way she looks at me like we were supposed to spend a lifetime together.

Our moments are smothered by the weight of what Sammy told me, and it sits like an elephant on my chest. Dominic controlled and isolated her. Made her believe she was nothing without him. Stole her work and claimed it as his own.

I also notice the damage that piece of shit left behind. Holiday second-guesses herself in ways she never did before. Every day, she's genuinely surprised when people line up for her cookies. Sometimes she shakes her head when someone gives her a compliment, like she doesn't believe it.

It makes me want to fly to Paris and punch his fucking face for trying to break her. Instead, I do what I can. I show up. I help. I try to make her see the reality right in front of her.

"Lucas? Did you hear me? You're very distracted," she says, flattening the dough with a candy cane-striped rolling pin. "Everything okay?"

"Yeah," I offer, but I don't think she believes me. The problem is, I know too much.

Holiday places the dough in a pan, then pops it in the oven.

"What's really going on?" she asks, moving in front of me.

I force a smile and place my hands on her shoulders. "Just have a lot on my mind."

"About?"

"Life," I say, being philosophical as I fight an internal war, one I will probably lose.

"If you want to quit—"

"No." I shake my head. "I won't be your excuse."

She pulls away from me. "What? I'm actually looking forward to this contest."

"Really?" I ask.

"*No.* I'm *dreading* it. But I'm trying to reprogram my thoughts," she says with a shrug.

My smile fades, and the quietness lingers.

"Did he hurt you?" I ask with my voice lowered, needing to hear it from her lips. "Don't lie. Please."

"Just emotionally," she admits. "But that's my fault for staying."

"No, it's fucking not." I take a step forward, holding my arms out, and she falls into me. I hold her tight, my fingers threading through her hair. "He's never going to hurt you again."

"You shouldn't care," she whispers.

"I'm aware." I rest my chin on the top of her head and don't move until she's the one to pull away first. "But for some reason I do."

She loosens her grip and looks up at me, and I wipe away her tears. "You're too pretty to cry."

"You don't mean that," she says, breathing me in.

I tap her button nose. "I don't give pity compliments to anyone. Not even you, Peaches."

"You're the only person I can trust to keep me honest," she says. "It's why I've tried to avoid you. It's like a vampire looking into the sun."

"Dramatic, don't you think?"

She immediately smiles. "Stop calling me Peaches or I'm going to fuck you up."

"Make me," I mutter. She elbows me in the stomach, and a laugh spills out of me.

"*Oof.* I'm going to make a complaint with Emma."

Holiday gives me a smug look. "Go ahead."

The mood immediately shifts as we clean our mess. Eventually, the timer buzzes, and she removes the shortbread from the oven to let it cool. Her eyes drift up to the clock on the wall.

"You think we should bring Mawmaw other options?"

"Nah. This is it, and you know it." I lean against the counter. "Stop second-guessing yourself."

She nods. "You're right."

Holiday shaves semi-sweet chocolate from a bar as I put the double boiler on the stove.

I place butter on the top as Holiday drops in the chocolate. My job is to stir while she pours the condensed milk into the pot. She's standing so close to me that I can feel the warmth of her body. Before everything is completely melted, I remove it from the stove, and she dumps vanilla in. Once it's all incorporated, I drop the pecans into the mixture.

"Go ahead," she tells me, and I empty the fudge mixture on top of the shortbread. Holiday sprinkles it with salt, then places a piece of parchment paper on top before shoving it into a spot she saved in the fridge.

She lifts her hand, and I give her a high five. "We prepped that in twenty minutes."

"'Cause we kick ass." I take the broiler to the sink and wash it. She grabs a towel and dries it, placing it back on the shelf where it lives.

"Go home and get ready. I'll bring this when I pick you up in two and a half hours," I tell her as I wipe down the counter. There's not much more to be done because we cleaned after we prepped for tomorrow.

"I can meet you there."

"Yeah, I know you can. But I'm not letting that happen." I finish wiping down the counter, then throw the rag in the dirty hamper.

She gives me a suspicious look. "Okay?"

"Okay. I'll be at your house at four thirty."

"Um."

I wrap my arm around her and force her to leave the bakery with me so she doesn't get distracted. One of her problems is that she doesn't know how to cut it off and stop working.

Back home, I shower and try not to think about tonight.

The two of us need to talk and clear the air about what's festering. And we need to do that without interruptions.

I change into dark jeans and a charcoal sweater. I run my hands through my hair, trying to make it look like I didn't try too hard, which is fucking ridiculous because it's just dinner at Mawmaw's. Except it's not *just* dinner.

It's the first time Holiday has been by my side at a family event in over a decade. At one point, she was my automatic plus-one to everything. I pull up to her parents' house ten minutes early and send her a text instead of going to the door. If her dad answers, he's going to give me *that* look.

A few minutes later, the front door opens and Holiday steps out.

Every thought in my head disappears.

She's wearing a red sweater that's a soft cashmere, and it

makes her look like she fell out of one of my dreams. Her hips shake as she struts toward the truck with her hair down in loose waves.

She's fucking gorgeous. This is torture.

My eyes slide over as she stares at me.

She reaches the truck and I get out to open the door for her.

"What?" I ask as she openly eyefucks me.

"Nothing. You look—" She stops herself, then continues. "Good."

I pop a brow at her as she steps on the running board, then slides inside, smelling like gardenias. I force myself to close her door and walk around to my side like a normal person, but my heart is racing.

"You sure you're ready for this?" I ask when I put the car in reverse.

"Absolutely not."

"Agreed." I back out of her driveway. I glance at her and she shyly looks away. I force my eyes back to the road and adjust my grip on the steering wheel.

At this rate, it's going to be a long fucking night.

A few minutes later, I take the entrance to the Christmas tree farm and drive down the loop to where Mawmaw lives. Our cookie bars sit in the back seat.

"What's the plan? We eat dinner, share our dessert, then get out before anyone can corner us?" she asks, twisting the hem of her sweater.

"Something like that."

"You're hiding something."

She always could read me too well.

"We're doing something afterward. It's a surprise," I say.

"I *hate* surprises," she mumbles.

"Since when?"

"Since always."

"That's bullshit. I used to plan things all the time and you'd —" I stop because I'm saying too much.

"Finish the sentence you started," she says.

"It doesn't matter."

"Lucas."

"You'd get this look on your face like I'd just given you the best gift in the world, even if it was flour and butter and a platonic sleepover at my grandma's." I keep my eyes on the road because if I look at her right now, I might say something I can't take back. "You'd smile like I hung the moon."

The silence stretches between us, but it's not uncomfortable. It's heavy with words and old feelings we've only danced around.

"I loved your surprises," she says quietly. "I knew they came from a good place. Can't say that about anyone else who's surprised me in the last decade."

"So that means you're in?" We pull into Mawmaw's driveway that's lined with cars. I kill the engine.

"Are you peer pressuring me?"

"Absolutely." I smirk.

"Better be worth it," she says, but does a terrible job of holding back her excitement.

"Isn't it always?" I park and go around to open Holiday's door before she can do it herself.

"Quit being so polite," she says, taking my hand as she steps down.

"Hell no. My mama taught me manners."

She looks up at me, and her eyes look impossibly blue. Her lips part like she's going to say something more, but Jake's voice cuts through the night, interrupting us.

"Hey, lovebirds! You coming inside, or should we start without you?"

"We're coming," I say over my shoulder, then turn back to Holiday. "Ready?"

"No. But it is what it is." Holiday's cheeks turn bright red, and we head toward the house.

Inside is the chaos I expected. The first thing Mawmaw does when she sees Holiday is pull her into a tight hug.

"Oh, sweetheart, look at you! Haven't changed a bit." She holds Holiday at arm's length and beams. "Doesn't she look beautiful, Lucas?"

"Yeah, Mawmaw. She does."

Holiday's eyes widen with a *Help me* look, but all I can do is chuckle. There is no saving her. My mom swoops in next, hugging Holiday and asking questions about the bakery. Then Emma and Claire both shower her with compliments. Hudson makes some comment about how we look good together and earns an elbow from Holiday. Jake just grins knowingly at both of us.

I watch Holiday light up around my family, like she used to, like she's craving genuine conversations and appreciation. I think about her ex and clench my fists, thinking about what I'll do when I meet him. Because now it's inevitable that I will.

We settle around Mawmaw's massive dining table that can fit twenty people. Holiday ends up next to me, close enough that our arms brush every time she reaches for something. It's almost too much.

My dad launches into a story about what a kid asked for Christmas.

"He said a billion dollars," Dad says. "I remember the days when remote control cars were in."

Hudson makes comments under his breath that have a very pregnant Emma shooting him warning looks. Jake and Claire are wrapped up in wedding plan conversations with my mom. Colby is drawing in a notebook while refusing to eat broccoli.

And I can't stop glancing at Holiday as she listens to Mawmaw like every word matters. She's adorable without even trying.

I'm so completely fucked.

"Lucas, honey, for the third time, could you please pass the potatoes?" my mom asks.

"Oh, sure," I say, realizing I'm too distracted.

It's just hard for me to believe any of this is real, after wishing for this for so long. I grab the bowl and pass it, catching Emma's knowing gaze from across the table.

I know I'm going to get shit for this later.

"So, Holiday," Mawmaw says, cutting into her pot roast. "How's it feel to be back home?"

"Great, actually," Holiday tells her with a sweet smile. "Strange sometimes, but I'm blessed and have a lot to be thankful for. Friends, family, a fun job. No complaints."

"Fifteen years is a long time to be away from the people who love you." Mawmaw's eyes flick to me for just a second, and I try to ignore her. "You being here now is what matters most."

"Yes, ma'am," Holiday offers between small bites. "This is delicious. The roast is perfect."

"Thanks, honey. Means a lot coming from someone like you. Makes this old woman very happy. Not to mention, you're baking with my Lucas again."

Holiday's eyes soften, and it makes my chest flutter. "Yeah. We make a good team."

"You always did." Mawmaw takes a sip of wine. "Even when you were teenagers sneaking into my kitchen at midnight to bake and drink my nog."

"No, we didn't," I say, but it's impossible to hold back my grin.

"Oh, you think I didn't notice my rum was half gone in the morning?" She laughs. "Plus, you were always so loud. I just pretended to be asleep because I knew you two were being safe and making good choices."

Holiday chokes on her water. "Yes, we were safe in the kitchen."

"That's right." She looks at Holiday with warm eyes. "I'm glad you're back, sweetheart. Truly. This town hasn't been the same without you. Neither has Lucas."

"Mawmaw," I warn.

A VERY MERRY ENEMY

My brothers and parents eat, watching us chat like it's a tennis match.

"Don't be shy about it," Mawmaw tells me, reaching for my hand.

My mom clears her throat, but she just acts innocent. This is a part of the matchmaking games she likes to play.

"So, I've heard you've been helping Holiday prep," Emma says. "Ready to quit the farm and come work at the bakery?"

"Hell no," Lucas tells her.

Hudson laughs, knowing Emma's just trying to rile me up.

Under the table, Holiday's knee bumps against mine, and she doesn't move away. I don't know if it's intentional or accidental, but I stay in place.

The wine flows, along with the conversation, and by the end of it, we're laughing.

"Oh shit. I forgot the dessert in the truck. I'll be right back," I tell them.

As soon as I walk out of the dining room, Mawmaw says loudly, "Now that he's gone, give us all the tea."

I chuckle, not remembering the last time I felt this at ease. For once, it feels like things are clicking into place in my life. Holiday returning has always been on my wish list, but it was never expected. In my mind, she'd marry that man, start a family, and fade away from my life forever.

I don't know why it feels like a second chance. But I also don't know if I can let her in again. The heartache I experienced from losing her the first time nearly destroyed me. Not sure I'm strong enough to survive that hell again. It took years. And her being here is a reminder of that.

After dinner, we clear the table, and Mawmaw cuts into *The One*. The room goes silent as everyone chews, then swallows. It's the only time I've heard all of them speechless at once.

"Holy shit," Hudson finally says around a mouthful.

"Hudson!" Emma hisses, nodding at Colby.

"Holy shit, Dad!" Colby says, beaming.

"That's a bad word," Hudson tells his son, who repeats it again with a little giggle behind it.

Jake nods. "These are definitely better than last year's winner."

"Ugh! That was us," Emma says. "But truthfully, these would've kicked our ass."

Mom and Dad are just as delighted.

Holiday and I focus on Mawmaw. She sits with her eyes closed, chewing slowly.

Everyone waits.

Finally, she looks at me, then at Holiday.

"These will absolutely win," she says, like she's predicting it.

Holiday chuckles, like she's relieved. "Really?"

"The shortbread is perfect. The fudge is balanced. The pecans add texture. And that salt. Chef's kiss." She takes another bite. "This is a winner. What did you name it?"

"Chef's kiss would've been cute, but we chose The One, because you can't just have one serving, and it's the only cookie you'll ever need during the holiday season." She's beaming with happiness. And fuck me, I want to kiss her right here in front of everyone.

What would happen if I pulled her onto my lap and tasted her sweet lips?

Instead, I stay seated and push that thought away. "Told you they were great."

"You did," she mutters.

"Now, don't y'all get cocky," Mawmaw says. "There are a lot of people competing. Last I heard, over thirty."

"There could be fifty teams. I know this is gonna win. And before anyone says anything, I'm not cocky. I'm confident. There's a difference. I know what we've got," I say.

Mawmaw tilts her head.

"You two, just…wow," Mom says. "Created a masterpiece."

Emma mouths *You're fucked* with a laugh.

I mouth *Fuck you* back to her.

This makes her laugh harder.

Once every last crumb of our cookie bar is eaten, Holiday and I help clean the kitchen since we're the youngest in the family. By the time we're done, it's after eight. Everyone settles in for a movie, and Mawmaw plays games with Colby.

"We're gonna head out," I tell everyone.

"Already? Feels like you just got here," Dad says.

"Hours have passed," I say.

"Are you going home?" Mawmaw asks.

Every single person in the room goes silent. Hudson is grinning. Jake is trying not to laugh. Emma looks delighted.

"That's no one's business," I say, glancing around the room.

"Bye, everyone," Holiday says, offering a wave.

Mawmaw pulls both of us into hugs. "Go on, just behave yourselves."

"Always," I say. "Goodbye!"

I place my hand on the small of her back and lead her outside. The temperature has dropped, and Holiday wraps her arms around herself against the cold. I give her my jacket from the back seat, then start the engine. Her breath fogs in the air, and I crank the heat.

"This is ominous," she says as I take the old dirt road that leads behind Mawmaw's house.

"Just trust me," I tell her, driving down the trail, deeper into the woods, at the far edge of our property.

"I do."

CHAPTER 17

LUCAS

My hands tighten on the steering wheel as we get closer. This could be a mistake, but I have questions that I need answers to. Because Dominic will show up in less than a week, and his presence will inevitably complicate things.

I can feel her watching me as I navigate the dirt roads that didn't exist fifteen years ago. My brothers and I spent several summers in my early twenties cutting drivable trails to our favorite places on the property. After five minutes of driving, the road gets narrower and the trees get thicker.

My heart is pounding now. I realize I'm nervous and second-guessing this whole plan. What if she doesn't want to be here? What if bringing her back to this place hurts more than it helps? What if I learn something tonight that I can't ignore?

Maybe I should turn around. Maybe—

But then I'm pulling onto the barely there path that leads to a clearing, and it's too late to back out now. I park and kill the engine, glancing over at Holiday. She's staring out the windshield into the darkness.

"Ready?" I ask.

"No." She shakes her head.

When we were kids, she was afraid of the dark. Some things never change.

I smile. "I've got you."

"You always did."

I get out of the truck, and I open the door for her, taking her hand. The November air is cold and crisp, carrying the scent of pine and distant wood smoke. Holiday looks up at the starry sky, and I watch her breath fog in the air. The stars are brighter out here, and it's hard to believe they're the same ones we used to wish on.

I lead her forward, and she stops dead in her tracks when we move closer to our destination.

The tent sits exactly where it always did, the same spot we claimed as ours when we were seventeen. Two camping chairs face the firepit with an extra stack of wood nearby. Bourbon sits in one of the chairs, chilled by the late November temperature.

"Lucas," she whispers, and her hand tightens on mine.

I can see recognition flash across her face as memory after memory hits her. Her eyes go from the tent to the firepit to the exact spot where we spread a blanket under the stars fifteen years ago. The place where I told her I loved her for the first time and where we made promises we couldn't keep.

She takes a few steps forward, her hand slipping from mine. She moves toward the tent and reaches out to touch the canvas like she's making sure it's real.

"I feel like I've stepped back in time," she says.

"Yeah." My voice comes out rougher than I intended. "Haven't really been back much, either. Just a few times."

The truth is, it was always too hard to visit. There were times when I was in my feels and sat out here, drinking alone. But I never brought anyone else here. This place has always been ours.

I light the wood I stacked earlier. The kindling catches quickly, and flames lick at the larger logs. The fire grows, casting dancing shadows across the clearing and pushing back the darkness. The firelight catches her face. For a second, she looks exactly like she did when we were teenagers—all hope and possibility, with that perfect smile that used to easily undo me.

"I can't believe you remembered all the details," she whispers.

"Our time together was unforgettable." The admission costs me, but I give it anyway.

I remember the first time I brought her here and how nervous I was. Back then, we rode a four-wheeler down the path I'd carved out when I found this natural meadow. We stayed up all night talking about our dreams—her bakery; me expanding the farm; us building a life together.

We made love for the first time right here, under these same stars. Both of us nervous and excited and fumbling through it, promising to keep one another like a secret. She looked at me afterward like I'd given her something precious. We held one another through the night and then spent three months fooling around. Best summer of my damn life.

I remember the last time we were here, before she left for culinary school. We lay in this exact tent, and she cried because she was scared to leave. I believed distance couldn't touch what we had. How wrong I was.

Holiday walks around the area, taking it all in. She stops at the firepit and runs her fingers along the stones we carefully arranged all those years ago.

"Wow," she says.

"Yeah." My throat is tight.

"We were both so nervous and excited and so in love." She looks at me; her eyes are shining with unshed tears.

"Come on. Let's get warm."

Holiday sinks into one of the chairs, putting distance between us. Smart. Because right now, with all these memories pressing in, I'm not sure I can be trusted to keep my hands to myself.

"Why did you bring me here?" she asks.

A VERY MERRY ENEMY

I uncap the bourbon and take a long drink. The burn reminds me of all the lonely nights I spent thinking about her, wondering where she was and if she ever thought about me. About this place. About us.

I hand her the bottle. "We need to talk."

"We've been talking all week."

"No. We haven't." In the night, her eyes seem darker; it makes her look like she did when we were young and stupid and thought nothing could tear us apart. "We've been dancing around things. Being careful. I'm tired of it."

She takes the bottle but doesn't drink yet. "What do you want to know?"

"Everything." I lean forward, elbows on my knees.

"Lucas—"

"Want to play a game?"

She goes very still. "No."

"Yes, you do," I tell her, taking the bourbon and gulping it down. "Confessions. Remember the rules?"

She stares at me for a long moment, and I can see her considering it. Weighing the risk. Wondering what truths might come out in the next hour that we can't take back.

"This is a very bad idea," she finally says.

"Probably. But we're doing it anyway. I'm tired of walking on eggshells around you. Tired of not saying what I really think. Tired of pretending everything is fine."

She snatches the bottle and drinks. "You asked for this. The answers might not be what you want to hear."

"Right back at you."

It's a game we invented when we were sixteen. Simple rules: steal alcohol from Mawmaw's liquor cabinet, set a timer for one hour while getting drunk enough that the truth comes easy, and then take turns asking each other anything for another hour. The catch was that when the game was over, everything said during Confessions stayed in Confessions. Nothing changed. We went back to being who we were before we played.

It was our way of being honest when we were too scared to say what we meant.

The pulse in her neck increases, and I set an alarm on my phone for one hour. For the first fifteen minutes, we drink without speaking. I think about everything I want to know, all the questions that have been burning in my chest. We keep passing the bottle back and forth, the bourbon going down easier with each sip.

My throat and chest are burning, and I'm sure Holiday's are, too.

I glance at her and notice how damn pretty she is, how she's always been, without even trying. It makes me drink more.

Forty minutes in, I stand to add more wood to the fire and don't walk in a straight line. The world tilts slightly.

Holiday giggles and stands, too, but she stumbles over nothing.

Without thinking, I wrap my arm around her to steady her. She's warm and soft and smells like gardenias and wood smoke. Having her this close, in this place, with bourbon making everything feel more dangerous—it's almost too much.

"You're always saving me," she whispers, looking up at me.

"Only when you let me."

Her face is inches from mine. I can see the firelight reflected in her eyes and can feel her breath on my face. I remember exactly what it felt like to kiss her fifteen years ago in this exact spot.

I force myself to step back. "Sit."

She plops down in the chair, and I add more firewood, taking my time to get myself under control. When the fire is blazing again, I rejoin her. The heat from the flames does nothing to chase away the cold awareness between us.

We're drunk now. The kind that makes consequences feel like they're in a galaxy far, far away.

Being here with her, in this place, is more dangerous than I thought. We're about to say things we can't undo and learn things we can't deny.

And I did it anyway.

Fuck it, right?

A few minutes later, the timer on my phone goes off. The drinking portion of the game is over.

Holiday looks at me, and something passes between us. It's understanding, fear, and anticipation. We're officially at the point of no return.

"Ready to start confessing?" she asks with a hiccup.

"Yep, there's no backing out now." I lift the bottle to my lips and take one long pull for courage. "Thoughts and prayers."

CHAPTER 18

❄

HOLIDAY

I take another drink of bourbon, and it goes down like water. That's when I know I'm in big trouble.

We've been out here for an hour, and I've thought about every question I've wanted to ask Lucas since I arrived in town. So far, we've only really discussed safe topics and skirted the ones that would force us to dig deeper.

The silence growing between us is almost too much. We're both drinking faster now, building up courage for whatever comes next.

"You first," Lucas says, setting the bottle down.

My heart kicks up, and I wipe my sweaty palms on my jeans. "Actually, I don't know if I'm drunk enough for this."

"Can you taste the bourbon?" He shifts the camping chair so he's directly in front of me. The firelight catches his face, all angles and shadows and scruff.

"No," I confess.

"Great. Then I'll start. Make it easier."

"Okay."

He takes a breath. "Why did you really come back to Merryville?"

"I told you. My contract ended and—"

"No surface-level bullshit, remember? Real answers."

I look at the flames dancing and hear the wood crackling. "Because I didn't know where else to go. Because I was so tired of pretending to be someone I wasn't. Because I needed to remember who I was before…" I trail off.

"Continue."

"Before Paris. Before I let someone else define who I was supposed to be." I take another drink. "Before I forgot what it felt like to be proud of my own work."

Lucas does nothing but listen and suddenly it's spilling out. The bourbon and the firelight and the fact that this man—the one person I've always been able to tell my secrets—makes it impossible to hold back anything.

"Dominic took credit for everything I created. My recipes. My techniques. My ideas." I shake my head. "And I let him. I actually let him because I thought that's what you did when you worked with someone you cared about. You supported them and lifted them up. I didn't realize he was standing on my shoulders only to elevate himself."

"Holiday—"

"I finally left when I overheard him talking to a food critic about his signature lavender honey cookie. The one I spent a year perfecting." I swipe at unexpected tears. "He was laughing about how easy it was to create, like it came to him in a dream."

Lucas's jaw tightens. "That's fucked up."

"A week later, I packed my bags and told him I was done. He laughed at me and said I was no one before him. That I'd failed him and I'd fail again. He called me selfish. Listed his accolades against my blank slate."

"You didn't fail, HoHo."

"Didn't I? I lost everything." I take a shaky breath. "I barely know who I am as a baker or a person without someone telling me what to do. For years, I was a robot."

"That's why you keep second-guessing yourself."

"Yeah, but..." I look at him, knowing he deserves the whole truth. "I also came back for you."

Lucas inhales a deep breath, and I know he wants to ask another question, but he can't because it's my turn.

We sit in silence for a moment. The fire pops and sends sparks into the night.

"Did you date anyone seriously after I left?"

He chuckles. "Fifteen years and *that's* the question you ask?"

I groan. "Yes. Now answer it."

"Okay. Yeah. A few."

My stomach clenches. "How many?"

"That's two questions."

I take another sip of bourbon and remind him of the rules of our made-up game. "Confessions are deeper than surface-level bullshit. Tell me."

"Three serious relationships." He leans back. "One lasted a year. One lasted eight months. The other lasted six months before she told me I was clearly in love with someone else and was tired of competing with a ghost."

The truth hangs between us. It's simple, honest, and devastating.

But jealousy isn't what I expected to feel. It nearly swallows me whole.

"Was that true?" I whisper, my heart pounding.

I never took into account that Lucas could be in love with someone else. Maybe that's why he's refused to let me in. He looks at me. Really looks at me. "I answered your first question. Save it for the next one."

My heart is pounding.

"What do you want from me, Holiday?" It's direct.

"I don't know. I don't have any expectations. I'm fucked up, Lucas. Honestly, your gut instinct to stay away from me is right. You probably should," I tell him, knowing the truth serum is working.

"That's not happening," he says matter-of-factly, and it eases some of my fears that after this contest, he'll go back to ignoring me.

I sip more bourbon.

"Do you ever think about us and what might've been?"

"Every fucking day." He glances at the fire, and I see years of hurt in his eyes. Guilt nearly swallows me whole. "You were the ghost who haunted the hallways of my heart. You were the reason I couldn't commit to anyone."

He looks back at me. "I'd think about your laugh when I told terrible jokes. The way you'd steal my hoodies and how they'd smell like you for days. But I mostly missed when you looked at me like I was the only person who mattered in your world. You made me believe love existed, but you also made me hate it."

His jaw clenches.

"You have every right to be angry with me," I whisper, drinking more bourbon.

"I'm not angry with you, Holiday. I just can't lose myself again. You make me weak. You make me believe things that you never believed were possible."

My brows furrow. "Like what?"

"Uh-uh. Not your turn," he says. Seconds turn into minutes. "Did you ever think about me, us, and what could've been?"

I nod. "All the time. Usually around the holidays, when people were decorating trees. But there were other times, too. Like when I'd hear a song on the radio that reminded me of our summer together. And…"

My body burns, and I tuck my lips into my mouth.

His eyes don't leave mine. "Tell me."

I put the bottle to my lips and drink until bubbles appear. "Anytime I touched myself."

A cocky smirk plays on those perfect lips, and his gaze narrows. "Mm. Bad fucking girl."

"You were the best I ever had."

"Wow," he says, taking the bottle from me. Our fingers

brush, and goose bumps trail over my arm. "Truthfully, you'll probably be the best I'll ever have, too. I can count on my hands how many times Dominic made me, you know, the seven years we were together."

His eyes darken. "Sad."

"Tell me about it. Maybe it was always supposed to be you. I don't know." My face burns.

He reaches out to cup my face. "Fuck. Your turn," he says after a moment, his thumb stroking my cheekbone.

"Do you think you'll ever be able to forgive me for hurting you?"

"I've forgiven you, I just haven't forgotten. I thought what we had was enough, and it wasn't. So, forgive me if I'm cautious. I don't think you know what you want in life, and I cannot be your rebound, Holiday. You taught me that a man should never try to build a house on unstable ground unless he wants it to collapse. I can't do that again."

The truth makes my tears prickle my eyes.

"That's fair," I whisper. "I'm a mess."

"Give yourself credit. You just stood up to a bully, and it takes time to heal. You can't rush that." His voice is fierce. "Are you leaving again?"

"I don't know," I say. "No one will hire me because of Dominic. If an opportunity arose, depending on where it is, I'd consider it. I feel like I have so much to offer in my career. But then I ask myself if I'm going to spend my entire life working for someone else. I dreamed of having my own bakery. Calling all the shots. Shipping cookies around the world. I don't know if that will ever happen now. I could never open a cookie shop in Merryville to compete with Emma. I have no options."

Lucas glances down at his phone, and I see we have fifteen minutes of asking questions left.

"Do you still want me?" I ask, ripping the Band-Aid off so hard it takes skin.

"I want you to be happy," he says.

"That wasn't my question. No dodgeball."

He stares at me for a long time. The flames dance across our bodies as the wood crackles and pops.

"I want you so bad it fucking hurts," he finally admits. "But I won't touch you, Holiday. I won't kiss you. I will refuse your every move until you know what *you* want in life. I'm not a toy."

"I want—"

"Don't you dare say *me*." He leans closer. "Figure your shit out."

"Will you wait for me?"

"I've been waiting fifteen years."

Our gazes lock, and in that moment, I believe everything will be okay. Tears fill my eyes and I wipe them away. "I don't deserve you."

"And see, that's where you're wrong. You do. But we have a lot of catching up to do. We're the same at our core, but we're also different, older. We've been apart for almost as long as we knew each other."

The timer goes off, and I know our game time of Confessions has closed.

He stands and holds out his hand. "Come on."

I take his hand and let him pull me up. My body is buzzing with bourbon as he leads me to the small tent.

"We need to sleep off this booze," he tells me, unzipping the flap. I climb inside, and I'm taken back to a time in our past. It's too intimate, with one large sleeping bag and blankets on top. I slide inside the bag, and he joins me until we're chest to chest.

"You clearly didn't think this through," I whisper, hearing his breath in my ear.

My entire body hums. We're inches apart in the darkness. Being next to him is the only time I'm not afraid.

"I missed you," I say.

He reaches out and tucks a few strands of hair behind my ear. "Don't you fucking break my heart again."

"I don't want to."

His hand slides to my hip.

I shift closer. "Lucas?"

"Mm?"

"I can feel how hard you are."

"I know." His hand tightens on my hip.

I rock my hips against him, and he makes a sound, low in his throat. His hand slides under my sweater, fingers on bare skin.

"I won't," he says, but his body is saying otherwise. "Fuck, you're tempting."

I press fully against him, and I can feel every inch of him. His thumb strokes my hip under my sweater.

We lie there, pressed together, breaths ragged.

"I won't touch you," he whispers against my ear. "But you can touch yourself."

My breath catches. Heat floods through me.

"Close your eyes."

I do.

"Do you remember the first time I showed you how?" His voice drops lower.

"Yes," I whisper. "I remember everything." My breathing quickens.

His bourbon breath is hot against my ear. "You were a bad influence."

"You were, too." I breathe out.

My hand trembles as I slide it inside my jeans, but outside my panties. I can feel how wet I am through the fabric. A gasp escapes me as I add pressure.

"That's it," he whispers.

I unbutton my jeans and move a hand inside my panties. "I want you so bad."

"I know." His lips brush my ear. "Slow circles."

Overwhelming pleasure overtakes me. It's been so long since I've felt this.

"That's my girl," he murmurs. "Feel good?"

"Yes."

"Keep going. Imagine it's me touching you. Just like you've been doing."

A moan escapes, and he buries his face in my neck. His lips are hot against my skin as they trail down my throat, kissing and sucking.

"So fucking sexy," he whispers against my neck.

I whimper and move faster as pleasure builds tight in my belly. His mouth is everywhere—my neck, my ear, the sensitive spot below my jaw that makes me gasp, but not on my lips.

"Chase it. Your body is yours. Your pleasure is yours." His voice is rough against my skin. "No one else gets to tell you what to do anymore. Claim it."

The words break something open. Tears stream as pleasure builds higher. His mouth is relentless on my neck.

"Lucas," I gasp. "I'm—"

His teeth graze my earlobe. "Come for me, Holiday. Let go."

I unravel as the orgasm rips through me, and I cry out into the darkness of the tent. Lucas's mouth is on my neck, kissing me through it as I shake and tremble in his arms.

Wave after wave. My body remembers. Remembers this. Remembers him.

When I finally come down, I'm nearly gasping for air, but Lucas never lets me go. His face is still buried in my neck, whispering soft words against my skin as he inhales me.

"I've got you." I feel him smile against my neck and pull away.

He takes my hand—the one inside my panties—and brings it to his mouth.

His eyes lock on mine as he sucks my fingers.

He hums. "After all this time, you still taste like peaches."

I laugh-sob. "Lucas."

He pulls me against his chest. I can feel how hard he still is. But he doesn't push.

Just holds me.

"Thank you," I whisper. "For giving that back to me."

He kisses my forehead. "Watching and hearing you come apart? A fucking fantasy."

I snuggle into him, just wanting to be held by him. He's safe. For the first time in years, I feel like myself.

His arms tighten around me. "Nothing changes."

"Promise?"

"Promise."

And I know for a damn fact, he'll keep it. He always has.

CHAPTER 19

❄

LUCAS

I wake up to the rumble of a truck engine getting closer.

My eyes snap open, and I tighten my arms around Holiday, who's still sound asleep against my chest. She's warm and soft, and her body curves perfectly into mine like it always used to. Like a decade and a half didn't pass. Like we never stopped doing this.

Early morning light filters through the tent fabric, and I can hear tires on gravel getting louder.

Shit.

A truck door slams, and I hear boots crunching across gravel.

Holiday stirs against me, moaning, a sound that goes straight through me. Her hand is under my shirt, resting on my chest. I'm acutely aware that I'm growing hard having her pressed against me. Then I think about last night and tasting her.

"Morning." Her voice is rough with sleep.

"Shh. Someone's here," I whisper.

She freezes as footsteps approach the tent. Then someone starts unzipping it from the outside.

"Rise and shine, lovebirds," Jake's voice says cheerfully.

Holiday sits up fast, her hair falling out of what used to be a bun. She looks gorgeous in her wrinkled red sweater with eyes still heavy from sleep. I have to resist the urge to pull her back down and kiss her until she makes those sounds she made last night.

"Oh my goodness," Holiday says when Jake's grinning face appears.

"Well, well, well. What do we have here?" His brow pops up.

"Go away," I say, running my hand through my hair and trying to clear my head.

"Wish I could, but I was put on the search crew to find you. Both of you, actually." He glances at his watch. "It's almost eight. The bakery is supposed to open in an hour. Holiday's mom has called everyone in the fam since you didn't come home last night. Emma called Bella, Wendy, and Bethany to come in and put up a sign saying they're opening late."

Holiday's face goes pale.

"Shit." She scrambles out of the tent. "I have to go right now."

Jake takes a step back and picks up the bourbon. "Ah, the culprit. Lucas, you realize you were supposed to help Dad with charity deliveries at seven. Way to piss off Santa."

"Dammit." I crawl out of the tent and stretch. Instantly, my head pounds. Holiday is frantic, moving at lightning speed. Her sweater has ridden up slightly, and I can see a sliver of bare skin at her waist. I force myself to look away.

Jake crosses his arms as he looks between us. His eyebrows shoot up, and he tucks his lips inside his mouth to stop himself from laughing.

"Y'all have a good night?" Jake asks.

I glance at Holiday, and I see her neck has three dark purple marks trailing from just below her ear down toward her collarbone. One is partially hidden by her sweater collar, but two are very visible against her skin. And she has absolutely no idea.

My marks. My mouth. *Mine.*

Something primal in me is satisfied by it, even though I know it's going to be a problem. She's completely oblivious to the fact that the evidence of what we did last night is branded on her skin.

"I never oversleep," Holiday mutters. "Bella and Wendy and Bethany are currently baking without me. This is so unprofessional. Shit. Have you seen my phone?"

"In the chair," I say, my voice raw.

She grabs it and immediately starts typing a text. I'm sure it's to Emma.

"Holiday." Jake is fighting a smile. His eyes keep flicking between her neck and my face. "What did y'all do here?"

She stops moving for just a second to look at him. "We didn't do anything. We just talked and drank too much. That's it."

Jake's eyes drop to her neck again, and he clears his throat. "Just talked, huh?"

"Yes." Holiday stands beside me. "I know how this looks, us being out here all night, but nothing happened."

"You heard her," I say, even though the marks on her neck are clearly screaming otherwise. Even though I can still taste her. Even though my body is still humming from having her come apart in my arms to thoughts of me.

"We're just friends. Lucas has made that very clear." She's already moving toward my truck with her arms full of her things.

"Yeah, it's crystal fucking clear right now," Jake says, and he's full-on grinning. "But sure, whatever you say."

She's at my truck now, opening the door.

"I'll pick this shit up," Jake tells me, squeezing my shoulder. "Didn't realize friends sucked each other's necks like that."

"Fuck off," I tell him. "Dad get help?"

"Yeah, Hudson went with him."

I shake my head. "I've been occupied."

"Apparently," he says. I move to the truck and climb in. I reach over and grab her hand. "It's not the end of the world, okay? Repeat after me. Shit happens."

She's vibrating with stress. "Emma is going to be so upset."

I laugh. "She won't."

The trail through the woods looks much different during the day. The golden sunlight sneaks through the branches and it makes me smile. My body remembers last night and how she felt in my arms. The sounds she made when she came and how she tasted.

My heart is pounding as she types another message to Emma.

She still hasn't noticed the hickeys, and I know she'll lose it when she sees them.

"Mondays are always so busy," she whispers. And I count down to the day when her ex is to arrive in town.

Five days.

When he arrives, he'll absolutely see those marks on her skin, knowing someone has been touching her, knowing she's not his anymore. If she ever really was. Doesn't sound like that was the case.

Love that for him.

"Emma says the girls have it under control, but I still feel awful," Holiday mutters. "Wendy had to come in on her day off because of me."

"They'll be fine. My cousins love this, trust me."

"That's not the point." She's typing out a response. "I've never been late to work."

I glance at her. Morning light is streaming through the windshield. I think about my mouth on her throat while she touched herself. Loved hearing the way she gasped when I sucked that sensitive spot below her ear.

I shift in my seat, knowing this could get awkward, but go for it anyway.

A VERY MERRY ENEMY

I reach up and pull down her sun visor. The lights on the small mirror flick on.

"What are you—" She stops midsentence as she catches sight of her reflection.

Her eyes go wide. She leans forward, tilting her head to see her neck better. Her hand flies up, fingers gently touching one of the marks.

"Oh my—" Her voice comes out strangled. She glares at me. "Lucas! What have you done!"

I wince. "Yeah. Whoops."

"Whoops? This isn't a whoops! Everyone is going to know."

"Sorry?"

"Three hickeys? Look how purple they are! Are you a fucking Hoover vacuum?" She's twisting the visor, trying to see all of them. Her face is bright red, but there's something else in her eyes, too. Something heated that makes my blood run hotter. "I just told Jake nothing happened!"

"Yeah, I think he knew you were lying."

"While I have this all over my neck!" She finally looks at me directly, and there's heat in her gaze along with a dash of annoyance. Or is that awareness? "I was like a kid with chocolate all over her face, insisting she didn't eat any cookies."

I can't help it, and I laugh. The image is too perfect.

"It's not funny!" But she's fighting a smile now, her eyes still locked on mine. There's something electric in the air between us. Something that didn't get resolved last night.

"It's hilarious," I say with a shrug. "So, HoHo. What will you say when people ask who marked you as theirs?"

"You're impossible." She touches the mark near her ear, and her cheeks flush darker. Her fingers linger on it, and I remember tasting her skin, enjoying it. "You always did this. Even in high school. Senior year, you gave me a hickey right before school pictures! I had to lie and say it was someone from Valentine that I met at the rodeo!"

191

"In my defense, I was young and dumb."

"And the only difference is that now you're thirty-four." She's not really mad, though. I can see it in her eyes and in the way her lips are curving up. It's also not lost on me that she keeps looking at my mouth.

We turn onto the main road through the farm and pass the line of cars trying to enter the property.

Holiday's eyes widen even more. "We're going to get slammed today."

I turn onto the country road and drive the two miles to her parents' place.

I smirk, knowing those marks on her neck prove she's mine.

Except, she's not yet. Not until she chooses me. And not after drinking half a bottle of bourbon together, either.

"For what it's worth," I say, "I'm actually not sorry I did it."

She turns to look at me. The morning light makes her eyes look impossibly blue. "I know you're not. That hasn't changed either."

I keep my eyes on the road because if I look at her too long, I'm going to pull over and kiss her until those marks are everywhere. "I'm not sorry about last night, either."

"I'm not either."

The air in the truck feels charged, like last night never really ended, and those secrets did change things. A part of me wishes we were still in that tent.

"Fucking Jollys," she says, but there's no heat in it. Just affection and want.

"Your favorite family," I say, grinning. I ache everywhere for her.

I pull up to her parents' house and put the truck into park. Even though she's hours late, Holiday doesn't get out right away. Her expression makes my heart kick up, makes me want to say *fuck it*. But I can't. Not yet.

Being reckless is the last thing either of us needs, and it seems like I'm going to have to stay strong for us both.

"So," she says quietly. "Do you think I'm desperate and pathetic? Like you said to me at Moonshiners?"

"No," I admit. "I was being cruel, and I didn't know the whole story. I'm sorry for that." My heart is pounding now. My whole body is tense.

Her eyes are steady on mine. Direct. "Thank you."

I reach across the console and cup her face, then brush my thumb over one of the marks on her neck. Her skin is so soft. Warm. *Mine.*

"I want you to figure your shit out, Holiday. But I won't wait forever."

"One thing at a time," she whispers. "This is a start."

I press a kiss to her forehead, letting my lips linger. Breathing her in. Memorizing this moment. Is this the beginning of forever?

She smiles and it does something to my chest. Makes it hard to breathe.

"Thank you for not using me," she says. "Most guys woul—"

"I'm not most guys," I tell her.

"Oh, I'm aware," she says with a laugh. Holiday reaches for the door, then leans back. Her eyes drop to my mouth for just a second before meeting my gaze again.

"Stop," I mutter.

"Stop what?" That cocky as fuck smile grows.

"Confessions aren't supposed to change anything," I remind her.

"Have a good day," she says with a brow lifted.

I watch her walk toward her parents' house with a rush to her step. She turns to look back at me, waiting on the sidewalk.

I shake my head at her, knowing what she's doing. Trying to break my control.

"Already fucking ruined," I mutter to myself as I back out of the driveway, then head home.

She knows I'm not like anyone else she's ever been with.

I give instead of take.
I support instead of control.
I love instead of manipulate.

And I'll have her begging me to slide down her chimney before it's over.

CHAPTER 20

❄

HOLIDAY

I barely wait for Lucas's truck to disappear down the street before I'm bolting up the front steps of my parents' house.

Please don't be awake. Please don't be awake.

I slip through the front door and say a little prayer that the curtains are still pulled. It's dark, except for the stove light my mom always leaves on. I can hear my dad snoring from their bedroom down the hall.

I tiptoe up the stairs, skipping the one that creaks, and make it to my childhood bedroom without getting caught. The door clicks shut behind me, and I lean against it, letting out a breath I didn't know I was holding. When I look up, I catch a glimpse of myself in the full-length mirror across the room.

I flick on the light and move closer to it, tilting my head to see my neck better. Three very purple hickeys trail down my neck from below my ear to my collarbone.

My hand flies up to touch the darkest one. The memory of Lucas's mouth on my skin floods back, and heat rushes through me. He sucked and bit my skin while I touched myself. I can almost hear his whispers in my ear. Then I remember Jake found us, and I lied to his face with these marks trailing down my neck. Hopefully, he'll keep it to himself, and his whole family won't know by noon.

Regardless, I can't deny I'm smiling like an idiot over Lucas Jolly marking me as his. Some primal part of me loves it.

The smile fades as reality crashes back in, and I remember what Lucas said. He's waiting for me to be ready, to be sure, to not break his heart again.

He's always waiting on me.

Guilt slams into me and I sink onto my bed.

I hurt him so badly, and that's something I wish I could take back. Hearing the pain in his voice when he talked about how he couldn't commit because none of those women were me was heartbreaking.

I don't like myself for killing something so kind inside of him.

If I could go back in time and shake eighteen-year-old me, I would. I'd grab her by the shoulders and scream at her not to leave. Not to get on that plane. Not to throw away everything for some dream that would actually become a nightmare.

I'd tell her that she already had everything she could ever want and need.

I had a good man who loved me at my rawest form, someone who never wanted to change me. A town that supported my baking with a future full of possibilities.

I was too young to understand the opportunities that were already in the palm of my hand. There was a stupid part of me that was convinced bigger meant better, and education meant appreciation. I was too desperate to prove myself to a world that only wanted to make me someone I wasn't, with people who never mattered.

For what? For me to pick back up where I left off?

Now I'm thirty-four years old, covered in hickeys from my secret ex-boyfriend, in my childhood bedroom, trying to figure out if I can trust myself not to fuck this up again.

How sad is it that it took losing everything to recognize how great my life was before? And now, I'm so terrified that I'll get everything back, and I still won't appreciate Lucas. What if he decides I'm not what he wants? What if I'm not capable of being the person he deserves?

The thought almost destroys me.

I move to my closet, grabbing clothes for the day. A turtleneck will solve some of this problem, except for the one right below my ear. I settle on a dark green one that hugs me tight. I rush through getting ready, trying to scrub away the smoke from my skin while in the shower. After I dry my hair, I pull it into a side braid, hoping it'll cover more. Then I try to hide the hickey not covered by my shirt with some cheap concealer that expired a decade ago. It's better than nothing and kinda works.

This will have to do.

I check the time and see it's already eight thirty. The bakery usually opens at nine, and I'm usually there by five thirty at the very latest to bake thousands of cookies. I've never been this late.

I grab my phone and see two texts from Emma.

> EMMA
> Heard you were found.
>
> EMMA
> Jake told Hudson EVERYTHING. 🫣

My face burns thinking about Hudson and Emma knowing what happened. Without responding—because what the hell would I say?—I shove my phone in my pocket and head downstairs. Mom's in the kitchen making coffee.

"Morning, sweetie," she says without turning around. "Where were you?"

"Out." My voice sounds too high.

"With Lucas?" She glances over her shoulder at me. Her eyebrows shoot up.

"Mom—"

"I'm not saying anything." But she's smiling as she pours her coffee. "Just that it's nice to see you two together again."

"I really have to go. I'm late." I'm already moving toward the door.

"HoHo?"

I stop and turn back, remembering the first time she called me that in front of Lucas. He had everyone calling me HoHo at school. Went over really well.

"Don't you hurt that boy again," she warns.

I nod because I don't trust my voice. The words hit me square in the chest because I was naive to think no one noticed Lucas had changed after I left. The whole town watched him break, and now they're watching to see if I'll do it again.

Seconds later, I'm out the door and in my car on the way to the farm before my thoughts can spiral any further.

The morning is beautiful, and I can still see some frost on the ground, sparkling like glitter.

The sky is bright and clear blue without a cloud in sight. The sun seems brighter somehow, like the whole world shifted on its axis last night. Everything seems different now. Maybe it is. Confessions is always a dangerous game.

I pull into my parking spot at the bakery and take a deep breath. Through the windows, I can see Bella, Wendy, and Bethany moving around the kitchen effortlessly. Bethany is pulling cookies from the oven. Bella is stocking the front while Wendy puts dough on baking trays.

My mouth falls open because the shop is running like a well-oiled machine. This whole time, I've been micromanaging everything. Even though I'm away from Paris and Dominic, I've been trying to control every tiny detail. I've trusted no one but

A VERY MERRY ENEMY

myself, assuming this place will fail without my constant supervision. But these girls are crushing it.

They're talented and capable, and I've been treating them like they might burn the place down if I'm not there. I've been so afraid of losing control that I haven't given them more responsibilities.

I take a deep breath and get out of the car. The bell jingles when I push open the door, and all three girls look up.

"Holiday!" Bella's eyes narrow as she studies my face. "You look...different. Rough night?"

I ignore her question. "Sorry I'm late. I never oversleep and—"

"We've got it covered," Wendy says, gesturing around the immaculate kitchen. "We're actually not far behind."

"Amazing." I move closer and survey their work. The dough is portioned perfectly on the baking sheets. The cookies coming out of the oven are golden and baked evenly. The workspace is clean and organized. It's exactly how I would have done things. Maybe better.

"See?" Bethany grins. "We can handle things when you're not hovering."

She laughs, but her words are true. I haven't been trusting them. I've been controlling things because I couldn't let go.

"You're right. The three of you have done an incredible job. Thank you." I tie on an apron and move to wash my hands. "I've been—"

Bella is staring at my neck with wide eyes. "Wait. What's that?"

My hand flies up, and she moves closer, peeling my turtleneck down to reveal the other dark marks that I didn't bother covering. All three of them are staring now.

"Is that a hickey?" Wendy gasps.

"Multiple hickeys?" Bethany asks.

"No. It's—I burned myself. With a curling iron."

"Four times down your neck?" Bella crosses her arms and fights a smile. "You suck at lying."

My face is on fire. "Can we just—"

Bella squeals. "You and Lucas! Finally!"

"We didn't—nothing happened. We just—" But I can't finish the sentence because what can I say? *We just got drunk and I touched myself while he sucked on my neck?* That's something I'm going to keep to myself. This is proof that something did happen, something I can't deny.

Wendy is already digging through her purse. She pulls out a makeup bag that's bigger than my entire collection of cosmetics. "Here. Let me actually cover those for you because whatever you tried to use isn't working."

She guides me to a stool and tilts my head to examine the damage. "Wow. He really went for it, huh?"

"Shut up."

"I'm not judging. *Too much.*" She uncaps concealer and starts dabbing it on my neck. "You never forget your first love, do you?"

"No," I whisper. "You really don't."

Wendy meets my eyes in the small compact mirror she's holding. "There you go. Can't even tell. This stuff will cover up anything."

"Thank you," I say, letting out a relieved breath.

"Don't mess it up this time," Bella says, examining her older sister's work. "Can't even see them now."

"What is that stuff called?" Bethany asks.

I glare at her. "No, ma'am."

I bring the turtleneck back up, happy they're now invisible.

Wendy squeezes my shoulder. "Now let's bake some cookies."

The rest of the day flies by. We sell out right after lunch, and I'm not even stressed about it. The girls handle the disappointed customers with grace. Bethany leaves for her afternoon classes while Bella and Wendy take the lead on prep. I only step in when they ask for help.

It feels good to let go and actually manage. It's almost like I've been carrying a weight on my back and someone just lifted it off me.

Customers comment on my good mood all morning. One woman says I'm glowing. Another asks if I'm in love. I deflect and smile and box up cookies while humming along to the Christmas music playing overhead. Lucas would notice and make a comment about it. The thought makes me smile wider.

Around two, I lean against the counter, watching Bella and Wendy clean up. Through the window, I can see how packed the farm is. There's a line leading to Santa's workshop, where Lucas's dad is posing for photos with customers.

This place. This town. This life. It's everything I ran away from and everything I spent fifteen years trying to recreate somewhere else. The magic of Merryville was always here, waiting for me to be ready for it.

My phone buzzes in my pocket.

> LUCAS
> How's your neck?

I bite my lip to keep from grinning like a lovesick fool.

> HOLIDAY
> I owe you one. Actually, three.

> LUCAS
> Don't tempt me with a good time, Peaches.

> **HOLIDAY**
> You couldn't handle it.

> **LUCAS**
> Probably. Good day?

> **HOLIDAY**
> Actually yes. Really good. Don't need help prepping.

> **LUCAS**
> Can I still see you?

The text sits there between us, and I stare at it for a long moment. Last night shifted something between us. Showed me that maybe, possibly, we could have a second chance if I don't screw it up.

> **HOLIDAY**
> You want to?

> **LUCAS**
> Don't make me beg.

> **HOLIDAY**
> Kinda wish you would.

> **LUCAS**
> Come to my place after work.

> **HOLIDAY**
> That's not begging.

> **LUCAS**
> Oh please, Holiday. You know I don't have to.

My heart does something stupid in my chest.

A VERY MERRY ENEMY

. . .

HOLIDAY
> Fine. But only because you used your manners and said please like a good boy.

LUCAS
> Yeah, you're gonna think good boy. See ya at 6.

I'm still smiling when Bella appears at my side. "You're texting him, aren't you?"

"Maybe."

She does a little happy dance. "Lucas and Holiday, sitting in a tree—"

"Do not finish that sentence," I warn.

"F-U-C-K-I-N-G!" she sings anyway.

I shake my head. "Lies. Trust me. Lucas is cockblocking himself."

"Sounds about right."

As we finish up and I lock the bakery, I can't help wondering if I can have this.

The lightness I was feeling dims just a little and fear creeps back in. The doubt that's been my constant companion since I met Dominic whispers that I'm not good enough, not strong enough, not worthy of anything good.

But then I catch my reflection in the front windows of the bakery. And I look like my old self.

Maybe that's enough.

Maybe being me is exactly what I need to survive this.

I let myself be present in the moment instead of spiraling while thinking about the future.

Right now, I'm happy. And it's Lucas's fault. He was the only one who could ever turn my frown upside down. Seems like that still stands true.

CHAPTER 21

❄

LUCAS

I've changed my shirt three times, like I'm seventeen again and trying to impress Holiday Patterson before taking her to the county fair. Except now, I'm thirty-four and should know better than to care this much. Clothes have never impressed her, but I can't help but notice how her eyes slide over me when we're together.

I settle on a black button-up and jeans. It's casual and cool, like I'm not trying too hard, even though I absolutely am.

At five forty-five, I look up at the clock, almost nervous about tonight. The last time we were alone, she confessed she came back to Merryville for me, and I admitted that I never stopped having feelings for her. We both said things we can't unsay, and I have to pretend like it didn't happen. But I know the truth and I'm fucking shook.

Headlights sweep across my front window, and my pulse gallops in my chest. I watch as she parks next to my truck and takes a few extra seconds to study her as she pulls her visor down to check herself. Her hair is down in soft waves, and she's wearing deep red lipstick that makes my mouth go dry. She's still in that dark green turtleneck she wore to the bakery this morning.

A VERY MERRY ENEMY

Holiday eventually gets out of her car, and I meet her at the door before she can knock.

"Hi," she says, and when she smiles at me this time, it actually touches her eyes. It gives me butterflies.

"On time, per usual." I grab my jacket, then pull the door closed as I walk out with her. "Ready?"

"Where are we going, exactly?"

"It's a surprise."

She narrows her eyes. "I told you, I *hate* surprises."

"Yeah, yeah. Come on," I say with a laugh, placing my hand on her shoulder as I lead her to my truck. I open the door for her and she climbs in. I catch the hint of her perfume, the same one she's been wearing since high school. The one that used to linger on my clothes after I'd sneak into her bedroom and hold her when she couldn't sleep.

I close the door and walk around to my side, taking a second to get my shit together as her eyes follow me. Being alone with her feels like a dream. And if it is, fuck, I don't want to wake up.

I start the engine and pull out of the driveway. The radio is already on the local station that's been playing nothing but Christmas music since November first.

"So," Holiday says as we turn onto the country road that leads to Merryville. "We're going into town?"

"I thought we'd look at Christmas lights."

"Like we used to." She glances over at me with appreciation. "That sounds perfect."

We drive down Main Street, and it's like the whole place has been dipped in red and white twinkling lights. Every storefront is already decorated, shining in the darkness—it's city code, required by the Monday before Thanksgiving. Garland and red ribbons wrap around light posts with big wreaths on every door. Glenda's Diner has the windows painted with snowmen and a Santa that looks just like my dad. It's packed inside.

"Wow," Holiday says. "It's better than I remember."

"It's legendary."

She laughs and the sound fills the truck. I realize I'm at ease in a way I haven't felt in a long time.

Her hand rests on her thigh, and I'm mildly aware of how easy it would be to reach over and lace our fingers together. But I keep my hands to myself.

We drive past the square where the festival is being set up. It kicks off this weekend, and once it does, downtown will be impossible to enjoy. Tourists and vehicles will line the streets and sidewalks; that's why I wanted to do this now. This year's theme is Winter Wonderland, and a Christmas village has been constructed to give the full North Pole experience.

"It's beautiful," Holiday says, staring out the window.

"I agree," I say, but I'm not talking about the town. She's breathtaking, without even trying.

I take the long way through the residential neighborhoods, starting with Candy Cane Lane. Some houses have simple white lights strung along the roofline. Others look like Christmas threw up on them with every color imaginable and enough wattage to power a small city. But every home is decorated.

We turn onto South Pole Street, and when we reach the end, Holiday gasps. The mayor's house is covered in lights with a motion-sensor twerking Santa, reindeer, snowmen, penguins, and what appears to be a disco ball, spinning along with a stripper pole in the front yard.

I reach forward and turn the stereo to the AM station listed on the sign. We watch the lights dance and Santa pop his ass to Cardi B's "WAP."

Her mouth falls open, but she's giggling. "I cannot believe the mayor did this. I love it."

"Thought you would."

She's entranced by the light show, but I can't stop watching her and how the colorful lights splash across her face. The song ends, and cars pull up behind us, so we drive away.

"Thank you for this." Her fingers brush my forearm, leaving heat in their wake.

"We're just getting started," I say.

We drive past our old elementary school, where candy canes line the fence. Even the little white church has lights on the steeple.

Five minutes later, I'm taking the highway that leads to the overlook on the edge of Merryville. It's just a small parking area where people go to fool around. It's on a hill above the town, where all of Merryville can be seen spread out down below, twinkling and glowing.

We sit in comfortable silence, taking in the view, as the radio plays in the background.

"Some things don't change," I say. I've come up here every year since I could drive.

She looks at me, and there's something dancing in her gaze. "Some things do."

The moment sits between us, full of memory and meaning.

I suck in a deep breath, knowing I need to say what's been on my mind all day. Because it's the right thing to do.

"Holiday, I know you're not going to like this, but I think we should take some space away from one another this week."

She turns to look at me, eyebrows raised. "Why?"

I keep my voice soft. "Tomorrow and Wednesday, I'll be with my dad, delivering trees until eight. Thanksgiving will be hectic with family, then getting ready for Black Friday and the chaos that comes with that. Not to mention, Jake and Claire's wedding is Saturday."

"So, you're saying we're too busy to see each other?" There's an edge in her voice.

"There's no rush." I shift to face her better. "Three weeks ago, I wanted to keep my distance from you. Now we're here."

She studies me, then a cute smirk tugs at her lips. "Scared you're falling for me, Jolly?"

The question catches me off guard. She's not backing down. She's calling me out.

"Excuse the fuck outta me, but I'm being *smart* about this."

"That's not an answer." Her smile grows.

"Holiday—"

"What about our baking sessions?" She tilts her head, all innocent. "The contest is in two and a half weeks."

I can't help it, but I sarcastically laugh. "Come on. You could bake those cookies in your sleep at this point. With your skills, we could compete tomorrow and win. The joy of having a perfectionist as a partner. I just need to show up."

Her face flushes. "Ugh."

I lick my lips. "You're just looking for excuses to see me."

"Maybe I want to make up for lost time." She's not embarrassed about it. "Is that so bad?"

"No. But that's exactly why we need space."

"Yeah, we're not astronauts, Lucas."

I chuckle, reaching over and taking her hand because I need her to understand this. "Look at me. You've spent over a decade with a man who controlled every aspect of your life. You need time to figure out who you are and what you want, without someone else constantly around."

"I want you in my orbit."

"But you still need to figure out what Holiday wants without someone else influencing you." I squeeze her hand. "That includes me. I don't want you waking up in three months, realizing you rushed into something you weren't ready for again." Silence draws on. "I can't be yours for only a season again. Do you understand?" I study her, memorizing the twinkle in her eyes.

"Okay." She glances down at our joined hands, then sighs.

"We both need to think this through. Right now, we can walk away, stay friends, and move on with our lives. If we cross any more lines, that will be a lot harder," I say. "I'm protecting us because you, while I adore it, are often like 'consequences be damned.'"

She pulls her hand away from me and tucks her hair behind her ears. "Are you having doubts?"

"I'm taking everything into account," I admit. "One day at a time."

"I can respect that," she says.

We both turn and look out at Merryville. "I could use some of Mawmaw's eggnog right now."

"Great idea for next time." I chuckle, and she nods.

"Will you be at Jake and Claire's wedding on Saturday?" I ask, realizing we haven't discussed it yet.

"I'll be there. Your brother invited me last week. Already RSVP'd with a plus-one," she says.

My jaw tightens. "I think the fuck not."

Her eyes light up with mischief. "I'm just messing with you."

"You're evil." I shake my head.

She gives me a look that's pure challenge. "I'll be there—alone—trying not to stare at you."

A smirk touches my lips. "There will be a lot of people there. It's probably best if we keep things platonic. Last thing we need is more rumors spreading around, you know?"

She tilts her head. "*More* rumors?"

"Yeah, so about that," I say, pulling my phone from my pocket and opening the browser window. "There are pictures of us on the internet."

Holiday's eyes widen as she scrolls through the articles written about me and her with pictures of my arm around her at the community center. There are other pictures someone took of us inside the bakery, standing close and flirty. There are a few pictures that someone plucked from my social media when we were teenagers.

I watch the color drain from her face.

"'Anonymous source claims Holiday Patterson and Lucas Jolly had a secret romance before she left for culinary school,'" she reads aloud and gasps. "'What will Dominic do to win back his ex-fiancée?'" She scrolls further. "'Lumberjack hottie wants to put a bun in Holiday Patterson's oven.'" Her mouth falls open. "Oh my goodness. This is a nightmare!"

She drops my phone.

"Hey, it doesn't matter. But this is pressure we didn't sign up for or need."

"After the contest, when Dominic returns to Paris without me, everyone will leave me alone," she promises. "I'm so sorry. I-I—"

"Not your fault, HoHo. Just be aware that we're being watched and talked about. The farm isn't safe. I want this to die down," I admit. "Emma had a lot of PR training in her influencer days, and she suggested we don't feed the beast. Don't give people anything to talk about, and they'll get bored."

Holiday leans her head back and closes her eyes. "I hate that he's coming here and bringing this mess with him."

"I do, too," I admit.

Holiday turns to me. "Speaking of exes…do I know any of the people you dated?"

I swallow hard. "Do you really want to have this conversation?"

The smirk on her lips fades. "Yes. Because of *that* response."

My heart races because I know this won't make her happy. "Lindsay Moore, Kristin Benford, and Amanda Hartly."

Holiday glares at me, and I see her nostrils flare. "You dated my *friends*?"

I cross my arms over my chest. "Oh no, you don't get to be pissed about that, babe. You were hardly friends with any of them. And you were *engaged*. Anyone who could hold a conversation with me got a chance," I explain. "I broke it off with each one of them because at the end of the day, they weren't *you*. I was happy for a little while, but it never lasted. I could've married any of them, and it would've been zero fucking prerogative to you. I really never believed you'd come back."

"But here I am," she says.

"Here you are, *always* proving me wrong," I tell her. "Showing me that my wishes on stars came true."

She lets out a laugh. "You didn't."

"Yes, I fucking did. Every chance I got," I confess.

Holiday licks her lips and I can't help but notice. "Surely you didn't wish for my relationship to end in flames?"

"Maybe a little," I say, starting the truck with a chuckle.

"You're terrible."

We drive back to my house in comfortable silence. She hums along to the radio, and I steal glances at her when I think she's not looking. She catches me twice and smiles like she knows exactly what she does to me.

I pull into my driveway and park next to her car. Neither of us moves.

"This isn't goodbye, is it?" she asks, but she doesn't reach for the door handle.

"Hell no."

The cab feels more intimate in the darkness.

"Okay, then enjoy your five days without me," she says.

"Enjoy? You'll be the only thing on my mind." I want to pull that turtleneck down and put my mouth back on those marks or add more. Want to make sure everyone who looks at her knows she's mine.

We get out, and the November air is cold enough to make our breath fog. I follow her to her car, and we stand in the space between our vehicles.

Holiday looks up at me, and her lips are parted slightly. Her eyes are full of want and challenge.

I reach up slowly and tuck a strand of hair behind her ear. My thumb grazes the side of her neck, and she sucks in a breath.

"Lucas," she whispers.

I want to kiss her. I want it so bad, my body aches with need. Right now, I could back her against her car and taste her mouth, make her forget every doubt she has.

My hand slides from her neck to cup her jaw and her eyes flutter closed.

"After fifteen years, you'll survive five days," I say close to her mouth.

"Asshole." She opens her eyes, but grins.

"You haven't seen anything yet."

She steps back and opens her car door. "Good luck, Lucas. You're going to need it."

"You, too."

She climbs into her car and starts the engine. Her headlights come on as she backs out of the driveway with a wave. I watch her taillights disappear and go into my dark house.

I add logs to the fireplace and start it. When flames are licking up the side, my phone dings.

HOLIDAY
Made it home safely. And just so you know, I'm not mad that you dated my friends. I'm jealous that you gave yourself to them.

LUCAS
We don't want to talk about jealousy, sweetheart. It killed me seeing you plan a wedding with someone else.

HOLIDAY
You know, I have to confess something. All those years I didn't come home, it was because I was scared I'd see you and give it all up. What if I just need to get you out of my system?

LUCAS
Oh, that will never happen. I'll linger under your skin for eternity.

HOLIDAY
That's what I'm afraid of. You ruined me, Lucas Jolly. For anyone else.

LUCAS
More proof my wishes always come true.

A VERY MERRY ENEMY

. . .

I set my phone down and lean back on the couch, grinning.

Holiday Patterson wants me, and she's making damn sure I know it.

Now I just have to make it five days without breaking my own rules by going to see her.

I want her to be absolutely sure that I am what she wants.

CHAPTER 22

❄

LUCAS

I'm standing in front of the mirror in Jake's old bedroom at our parents' house, adjusting my tie for the third time. It's been five days since I've seen Holiday, and I'm losing my mind.

We've texted short and sweet messages that feel like breadcrumbs when what I really want is the whole damn meal. There were several *good morning* and *how's your day going* texts.

The bakery is insane.
The farm is chaos.
Black Friday nearly killed me.
Hope you're surviving.

There was nothing substantial. Nothing that crossed any lines that we agreed not to cross right now. But every time my phone buzzes, my heart jumps, hoping it's her.

I almost broke twice. Wednesday night, I was in my truck with the engine running, ready to drive to her house. Friday afternoon, I found myself standing outside the bakery like a creep, watching her laugh through the window before I forced myself to leave.

Five days felt like years.

And now, the talk of the town is about Dominic, who arrived in Merryville this morning. Emma sent the group chat a text saying he checked into the Merryville Inn. The newspaper already interviewed him, and he was walking around town like he has a right to be here.

I haven't heard from Holiday in twenty-four hours.

There has been no mention of Dominic or if he's tried to contact her. *Nothing.*

And it's killing me.

"You look like you're about to throw up," Hudson says from where he's lounging on Jake's bed, already dressed. He looks annoyingly comfortable in the custom-made Italian suit that costs more than my truck.

"Oh, I'm fine," I say, looking at him from the reflection of the mirror.

"You've been staring at that tie for ten minutes. It's straight. You're just stalling."

"No, I'm not."

"You absolutely are." Jake appears in the doorway already dressed and ready. He looks different somehow. More mature, even though he's only three years older than me. He's about to marry the love of his life and has zero doubts about his future.

Claire's family spared no expense on this wedding. The formal wear is custom, tailored to perfection, all designed by her friends at Bellamore. My suit was custom-made for my body. It's black with subtle details and is lined with red silk.

My phone buzzes in my pocket, and it's Emma.

EMMA
Still no Holiday.

The jacket makes my shoulders look broader, and I've been working on the farm enough that I'm in the best shape of my life. But none of that matters if Holiday doesn't show up. She's never late.

I'm concerned Dominic's presence is messing with her head.

"Dude." Hudson sits up. "You need to chill."

"Yeah, what's the problem?" Jake asks.

The problem is, I haven't seen her in five days, and I'm supposed to act like we're casual acquaintances who just happen to bake cookies together when the world knows the truth. Dominic Laurent is in town, and I know he will try to contact her. I stupidly gave her space when every instinct I have is screaming to go to her.

I don't tell them that, though. My relationship issues aren't a concern for either of my brothers.

"Zero problems," I tell him. "Just want everything to go smoothly tonight."

"Oh, it will. Claire has planned this down to the minute." Jake gives me a smile. "But that's not your issue. You've been walking around like a ghost all week. We should talk about Holiday."

"There's nothing to discuss," I say.

"Bullshit." Hudson stands and crosses his arms. "You gave her hickeys and then ignored her all week."

"I didn't ignore her," I correct him. "We hung out the next night."

"And then you ignored her, right?" Hudson grins. "You're keeping track like some lovesick teenager."

I want to punch him.

"Speaking of," Hudson continues, clearly enjoying himself, "I couldn't believe Mawmaw brought the hickeys up at Thanksgiving dinner. Love that the whole family knows you marked her like a caveman."

"Yeah, well, Jake should've kept his fucking mouth shut."

This makes him laugh. "No, I shouldn't have. It's a lot more fun to watch you squirm."

"Can we please not do this right now?" I say, glancing between them.

"We are absolutely going to do this right now." Jake moves closer, but his expression is gentler now. "Look, I'm marrying the love of my life tonight. And you know what I've learned from being with Claire?"

"What?"

"Life's too short to play it safe when you know." He puts his hand on my shoulder. "You've been in love with Holiday Patterson since you hit puberty. That's two decades, Lucas. And you've spent a long fucking time waiting and wondering and wishing she'd come back."

"I know how long it's been."

"Then why are you acting like this?" He squeezes my shoulder. "She came back. She's here. She's single. And every time you two are in the same room, it's obvious she wants you just as much as you want her."

I sigh. "It's complicated."

"Love is complicated. That's what makes it worth it." Jake steps back. "I'm not telling you to rush into anything. Just don't waste any more years being scared of what might happen when you could be living the life you want."

Hudson nods. "For once, I agree with Jake. You've been miserable. Just admit you're crazy about her and do something about it."

"I'm being respectful. Giving her space to figure out what she wants."

"Has it occurred to you that maybe," Jake says slowly, "she already knows what she wants? And she's waiting for you to stop being so damn noble about everything?"

I think about the texts. The way she's tried to restrain herself because I asked her to.

"I can't be hers for a season again," I say. "I won't fucking survive it."

Both of them go still.

"You think you're a rebound?" Hudson asks, and his voice has lost all of its teasing edge.

"I don't know. Her ex fucked her head up." I run my hand through my hair. "She has a lot to work through."

"Fuck that," Hudson says. "Help her heal from it."

Jake's jaw is tight. "She needs you, Lucas. Pushing her away is the last thing you should be doing."

The words hit like a punch because he's right.

"Space is one thing. But her ex just arrived, and you're like…let's ignore one another?"

"It's not like that."

"No? 'Cause that's what it looks like." Hudson's voice is firm now. "Seems to me like you're the one who isn't sure what you want. She came back for you, Lucas. That's pretty fucking obvious to everyone."

I stare at him, my chest tight.

"Agreed," Jake says. "Now stop overthinking everything and just…be with her."

"There are articles online about us."

"And? There were articles about me and Hudson when we started dating the Manchester sisters. You'll get over it. You'll learn to ignore it. Build a fortress where the two of you can escape it all. And who gives a damn what anyone says or how it looks. Stop hiding behind needing space and being respectful, and just be honest with yourself," Jake says. "You deserve to be happy, too."

"Yeah? And what if what I want scares her off? What if she runs back to Paris, and I'm left here to pick up the broken pieces alone again?"

"Then at least you tried." Jake adjusts his jacket. "But I'd be willing to bet that she's been waiting for you to stop holding back just as much as you've been waiting for her to come home."

Hudson claps me on the shoulder. "Plus, you look good today. Use it to your advantage."

I let out a rough laugh. "You're both terrible at pep talks."

"We're excellent at pep talks, you're just a stubborn asshole who thinks he knows it all." He claps me on my shoulder again. "Now come on. We have a wedding to get to, and you have a woman to impress."

We drive out to the opposite side of the farm by the big storage barn in a convoy of black SUVs that Claire's family arranged. Everything about this wedding is extravagant in a way that should feel out of place in Merryville, but somehow, Claire made it work.

The large venue is set up in the north field, the one with the best view of the rolling hills and Christmas trees beyond. It's been transformed into something that belongs in a magazine, not on a working tree farm.

Three massive white tents are connected by heated walkways lined with evergreen garland and thousands of white lights. The main ceremony tent is in the center, with clear panels on the sides so the farm can be seen. Crystal chandeliers hang from the ceiling, and more white lights are strung everywhere, making it look like we're standing under a sky made of stars.

The tent on the left is for cocktails and appetizers. Ice sculptures of swans and Christmas trees are on the opposite side of the entrance. Their surfaces glisten with condensation from the heat lamps. There are several bars being tended by bartenders in formal wear, mixing signature cocktails and serving appetizers on silver trays.

The tent on the right is set up for dinner and dancing. A quartet is doing sound checks in one corner, the soft sounds of a violin floating through the space. Tables are draped in white linen with gold accents. Centerpieces made of white roses and evergreen branches smell like Christmas and elegance combined.

Heat lamps disguised as elegant standing candelabras keep the temperature comfortable, despite the late November cold outside. This had to have cost more than most people make in several years, but it's beautiful. Exactly what I'd imagine Claire would do.

"Your fiancée went all out," I tell Jake as we walk through the ceremony tent doing a final check.

"She's been planning this for a year. I just showed up where she told me to and said yes to everything." But he's grinning, clearly happy to let Claire have whatever she wants.

Claire appears from behind a curtain where the bridal party is getting ready. Even though Jake's not supposed to see her, she walks right up to him in her silk robe and kisses him like they're the only two people in the world.

"Everything okay?" she asks when she pulls back.

"Perfect." Jake's looking at her like she hung the moon. "You look incredible."

"You haven't even seen the dress yet."

"Don't need to."

She smiles and touches his face gently. "I love you."

"Love you, too. Now go finish getting ready so I can marry you already."

She laughs and disappears back behind the curtain, and I feel something twist in my chest watching them. That's what I want. That certainty. That ease. That absolute knowledge of being with the right person. And I had it once with Holiday, but we were kids who didn't know any better.

Maybe we could have it again. I want to believe that.

Hudson elbows me. "That's going to be you and Holiday in about six months. Calling it now."

"Shut the fuck up."

"Tell me I'm wrong."

"I don't know what the future holds," I tell him.

"Ah, you're in the uneasy stage. Enjoy the ride, little brother," Hudson says, pulling a flask from his inside pocket and handing it to me. I take several gulps, needing it to calm my nerves.

Guests start arriving around four thirty. Vintage white horse-drawn carriages bring them from the parking area to the venue. They're heated inside, with white leather seats and gold trim, and there are blankets embroidered with Claire and Jake's initials for anyone who wants them.

Christmas music plays from hidden speakers as the carriages glide along the path. Each arrival feels like an event, guests stepping out in their finest, looking around at the transformed farm with surprised reactions.

I'm standing with Hudson near the entrance to the ceremony tent, greeting early guests, and my stomach is in knots. Every carriage that arrives, I watch. Waiting. Wondering if this is the one that's carrying Holiday.

Emma walks over to us, and Hudson immediately goes to her side.

"Babe, everything okay?" he asks her.

"Fine. I'm just going to the bathroom before this party starts. I swear the babies are using my bladder as a trampoline right now."

Everyone is worried her water is going to break tonight. Emma's very pregnant with twins and looks like she could pop any second, but she refused to stay home. She's stubbornly glowing.

"You clean up nice." She looks me up and down. "The ladies are going to lose their minds when they see you."

"Hush," I tell her.

"Aw, are you blushing?" Emma exchanges a look with Hudson. "Is he nervous?"

"I'm not nervous," I snap.

"Is that why you've been checking every carriage for

Holiday like your life depends on it?" she mutters close enough for me to hear.

"I'm not—"

"You absolutely are," Hudson confirms, walking with Emma. "It's pathetic. But also, kind of sweet."

I'm happy they both stopped riding my ass, it gives me a chance to calm my nerves as more guests arrive.

Photographers are everywhere, capturing candid moments and directing people into positions. I recognize faces from all over—Claire's family and friends from New York, their designer clothes and easy wealth obvious even from a distance. Jake's friends from high school, more casual but still dressed to impress. Half of Merryville is in their Sunday best, clearly excited to be part of something this extravagant.

But I notice how they look at me, and I overhear their conversations as they pass.

"That's Lucas Jolly, the one from the articles…"

"Is Holiday Patterson here?"

"I heard they had a secret relationship when they were teenagers…"

"My cousin saw them at city hall and said they couldn't stop touching each other…"

Great. Just great.

Another carriage arrives, and then another.

The ceremony tent is full of guests taking their seats. The quartet starts playing soft background music, and everything is moving forward according to the schedule.

But there's still no Holiday.

"You look like you're about to pass out," Matteo says.

"I'm fine," I tell him.

"You're really not." But he's smiling. "It's cute, though. In a pathetic sort of way."

Matteo laughs and I flip him off.

Ten minutes pass, and it feels like an hour as we get closer to the ceremony starting.

I force myself to greet more guests with a smile and make small talk, all while acting like I'm not constantly watching the path from the parking area. Like my entire nervous system isn't on high alert waiting for her to arrive.

The photographer wants photos of the groomsmen before the ceremony starts. We line up, and I try to focus, try to grin naturally, and be present for Jake's big day. But all I can think about is Holiday and what I'm going to say when I see her, or how I'm supposed to act like we're just friends when I've been counting down the minutes until I could see her again.

"Relax," Jake mutters as we pose. "You look constipated."

"Thanks. *Very* helpful," I say.

"I'm serious. Breathe. She'll be here."

I force myself to take a breath and relax my shoulders. Then I stop clenching my jaw.

The photographer finishes with us and we head back toward the ceremony tent entrance. Guests are still arriving, the carriages coming more steadily now. The ceremony starts in twenty minutes.

A white carriage travels down the path with bells jingling and stops. The driver opens the door, and my entire world narrows to that single point when Holiday steps out.

She's wearing a burgundy dress that should be illegal. It hugs every curve, with a neckline that shows off her collarbones and the graceful line of her neck. Her hair falls in waves past her shoulders, styled in a way that's both elegant and effortless. She's wearing just enough makeup to make her blue eyes look impossibly bright, and her lips are painted the same deep red she wore Monday night.

She looks like every fantasy I've had come to life.

Her parents step out of the carriage behind her, her mom adjusting her shawl, and her dad offering his arm. But I barely register them. All I can see is Holiday as she looks around at the transformed farm, her eyes wide, a small smile playing on her lips.

Then she looks up and our eyes meet across the distance.

Everything else disappears.

Guests walk past me as music floats from the tent. The photographer calls out instructions somewhere to my left. Then I think I hear Emma say something to Hudson behind me.

It's just me and Holiday, and five days of separation that suddenly feels like an eternity.

She stops walking. I watch her breath catch, watch her hand come up to touch her chest, watch color rise in her cheeks even from here.

And I know. In that instant, I know that whatever happens between us, we'll be okay. She's looking at me like I'm the only person in the world.

Around us, I'm vaguely aware that people have noticed us. That guests are turning to look, and I hear the whispers getting louder. This moment is being watched and will likely end up on the internet by tomorrow.

But I don't care.

She starts walking toward me, her heels clicking softly on the wooden pathway. Her parents follow behind, but her eyes never leave mine.

I can see the pulse jumping in her throat now. I can see she's wearing the necklace I gave to her for her birthday when we were seventeen. It's a simple silver star that I saved up for weeks to buy. She kept it.

Suddenly, she's ten feet away, then five.

When she's standing right in front of me, I can see the darker flecks of blue in her eyes and count every freckle on her face that I've memorized a thousand times.

"Hi," she says, and her voice is soft.

"Hi." It comes out rougher than I intended. "You look…"

I can't finish the sentence because no words can describe her.

"You too." Her eyes slide over me, taking in the way the suit fits, and I watch her swallow hard. "Really good. Like, unfairly good."

"*Unfairly?*"

"You'll be the death of me." She takes a breath, and I can see her trying to compose herself, trying to remember that we're supposed to be keeping a distance. "How am I supposed to act casual when you look like that?"

I make a face. "Are you kidding me? I should ask you the same thing."

We stand there, staring at each other, while people move around us. At least a dozen people have stopped what they're doing to watch us. Phones are definitely out.

Someone clears their throat nearby, but neither of us looks away from the other.

"I missed you," she says, and my chest feels like it's cracking open.

"Missed you, too, Peaches." I want to touch her and pull her against me. I don't know if I'll ever let go. I'm tempted to cup her face and kiss her until neither of us can think straight.

"Holiday—"

"Lucas!" Jake's voice cuts through the moment. "We need to start lining up. Ceremony's in ten minutes."

Reality crashes back in, and I know I need to go.

But I don't want to.

"Go," Holiday says, even though I can see in her eyes that she doesn't want me to leave, either. "I'll be right there. Third row, on the groom's side."

"Promise?"

"Promise."

I force myself to step back and turn away, even though every cell in my body is screaming to stay.

As I walk toward the ceremony tent with the other groomsmen, I glance back at her. Holiday's watching me with an expression that makes my heart pound.

Emma appears at her side immediately, and I watch them

hug around her big bump. Emma says something that makes Holiday laugh, and her cheeks turn pink.

Hudson elbows me as we line up for the processional. "Well, that was real fucking subtle."

"Shut up."

"You two might as well have made out in front of three hundred people."

"We were *just* talking."

"You were eye-fucking each other into oblivion, and you know it." He's grinning. "But hey, at least now everyone has confirmed that you're absolutely crazy about each other. Stop pretending."

The music changes, signaling the start of the ceremony. Guests hurry to find their seats. I give Jake a tight hug. He looks nervous and excited and ready.

From where I'm standing, I can see Holiday take her seat exactly where she said she'd be. Third row, Jolly side. The ceremony is about to start, and I have no idea how I'm going to get through it without staring at her.

This is going to be the longest hour of my damn life. And I can't fucking wait.

CHAPTER 23

❄

HOLIDAY

I adjust my burgundy dress as I sit behind Lucas's immediate family, wondering if I made a mistake wearing something this formfitting to a wedding. But then I remember the look on Lucas's face when I stepped out of that carriage, and I know I made the right choice.

My parents sit beside me. Dad is fidgeting with his tie, and Mom keeps dabbing at her eyes with a tissue even though the ceremony hasn't started yet.

"This is so beautiful," she whispers to me, squeezing my hand.

"You say that at every wedding," Dad teases.

"Because it's true." Mom looks at me and there's something knowing in her expression. "Weddings always make me emotional. Especially when they're between two people who are clearly meant to be together."

I know she's not just talking about Jake and Claire.

The tent fills with guests. White chairs are arranged in neat rows facing the front, where an elegant arch covered in white roses and evergreen stands waiting. Crystal chandeliers hang overhead, their light mixing with the thousands of white fairy lights strung across the ceiling. Through the clear panels on the sides of the tent, I can see the fading sunset over the Christmas tree farm stretching out into the distance. It's magical and romantic and everything a winter wedding should be.

I turn to glance at the entrance where the groomsmen are gathering. Lucas looks so incredibly handsome in his tuxedo that my chest aches. He's talking with Hudson and laughing at something, completely at ease. And when he smiles, I see that dimple, the one that only shows when it's genuine.

Then, as if he can feel me watching him, he turns his head and our eyes meet across the tent.

Everything else fades away for a moment. The other guests disappear. The music becomes background noise. It's just him and me with an eternity in front of us. He doesn't look away, and neither do I.

"Holiday," my mom says, grabbing my attention.

I blink at her. "Yes, ma'am?"

"Honey, you're staring." But she's smiling when she says it.

"I'm not—"

"You absolutely are, sweetheart." She pats my hand.

My dad clears his throat, but I can see the corner of his mouth twitching like he's trying not to smile.

Sammy slides in next to me. He had to work today and told me he'd arrive a little later. "Hey, sis. What's goin' on?"

"Nothing," I tell him.

"Mm-hmm," my brother says, chuckling. He pulls a flask from inside his suit jacket and hands it to me. "You need to relax."

I don't deny it and lean into him, taking a few gulps.

More guests fill in around us. I recognize people from town dressed in their finest. The Jolly family sits in the front rows looking proud and emotional. Claire's family and friends are sitting on the other side, looking elegant.

The energy in the tent shifts as the ceremony time draws closer. Conversations drop to hushed whispers. The photographers move into their positions with their cameras. The

A VERY MERRY ENEMY

quartet in the corner adjusts their instruments. And then the music changes.

Everyone turns toward the back of the tent as the procession begins.

My heart races as I watch the entrance, knowing Lucas will walk down that aisle any second now.

Wendy appears with her cousin Dean. They walk slowly down the aisle, smiling as they pass.

Hudson walks with Emma, who looks absolutely radiant even though she's very pregnant. She's moving slow, one hand on her belly, but she's smiling widely. When they pass our row, Emma catches my eye and winks at me before taking a seat in the front row. No way she can stand on her feet for the entire ceremony. Hudson gives her a quick kiss before moving next to Dean.

Then Lucas appears with Bella on his arm.

My breath catches in my throat.

He looks even more gorgeous up close. The suit fits him perfectly, emphasizing his broad shoulders and the strong lines of his body. His dark hair is styled but still has that slightly messy quality that makes me want to run my fingers through it. His jaw is set with determination, but there's something vulnerable in his eyes as he scans the crowd, wearing that soft smile.

Bella leans close and whispers something to him as they start walking. Whatever she says makes his entire face flush red, and he tries to hold back a wide smile but fails. She says something else and he actually laughs out loud, shaking his head at her like he wants her to stop talking.

I wonder what she said to make him blush like that. Knowing her, it was probably something completely inappropriate and exactly what he needed to hear.

When they pass my row, Lucas's eyes find mine again.

It's so damn intense, butterflies flutter. It's a good thing I'm not standing, or I might have gone weak in the knees. There's heat in his look, and longing, and something that looks dangerously close to love. Lucas and Bella separate when they reach the arch. She moves to stand with her sister on the left side, and Lucas takes his position on the right, directly next to Jake and Hudson. The three of them have always been close.

Lucas smiles at Jake and places his hand on his shoulder and squeezes. When Lucas looks out into the crowd, his eyes immediately find mine.

My mom squeezes my hand again, and when I glance at her, she's definitely crying now.

Colby and his best friend Evie walk down the aisle together, looking as cute as can be. It reminds me of when Lucas and I did that for my sister's wedding. I turn to my mom.

"Where's Tricia?" I ask.

"In the back," Mom tells me. "They just got here."

"Oh, okay," I say, turning to search for her. I immediately find Bethany and see my sister sitting next to her.

Jake looks nervous and excited and so incredibly happy as he waits for his bride.

Hudson says something that makes Jake smile and nod. The gesture is so tender and brotherly that it makes my throat tight.

The music shifts to the bridal march, and everyone stands.

Claire appears at the back of the tent on her father's arm, and she is absolutely breathtaking. Her dress is elegant and timeless, with an intricate lace detail on the bodice that catches the light from the chandeliers. Her cathedral-length veil trails behind her like something out of a fairy tale. Her face is glowing with happiness. She looks like a princess.

Jake's entire face transforms when he sees his bride. His green eyes are definitely wet with tears, like he cannot believe his luck.

Lucas smiles at Claire, then watches his brother with admiration. There's pride there, and happiness, and something soft and vulnerable that I don't often see on his face. He's watching Jake fall apart with joy, and there's so much love in that look.

Lucas's eyes shift from Jake to me. And I know exactly what he's thinking because it's on my mind, too.

I take in a deep breath, wondering if that could be us someday. Could we stand up there and make those promises with that kind of certainty? Or are we always meant to be chasing one another?

I want to believe it's possible. I want that so badly it hurts.

Claire reaches the front, and her father kisses her cheek before placing her hand in Jake's. Then he takes his seat, and Claire and Jake stand facing each other, hands clasped together, looking at each other like they're the only two people in the world.

"Please be seated," the pastor says, and everyone sits with a rustle of fabric.

Pastor John is an older man with kind eyes and a warm smile. "Dearly beloved, we are gathered here today to witness the joining of Claire Caitlyn Manchester and Jake Andrew Jolly in holy matrimony."

His voice carries through the space.

"Marriage is not to be entered into lightly, but thoughtfully, reverently, and with the understanding that it is a sacred bond between two people who choose each other, day after day, through all of life's seasons," Pastor John continues.

Lucas's jaw is tight, and his hands are clasped in front of him, but his eyes keep drifting toward me. When our gazes meet, something electric passes between us.

Choose each other. Day after day. Season after season.

Is that what we've been doing this entire time? Even when we were apart? Even when I was in Paris and he was here? Were we still choosing each other in some fundamental way that neither of us can really understand?

"Jake and Claire have chosen to write their own vows," Pastor John continues. "Jake, you're first."

Jake takes both of her hands in his and sucks in a deep breath. When he speaks, his voice is thick with emotion.

"Claire, I'm not good at fancy words or big romantic gestures. You know that better than anyone."

A ripple of laughter goes through the guests, and I find myself smiling even though tears are already forming in my eyes.

"But what I can tell you is this. From the moment I met you, you've been it for me. You literally walked into Merryville and everything in my life just clicked into place in a way I never expected."

Claire's eyes are watering as she rubs her thumbs across Jake's.

"You make me want to be better. Braver. More open to the world and its possibilities." Jake's voice cracks as he tries to hold on to his emotions. "You've taught me that love isn't about being perfect. It's about showing up every single day and choosing each other, even when it's hard. *Especially* when it's hard."

My vision is blurring. My mom offers me a tissue and I take it, dabbing my eyes.

Lucas glances at me, and I can barely breathe.

"I promise to choose you every day for the rest of my life," Jake continues. "I promise to support your dreams, even when they scare me. I promise to make you laugh when you're stressed, to hold you when you cry, and to always, always be honest with you, even if it's hard. I promise to love you through every season, every challenge, every triumph, and every failure."

Each word feels like a preview of what could be.

Jake takes a shaky breath. "You're my best friend, CeCe. You're my home. And I can't wait to spend the rest of my life proving to you that you made the right choice in saying yes to me."

The tent is silent except for the sound of people sniffling and trying not to sob out loud. Even some of the men are wiping their eyes.

Lucas's eyes are soft and full of longing as he smiles at me. He's not even trying to hide it anymore.

"Beautiful." Pastor John smiles. "Claire, your turn."

Claire takes a moment to compose herself, carefully wiping at her eyes so she doesn't smudge her makeup. When she speaks, her voice is clear, despite the tears streaming down her face.

"Jake, I knew from the very first moment we met that you were different. You refused to let me walk into Merryville after I ran out of gas. Getting in the truck with you changed my entire life." She squeezes his hands.

More laughter ripples through the room.

"You were the first person who made me feel like I didn't have to be perfect all the time. Like I could just be me, with my anxieties and overthinking. You taught me that you get what you give. I don't know what I did in life to deserve you."

Jake grins at her through his own tears.

"You've shown me what it means to be loved unconditionally," Claire continues, her voice getting stronger. "Not for what I can do or what I can provide, but just for who I am. You've been patient with me when I needed it, pushed me when I needed that, too, and never once made me feel like I was too much or not enough."

The words hit me like a physical blow because that's exactly what I've been afraid of. Being too much. Not being enough. Making the wrong choice again.

But as I watch Jake look at Claire like she hung the moon, I realize that real love doesn't keep score like that. Real love just *is*.

"I promise to be your partner in all things," Claire says. "To support your family and your farm and everything that matters to you. I promise to trust you, to communicate with you, and to never let the sun set on an argument between us. I promise to choose adventures with you, and I can't wait to build a life with you that's full of joy and laughter and most of all, love."

Lucas shifts his weight, and I watch his hand come up to adjust his tie like he can't quite breathe. I know the feeling.

"You're my greatest adventure, JJ." Claire's voice breaks on his nickname. "My Christmas miracle. You're the person I want beside me every single moment for the rest of my life. I love you more than I ever thought was possible."

My mom is crying so hard now that my dad wraps his arm tighter around her, and I'm crying, too. Not just for Jake and Claire, but for me and Lucas. For what we had and what we lost. For what we might still have if we're brave enough to claim it.

Pastor John lets the emotion of the moment settle before continuing. "Jake and Claire, you have declared your love and commitment to each other before what looks like the entire town of Merryville. Now, as a symbol of your promises, please exchange your rings."

Colby steps forward with the rings balanced on a small velvet pillow. He's grinning, clearly happy for his uncle. Jake takes Claire's ring with shaking hands.

"Repeat after me," Pastor John says. "With this ring, I thee wed."

Jake repeats it, his voice steady as he slides the diamond band onto Claire's finger.

Claire takes Jake's ring and repeats the same. The simple gold band slides onto Jake's finger and they both just stare at their joined hands for a moment, like they can't quite believe this is real.

Pastor John raises his hands with a smile. "By the power vested in me by the state of Texas, and before all of you, I now pronounce you husband and wife." He pauses for dramatic effect, his smile growing wider. "Jake, you may kiss your bride."

Jake doesn't hesitate. He pulls Claire into his arms and kisses her deeply while the entire tent erupts in applause and cheers. The quartet launches into something joyful that fills the space with celebration.

Jake and Claire break apart after a long moment, both of them grinning and crying at the same time. They look drunk on happiness. They join hands and practically run back down the aisle together as husband and wife.

The bridal party begins to follow. Lucas offers his arm to Bella again, and as they walk past my row, he winks at me. The expression on his face is full of longing and hope and determination.

My mom leans over and whispers in my ear. "Go to him, sweetheart."

"What?"

"After the ceremony. You two need to work this out," she says.

"I agree," Sammy says.

I turn to him. "What?"

"You and Lucas. Like I told him, you two deserve each other. Both stubborn asses and—"

"Hey. We don't need that," Mom says to him.

The rest of the bridal party exits, and guests move toward the cocktail tent. The ceremony is over. Jake and Claire are married.

And right now, I need to find Lucas.

I need to tell him that I've thought about nothing but us over the past five days, and I want a real chance. Truthfully, I want all of it. The vows, the certainty, the choosing each other every single day.

We have to try.

CHAPTER 24

HOLIDAY

The ceremony tent empties as guests make their way to the cocktail area, while the crew transforms the main space for dinner and dancing. I lose sight of Lucas in the crowd, which is probably for the best because if I find him right now, I might do something completely inappropriate in front of three hundred people.

White-gloved servers are already circulating through the cocktail tent with champagne flutes and silver trays of fancy appetizers. The bar is doing a steady business with a line of guests waiting for signature cocktails. The quartet has moved to this space and is playing soft jazz that mingles with conversation and laughter.

I grab a glass of champagne from a passing server and take a sip, barely tasting it.

"You okay?" Tricia appears at my side, and her eyes are full of knowing.

"I'm fine."

"You look like you're about to combust." She links her arm through mine. "Come on. Let's find somewhere you can breathe."

She guides me toward a quieter corner where Mawmaw is standing with Hudson, Emma, and Colby. She looks teary-eyed.

"That was beautiful," Mawmaw says when she sees me. "Wasn't it beautiful?"

"It was perfect," I agree, taking another sip of champagne.

"Jake did good." Hudson grins. "Didn't think he'd make it through his vows without completely losing it, but he held it together."

Emma grins. "It was sweet. Very sweet. I'm so happy for my sister. I couldn't stop crying."

"You cry at commercials these days, babe. The pregnancy hormones have you all over the place," Hudson offers, placing a kiss on her forehead.

"That's true," Emma agrees. "But those vows were moving."

All eyes turn to me and my face heats. "They were touching."

"Mm-hmm." Emma studies me.

"And you were definitely not staring at Lucas the entire time. Not at all," Hudson says.

"I will kick your ass, Jolly," I warn.

"What? I'm just saying what everyone else is thinking," he says. "You two were having your own moment up there. It was very obvious from where I was standing. Lucas looked like he was about to abandon his best man duties and go to you."

I don't know what to say to that, so I just take another sip of champagne.

Tricia moves me away from them. "You and Lucas?"

"No," I say. "I mean, not yet. Maybe? I don't know," I whisper.

She gives me a knowing look. "Go for it. What do you have to lose?"

"Him."

My sister takes a deep breath. "No way. I don't believe that."

The photographers are everywhere, capturing candid moments of people laughing, talking, and celebrating. Servers continue to circulate with drinks and food. The energy is festive and joyful and exactly what a wedding reception should feel like.

And then I see him.

Lucas is standing near one of the heat lamps with some of his old friends. His jacket is unbuttoned now and he looks relaxed as he laughs at something someone said. His head is thrown back, and that smile on his face makes my heart skip. He's so beautiful it almost hurts to look at him.

He's completely in his element, and it shows.

"You're staring again," Tricia says beside me.

"I can't help it." The words come out before I can stop them. "Look at him."

"Oh, I'm looking." Tricia sounds amused as she snags a glass of champagne from a server. "And he can't seem to keep his eyes off you."

I study my sister. "What?"

"He's been watching you since you walked in here. He's just better at being subtle than you are." She squeezes my arm. "This is harder than you thought it would be, isn't it?"

"What is?"

"Letting yourself have what you've always wanted." She tilts her head toward Lucas. "He's right there, and I can tell you want to go over there and climb him like a tree."

"Tricia!" But I'm laughing because she's not wrong.

"What? Am I lying?" She grins at me. "You heard those vows. You watched Jake and Claire promise forever to each other. And the whole time you were imagining Lucas saying those words to you."

"I wasn't—"

"Holiday, I know you better than you know yourself. Don't lie to me." She uses her big sister tone. "It's okay to want him. It's okay to be scared and want him anyway."

"I'm trying to be realistic about this," I confess.

"You're trying to be safe." She touches my arm. "But I know you came back to Merryville for him. You left Paris. You left

Dominic. You came home. And we both know it wasn't because you couldn't find a job anywhere else."

"Tri—"

"Stop overthinking everything." Her voice is firm now. "That man has been in love with you since you were teenagers. And you've been in love with him just as long. Everyone knows it. I saw the articles. I've read every one. The whole town knows. So, what are you waiting for?"

"For him," I say. "He's being cautious with me. Wants to make sure that I'm sure."

"Then be sure." She smiles. "Let yourself want him. Let yourself have him. Tell him. Stop being so afraid of being happy."

Before I can respond, someone calls Tricia's name from across the tent. She excuses herself with a knowing look, leaving me standing there with my champagne and my racing thoughts.

Mawmaw walks over. "She's right, you know."

"Mawmaw, please—"

"My Lucas has been in love with you your entire life. And you've been in love with him just as long." She touches my hair the way she used to when I was little. "I know you're scared, sweetheart. I know Dominic hurt you and made you doubt yourself. But Lucas isn't Dominic."

"I know that."

"Do you?" Her green eyes search mine. "Because it seems like you're punishing yourself for Dominic's mistakes. And that's not fair to either of you."

The words hit harder than I expect. "I'm not."

"What's stopping you?" she asks.

"I don't know," I whisper.

"Yes, you do." She squeezes my hand and then pulls me into a hug. "Stop being afraid, sweetheart. Stop letting your past dictate your future. Lucas would move heaven and earth for you. Let him."

She pulls back and wipes at my eyes before my tears can fall.

Then she drifts away to talk to some other guests, leaving me alone with my thoughts.

I take another sip of champagne and let myself look at Lucas again. Our eyes meet across the tent, and the heat in his gaze makes my mouth go dry.

He doesn't look away, and neither do I.

The moment stretches between us, loaded with everything we haven't said. Everything we've been holding back. Then someone says something to him and he's forced to turn away.

The spell breaks.

I drain the rest of my champagne and grab another glass from a passing server. The music continues, and time moves forward the way it always does at events like this. I make small talk with people from my past and several ask me about the baking contest in two weeks.

And then I see her.

Lindsay Moore walks through the entrance in a green dress that shows off her figure perfectly. Her blond hair is styled in loose waves that look effortless but probably took an hour. She's beautiful and confident and walking straight toward Lucas.

My stomach drops so fast, I feel lightheaded. Knowing that he dated her makes jealousy rage inside of me.

Lindsay was one of my friends in high school. We were on student council together. We went to the same parties. We studied together sometimes. And then, years later, after I left for Paris, she dated Lucas.

I watch as she approaches him where he's standing with his friends. I watch his expression change from relaxed to polite. She says something that makes him smile in that friendly way he has when he's being courteous but not particularly interested.

When she touches his arm, something hot and ugly twists inside me.

I've never experienced jealousy like this. It makes me want to cross the room and physically remove her hand from him.

"They dated," Sammy says beside me, sipping from his flask.

He appeared next to me without me even noticing. "For about a year."

"Yeah," I manage to say through gritted teeth. "I know."

"He considered marrying her," Sammy says.

I turn to him. "Why are you telling me this?"

"Because I want you to know what you almost lost," he tells me.

Lindsay leans closer to Lucas and says something. He laughs at whatever it is. She touches his arm again, more deliberately this time, letting her hand linger on his bicep.

My champagne glass is in serious danger of shattering in my grip.

They continue chatting and Lucas glances toward the reception tent where music has started to play. The dinner space must be ready because couples are starting to drift in that direction.

No. Please, no.

Lindsay is asking him to dance and Lucas is agreeing. He said yes to her.

I watch them walk toward the reception tent together. Lindsay's hand is still on his arm, possessive and familiar. They're both smiling and talking and I might be sick. Or commit murder. It's hard to tell at this point.

"You gonna let that happen?" Sammy asks.

I can't respond. I can't move. I can't do anything except watch Lucas disappear into the reception tent with my old friend, who also happens to be his ex-girlfriend. Lucas dated her after I left. She touched him and kissed him and was with him while I was in Paris pretending I was happy.

"March over there right now," Sammy says. "You're both being stubborn idiots."

He grins at me, and I recognize that look. It's his scheming face. "Okay then, give him a taste of his own medicine."

"What does that mean? Are you drunk?" I ask him, knowing he'd never ever support this.

He scans the cocktail area with purpose. "We need to find you someone to dance with. Someone Lucas will definitely notice and absolutely hate seeing you with."

"I don't think this is a good idea," I tell my brother.

"Trust me on this." He points across the room decisively. "There. Jake's friend. The tall one in the navy suit. What's his name? Derek? David? Dylan! That's his name."

I recognize him from earlier when I was moving into the seating area.

"Perfect. Dylan it is." Sammy looks him over. "He'll do. He's exactly the type that will make Lucas lose his damn mind. Plus, I saw him check you out earlier."

"What?"

"Yeah, I have eyes." He pulls me toward the reception tent entrance. "Come on. Time to remind Lucas Jolly that he's not the only one with options here."

"This feels petty and ridiculous."

But my brother is absolutely relentless. "It is petty."

Sammy doesn't sound bothered. "Sometimes you have to make a man a little crazy to motivate him to finally do something about his feelings. Trust me on this one."

He links his arm through mine and marches me toward the reception tent with the determination of a general leading his troops into battle.

We walk inside, and the first thing I see is Lucas on the dance floor with Lindsay. His hand is on her waist. They're swaying together to a slow song. She's smiling up at him and saying something animated that makes him laugh and nod. Seeing that makes something inside me snap.

"Okay," I say, and my voice is more determined than it was before. "Let's do this."

Sammy grins at me like I just declared war. "That's my sis. Follow my lead."

We find Dylan near the bar, talking with a group of guys. They're all tall and athletic looking, clearly former athletes, all

A VERY MERRY ENEMY

laughing about something. Dylan is probably the most attractive of the group with his dark hair and easy smile.

He looks up as we approach and his eyes slide over me. There's definite interest there.

"Hey guys, this is my sister, Holiday," Sammy says with a smile. "My single sister."

"Hi, I'm Dylan," he says with a grin that's friendly.

"Hey, nice to meet you," I offer.

"I remember seeing you earlier. That is definitely your color," he offers.

"Thank you." I take a breath and just go for it. "Would you like to dance with me?"

His eyebrows raise in surprise, but he recovers quickly. "Um, sure. I'd love to dance with you."

He offers his hand, and I take it, letting him lead me toward the dance floor. I'm aware that we're moving in the direction of where Lucas is dancing with Lindsay. I glance back at Sammy, who gives me a thumbs-up.

Dylan pulls me into his arms with one hand on my waist and the other holding one of my hands. He's a good dancer, keeping the movements smooth and comfortable. He smells like expensive cologne, and his suit is probably designer.

"So, how do you know Jake and Claire?" he asks as we start to sway to the music.

"I grew up with the Jollys." It's close enough to the truth without getting into the complicated history. "What about you?"

"Jake and I know each other from the farm. My family owns a ranch close to Big Bend. We became really good friends and keep in touch." He smiles. "Best guy I know. Claire's lucky to have him."

"They're lucky to have each other," I offer.

"True." He pulls me slightly closer. "Am I allowed to be happy I got to dance with the most beautiful woman at this wedding?"

Under different circumstances, I might be flattered. Dylan seems like a genuinely nice guy. He's attractive and charming.

I giggle. "Thank you for saying that, and sure."

Dylan twists me around, and over his shoulder, I see Lucas watching us. All of a sudden, I'm transported back to prom, when he watched me dance with Theo.

His jaw is tight and tense. His hand has moved from Lindsay's waist to a more appropriate and distant position on her upper back. He's barely looking at her anymore, even though she's still talking to him.

He's staring directly at me with an intensity that makes me want to jump out of my skin.

Our eyes meet, and the heat in his gaze makes me lose my train of thought. He looks like he's about three seconds from losing control.

Maybe Sammy was right.

Dylan says something about the song and pulls me closer than before. I tilt my face up toward his like he's the most fascinating person I've ever met.

Lucas's expression grows more dangerous. The song continues and we keep dancing. I keep my eyes on Dylan while feeling Lucas's stare burning into me from across the floor.

The song finally ends and Dylan speaks. "Thank you for the dance. That was really—"

He doesn't get to finish his sentence because Lucas is suddenly there beside us. His hand wraps around my elbow firmly, and his presence is completely overwhelming and commanding.

"Excuse us," Lucas says to Dylan. His voice is polite but there's an edge to it that makes it very clear this is not actually a request or a suggestion.

Dylan glances between us, clearly reading the tension radiating off Lucas in waves. "You good, Lucas?"

"Yeah," he snaps.

"Thanks for the dance, Holiday," Dylan says, walking away.

Lucas immediately pulls me farther onto the dance floor as a new song starts. This one is slower and more intimate than the last.

His hand slides to my lower back, pulling me against him until there's no space between our bodies at all. His other hand takes mine, and his fingers lace through mine in a way that feels possessive, like he's claiming me. We start moving together, and I can feel every inch of him pressed against me. His chest against mine. His thigh between my legs as we sway. His breath on my neck.

"You're trying to make me jealous," he growls. His voice is rough, and it sends shivers racing down my spine.

"Did it work?" I tilt my head back to look up at him defiantly.

"You know damn well it worked." His hand tightens on my lower back. "Dancing with Dylan fucking Mitchell like I'm not standing right there watching you. Like I haven't been watching you all night. Like I haven't been able to think about anything except you in that dress."

"You were dancing with Lindsay."

"That's different."

"You're right." I pull back to glare at him. "You were dancing with your *ex-girlfriend*. I don't know Dylan."

"I didn't want to dance with Lindsay." His eyes are on mine, burning straight through me. "I was being polite."

My breath catches in my throat. "You didn't think about me."

His jaw tightens. "I was trying to keep it platonic. I can barely be in the same room as you and not lose my mind."

"You're being irrational."

"Yeah, I am. Because I'm fucking obsessed with you."

Laughter spills from my lips. "Yeah? How's that working out for you?"

"Terribly." He manages to pull me even closer. "I lasted exactly five minutes watching you dance with him before I completely lost my shit. Better be glad I didn't break his arms for touching you. I can't pretend, Peaches."

"Good." I can feel his heart pounding against my chest, matching the rhythm of mine. "Now you know how I felt."

"I'm sorry." His voice is quieter now. "I didn't know how to turn her down without making it weird and awkward for everyone." His thumb traces slow circles on my lower back through the fabric of my dress. "I've been waiting for you all night. All week. All my fucking life, Holiday."

I can't breathe. "Lucas."

I want him so badly I can barely think straight.

"What are we doing?" I ask quietly, my voice barely audible over the music.

"I don't know." His thumb brushes across my bottom lip, and my knees nearly buckle.

My heart is pounding so hard, I'm sure he can feel it. "Okay."

"We'll figure it out," he says and it comes out like a promise.

I slide my hand up his chest to rest over his heart. "I've done a lot of thinking over the last five days."

"And?"

We keep dancing even though the song has moved into the next one. Other couples swirl around us on the dance floor but I barely notice them. All I can focus on is Lucas and the way he's holding me, and the way he's looking at me like I'm everything he's ever wanted. Like I'm worth waiting for.

"I want to try," I whisper.

His fingers brush under the silver star necklace and he looks down at it. "You kept it after all these years?"

"Yes," I whisper, bringing the charm to my lips and kissing it. "I've made many wishes upon this star."

"Holiday—"

"I know what I want." I cut him off before he can say whatever he was going to say. "I've been terrified that I will mess this up. That I'll hurt you again. After *that* relationship, I questioned if I was actually ready for this. But…"

"What?"

"I don't want to waste any more time. I don't want to keep my distance." I take a shaky breath. "I want you, Lucas. I want this. Whatever this is, whatever it becomes, I want it. I want you."

The smile that breaks across his face is so bright it could light up this whole town. "Are you sure?"

"Yeah. Absolutely, yes."

"Come with me." He takes my hand.

"Where are we going?"

"Somewhere we can be alone." He pulls me off the dance floor, and I notice how all eyes are on us. I follow him out of the tent, my heart racing, every nerve in my body on fire with anticipation.

This is happening. After so much pain and distance, we're finally choosing each other.

And I cannot wait.

CHAPTER 25

LUCAS

I pull her off the dance floor, weaving through the other couples. She keeps hold of my hand and follows me willingly. I'm convinced I can feel her heart racing through her fingers. Or maybe that's my adrenaline rushing. I can't tell anymore where I end and she begins.

All heads turn to watch us, but I have no more fucks to give. Holiday Patterson is mine and I am hers.

We push through the tent entrance into the cold November night. The breeze hits us like a shock after the warmth inside, but I don't care. All I can focus on is Holiday in that burgundy dress, and the way she looks at me like I'm rescuing her.

The vintage white carriages are parked in a line along the pathway. The interiors are still heated, with soft lights glowing through the windows.

I open the door of the nearest carriage and help Holiday inside. She climbs in, her dress rustling, and I follow her quickly, closing the door behind us.

Suddenly, we're in our own private world. The inside is heated and intimate, with white leather seats and gold trim. Soft Christmas music plays faintly from the reception tent but it feels miles away instead of fifty feet.

Holiday turns to face me, and the look in her eyes makes my breath catch. She wants this just as much as I do.

I don't give her even a moment to say a word. Instead, I pull her against me, and finally, *finally* kiss her the way I've been desperate to since I walked into the bakery and saw her for the first time.

She tastes like champagne, wishes come true, and home. Her lips are soft, and a sound escapes from the back of her throat. I lose whatever control I had left.

My hands slide into her hair, angling her head so I can kiss her deeper. Her hands fist in my shirt, pulling me closer like she can't get close enough. We're pressed together from chest to thigh and it's still not enough.

I've kissed her before. Hundreds of times when we were teenagers. But this is different. We're different. Fifteen years of wanting and waiting and wondering has built up between us, and now it's pouring out.

I back her up against the leather seat, and her dress rides up as I settle between her legs. My cock presses against her panties, and she gasps against my mouth.

"I've been waiting fifteen years for this," I say against her lips.

"Then stop talking," she says, tugging on my belt.

I kiss her harder, deeper, pouring everything I feel into it. My hands slide from her hair down her neck, across her collarbones, down her sides. The silk of her dress is smooth under my palms, but I want to feel her skin.

She tugs at my tie, loosening it, then starts working on my shirt buttons. Her fingers are shaking slightly and something about that makes my chest tight.

I help her with the buttons, shrugging out of my jacket and letting it fall to the carriage floor. She gets my shirt untucked from my pants, and her hands slide underneath, warm against my stomach. I suck in a breath at the contact.

I find the zipper at the back of her dress and slowly pull it down. The sound of it in the quiet carriage seems as loud as a crack in the night. She watches me with blue sparkling eyes as I slide the dress off her shoulders, revealing smooth skin and a burgundy lace bra that matches the dress.

"Holiday."

"You like it?" She sounds breathless.

"I love it. I love it on you. I'll really love it off you, too." I kiss along her collarbone, tasting her sweet skin. "I'm still in love with you."

The words slip out before I can stop them, but I don't take them back. They're true. They've always been true.

"I'm still in love with you, too," she confesses. She makes a sound that might be a laugh or a sob and pulls me back to her mouth. We're kissing like we're drowning and this is our air. Like we've been starving for fifteen years and this is our first meal.

My hands slide up her thighs, pushing her dress higher. Her skin is soft against my rough palms. I reach the edge of her panties, and she arches against me.

"Lucas." She gasps.

"Tell me to stop." I kiss down her neck, sucking at the spot that always made her crazy. "Tell me to stop and I will."

"No. I can't. I want you."

That's all the permission I need. My fingers slide under the edge of her panties, and she's so wet, so ready for me. I groan against her neck, and she makes this desperate sound that goes straight through me.

We're really doing this, right here in this carriage at my brother's wedding, and I don't care. I need her like she's my only sustenance.

I'm fumbling with my belt when there's a knock on the carriage door.

We both freeze.

"Lucas!" Hudson's voice comes through the door. "You in there?"

"Fuck," I breathe against Holiday's neck.

"Ignore him," she whispers, her hands still working at my belt.

The door opens and Hudson's face appears in the gap. He takes one look at us and his eyebrows shoot up to his hairline.

My shirt is untucked and half unbuttoned. Holiday's dress is unzipped and pulled down to her waist. Her hair is completely destroyed, not to mention me being positioned between her legs. Our lips are swollen and red. We look exactly like what we are—two people who were about thirty seconds away from having sex.

Hudson grins slowly. "Well. This is very interesting."

"Go away," I say.

Holiday closes her eyes tight, like she can wish Hudson away. She lifts her dress to cover herself.

"No can do, little brother. Jake's looking for you. Best man speech in five minutes. Then garter and bouquet toss and cake." His grin gets wider. "So maybe make yourselves presentable and get your asses back inside."

He closes the door, and we hear him laughing as he walks away.

Holiday covers her face with her hands. "Oh my gosh."

"He's never going to let me live this down."

"The whole town won't."

He sighs. "Well, let's take our walk of almost shame together." I tilt her chin up so she's looking at me. "I'm fucking done hiding how I feel about you."

She searches my face. "Lucas—"

"I mean it. I don't care who knows. I don't care if it ends up in more articles or if people talk." I kiss her softly. "You're mine and I want everyone to know it."

"What about Dominic? I thought we were going to keep things quiet until after the contest."

I pause, considering. She's right. Dominic is still in town. Still judging the contest. If we're too public about this, it could cause problems.

"I don't want to hide you, either," she admits. "But we should be modest about it."

Looking at Holiday with her lips swollen from my kisses and her eyes sparkling with want, I can't bring myself to care about her ex.

"We'll figure it out," I say. "But right now, we need to get back inside without causing a scene."

She laughs and it's the best sound I've ever heard. We help each other get dressed, trying to make ourselves look presentable. I button my shirt, then I help her zip her dress. She tries to fix her hair in the reflection of the carriage window but it's hopeless.

"You look like you've just been fucked," I tell her.

"I wish." She reaches up and wipes lipstick off my mouth with her thumb. "There. Better."

"Everyone's still going to know."

"We confirm nothing and give them nothing that can verify it. The way we look is just speculation."

"It's almost adorable how naive you're acting. Just be prepared for the whispers."

"They're a turn-on," she says, pulling me back to her. "I like people whispering about us."

"Peaches," I groan, moving back to steal another kiss from her.

"Go," she says with a laugh, wiping more lipstick from my face.

I help her out of the carriage, and we walk back toward the reception tent. My hand is on her lower back, possessive and obvious. I can feel eyes on us as soon as we step inside.

Emma sees us first, and her face breaks into a huge grin. She elbows Hudson, who's standing next to her. Bella looks like she just won a bet.

Jake and Claire are standing by their wedding cake, waiting. When Jake sees us, he starts laughing. "There you are. We were about to send a search party."

"Sorry," I say, not sounding sorry at all.

Holiday's face is bright red but she's smiling. I keep my hand on her, and I don't move away from her side.

She slides into the back of the space, and I move to grab the microphone from the stand on the stage. "Hi. Wow. What an entrance, right?" I ask, and everyone laughs. Holiday does, too. "What can I say? My big brother and best friend just married the love of his life. I've never seen Jake so happy, and I've known him my whole life. Meeting you was a miracle, Claire. For the whole family. Even if sometimes you're a little mean, you're exactly the kind of big sister I always wished I had. The type of love you two have only happens once in a lifetime." I find Holiday's eyes in the crowd. "You both taught me that love finds a way, no matter the circumstances. That if it's meant to be, it will happen. How does it feel to have your greatest wish come true? I'm so happy for you two. Congratulations."

Hudson continues and then it goes down the line of different family members and friends telling stories.

I go to Holiday, who's at the back of the room, and slide in next to her. I hook my pinky with hers, like we used to do when no one was looking.

After that, we gather around as Jake and Claire cut the cake. It's beautiful, three-tiered, with white frosting and Christmas garland decorations. They feed each other bites and everyone applauds.

Holiday leans into me and I feel her relax.

This feels right. This is how it's supposed to be. I lean in and whisper in her ear, "After the wedding, I'm peeling this dress off you."

She glances over at me, biting her lip, trying to hold back a smile.

The rest of the reception passes in a blur. I don't leave Holiday's side. I'm constantly touching her waist, her back, or her hand. People are definitely staring. Phones are definitely taking pictures. By tomorrow morning, there will be articles about us online.

I don't give a single fuck.

When the reception finally winds down around midnight, guests start filtering out. Jake and Claire leave in a shower of sparklers and cheers, heading off to their place. They refuse to go on a honeymoon until after the twins are born. Claire said she won't miss her niece and nephews' birth. Jake agreed.

Holiday and I stand in the now mostly empty tent. The lights are still twinkling overhead, and soft music is playing. A few people are cleaning up around us.

"Come home with me," I say.

She doesn't hesitate. "I thought you would never ask."

We walk out to the parking area where my truck is waiting. We parked our vehicles at the venue beforehand.

I open the passenger door and help her in, then walk around to my side.

As I start the engine, I reach over and take her hand.

"You sure about this?" I ask.

"I've never been more sure of anything in my life."

"That's the correct answer." I bring her fingers to my lips and kiss her knuckles. Then I drive us home. The anticipation is almost too much.

CHAPTER 26

❄

HOLIDAY

The drive to Lucas's house feels like the longest ten minutes of my life.

My hand is in his, resting on the console between us. His thumb traces slow circles on my palm and every touch sends electricity up my arm. The radio is playing soft Christmas music, but I barely hear it over the sound of my own heartbeat.

Fifteen years of wondering what it would be like to be with him again. Fifteen years of missing him. Fifteen years of trying to convince myself I'd moved on when I never really had.

And now I'm in his truck on the way to his house, and in a few minutes, he's going to touch me the way I've been dreaming about since I left Merryville.

He brings my hand to his lips and kisses my knuckles. We turn onto his long driveway and my breath catches. I've been to his house before over the past few weeks but this is different.

He parks the truck and kills the engine but neither of us moves.

"We don't have to rush anything."

I turn to face him. "Whatever happens, happens."

The look he gives me is so full of heat and want that I feel it in my bones. It's the same words I said to him the first time we fooled around. I'll never forget the way he kissed me like I belonged to him. It was the same way he kissed me tonight.

Lucas gets out and comes around to open my door. I take his hand and he helps me down. A chill rushes over me as our eyes meet.

We walk up the steps to his porch, and his face glows in the Christmas lights he must've put up. "I thought you were going to be a scrooge."

"I did, too. Jake and Hudson helped me," he says.

When we're inside, he doesn't turn on the lights. Moonlight streams through the windows, casting everything in silver. His house is warm and smells like him. It's a mixture of pine, wood smoke, and leather gloves. The door closes behind us, and suddenly, we're alone in the darkness.

"Holiday," he says, my name like a prayer. "The past five days—"

I don't let him finish whatever he was going to say. I step forward and kiss him, pouring fifteen years of want into it. He makes a sound low in his throat, and his hands slide into my hair.

We stumble through the entryway, kissing and touching and trying to get closer. He backs me against the wall, and I gasp as his body presses against mine. I can feel how much he wants me and it makes me ache from the inside out.

He keeps kissing me like he can't stop. Finally, he pulls back enough to take my hand, and then he lifts me into his arms and carries me up the stairs.

"And you say I'm dramatic," I tell him, kissing his neck as he pushes open the door to his room.

His bed is made, and the lights outside on the top eave make the inside of his room glow.

For a moment, we just look at each other. His green eyes are full of want. His hair is messed up from my fingers. Lucas is so beautiful, it leaves me speechless.

"I've dreamed about this," he says.

"Me too. I didn't know if we'd still have anything left. Years have passed, but…"

"Somehow, it still feels like yesterday." He steps closer and cups my face in his hands. "I want to take my time with you. I want to make you feel good. I want—" His voice catches. "I want you to know how much I missed you."

Tears prick at my eyes. "I couldn't stop thinking about what might've been."

His thumbs brush across my cheekbones.

"I never stopped loving you," I whisper. "Even when I should have. There was always this secret compartment in my heart that was just yours."

He kisses me and it's full of everything we haven't said.

"I have loved you since we were kids. I loved you when I tried to move on and couldn't. No one can ever replace you, Holiday. You're it for me and I know that. I've known that from the moment we walked down the aisle together at Tricia's wedding," he says.

A smile touches my lips as I loosen his tie. "I promised you I would always love you. And I know you thought I broke that promise, but I didn't. I know you thought I wouldn't come back like I promised, but here I am."

"Here you are." He smiles, moving some hair out of my face.

"If I could go back in time," I whisper.

"All that matters is you're here now," he says against my lips.

His hands find the zipper of my dress—the same zipper he started to undo in the carriage. This time, there's no Hudson to interrupt us. This time, we can finish what we started. I pull it down and the dress slides off my shoulders and pools at my feet, leaving me in just the burgundy lace bra and matching underwear.

Lucas steps back to look at me and the expression on his face makes me feel beautiful and seen in a way I haven't felt in years.

"You're perfect," he says.

"I'm not."

"Pure artwork." He reaches out and traces his finger along the edge of my bra. "And mine."

I reach for his shirt and start unbuttoning it with shaking fingers. He helps me, shrugging it off and letting it fall to the floor. Then his hands go to his belt, and I watch as he undresses, revealing the body I used to know so well.

He's different now. Older. More muscled from years of working on the farm. There are new scars I don't recognize and tattoos up his arm and across his chest. But he's still Lucas. Still exactly what I want.

He walks me backward until my legs touch the bed, and then we're falling onto the mattress together. The sheets are cool against my back, but Lucas is warm above me. His mouth is on my neck, sucking and kissing across my collarbone, and between my breasts. His hands slide behind my back, and he unhooks my bra. When he removes it, I suddenly feel vulnerable.

Lucas looks at me like I'm a masterpiece.

"Beautiful," he whispers, his mouth finding my breast. "So fucking beautiful."

His hands are everywhere, touching and worshipping every inch of me. Like he's remembering every place that makes me gasp or arch or moan.

When his hand slides between my legs, I nearly come apart.

"Lucas, please don't tease me." I breathe.

"I won't, Peaches. I've got you."

He hooks his fingers in my lace panties and slides them down my legs. Then his mouth is settling between my thighs. The first touch of his tongue on my clit makes me cry out.

"So wet," he whispers as he kisses and sucks. Lucas unravels me slowly, devouring me until I'm shaking with anticipation.

"I'm so close." I gasp, surprised by how quickly he worked me up. "Lucas, please."

"Tell me what you need."

"Make me come."

He moves back up my body, kissing as he goes. I reach between us and slide my hand into his boxers, wrapping my fingers around him. He's hard and hot, and I want him inside me so badly, I can barely think.

He groans and buries his face in my neck. "You're so fucking pretty."

"You're teasing me," I say, running my fingers through his hair.

"Just a little," he mutters against my lips before moving back down my body. Seconds later, he's taking my clit into his mouth. He sucks and flicks until the orgasm rips through me. I'm groaning out his name, my cunt clenching so damn hard as he slides a finger inside me.

"Feels so good," I whisper, never having been worked so fucking good. He places his finger into his mouth, not wasting a drop. The orgasm nearly takes me under as he reaches for his nightstand and pulls out a condom. I watch as he rolls it on. He settles between my legs and the first inch of him inside me makes us both freeze.

"You okay?" he asks.

"Yes. Don't stop."

He pushes inside slowly and I feel myself stretch to fit him. This is how it always was with us; we have to take it slow. It's been so long and he's much bigger than I remember.

For a second, it's almost too much, and he reads me, waiting for me to relax before continuing. My back arches, and I try to steady my breathing until he's fully inside me. With Lucas buried deep inside, everything in the world seems right again.

"You feel like home," I whisper.

"Fuck, you do, too, sweetheart. You were made for me. Feel how good we fit together?" he asks against my neck. Then he slowly moves as our tongues twist together. I can taste myself on his mouth.

As he thrusts into me, I swear I see stars. This connection.

This intimacy. This feeling of being completely seen and wanted and cherished. The sensation is almost too much.

"Holiday," Lucas says, and I open my eyes to find him staring down at me with so much adoration it takes my breath away. "Stay with me tonight."

"I want to."

We move together, and his rhythm matches mine perfectly. Every thrust sends pleasure spiraling through me. Every kiss tastes like home.

The orgasm builds and builds until I'm right on the edge. Lucas keeps a slow pace, but thrusts into me deeper, exactly where I need him, and suddenly, I'm falling apart in his arms for the second time tonight.

I cry out his name as I come, my body convulsing around him. He follows seconds later, burying his face in my neck and groaning my name as he shudders above me.

For a long moment, we just lie there, breathing hard, hearts pounding against each other.

I curl into his chest and hold him, letting out a sigh of relief. I spent too long missing him and denying myself. I tried to be someone I wasn't, and I didn't like who I became.

"I never forgot you," he whispers, stroking my hair.

"I never forgot you, either." I press my face into his chest, smiling. "You were my best kept secret."

Lucas pulls out of me and slides on some joggers.

"I'll be right back," he says, running down the stairs.

I lie back in his bed and smile as I'm tangled in his sheets. I hear drawers clattering and a microwave going off. A minute later, Lucas is rushing into the bedroom with two bowls. He hands me one with a spoon. "You have to try our cookie bar with Blue Bell ice cream on top."

"You baked this?" I ask.

He smirks. "Yeah. I brought it to Thanksgiving dinner. It was a huge hit again. But I made us some, too."

"Well, let me try it," I say, dipping my spoon into the ice cream and cookie bar.

"Wow. That's really good," I say.

"Right. I think we should serve it with ice cream."

"We'd need to make the ice cream ourselves, but we'd have plenty of time. I have a recipe for vanilla bean that's close to this." I grin. "You did incredible. And you say I'm the perfectionist. Look at this cookie."

"I was taught by the best in the industry," he says.

We finish eating our dessert, then I lie back in his arms.

I take a shaky breath. "I feel like I've been lost for years, and I finally found my way back."

His arms tighten around me. "You were. I'm just so damn glad you woke up."

"I became this person I didn't recognize. I did things I didn't want to do. I gave up pieces of myself until I didn't know who I was anymore." I pull back enough to look at him. "But with you, I feel like me again. Like the me I was supposed to be."

"I'll always remind you of who you are," he says fiercely. "He may have tried to change you, but he couldn't. You're still you, Holiday."

"Thank you," I whisper.

"For what?"

"For helping me heal."

"Always." He tilts my chin up and kisses me. "I will always help you."

We lie there in the darkness, wrapped around each other, and I feel pieces of myself clicking back into place. Pieces of me that were taken. I thought they were gone forever.

My heart stutters. I search his face and see only sincerity. Only love.

"What are we?" I kiss him, and he pulls me up into his arms.

"I don't know," Lucas answers truthfully. "I don't want to rush things."

"I don't, either."

Our kisses grow more heated. We can figure out the logistics later. Right now, I just want to be here with him.

We make love again, slower this time. He takes his time exploring every inch of me, relearning my body. By the time we both come apart again, I can barely remember my name.

Afterward, we lie tangled together. My head is on his chest, and I can hear his heartbeat slowing to normal. His fingers trace lazy patterns on my back.

"I could get used to this," I say.

"Good. Because I'm planning on forever."

I smile against his chest. "Forever's a long time."

"Still somehow not long enough."

I'm drifting off to sleep when my phone buzzes from somewhere on the floor. I ignore it.

It buzzes again.

"You should check that," Lucas says.

"I don't want to move."

"It might be important."

Sighing, I untangle myself from him and find my dress. I pull out my phone from my pocket, and my stomach drops when I see the notifications.

Three texts from Dominic.

> DOMINIC
> We need to talk.
>
> DOMINIC
> I still love you.
>
> DOMINIC
> I'm staying at the Merryville Inn. Come see me tomorrow. We have things to discuss.

I stare at the messages and feel the happiness from tonight drain away.

"What is it?" Lucas asks, sitting up.

I show him the texts. His jaw tightens as he reads them.

"Don't go," he says.

"Okay, but he'll find me. He's relentless," I explain.

"I don't like this." Lucas takes the phone from my hands and sets it on the nightstand. "You don't owe him anything."

"He won't give up."

"He will because I'm not letting you out of my sight." Lucas pulls me back into his arms. "I won't let him hurt you again."

"What did I do to deserve you?" I ask.

"I ask myself the same thing."

I drift to sleep in his arms, feeling safer than I have in years.

Tomorrow, we can deal with reality. Tonight is ours.

CHAPTER 27

LUCAS

I pull into the bakery parking lot just after four and see Holiday's car is still parked out front. The lights are on inside, and I can see her moving around through the windows, her hair pulled back in a ponytail, wearing one of those aprons that makes her look like she belongs in a magazine.

She's already started working on prep for tomorrow, while I finished up my duties on the farm. Holiday mentioned she wanted to spend more time practicing for the contest, but we both know it's not needed.

I've been looking forward to seeing her since I dropped her off at her parents' house this morning. We've barely texted throughout the day, but each time we did, I'd grin at my phone like a lovesick teenager. I get out of the truck and walk to the front. It's locked, but Holiday sees me, and her whole face lights up.

She unlocks the door, and I step inside, pulling her against me before she can say a word.

"Hi," I say against her hair.

"Hi, yourself." She melts into me. "I thought you were working late."

"This is late," I tell her.

She pulls back to look at me with a teasing smile. "I'm almost done with the dough."

"Great." I bring her to the back and kiss her because I can. Because she's here and she's mine and I don't have to hold back anymore. She tastes like sugar and coffee.

"Last night was…" She bites her lip.

"I've been thinking about it all day."

She swallows hard. "Me too."

We move into the kitchen and she places the dough she was working on in the fridge.

"I was thinking we could make some ice cream today," she tells me, pulling out ingredients. "We'll have to time it perfectly because it tastes like shit when it's refrozen."

"If it's too much, we can ditch the idea," I say.

"We'll try it," she tells me. "It was delicious. But I have a recipe that would work perfectly." She's already flipping through her notebook with handwritten notes. "We'll want to make sure the texture is right."

I love watching her work and seeing her in her element, completely focused and confident. This is who she is—passionate and driven and so fucking talented.

We work side by side for the next hour, mixing heavy whipping cream, sugar, and vanilla.

She precisely measures ingredients while I follow her instructions. We've fallen into an easy rhythm, moving around each other like we've been working together for years instead of weeks. It's wild how easily we picked up where we left off. Never could've predicted it.

Every so often, I steal a kiss because I can't help it. Or she'll brush against me and I'll pull her close for a moment before we go back to work. It's everything I've ever wanted.

"What are you smiling about?" she asks, catching me watching her.

"Nothing."

She reaches up and kisses my cheek. "Horrible liar."

Holiday pulls the ice cream out of the churner and dips a spoon inside it, feeding it to me. My eyes go wide. "Wow, HoHo. That's amazing."

"It's no Blue Bell, but…"

"It's incredible," I tell her, stealing an ice cream kiss. "I want to eat it off your body."

"Oh, well, we can arrange that," she says, pulling me close, when there's a knock on the front door.

Holiday looks toward the front and then freezes.

"Fuck," Holiday whispers.

I turn and see *him* standing outside. Dominic Laurent is wearing a fake, charming smile that makes me want to punch him in the face.

"I'll handle it," I tell her and head for the door.

"Lucas—"

"Just stay here," I say.

I unlock the door and step outside, pulling it closed behind me so Holiday's blocked from view. The temperature has dropped significantly since earlier in the day.

"We're closed," I say, towering over him. I honestly imagined he'd be taller.

"I can see that." Dominic's smile doesn't reach his eyes. He's dressed in clothes that look designer—dark jeans, a cashmere sweater, and a leather jacket. Everything about him screams money and sophistication. "I came to see Holiday."

"She's working."

"Yeah, she can take a break." His eyes flick past me.

"Yeah, don't think she wants to," I say, stepping to block his view of Holiday.

"And who are you? Her boss?" He looks me up and down like he's assessing livestock.

"I'm Lucas Jolly," I tell him.

Recognition flashes across his face. "Ah. Jolly. I've heard about you."

The way he says it makes my jaw clench, like I'm beneath him.

"What do you want?" I ask.

"To speak with Holiday. Privately." He emphasizes the last word. "This doesn't concern you."

"Ah, see, that's where you're wrong, bud."

His smile transforms into something more sinister.

The door opens behind me and Holiday steps out. She's taken off her apron and her arms are crossed over her chest. Her face is neutral, jaw locked tight, but I notice the tension in her shoulders.

"Dominic," she says coolly.

"Holiday." His whole demeanor changes, but it seems rehearsed. "I had to see you today. I've texted you several times and have received no response."

"Yeah, it's because I have nothing to discuss with you," she says.

"Please." He glances at me. "I didn't fly across the world for nothing."

"Go on, then," she says. "What do you want?"

"I wanted to speak to you alone," he mutters.

"No thank you," she says firmly.

Something flashes in his eyes—anger, maybe, or jealousy—but he covers it with that charming smile.

"Okay, then. I can't get you off my mind, Holiday. I think about you every day," he says. "I've been in town for a day and have heard the most interesting gossip."

Holiday doesn't respond, just stares at him.

"Apparently, there was quite a scene at a wedding last night." He looks at me. "With him?"

"Last time I checked, she can do whatever the fuck she wants," I say, and not very nicely.

Dominic ignores me, bringing his attention back to Holiday.

"People are talking." He stares at her. "I've seen the photos online. I read the articles."

Hearing him say it makes it real.

Holiday doesn't seem to care. "And?"

He steps closer to her, and I immediately take a step forward. He stops, raising his hands in mock surrender. "I'm just trying to understand. Two months ago, you were planning our wedding. Now, you're here with him."

"Two months ago, you were stealing my recipes and making me feel worthless," Holiday says, and I want to applaud her. "Things change."

"Do they?" His eyes narrow. "Or were you just waiting to end things? Tell me, is this why you came back to Merryville? For him?"

"I came back because this is my home."

He sarcastically laughs. "I find it convenient that you're baking partners." He looks between us. "Are you sleeping with him?"

"That's none of your damn business," I say before Holiday can respond.

"Oh, I think it *is* my business." Dominic's charm is cracking now, showing something uglier underneath. "I came here for you, Holiday. I want to fix what we had. I'm sure you've seen the articles about us. I do want you back."

"There is nothing you can say or do that will make me change my mind, Dominic," Holiday snaps.

"This is nothing but a rebound." Dominic's smile is cruel now. "Come on, Holiday. Remember all the good times. All the mornings we spent tangled together. The trips we took. We were in love."

My adrenaline rushes, and I ball my hand into a fist, ready to fuck him up. Holiday reaches for me, to stop me.

"You need to leave," she says.

He straightens his jacket. "Come see me at the inn. I'm in room D."

"Not happening," Holiday says. "We're over, Dominic. There won't be a second chance."

"I don't believe that." For a second, his mask slips completely, and I see real anger flash across his face. But he controls it, forcing that smug grin back into place.

He looks at me. "Enjoy your little bakery romance. It won't last."

He turns and walks away, getting into a black Mercedes. We watch until his taillights disappear.

We go back inside the bakery, and Holiday lets out the breath she's been holding. "That went well."

"I'd say so, considering he left without getting his face bashed in," I say.

I pull her against me, and she buries her face in my chest. I can feel her shaking—not with fear but with anger.

"I *hate* him," she says, her voice muffled. "I hate that he still has power over me. That he can just show up and—"

"You shut him down. You didn't let him guilt you or manipulate you. You were incredible."

She pulls back to look at me. "He's jealous."

"I would be, too," I admit.

"He's going to keep showing up, keep trying to—"

I kiss her to stop the spiral. When I pull back, she's breathless. "We can handle two weeks of him. And then he goes back to Paris, and we never have to see him again."

We're standing in the middle of the bakery kitchen when she kisses me again. It's soft at first, gentle, but then it deepens, and suddenly, we're pressed against the counter. My hands are in her hair, pulling it out of that ponytail, like nothing else matters.

She pulls back just enough to look at me, her pupils blown wide. "I want you."

"Here?"

She nods.

I lift her onto the counter and step between her legs. She wraps them around my waist and pulls me closer. We're kissing like we're starving for each other, hands everywhere, breathing hard.

I reach for the button on her jeans when there's a loud bang on the window.

We jump and turn to see Sammy standing outside, grinning and giving us a thumbs-up.

"You've got to be fucking kidding me," I mutter.

Holiday drops her head to my shoulder and starts laughing. "I want to be left alone."

I help her down from the counter, and we try to compose ourselves before she unlocks the door. Sammy walks in, grinning.

"Guess you're not even trying to hide it anymore," he says.

"What do you want, Sammy?" Holiday asks, her face bright red.

"I heard Dominic was heading this way. Thought I'd come check on you." His eyes flick between us. "Looks like you're just fine."

"We were working," I tell him.

"Sure, you were." He leans against the counter. "So, what is this?"

Holiday and I exchange a look.

"What do you mean?" I ask finally.

"The two of you. Seems you've got some explaining to do," he says, crossing his arms over his chest.

"I—uh—we." Holiday stops talking. "We're just..."

"Figuring things out," I finish.

"You know the whole town's talking about you, right? After what happened at the wedding, it's pretty obvious."

"We know," Holiday says.

"So, what's the plan? You hooking up? Dating? Because if you get together and then break up, I'm going to be fucking pissed," Sammy says. "I can't deal with you two being at each other's throats."

"We're figuring things out," I repeat myself. "Without any pressure."

"And while Dominic is in town, I think it's best we don't give him any more ammunition to make things complicated," Holiday says.

Sammy's expression hardens. "What did he say to you? What did he want?"

"He wants me back," Holiday explains.

"That's not happening," Sammy says, and I can see the same frustration on his face as I did the night he told me about Dominic. "I'm just going to say this. If you two are going to do this, go all in. No games. No bullshit. You either commit to each other or you don't, but I'm not going to watch you hurt each other again."

The words hit me harder than I expect. We destroyed each other and everyone around us felt the fallout.

"We're not playing games," I say. "We just want to get through the contest without drama. After that, we'll be public about it."

Holiday clears her throat. "I think that's for the best. I want to avoid drama and more articles being written about me. This is overshadowing my career, again. I'm growing exhausted by it all," she says.

Sammy considers this. "I get it. Dominic's a judge. Keep it low-key until after the contest." He points at both of us. "But after that? No more hiding."

"You support us being together?" Holiday directly asks him.

"I always have," he tells her. "As weird as it is, you two were always meant to be together. Anyone with eyes can see that." Sammy's expression softens. "If Dominic tries anything—and I mean anything—you tell me. Lucas isn't the only one who'll protect you."

"Thanks, Sammy," Holiday says, moving to her brother and hugging him.

"Yeah, yeah. Don't get all emotional on me." He squeezes her.

"And what if I told you I gave Lucas my virginity?" she asks, and my mouth twitches.

Sammy's jaw tightens as he looks between us. "What the fuck?"

The silence draws on.

"Yeah, I thought I might go ahead and rip that Band-Aid off since we're here together," Holiday says, her arms still around her brother.

Sammy slowly turns his head to look at me. His expression is unreadable, but I can see the calculation happening behind his eyes.

"What the fuck, Lucas," he says, pointing at me.

"Yeah, so about that," I confirm, not moving.

He releases Holiday and takes a step toward me. Then another. His hands ball into fists at his sides.

I don't move, just wait for whatever's coming.

Sammy gets right in my face, close enough that I can see the vein pulsing in his temple. He draws his fist back like he's about to punch me.

I don't even blink.

His fist stops an inch from my face. We stare at each other for a long moment.

Then Sammy drops his hand and steps back, shaking his head. "That explains a lot."

"What does?" Holiday asks.

"Why you were both so fucking weird when I got home from camp." Sammy runs his hand through his hair. "Why you"—he points at me—"couldn't move on. And why you"—he points at Holiday—"always asked about Lucas when you were engaged to someone else."

Holiday touches the silver star at her throat instinctively.

"You were both each other's...first?" Sammy looks at me.

"Yeah," I say.

Sammy takes a step back. "I'm shook."

"Sammy—" Holiday starts.

"No, I want to know. When did this happen?"

"Fourth of July," I tell him.

Sammy stares at me. "So, all that talk about some tourist was a fucking lie?"

"Look. I made him promise not to tell anyone. Not even you," Holiday says. "So, if you're pissed at someone—"

"Bros before hoes," Sammy says.

Holiday scoffs. "I am not a ho! What the hell!"

"I'm sorry I didn't tell you," I offer. "It's weird to talk about with you."

Sammy shakes his head, and I can tell he's actually shocked. "This is why you were both a mess. It wasn't a crush."

"No," Holiday confirms. "It was honestly the best summer of my life."

Sammy looks at his sister. "How could you leave and forget that happened?"

"I didn't forget anything," Holiday says, her voice breaking slightly. "I thought about Lucas every single day."

"But you still stayed away for fifteen years. You still got engaged to someone else."

"Okay, that's enough," I say, crossing my arms over my chest. "Rehashing old shit does no one any good. But now you know. Consider yourself the third person on the planet who's aware."

Sammy is quiet before he sighs deeply.

"Okay," he says. "This explains everything."

"Are you mad?" Holiday asks quietly.

"Mad?" Sammy considers. "No. I'm pissed at both of you for not choosing one another."

"Sammy—" I start, but he interrupts me.

"Just don't fuck it up this time," he says.

"Don't plan on it," I tell him.

"Good." Sammy heads for the door, then pauses with his hand on the handle. He turns back. "One more thing."

We both look at him.

"This means we get back to how we used to be. The three musketeers?"

Holiday grins. "You want that?"

"You know I do. I miss hanging out with you two without all the weird tension and drama." He shrugs. "You're both my best friends. I want my family back."

"Yeah, I'd like that," Holiday says.

"Me too." I give him a smile.

"Good." Sammy grins. "And Holiday? Maybe don't ever tell Mom and Dad about the virginity thing. I don't need that image in my head, and neither do they."

He leaves and I hear his truck start up outside.

Holiday and I just stand there, staring at each other.

"Well," she says finally. "That went better than expected."

"Did you really just tell your brother about that?"

"I didn't mean to blurt it out, but it felt good to get it off my chest." She's smirking. "Did you see his face?"

"I thought he was actually going to fuck me up."

"He wouldn't have."

"You don't know that."

She walks over and wraps her arms around my waist. "Was hot that you didn't flinch."

"Why would I?"

"Most guys would have."

"Not sure why I have to keep reminding you, but I'm not like most guys." I kiss the top of her head. "And I'm not afraid of your brother."

She looks up at me. "Because you could kick his ass."

"You're damn right about that," I say with a laugh.

She runs her fingers through the back of my hair as she looks up at me. "The three of us were inseparable back then."

"We were. I'd like to have that back, HoHo."

"So would I."

She steals a kiss. "Well, now that the ice cream is completely melted, maybe we should clean up this mess and try again later?"

"Sounds like a plan."

We quickly clean up, then Holiday locks up the bakery.

"In two weeks, we tell the world," she says with a yawn.

"I can't wait." I pull her close one more time. "Go home, Peaches. Get some sleep."

"I'd rather go home with you," she whispers.

"Meet me at my house," I tell her.

"Is that a pity invite?"

"Hell no," I tell her, opening her car door.

"Just making sure," she says, climbing inside. "I'm going to go home and take a shower first."

"Maybe we should conserve water?"

"Great idea. Love that you're thinking about the planet." She shoots me a wink as I close her door.

Holiday backs out of her parking spot, and her taillights disappear into the dark.

I'm looking forward to two weeks of stolen moments. Two weeks of being careful around Dominic.

But at least now we have Sammy on our side.

This is a start. Maybe we really can get back what we lost all those years ago. Not just each other, but the friendship that made us who we were.

Long live the three musketeers.

CHAPTER 28

HOLIDAY

I pull into Lucas's driveway and kill the engine, my heart racing. The Christmas lights glow warmly through the windows.

I grab my phone and quickly text my mom.

> **HOLIDAY**
> Staying at a friend's house tonight. Love you.

> **MOM**
> Okay, sweetie. Have fun! Love you too!

I'm thirty-four years old, and my parents don't care where I am. But after the bourbon and tent incident, when no one could find me, I'm trying to communicate if I won't be home. I don't want my parents to worry, though it does make me feel like a teenager again, sneaking around with Lucas. Which, I guess, is exactly what I'm still doing.

Some things do stay the same.

The overnight bag I packed this morning, just in case, comes with me as I step out of the car. The night air bites at my skin, and I wrap my arms around myself, wishing I'd grabbed a heavier jacket. Before I can make it to the porch, headlights sweep across the driveway. Lucas's truck pulls in next to my car, and he's out in seconds, walking toward me with that sexy look in his eyes.

"Beat me here," he says.

"I left first."

"You did." He reaches me and immediately pulls me against him, his mouth finding mine. The kiss is hungry and impatient, and I drop my bag to wrap my arms around his neck.

When he pulls back, he's grinning. "Come on. Let's get you inside."

Before I can respond, he bends down and throws me over his shoulder in one smooth motion.

"Lucas!" I shriek, the sound turning into laughter. "What are you doing? I dropped my bag!"

"Your bag?" he asks, looking over his shoulder. "You moving in, Peaches?"

"Don't tempt me with a good time," I tell him as he easily picks up my duffel and carries me up the steps. Before we walk in, his hand comes down on my ass in a playful smack.

"Temping you is fun," he says.

"You can't just be a caveman and throw your woman over your shoulder whenever you want!"

"But I did." He types in the code to his house and shuts the door behind him. "Seems to be working pretty well."

I'm laughing so hard I can barely breathe. "Put me down!"

"Nope. Not until we're upstairs."

"You're ridiculous."

"You love it."

God help me, I really, really do.

As promised, he doesn't set me down until we're in his bedroom. When my feet hit the floor, I'm unsteady.

"You're so pretty." He cups my face, and the playfulness fades from his eyes, replaced by something hungrier. When he kisses me this time, there is no rushing. He takes every sweet second, and I moan against him.

When he finally pulls back, his eyes twinkle. "Wait here."

Before he goes, he turns on the bedside lamp so I'm not standing in the dark, alone.

He disappears into the bathroom, and I hear him moving around. A moment later, he comes back and takes my hand, leading me. I stop in the doorway, and my breath catches. Candles are lit on the counter. The room glows.

He moves to the shower and turns it on. Steam billows and the glass begins to fog. I take several steps toward him, and he gently kisses me as his fingers grab the hem of my sweater. As the fabric rises, his knuckles graze against my skin, causing goose bumps to trail over me. I raise my arms, and he pulls my top over my head, letting it fall to the floor. His hands slide down my bare arms as he kisses the ghosts of the hickeys he gave me.

He brushes my hair back from my face as I remove his belt, then unbutton and unzip his pants. I push them down along with his boxers. My fingers slide up his shirt, and he removes it. The two of us shimmy out of the rest of our clothes and stand in front of one another naked. Lucas wants to take his time, not rush the motions. He wants to kiss me and touch me and memorize every inch of me.

The thought breaks something open in my chest. This is what it's like to be wanted, desired.

With Dominic, sex was about performance. About fucking to fuck. It was always about him and what he wanted. My satisfaction didn't matter. Pleasing him should've been enough.

I squeeze my eyes shut tighter.

"What?" Lucas asks, pulling away.

I shake my head. "Nothing. I was in my head."

Lucas looks at me like I'm the only thing in the world that matters. "Be with me, right here, right now. Get out of there." He taps on my temple. "Okay? Little Miss Overthinker."

"Okay," I tell him as we step into the shower.

"I've missed this," he says as the stream falls over us. "Being close to you. Touching you. Having you in my space. I didn't realize how much until now."

He reaches for the shampoo and pours some into his palm, then his fingers slide into my hair. He massages my scalp in circles that make my eyes drift closed. No one has ever touched me with as much care and attention as Lucas. The man is a lover.

"What are you thinking about?" he asks.

"You," I tell him.

This makes him smile.

He takes his time, working the shampoo all the way through my hair before guiding me under the spray to rinse. When my hair is clean, he grabs the conditioner. By the time he's done, I'm overly relaxed, leaning against him for support.

"Now let me wash you," he says.

"Princess treatment," I whisper.

"Queen treatment," he says, kissing my shoulder.

Lucas grabs the body wash and loofah, then starts at my shoulders. His touch causes heat to rise throughout me as he moves down my arms, across my collarbone, and over my breasts. When his thumbs brush over my nipples, I gasp.

"Sensitive?" he asks.

"They've always been."

"I remember." His hands continue exploring me. Light fingertips slide down my ribs, across my stomach, over my hips. "I remember everything about your body. Every place that makes you sigh. Every spot that makes you moan."

His hand slides between my legs, and I have to brace myself against the tile wall. His fingers move in slow, torturous circles, and I feel my knees go weak.

"Are you with me, Peaches?"

I laugh and smile. "Yes. I was just thinking about how, with you, it's different. I'm not a box to check off your list. You care about my pleasure. You—"

"Shh." Lucas places his hands on my shoulders and meets

my eyes. Suddenly, we're eighteen again, and he's about to give me life advice.

"I'm sorry that you only dated pieces of shit after me. I'm sorry they treated you like a condiment instead of a precious commodity." He kisses down my neck, between my breasts, and drops to his knees. "Look at me."

I meet his green eyes and he smiles. "You deserve to be worshipped, Holiday."

When he presses a kiss to my hip bone, I thread my fingers through his hair. He studies me like he would a piece of art. We look at each other in the candlelight and steam, both breathing harder now. Carefully, he lifts my leg and steadies me as he devours me.

"Fuck," I whisper as he focuses on my clit. He hums when I rock my hips, loving the way his stubble feels against me.

"You're trying to make me come," I whisper.

He nods, slowing down his pace, burying his face in my pussy. I'm greedy for him, almost too greedy. Two fingers slide inside me, and when he curls them, I nearly lose myself.

"Not yet," he tells me.

I tip my head back, letting the water run over my face and hair. "I'm so close."

"I know, I can taste you," he says.

"Lucas, please."

"Please what?"

"I need more."

"Tell me what you need, Peaches."

"You. Inside me."

The look in his eyes steals my breath.

"We're getting there, babe." He closes his eyes and continues to work my clit with his mouth while giving me two fingers. The combination is overwhelming in the best fucking way possible.

I steady myself on his shoulders as the pleasure builds.

"That's it," he says against my pussy. "Let go. I've got you."

The orgasm hits me hard, and I cry out his name, my body

clenching around his fingers. He holds me steady against the wall, whispering how sexy I am. I ride his fingers, loving how it feels, even if it makes me blush.

"That's it, Peaches. Take what you want, like old times." He continues to tease my clit, and the heat builds again.

"Fuck, Lucas," I whisper.

"Oh, my greedy girl has returned," he mutters against me. "Welcome back, sweetheart."

I squeeze my eyes shut.

"Yes," I say breathlessly, wanting and needing to come again.

"So fucking wet," he says, grabbing my ass. "So fucking mine."

I tug on his hair when he claims me, guttural groans I've never heard before release from my throat.

"You belong to me now," he says against me. "Don't you?"

"Yes," I confess into the quiet. "I've always belonged to you, Lucas."

My body can't take any more, and I nearly lose my balance as the second orgasm rips through me. He holds on to me, steadies me. Lucas laughs as he kisses back up my body to my ear. "Love the way you taste."

Once I've come back to reality, I take my time washing his hair first, running my fingers through it like he did for me. He closes his eyes and leans into my touch, and I love seeing this big lumberjack of a man so vulnerable with me.

When his hair is clean, I lather my hands with body wash and explore his body. I take my time, learning the new scars and the way his muscles shift under my touch. When I wrap my hand around his cock, he groans, and his head drops back against the tile.

"Feels so good," he says.

I drop to my knees in front of him, the shower water cascading over both of us.

"Holiday—"

"Let me." I look up at him, and his eyes are full of want. "I want to taste you."

His hand slides into my wet hair. It's gentle but so damn possessive, I squeeze my thighs together. "Okay."

The first taste of him makes me hum with satisfaction. I take him into my mouth slowly, savoring the weight of him on my tongue. His fingers tighten in my hair, and I hear him groan above me.

"Fuck, Holiday."

I work him slowly, finding a rhythm that makes his breathing ragged. My hand wraps around what I can't take, stroking in time with my mouth. The sounds he makes…they're desperate, guttural groans. They go straight between my legs.

"Look at me," he says.

I do, meeting his eyes while I take him deeper. His eyes are full of want, need, adoration, protection, and…love, maybe?

"You're so beautiful," he says. "On your knees for me. Taking me like a good girl."

I moan around him, and his hips jerk slightly. One hand braces against the shower wall while the other stays in my hair, guiding me but never forcing.

"Fuck, Peaches," he says. "You're working me so fucking good."

I pull back just enough to tease him.

I take him as far back as I can, nearly gagging on him. His breathing increases, and I work him faster, wanting to watch him fall apart.

"Holiday, I'm—fuck—"

He pulses in my mouth, and I drink him down, watching him lose himself. I love the way he looks when he comes completely undone.

I stand and wrap my arms around him, kissing him, allowing the taste of both of us to mix into our mouths.

"I think I want to conserve water every day," I whisper across his lips, smiling.

"Fuck, me too." Then he cups my face and kisses me deeply under the hot stream.

We finish rinsing our bodies, and he turns off the water. Lucas wraps me in a towel and then wraps one around himself.

We're both still trying to recover from our shower, smiling at each other in the candlelight, when our phones buzz from the bedroom at the same time.

We look at each other, and then we rush into the bedroom where our phones are lighting up with notifications. I grab mine and see I've been added to the family group chat. I look at it, and then I look at Lucas. He shrugs.

HUDSON
> Emma's in labor. Going to Merryville General now.

CLAIRE
> Emma's having the twins! Everyone's heading to the hospital!

MOM
> Holiday, Emma's in labor. We're all going to the hospital. Are you?

Lucas is already pulling on jeans and a T-shirt. "We need to go right now."

I drop my towel and scramble to get dressed, throwing on the clothes I brought. My hair is still wet, but there's no time to dry it. Lucas is fully dressed in less than a minute and grabbing his keys.

"You ready?" he asks.

"Yeah. Let's go," I tell him, trying to slide on my flats as I walk down the stairs. We both walk as fast as we can to his truck. He drives faster than usual, but his hand finds mine.

I text the family group chat back quickly.

HOLIDAY
On the way to the hospital now. Be there in ten minutes.

JAKE
Lucas with you?

MAWMAW
Ooooohhh!

I blush and swallow hard.

"Oh, no, they're giving you a hard time already?" Lucas asks. "You know how they are, so it's kinda your fault."

"True," I tell him.

HOLIDAY
Yep!

CLAIRE
Is that wedding bells I hear?

HOLIDAY
I can absolutely leave this chat.

I'm bombarded with several *not an option* and *no* replies.

We pull into the hospital parking lot, and Lucas finds a spot close to the entrance. We practically run inside, following signs to the maternity ward. I haven't known Emma for too long, but she became a fast friend, and I care about her well-being. Plus, this is Lucas's niece and nephew being born, which is a big deal.

The waiting room is already packed. Hudson's parents, Emma and Claire's dad, Jake, Claire, and Mawmaw are all present. It feels like half the town is here.

Mawmaw sees us first. "There you are! Got here in record time. I hope you weren't speeding. You know the troopers are out this time of year."

"You both showered," Jake says conveniently. I see several pairs of eyes go to mine and Lucas's hair.

"Yes? And? Is that not allowed?" I ask, challenging him.

"Together?" Jake adds, giving Lucas a hard time.

Mawmaw speaks up. "Hudson's with Emma now. Doctor said it could still be a few hours."

"Or it could be any minute," Dad adds. "Twins don't follow a schedule."

"How would you know?" Lucas asks him.

"I'm Santa. I know everything." He blinks at him.

We find seats at the end of the row, and Lucas drapes his arm across the back of my chair. Everyone notices but no one says anything directly. Bella slides into the chair next to me with a knowing smile.

"You both look guilty as sin," she whispers.

"Shut. Up," I tell her. "You're annoying."

"I know," she says. "I'm like an annoying little sister. Which is great, because when you'd babysit me and Wendy, we'd pretend like you were our meaner older sister."

I turn to her. "Oh really? I let you do whatever you wanted."

She chuckles. "You're right."

Jake brings us coffee from the vending machine and settles in on Lucas's other side. I lean into Lucas without thinking about it, and his arm comes around me naturally. Mawmaw is definitely watching but I don't care anymore. I'm in the family group chat. They all know at this point.

When he thinks no one is looking, he presses a kiss to my damp hair.

We wait for what feels like forever. People doze in their chairs. Someone orders pizza that arrives around midnight. Mawmaw tells stories about when her own children were born, making everyone laugh. Lucas's dad paces, and each time he walks, his shoes jingle.

Lucas traces circles on my palm. Every so often, I catch his mawmaw watching us with a soft smile on her face.

Around one in the morning, Hudson finally bursts through the doors with the biggest smile I've ever seen on his face.

"They're here!" he announces. "One healthy baby boy and one healthy baby girl!"

The waiting room erupts in cheers and congratulations. Hudson's eyes are wet with tears, but he's grinning from ear to ear.

"Emma's incredible. The babies are perfect. They're so tiny and beautiful and—" His voice cracks. "Colby is in there holding them before anyone else. He's going to be such a good big brother."

Jake pulls Hudson into a hug and they're both crying and laughing at the same time. Hudson's parents rush to embrace him. Everyone is talking at once, asking questions, and congratulating him.

"How much do they weigh?" Mawmaw asks.

"Five pounds, three ounces for Evan and five pounds even for Ella," Hudson says. "They're small but strong."

"And Emma?" his mom asks.

"She's tired but wants everyone to meet them before she goes to sleep."

We wait another thirty minutes while the nurses get Emma and the babies settled. The energy in the room is completely different now. It's joyful and full of anticipation.

Finally, a nurse comes out and says we can go in to see them in small groups. Lucas's parents go first, then Mawmaw. After her, Mr. Manchester, Claire, and Jake go. When it's finally our turn, Lucas takes my hand and we walk into Emma's room together. He smiles at me, and I can't help but smile back, feeling that electric pull between us. This is a very close family thing, and I'm his plus-one. The significance of that isn't lost on me.

Emma looks exhausted but absolutely gorgeous, and she sits up in bed. Hudson holds a swaddled baby and so does Colby, who's looking prouder than I've ever seen anyone look in my life.

"Holiday! Lucas!" Emma smiles when she sees us. "Come meet your niece and nephew."

There's no question in her voice when she says it.

Lucas goes to Hudson first, and he carefully transfers one of the tiny bundles into his arms. I watch as he cradles the baby against his chest. The baby is so impossibly small in his big hands, wrapped in a blue blanket with a little knit hat on his head.

The look on Lucas's face has my blood pumping much faster. Wonder and tenderness and something that looks almost like fear—like he can't believe he's being trusted to hold something so precious.

"This is Evan," Hudson says. "Evan, meet your uncle Lucas, who's absolutely not going to be a bad influence on you."

Lucas chuckles. "Yes, I will."

"Colby, give Holiday your sister, okay, buddy?" He nods as Hudson does a successful transfer.

"You make a good dad," I tell him.

"Thanks, Holiday," he says, putting her in my arms.

I cradle Ella carefully, surprised by how impossibly small she is. She weighs almost nothing in my arms. Her face is red and scrunched up, her tiny fists curled near her chin. Not to mention she has the tiniest fingernails I've ever seen.

"She's beautiful, Emma," I whisper, afraid to speak too loudly.

"How did these two miracles come out of you demons?" Lucas asks with a soft laugh.

"Oh, just you wait," Hudson warns him. "Both of you. But still, even I can't believe we made perfect little humans."

"Am I perfect, Daddy?" Colby asks.

"Oh, the most perfect, Colby. The perfect son. The perfect big brother. You're the absolute best."

"You totally are! And you know what, because you're so amazing, I'm going to make you some very special cookies just for being the best."

"Oh, really? Aunt Holiday, you're baking me big brother cookies?" His voice goes up an octave.

"Yes, I am," I promise him.

Emma watches Lucas and me hold the babies with tears in her eyes. "The kids are lucky to have you."

I glance over at Lucas and find him already staring at me. I give him a smile and he returns it. Something passes between us. It's understanding, and a promise that someday this could be us.

CHAPTER 29

❄

HOLIDAY

The past week has been a blur of flour, sugar, and stolen moments with Lucas.

We've been working ourselves to exhaustion, trying to maintain the farm and the bakery with the crowds of customers on the property. I've obsessively been trying to perfect every detail of our contest entry because I won't give those professional judges one reason not to choose us. The shortbread fudge cookie base will be exactly right with crispy edges, a chewy fudge top, with just enough chocolate to balance the buttery shortbread. The homemade vanilla bean ice cream needs to be churned at an exact time so it doesn't melt and turn into a sloppy mess.

Every practice run we've done this week has been timed down to the second. We have exactly three hours to prepare everything from scratch in front of the judges, and we've been rehearsing until we can do it in our sleep. The contest itself isn't that serious. Any other time, I wouldn't go to these lengths, but Dominic discredited me very publicly, and now I have something to prove. I won't allow him to embarrass me in front of four other industry professionals. This is one example of my being overqualified that I will happily accept.

"You're so pretty," Lucas tells me, tucking loose hair that's fallen out of my bun behind my ear.

"You are, too," I tell him as we work around the kitchen in perfect sync, like we can predict one another's moves.

This past week, baking consumed us, but sneaking around did, too.

We've exchanged many stolen kisses in the back of the bakery when we think no one's watching. I've spent too many late nights at his place while we try to keep our relationship private. But the whole town seems determined to expose us.

We couldn't even have breakfast at Glenda's Diner without people staring. Right after, pictures surfaced of our fingers touching across the table. I'm almost convinced that not going public has made the articles worse. They're full of speculation, even though we've shown incredible restraint while out and about.

Old pictures of Dominic and me have surfaced from some internet black hole, making it seem like I'm dating them both, even though those photos are five years old. This love triangle is a scandal that's been fabricated to get more views. My life went from a Hallmark movie to reality TV entertainment in weeks. I'm neither.

According to Bella, who's friends with someone who works at the Merryville Inn, Dominic's been asking about Lucas and me. He wants to know when this relationship started. I came home to escape him, and now it feels like the walls are closing in. Thankfully, I've been so busy, I've barely been able to think straight. Days and weeks have melted together, and I know I just need to survive the holidays.

Today's practice run was supposed to be one of our final dress rehearsals before the contest next Saturday.

Lucas and I make it through the shortbread cookies and fudge in the first ninety minutes. The ice cream base is prepared and churning by the two-hour mark. We're on track, working in perfect sync, when Lucas pulls me close against the counter and kisses me.

"Mm," I hum against his mouth, wrapping my arms around his neck. "Don't get used to this."

"Why not?" He kisses down my neck, making it hard to think.

"Because when we're actually competing, we can't do this as much as I want to," I remind him. "We have to be professional."

Lucas steals another kiss and smirks. "Okay. Sure."

"Lucas...come on. I don't want any drama."

"There won't be any. I'll behave. Promise." He shoots me a wink.

"One more week," I say, cupping his face.

He pulls me close again, resting his forehead against mine. "I know, Peaches. We've got this. Now, let's finish this so you're not late for dinner with your parents."

"You're right," I tell him, glancing up at the clock on the wall.

We finish the practice run in two hours and fifty-six minutes—four minutes to spare. The cookie base is perfect, and the fudge is soft. The ice cream is creamy and smooth with visible vanilla bean flecks. After we've got the presentation down, I pull out my phone and take a picture.

"Shall we?" Lucas asks, and I grab two spoons. We tap our utensils together.

Lucas takes a bite and closes his eyes. "This is it. It's incredible."

I taste mine and have to agree. There is just enough richness from the ice cream without overpowering the other flavors. The shortbread and fudge with the ice cream makes it melt in my mouth. The combination of textures is perfect.

"We're ready," I say, but my anxiety about competing twists in my stomach. I know how cruel Dominic can be, how particular he is. He will not go easy on me.

"Hey." Lucas turns me to face him. "We've got this. Stop overthinking."

"I can't help it. It's what I do."

He kisses my forehead. "We're going to walk in there Saturday, bake our asses off, and win."

I want to believe him.

We clean the kitchen together, and I gather my things. "I should go. Don't want to be late."

"You sure you don't want to skip?" His hand slides to my hip. "Come back to my place instead?"

"Tempting. *Very tempting.* But they've barely seen me this week. I should probably show my face."

"Fair enough." He steals one more kiss. "Text me later?"

"Of course."

Lucas watches me with that soft expression.

I love you. The words sit on my tongue, desperate to come out.

But what if it's too soon? What if he thinks I'm rushing things? We just started this—really started this, even though it's been decades in the making—a week ago. So, I swallow the words down and just smile. "Great job today."

"You too." Something flickers in his eyes, like he can sense what I'm not saying. "See you tomorrow?"

"See you tomorrow."

We lock up the bakery and leave at the same time.

As I drive home in the setting December sun, I should feel accomplished and proud. Instead, I feel like I'm standing on the edge of a cliff, waiting to fall.

When I pull into the driveway, the first thing I notice is the black Mercedes parked next to my mom's SUV.

My stomach drops.

No. No, no, no.

I sit in the driveway for a long moment, gripping the steering wheel, trying to calm my racing heart. Maybe I'm wrong. Maybe it's just someone else's Mercedes. Maybe—

Through the window, I see him. Dominic Laurent, standing in my parents' kitchen, laughing at something my father just said.

Rage floods through me.

I get out of the car and walk up the driveway on shaking legs. After a deep breath, I walk inside. Dominic sees me and his face lights up with the charming smile that used to make me weak. Now, it just makes me want to throw something at his head.

"Ma chérie!" He opens his arms like he expects me to hug him. "What perfect timing. Your parents and I were just having the most delightful conversation."

"What are you doing here?" The words come out harsher than I intended but I don't care.

"Holiday!" My mother appears behind Dominic. "Look who stopped by! Isn't this a lovely surprise?"

Lovely isn't the word I'd use.

"Dominic was in the neighborhood and thought he'd stop by to say hello," my father adds.

"In the neighborhood, five miles outside of town? That's convenient," I say, shocked this is happening.

"We've been having a wonderful chat about your time in Paris," Dad says.

Of course, they have. Because my parents don't know what Dominic really is. Mom knows the PG-rated version, but I never told them how poorly he treated me and how he controlled me. All they see is the charming French chef who swept their daughter off to Europe.

"Have a glass of wine, sweetheart," my mother says. "We were just about to have lasagna, and I made your favorite bourbon chocolate cake."

I want to refuse. I want to grab Dominic by his expensive jacket and throw him off my parents' property. But they're looking at me with smiles, and I can't make a scene.

"Fine," I manage through gritted teeth.

We move to the dining room, and the situation feels surreal. Dominic sits at the table like he belongs here. My mother serves him sweet tea in her crystal glassware. My father chats about how successful the bakery has been since I started managing it.

This is a living nightmare.

I sink into the chair across from Dominic, and he gives me that smile again.

"Dominic told us about your scuba diving trip to Belize. It sounded incredible," Mom says.

"It was a long time ago," I tell her flatly.

"Indeed." His eyes hold mine. "So many things were different then."

My mother brings out the lasagna and cuts us each a slice. She places garlic bread on the table. I chug wine and end up filling up my glass as I glare at him.

"Why are you here?" I finally ask.

He glances at my parents, then back at me. "Because I miss you."

"No, you don't."

"Holiday," Dad says. "You're being rude."

"You're absolutely right. Apologies." For the rest of dinner, I don't say a single word. I eat, I drink, and I don't engage in any of the conversations around me.

"Honey, you're so quiet," Mom eventually says when our plates are cleaned.

"You taught me if I don't have anything nice to say, then I shouldn't say anything at all," I say as she brings out the chocolate cake. I watch in horror as she cuts Dominic an enormous slice. He takes a bite and practically moans.

"Mrs. Patterson, this is divine. Absolutely exquisite. Would you be willing to share the recipe?"

"Oh, of course!" My mother is glowing under his attention. "It's been in our family for generations."

I want to scream. I want to flip the table over. I want to tell my mother that Dominic Laurent doesn't deserve her recipes, doesn't deserve her kindness, doesn't deserve to be sitting in our home, pretending to be a decent human being. But I sit there, fork clenched in my fist, and suffer through dessert while Dominic charms my parents with stories from Paris. He's funny and gracious—everything he was when we first met. Everything he stopped being once he had me under his control.

My father laughs at his jokes. My mother asks about his bakery. They're completely enchanted by him and it makes me sick.

Finally, my father glances up at the clock. "Well, it's getting late. We should probably let you get back to the inn, Dominic."

"Of course." Dominic stands. "Thank you so much for your hospitality. It's been a true pleasure."

"Pleasure was ours," my dad says. "You're welcome anytime."

Over my dead body.

Dominic looks at me. "Holiday, would you walk me out? I'd love a moment to speak with you privately."

"Oh, I would *love* to," I say, the wine streaming through my system.

We step out onto the front porch, and I immediately put distance between us. The night has turned frigid, and I wrap my arms around myself.

"Now I see why you always wanted to visit home," Dominic says, looking out at the land. "Lovely place. Merryville is wonderful. Very…quaint."

"Cut the shit, Dominic. What do you want?"

"Such ugly language for a pretty girl." His face glows in the Christmas lights. "I wanted to see you. Talk to you. Alone. You've been avoiding me."

"I've been *busy.*"

"With your lumberjack." It's not a question. "I've seen the pictures. The articles. You and Lucas Jolly, small-town sweethearts." His voice drips with condescension. "Is this really what you want? To throw away everything we built for some provincial nobody?"

"Don't talk about him like that."

"Why not? It's the truth." He steps closer, and I take a step back. "Holiday, please. I came here to apologize. To make things right between us. I've made mistakes, I know that. But we can fix this. We can start over. Come back to Paris with me. I'll help you open your own bakery. I'll give you everything you and your talent deserve."

"No."

"No?"

"Fuck no, Dominic. What you did to me can't be fixed. There is no *us* anymore. There never really was, though, was there? It was always just you using me and calling it love."

His expression hardens. "That's not fair."

"Fair? I don't think you have the right to speak about fairness." I laugh bitterly. "You took credit for my work. You made me feel worthless unless I was serving your ambitions. That's not love. That's exploitation."

"I gave you a stage to test your recipes," he says, his voice rising. "Everything you have is because of me. I gave you Paris. I gave you a career. I gave you opportunities you never would have had otherwise."

"You took *everything!*" The words explode out of me. "You took my confidence, my sense of self, my connection to my family. You isolated me and controlled me and made me doubt my own talent. And now you have the audacity to come to my parents' house and play the charming ex-boyfriend? What is wrong with you?"

"I love you," he says, and for a moment, he almost sounds sincere. "I've always loved you. I know I didn't show it all the time, but—"

"Love?" I shake my head. "You don't know what love is."

He reaches for me then, grabbing my arms and trying to

pull me against him. "Holiday, please. Just give me another chance. Let me prove—"

Instinct takes over.

I shove him away from me, and he stumbles backward, losing his balance. His expensive shoes slip on the porch steps, and he tumbles down, landing on his ass on the front lawn.

For a second, I just stare at him, not realizing how much strength I have.

The front door opens and my mother appears. "Holiday? Is everything okay out here?"

I don't take my eyes off Dominic. "Everything's fine, Mom. Just telling Dominic goodbye."

"Oh. Well...don't stay out too long, sweetheart. It's getting cold."

The door closes, and I move to the edge of the porch.

Dominic stands slowly, brushing grass and dirt off his expensive slacks. "You've changed."

"No, I haven't. I just remembered who I am."

"This isn't you, Holiday. This violence, this anger—"

"Leave me alone, Dominic." My voice is cold. "Go back to Paris and forget about me."

"Forgetting you is impossible." His voice cracks. "And if you don't stop this charade with that tree farmer, I'll make sure everyone knows about everything."

Ice floods my veins. "I'm not afraid of you."

"You should be. After everything you did. I'll make sure everyone sees you for who you really are. Every intimate moment. Everything we did together. Your precious small-town reputation will be destroyed. Your parents will never look at you the same way." He straightens his jacket. "You think you can just walk away from me? From everything we built? I made you, Holiday. I can destroy you just as easily."

For a moment, fear grips me so tightly, I can't breathe. I'd forgotten about the videos he'd recorded of us. He still has them all—the ones I knew about, the ones I didn't consent to, but he promised they were just for us.

If those videos get out, if anyone in Merryville sees them, I'm done. My parents would be devastated. The town would never look at me the same way. My career would be over. And Lucas—

Lucas. How do I even begin to explain this to him?

Before I spiral, something shifts inside me. The fear burns away, replaced by anger.

"You're right," I say. "You could release our most private moments. You could try to humiliate me, embarrass my family, destroy whatever reputation I have left after you tried to ruin me, but—"

"Then you understand—"

"But here's what you're forgetting, Dominic. You stole *my* recipes. And sure, we have an NDA." I take a step closer to him. "But if you release those recordings, I'll tell everyone and show proof that your Michelin star was earned with my recipes. How would the world like to know your entire empire was built on stolen work from southern trash?"

His face goes pale.

"Oh, and there's more," I continue, my voice getting stronger. "Releasing those videos without my consent is illegal. Revenge porn laws exist in the US, Dominic. You will face criminal charges, and I will take you for everything you're worth."

"You wouldn't—"

"Try me." I cross my arms over my chest.

"Go ahead. Just know, I will take you to the pits of hell with me. I will tell every food critic, every journalist, every chef who respects you that you're a thief and a fraud. I will make sure your legacy is as stained as mine. And then I'll press charges and take you to court. You do not want this fight with me."

He's shaking now, his mask of confidence shattered.

"Who are you?" he asks.

"Your biggest mistake. I'm not that timid girl you controlled in Paris anymore. I won't let you threaten me or manipulate me or use my past against me." I turn toward the house. "So leave me alone. After Saturday's contest, go back to Paris and forget I exist."

"And if I don't?"

I look back at him over my shoulder. "Then I'll have the satisfaction of taking you down with me."

"Holiday. I don't want to do this. You're the love of my life."

"No, I'm not. No one would treat the love of their life the way you've treated me."

"I'm sorry," he says.

"It's too late," I tell him, walking up the porch steps and into the house without looking back. My whole body shakes with adrenaline and anger and something that feels almost like freedom.

Inside, I lean against the closed door, trying to catch my breath. My parents are in the living room with the TV on, pretending they didn't just witness whatever that was through the window.

"Everything all right, honey?" my mother calls.

"Fine," I manage. "Dominic's leaving."

"He seemed like such a nice young man."

I don't have the energy to explain. I mumble something about being tired and head upstairs to my childhood bedroom.

Once the door is closed, I sink onto the edge of my bed and let the reality of what just happened wash over me. Dominic has those videos and he could release them at any moment. He could destroy my image after destroying my career.

But I called his bluff.

I threatened him right back.

And for the first time in years, I didn't let him win.

I'm no longer a pushover.

My hands are still shaking as I pull out my phone.

HOLIDAY
Dominic was at my house and joined me and my parents for dinner. Afterward, we had words. I'm so pissed I can't see straight.

His response comes within seconds.

LUCAS
Are you okay?

HOLIDAY
I'm fine. I pushed him off the porch.

LUCAS
You what?

HOLIDAY
Long story. Can you come over? We need to talk.

LUCAS
On my way.

I stare at my phone, at Lucas's name on the screen, and I feel tears prick at my eyes. He's coming. He'll be here soon. And I'm going to have to tell him about all of it.

The thought makes me nauseous, but I can't keep hiding this. Not from him. Not anymore.

If we're going to be together—really together—he deserves to know the truth about my past. Even the ugly parts. Even the parts that make me ashamed.

I just hope he doesn't look at me any differently.

CHAPTER 30

LUCAS

The text comes through while I'm sitting on my couch, eating macaroni and cheese, trying not to think about how stupidly in love I am with Holiday.

My phone buzzes, and her name lights up the screen. It's almost like she knew she was on my mind.

> **HOLIDAY**
> Dominic was at my house and joined me and my parents for dinner. Afterward, we had words. I'm so pissed I can't see straight.

Every muscle in my body goes rigid. That French bastard was at her house? With her parents? My hand tightens around the phone.

> **LUCAS**
> Are you okay?

The three dots appear, disappear, and appear again. Each second feels like an hour.

HOLIDAY
I'm fine. I pushed him off the porch.

That's my girl. Always has been.

LUCAS
You what?

HOLIDAY
Long story. Can you come over? We need to talk.

The last three words make me feel like I've missed a step in the dark. Nothing good comes from a *we need to talk* conversation. But she needs me, and that's the only thing that matters.

LUCAS
On my way.

I grab my keys, and head for the door, then stop with my hand on the knob. If I pull into her driveway, her parents will know I'm there. They'll see my truck, invite me in for small talk and hot chocolate, while Holiday wants to discuss something. She needs privacy.

A memory surfaces. Me at seventeen, sneaking through the woods to climb up to her window because we couldn't get enough of each other. Back when everything was simple and we believed love could conquer all. That was before the world proved us wrong.

I slide my phone into my pocket and head to the garage. The old golf cart sits in the corner, buried under Christmas decorations that never made it into the yard. I haven't touched it since earlier this year.

The engine sputters, then catches on the second try. I navigate out of the garage and turn down the back road that leads through the woods. The headlights barely cut through the darkness. The trail is overgrown now, branches scraping against the cart's sides like fingers trying to pull me back. But the path is still there, still connecting my property to hers like a scratch that never quite healed over.

The December wind freezes me through my jacket, and my hands are already going numb on the steering wheel, but I don't care. All I can think about is Dominic being at her house and putting his hands on her. That's the only reason she would've pushed him, if he touched her.

My jaw clenches so hard my teeth ache.

What did he say to her? What did he do? The questions loop through my head as I wind through the trees, following the trail from memory more than sight. Branches slap against my arms, but I don't slow down.

The cart finally breaks through the tree line behind her house, and I kill the engine, letting my eyes adjust to the darkness. The Patterson house glows with warm light, Christmas decorations twinkling in every window like something out of a catalog. It looks peaceful.

I approach the side of the house where Holiday's bedroom window is located. I look up at the second floor, my breath coming out in clouds. The white lattice is still there, painted fresh and looking sturdy. Mr. Patterson keeps it maintained, probably not realizing he's preserving the very thing that helped his daughter sneak out for years.

I test my weight, since I weigh so much more than I did in my teens, and the wood creaks but holds. My hands are freezing, and the frost makes everything slippery, but muscle memory takes over.

The curtains are drawn but light glows behind them. I tap gently on the glass at first, then a little harder when she doesn't respond. My heart is hammering against my ribs.

The curtain pulls back and Holiday's face appears. Her eyes are red and swollen, her hair falling out of its bun in messy waves, and she looks absolutely exhausted. When she sees me clinging to the side of her house like some kind of deranged Romeo, her mouth drops open.

She shoves the window up and cold air rushes inside. I climb through less gracefully than I used to in my teenage years, nearly knocking over a lamp on her desk.

"Lucas, what are you—" She's staring at me like I've lost my mind, and maybe I have.

I shove my hands in my pockets. "Surprise."

Something shifts in her expression, and surprise melts into appreciation. Her chin trembles. "Blast from the past."

"Remember when I used to sneak into your room?" I close the distance between us in two steps, framing her face with my frozen hands. Her skin is warm, and I can feel her pulse racing under my thumbs. "Are you okay? Tell me what happened."

She reaches past me to close the window, shutting out the cold, then sinks onto the edge of her bed like her legs won't hold her anymore.

The room smells exactly as I remember. Vanilla and clean laundry with a hint of her perfume. I glance around, and it's like walking into a time capsule. She has the same purple comforter on her bed, the same posters on the walls, and the same desk in the corner where she used to do homework while I distracted her.

"He showed up for dinner," she says, her voice low. "Just appeared in my parents' kitchen like he belonged there. Charmed them. Ate my mom's lasagna. Told stories about Paris. They have no idea who he really is."

Rage builds in my chest, and it spreads through my veins like poison. "What did he say to you?"

"After dinner, we spoke privately on the porch." She's twisting her fingers together and won't meet my eyes. "He tried to convince me to come back to Paris with him. Said he made mistakes, that he wanted to start over, that he'd give me everything I deserve. When I refused—" Her voice cracks. "He grabbed me and tried to pull me close to him, so I pushed him. He fell off the porch onto his ass."

This makes me grin. "I'm proud of you."

Proud because she stood up for herself, and that she's stronger than he ever gave her credit. I can't believe he had the audacity to put his hands on her like he had any right to touch her.

My voice comes out rougher than I intended. "He's lucky that's all you did. If I'd been there—"

"Lucas." She looks up at me, finally, and there are tears streaming down her face. "There's more. Things I need to tell you. Things about my past with Dominic that you don't know."

The fear in her voice makes my stomach turn. I sit beside her on the bed, and the old springs creak under my weight. I take her hand in mine, and her fingers are ice cold. She's trembling like leaves in the autumn wind.

"Okay," I say, trying to keep my voice steady. "But I want you to know, no matter what you tell me, it changes nothing. I don't care about your past."

"I know. But I don't want you to be blindsided if Dominic decides to retaliate against me." She takes a shaky breath, then another, like she's trying to gather her courage. "When Dominic and I were together in Paris, he liked to record us. Our intimate moments."

The words come out rushed, like she needs to get them out before she loses her nerve.

"I consented to it at first because I trusted him. I thought it was just for us, something private. But now—" She stops, swallows hard. "Now, I'm not sure how many there are. Or if I even knew about all of them."

My jaw tightens so hard, I hear my teeth grind together. I force myself to breathe through my nose, to stay calm, to let her finish. But inside, I'm already planning how to find Dominic Laurent and break every bone in his smug French body.

"And there was one night—" Her voice breaks completely,

and she has to stop. She's shaking now, her entire body trembling. I squeeze her hand, trying to calm her.

"Take your time," I say, even though waiting is killing me.

She nods, wipes her eyes with her free hand, then tries again. "There was one night with his best friend. We fooled around, and apparently, Dominic recorded that, too, and…" She can't continue, and I'm thankful because I don't want to know.

White-hot anger explodes through my chest like a bomb detonating. My free hand clenches into a fist so tight that my nails press into my palm, hard enough to leave marks. I want to find Dominic Laurent and fuck him up.

But Holiday is sitting beside me, shaking and terrified and waiting for my reaction, so I force myself to breathe. In through my nose, out through my mouth. Again. Again. The rage doesn't disappear, but I push it down and lock it away for later.

"Tonight, when I refused to return to Paris…" Her voice is barely a whisper now. "He threatened to release the videos. All of them. If I don't stop seeing you, he'll make them public. He'll show everyone. My parents, the town, everyone in the culinary world. He will destroy my reputation and make me look like a whore. My parents will never look at me the same way. I'm so scared that you—" She chokes on a sob. "That you will walk away from me over this."

I have to physically restrain myself from standing up, putting my fist through her wall, and getting in my truck and driving straight to the Merryville Inn to find that bastard. The thought of her with him and those videos being posted on the internet for everyone to look at makes me see red.

"Lucas." Her voice is so small, so unlike the confident woman who pushed Dominic off the porch. "Say something. Please."

I turn to face her, taking her other hand in mine so I'm holding both of them. "Look at me, Holiday."

She does, her eyes swimming with unshed tears, shame, and fear.

"None of that changes anything," I tell her. "Not one single thing."

"But—"

"You were manipulated. You were taken advantage of by someone you trusted, someone who was supposed to care about you. That's not your fault. That's on him." I cup her face in my hands, making sure she can't look away, making sure she hears every word. "I don't care about your past relationships at all, or the videos, or anything else Dominic is holding over your head. The only thing I care about is you. Right now. Do you understand me? None of it matters. Nothing he could ever say or do will change my mind about you. Ever."

A tear spills down her cheek, and I brush it away with my thumb, then another, and another, until I'm just holding her face while she cries.

"You don't think less of me?" Her voice breaks on every word. "You don't think I'm ruined or—"

"Stop." The word comes out harsher than I mean it to, but I need her to hear this. "Holiday Patterson, I think you're the bravest person I've ever met. You're smart. Beautiful. You came home and you rebuilt your life. You didn't let Dominic destroy you, even though he tried." I lean my forehead against hers, breathing her in. "I love you."

The words slip out before I can stop them, hanging in the air between us like something fragile and vital.

Her breath catches. "What?"

My heart is racing now, pounding so hard I'm sure she can hear it. But I've said it and can't take it back. I don't want to, anyway.

"I love you," I repeat, and saying it again feels like jumping off a cliff, but this time I have a parachute. "I've loved you since we were kids. I loved you when you left for Paris, even though I was so angry I could barely see straight. I loved you when you came back, and I pretended I hated you. I love you right now, sitting in your childhood bedroom, telling me about the worst parts of your past." I pull back just enough to look her in the eyes. "I love all of you, Holiday. The good parts and the messy parts and the parts you think are too broken to love. All of it. All of you. I always have, and I always will."

She's really crying now, her whole body shaking with sobs, and I pull her against my chest. She wraps her arms around me and holds on like I'm the only thing keeping her from drowning. Her fingers curl into my shirt, and I can feel her tears soaking through the fabric.

"I love you, too," she whispers against my chest, so quiet I almost miss it. "I've been trying not to say it because I thought it was too soon, because I was scared you'd think I was moving too fast. But I can't hold it back anymore." She tilts her head to look at me. "I love you, Lucas. I never stopped. Not once. Not ever."

Something inside me splits open.

All the years of hurt and resentment and anger toward her just drain away like water through a broken dam, leaving nothing but this—her in my arms, both of us finally saying what we should have said over a decade ago.

I kiss her, pouring everything into it that I can't put into words.

I give her my love and my gratitude that she trusted me enough to tell me the truth. She kisses me back just as desperately, her hands sliding up to tangle in my hair.

When we finally break apart, we're both breathing hard. She rests her forehead against mine.

"What do I do about this?" she asks. "About the videos?"

"You need to talk to a lawyer. What he's threatening is illegal. He can't just release that stuff without consequences."

"I told him that. I threatened to press charges and expose evidence that he stole my recipes for his Michelin star." A ghost of a smile crosses her face. "I called his bluff."

Pride swells in my chest again. "That's my girl. But we need to be smart about this going forward. Document everything. Save all his texts and emails. If he shows up here again, you call the sheriff. You don't talk to him, you don't engage. Tell your parents, too."

She nods, some of the tension finally leaving her shoulders. "Okay. What about the contest?"

"We go in there Saturday and we destroy the competition." I tuck loose hair behind her ear, letting my fingers linger against her cheek. "We show him and everyone else what you're capable of because I think that's what he's ultimately scared of. Everyone finding out the truth." I pull her close again, breathing in the vanilla scent of her shampoo. "You're not alone anymore, Holiday. Whatever happens, we'll face it together."

She looks up at me and more tears come. "You climbed the lattice."

"Yeah."

"You took the golf cart through the woods like we used to."

"Seemed faster."

"You came because I asked you to." Her voice cracks on the words and fresh tears spill over. "You didn't ask questions or tell me to wait until morning. You just showed up."

"Of course, I did." I wipe away her tears with my thumbs, trying to memorize her face. "Holiday, you could call me at three in the morning from the other side of the world and I'd find a way to get to you. That's what you do when you love someone. I will always show up for you. Always."

She kisses me again, and it's full of relief and love. When we break apart, she's smiling through her tears.

"Stay tonight?" she whispers. "Please? I don't want to be alone."

"Your parents—"

"Will never know. Once they finish their show, they'll sleep like the dead. Besides, we can lock ourselves in." She glances at her closed bedroom door, then back at me. "I just need you here. I need to know you're real, that you meant everything you just said."

"I'm not going anywhere."

We lie down together on her narrow twin bed, the springs creaking under our combined weight. It's too small for both of us and we have to press close together just to fit, but I don't mind. Holiday snuggles against my side with her head on my chest, right over my heart. I wrap my arms around her like I can shield her from everything that's trying to hurt her.

I run my fingers through her hair, feeling the tension slowly drain from her body. Her breathing evens out and deepens, and I think she might be falling asleep.

"Lucas?"

"Yeah, Peaches?"

"Thank you. For not judging me. For still loving me after everything."

I press a kiss to the top of her head, breathing her in. "There's nothing you could tell me that would make me stop loving you. Nothing. You understand? You could tell me you robbed a bank or joined the circus or decided you hate Christmas. Wouldn't matter."

She laughs, and I start to relax along with her.

"I don't hate Christmas," she whispers.

"Good. Because that might actually be a deal-breaker."

She shifts closer, her fingers twisting into the hem of my shirt. "I'm scared about Saturday. About seeing him again. About what he might do if I don't comply with his demands."

"I know. But I'll be right there beside you the entire time." I tighten my arms around her. "And if he tries anything—if he so much as looks at you wrong—he's going to have to deal with me."

"You're my hero," she says, but there's affection in her voice rather than mockery.

"I'm all yours," I confess.

Outside, Christmas lights twinkle through her window,

casting red and green shadows across the walls. Downstairs, her parents' TV hums faintly through the floorboards. Inside this room, we're wrapped up in each other.

"Is there anything else I should know?" I ask.

"No," she tells me. "That's the only skeleton in my closet."

The contest is in six days, and Dominic is a bigger threat than he was before. There are a thousand things we still need to figure out, but mostly how to protect her from what he might do next.

Nothing will come between us because we have each other. We have the truth between us. We have our love. And that's more than enough.

Holiday's breathing deepens and evens out, and I know she's finally asleep.

I stay awake longer, listening to the old house settle around us, feeling the weight of her in my arms, as I stare up at the glowing green plastic stars on her ceiling. My childhood memories are full of moments in this room—sneaking in through the window, stolen kisses while her parents watched TV downstairs, whispered conversations about the future we thought we'd have together.

We lost that future once, and I'll be damned if I lose it again.

I close my eyes and let myself drift off with Holiday safe in my arms, and I sleep without dreaming about what I lost. Because we've found each other again.

CHAPTER 31

HOLIDAY

I wake up at three forty-five in the morning, and for a moment, I don't know where I am.

My childhood bedroom comes into focus slowly. I see the glow-in-the-dark stars on the ceiling that Lucas put up when we were sixteen. I reach for my phone on the nightstand, and the light from the screen hurts my eyes.

Friday, December 13th.

Spooky.

Tomorrow is the contest, the day I've been counting down to for weeks.

My stomach turns itself inside out, and I have to breathe through my nose to keep from getting sick. Tomorrow, I'll stand in front of hundreds of people and bake while Dominic Laurent watches my every move. The entire town will see if I'm as good as everyone believes me to be. Tomorrow, everything I've worked for over the past decade will come down to those three hours. Because, while this contest is in Merryville, the entire world is watching my relationship with Lucas unfold.

They even discussed live streaming it. It's something I didn't learn about until yesterday. I'm not ready for this level of exposure, and the thought makes me sick.

I force myself out of bed and into the shower, letting the hot water run over me until it turns lukewarm. When I catch my reflection in the foggy mirror, I barely recognize myself. I look like I haven't slept; probably because I haven't. The only time I can rest is when Lucas is holding me.

When I'm alone and I close my eyes, I see Dominic's face. I can hear his threats and remember how he controlled me. I imagine those videos being released, my parents seeing them, and the whole town knowing every intimate detail of my past. This is a game of cat and mouse, except I don't know which one I am. Right now, I feel like I'm being hunted.

I get dressed in the dark, and by four fifteen, I'm in my car, driving down the empty country road that leads to the Christmas tree farm. When I turn onto the property, Christmas lights twinkle in the predawn darkness. Usually, it makes me smile, but today I just feel lonely.

The lights are already on at the bakery when I pull up. Bella's car is in the parking lot, and when I walk inside, she's already wearing her apron and pulling ingredients from the walk-in fridge.

"Why are you here?" I ask.

"Wanted to get started and give you a break," she says. "You're mentally exhausted, Holiday."

"I am," I say. "Will be happy when this contest is over and everything can go back to normal."

Normal. I don't even know what that is.

"Yes, tomorrow is going to be a big day!" She's way too cheerful for four thirty in the morning. "Are you excited? Nervous? Both?"

"Both," I manage, tying on my apron, barely awake.

I move to the coffee maker and brew some coffee, hoping it jolts me awake. Right before I take my first sip, my phone buzzes in my pocket. I pull it out, expecting a good morning text from Lucas. But it's not.

> **DOMINIC**
> Look what I just came across on my phone.
> Missing you terribly.

Below the text is a thumbnail file of a video. My stomach drops because I recognize the setting immediately. It's our condo in Paris. More specifically, the bedroom with the exposed brick wall, and in the thumbnail, I can see myself on the bed.

My hands start shaking so badly that I almost drop the phone.

This is his warning shot. His reminder that he has power over me. That tomorrow, when I'm standing in front of everyone, he'll be watching me while lording this over my head.

I don't watch the video because I can't. I know what's in it and seeing it will destroy me. With trembling fingers, I text Lucas.

> **HOLIDAY**
> He sent me one of the videos.

The response comes within seconds.

> **LUCAS**
> Fuck him. He's just trying to get into your head and play mental games. Don't let him, HoHo. You hold all the cards.

> **LUCAS**
> Also, good morning. Can't wait to see you.

I force myself to focus on work as I make the icing. Today, I'm making Double Doozie gingerbread men, peanut butter blossoms, and red velvet cookies. I know they'll all be bestsellers, and we'll sell out in hours, but there is nothing I can do until the bakery is expanded. My hands know the measurements to the icing by heart, even when my brain is somewhere else.

Bella pulls the first batches out of the oven, and they come out perfectly.

"I have to run home real quick," Bella tells me. "I forgot my headphones, and I want to listen to my audiobook."

"Okay, no problem," I tell her.

"Ten minutes, max," she says, rushing to the door.

I add the dough to the trays and place it inside the oven as I work on the rest of the prep. When I smell the cookies, I realize I forgot to set a timer. When I pull them out, they're burned with black edges. The gingerbread men look more like corpses. I stare at the ruined cookies and something inside me cracks. I've been baking since I was eleven years old. I've worked at Michelin-star restaurants. I don't ever burn cookies like this. But I just did.

I'm too distracted.

"It's okay," Bella says quickly as she rushes inside. "We'll make another batch. No big deal. No use crying over burnt cookies."

How am I supposed to perform tomorrow in front of the judges, cameras, and Dominic if I'm making mistakes like this?

I force myself to focus. The next ones come out perfect. By the time Wendy arrives at seven, we've got a few thousand cookies cooling, and more in the oven.

By nine, the line is wrapped around the building. Everyone wants to wish me luck, take photos with me, and tell me they're rooting for us. I force smile after smile until my face hurts. Every time my phone buzzes, I flinch, expecting another text from Dominic. But he stays silent.

We sell out by one o'clock, and Bella shoos me toward the door. "Go rest. You need it for tomorrow."

"Are you sure?"

"Yes," she confirms. "Wendy and I have this."

"Thank you," I tell her.

I drive home and force myself into the shower, trying to wash away the memory of that video thumbnail. It doesn't work, but I try to scrub away the feeling of Dominic's hands on me and his voice in my ear, along with all the things I did so he'd love me. I slide into some buttery-soft black leggings and an oversized cream-colored sweater, grab my overnight bag, and head to Lucas's house.

"Staying with a friend," I tell my mom and dad.

"Tell Lucas we said hi," Mom says with a smirk.

I grin, then leave. The drive over to his house takes longer than I want because there is still a line to get into the Christmas tree farm. In December, they do sleigh rides, photos with Santa, and have live bands play. It's an experience that everyone wants. Leaving the farm is easy, but returning is hard, even with the shortcut that leads to the Jolly loop where his entire family lives.

When I arrive, I look at the house he built, the one we talked about when we were teenagers. Christmas lights twinkle around the eaves. Before I make it to the porch, he's opening the front door, smirking at me. He's shirtless and wearing gray joggers. My eyes slide up and down his body, and I can't believe he's looking at me like this. It takes my breath away.

"Hurry, my nipples are so hard they could cut ice," he tells me with a laugh, shoving his hands into his pockets.

My face cracks into a smile, and I pick up my pace. I rush up the steps, and he pulls me inside, closing the door behind me. The warmth of his house wraps around me immediately, and I can smell something cooking that makes my stomach rumble for the first time all week.

"There you are," he says, taking my overnight bag and tossing it by the stairs. "Was starting to think you got lost."

"Traffic was insane getting back onto the farm."

"Yeah, December is nuts." He pulls me against him, and I

melt into his chest. "How are you holding up after this morning?"

"Better now that I'm here."

He tilts my chin up to look at him. "That video he sent was bullshit. You know that, right?"

"I know. I just—"

"Nope." He puts his finger over my lips. "We're not talking about him tonight. Tonight is about us. About getting you relaxed and ready for tomorrow. About reminding you that you're a badass who's going to destroy everyone at that contest."

Lucas always knows how to make me smile. "A badass?"

"The baddest." He grins and that dimple appears. "Now come on. I made dinner, and if you don't eat, I'm gonna have to kick your ass."

"I haven't been hungry lately."

Lucas takes my hand and leads me to the kitchen. "When's the last time you ate a full meal? Not that girl dinner bullshit."

I think about it. "I don't remember."

"That's what I thought." He guides me to the kitchen island, and I slide onto a stool. "I made your favorite."

When I get stressed, I lose my entire appetite. I've been so busy, the only reason I know the date is because the contest is tomorrow.

Lucas pulls a dish from the oven and my mouth actually waters. He made chicken parmesan with pasta and garlic bread. It was the first meal he ever cooked for me.

"I love this," I say, my throat tight.

"You haven't even tasted it yet. Could suck." He plates the food and sets it in front of me. "Now eat. Lumberjack orders."

I snicker. "There's something else you have that I want to eat."

"Oh, babe. There will be plenty of time for that. But I'm taking care of you first." Lucas shoots me a wink.

I laugh, actually laugh, for the first time all day. He grins at me, clearly pleased with himself, and sits beside me with a plate piled high.

I take a bite, and it's pure perfection. The chicken is crispy and the cheese is perfectly melted where it's still gooey. The marinara is tangy, and I didn't realize how hungry I was until now.

"Well?" he asks.

"So damn good. Like, wow."

"That YouTube video was a winner." His eyes are warm on mine.

We eat in comfortable silence, and I feel the tension from the day starting to drain away. With Lucas, I don't have to be perfect. I don't have to perform. I can just be myself.

"So," he says, stealing another piece of garlic bread off the stove. "You nervous about tomorrow?"

"Terrified," I tell him as he returns back to me.

"That means you care." He takes a bite. "Nothing to worry about. I'll be right there with you. Just promise me you'll have fun."

"What if I can't?"

"Then I'll quit tomorrow morning. This isn't worth it, Peaches." His voice is firm.

"Please do not do that," I say.

He smiles. "Then promise me you'll *try* to have fun. It's going to be me and you. My entire family will be watching and cheering us on—your fan club in the audience. We've always wanted to do this together, and I know how important this is to you, but I don't want you to give Dominic any power over us. Don't let him ruin something that could be a special moment for us. You know?"

Something in my chest loosens. "I promise I'll try to have fun."

He takes my hand in his and kisses it. "That's my stubborn girl."

I roll my eyes, but I'm smiling. We finish dinner and he takes our plates to the sink. I move to help, but he shoos me away.

"Go sit by the fireplace."

"Lucas—"

"Please?" He grabs a glass from the cabinet and pours me a glass of wine. "Relax for me."

"Okay," I say. I sink into the couch with a sweet red vintage. The fire is already going, crackling and warm. I curl up against the cushions and stare at the flames. For the first time all week, I feel like I can actually breathe.

A few minutes later, Lucas joins me with his own glass of wine and the bottle. He sits close enough that our thighs touch.

"Thank you," I say. "For this. For making me eat. For making me laugh. For just…being you."

"You're welcome. Thank you for being you, too." He clinks his glass against mine. "A toast to kicking ass. To the beginning of us."

"To us," I say, knowing nothing else on that list matters as much to me.

We drink, and the wine is warm going down. Lucas shifts and pulls me against his side, his arm around my shoulders. I rest my head on his chest and listen to his heartbeat.

"Can I ask you something?" I say after a moment.

"Anything."

"How are you so calm about this contest? Doesn't it make you nervous knowing so many people will be watching?"

"Hell yeah, it does." He smiles and kisses my nose. "But in the grand scheme of life, it's just a blink in time. We walk in there with our heads held high and we show everyone what we're made of. And then it's over. A little over three hours of our lives, and then we'll never have to do it again."

"You make it sound so easy."

"It's not. But it's going to fly by, and when we're eighty, we'll laugh about it." His fingers trace lazy circles on my arm. "You and me, we're a team. And we're going to remind this damn town why we're at our best when we're together."

I tilt my head back to look at him, admiring his features in the firelight. He leans down and kisses me, taking his time. When he pulls back, his eyes are full of mischief. "Now, I have a surprise for you."

"You know how I feel about surprises."

He chuckles. "Shut the hell up."

Lucas stands and holds out his hand. "Come with me."

I let him pull me up, and he leads me upstairs to his bedroom. Candles are already lit on the dresser and nightstand, casting the room in a warm glow.

"Lucas Jolly, did you set the mood?" I tease.

"Maybe." He grins. "Now lie down for me."

"Should I take off my clothes?"

He smirks. "If you want. But it's your choice." He cracks his fingers. "Thought I could give you a massage to loosen you up."

My breath catches as I lift my sweater over my head, then slide out of my leggings.

His brow lifts. "Lie down on your stomach for me, Peaches."

I do as he says and feel the bed dip as Lucas sits beside me. His warm hands rub on my shoulders, and he starts working the muscles with firm pressure.

"Holy shit, you're tense," he says.

"Yeah, stress will do that."

"Mm. Good thing I'm here to fix it." His thumbs dig into a particularly tight knot, and I groan. "That's it. Let it out."

His hands work from my shoulders, down my spine, finding every tight spot and coaxing it loose. The tension I've been carrying for weeks starts to disappear under his touch.

"Your hands are magic," I mumble into the pillow.

"I know. I conveniently have a few body parts that are magic." I can hear the smirk in his voice.

"*Cocky as hell.*"

"*Confident* as hell. There's a difference." His hands slide lower, working the muscles in my lower back. "How's that feel?"

"Like heaven."

"Good. That's what I'm going for."

His fingers trace along the waistband of my panties, and goose bumps trail over me.

"You cold?"

"No. The opposite, actually."

"Interesting." He continues the massage. When his hands slide up to unhook my bra, I lift slightly to help him. "This okay?"

"More than okay."

The bra comes off, and his hands return to my back, working higher now. His thumbs trace along my ribs, and I have to bite back a moan.

"You're trying to kill me," I say, grabbing the comforter, wanting him to touch me all over.

"Nope. Just trying to get you to relax." But his voice is rougher now. "Is it working?"

"Too well."

I roll over to face him, and his eyes drop to my bare chest before meeting my gaze again. The heat in his expression makes my breath catch.

"Hi," he says.

"Hi, yourself."

"You're beautiful, you know that?"

"You might've mentioned it once or twice."

"Well, I'm mentioning it again." He leans down and kisses me. When he pulls back, I'm breathless. "How are you feeling?"

"Better. So much better." I reach up and trace my fingers along his jaw. "Thank you for taking care of me."

"Always." He brushes hair away from my face. He kisses me again, this time with more heat. His hand slides up my side, his thumb brushing just under my breast.

"We don't have to do this if you're tired," he whispers.

"What are you talking about? I *need* you, Lucas."

"You've got me." His mouth moves to my neck, and I arch into him. "You've always had me."

His hand finally cups my breast, and I gasp. Everything about this feels different. Right now, I'm just here, present, with Lucas making me feel things I only feel with him.

"I love you," I whisper.

"I love you, too." He kisses down my throat, across my collarbone. "Tonight, I don't want you to think about anything other than us."

"Sweep me away with you," I whisper, pulling him back to my mouth. "Make me forget everything."

"Oh, Peaches, I plan on it."

And for the first time since Dominic arrived at my parents' house, I feel like everything is going to be okay. Because I have Lucas. And he has me. And that's what really matters.

CHAPTER 32

❄

LUCAS

I wake up before my alarm goes off.

Holiday is snuggled against my side with her head on my chest, one arm draped across my stomach. Her breathing is peaceful in a way it hasn't been in weeks. I don't move, just lie here watching the early morning light creep through the curtains.

Today's the day. Everything Holiday and I have been working toward for weeks comes down to the next few hours.

My phone says it's five thirty. We need to be at the venue by eight to set up our station. The competition starts at ten, and we have three hours to bake, present, and show everyone what we're made of.

Holiday shifts in her sleep and makes this small sound that I find so damn adorable. Last night was exactly what she needed. What we both needed. I made sure she forgot about everything except us. She fell asleep smiling, wrapped around me, and seemed like she was finally at peace.

I press a kiss to the top of her head, and her eyes flutter open.

"Morning," I say.

"Morning." Her voice is soft. She tilts her head back to look at me. "What time is it?"

"Five thirty. We've got plenty of time."

"It's contest day," she says.

"Sure is," I confirm. "You ready?"

"I think so." She pushes up on one elbow to look at me. "Are you ready?"

"Hell yeah. Ready to get this over with so I can worship you properly." I tuck her hair behind her ear. "But I'm also very excited."

She studies my face for a long moment. "Thank you."

"For what?"

"For last night. For reminding me why we're doing this." She leans down and kisses me softly. "Easy peasy."

She smiles against my mouth and kisses me again, deeper this time. My hand slides into her hair, and I'm about two seconds from saying screw the contest when she pulls back.

"We should get ready," she says, but she's grinning.

"Probably. But you're so damn tempting."

"That's what you keep saying," she replies.

We get up and move through our morning routine together. We shower together to save water, then I make coffee while she gets dressed. By six thirty, we're both ready and standing in my kitchen, trying to eat breakfast.

Holiday picks at the toast I made her, managing maybe three bites before pushing the plate away.

"I can't," she says, sipping her coffee. "My stomach is in knots."

I eat and watch her tap her fingers against the counter as she scrolls through her phone. She's wearing dark red jeans and a festive sweater with Christmas trees on the front. Her hair is pulled back into a braid, and she's wearing her signature red lipstick. She looks beautiful and stressed but also determined.

"Hey," I say, reaching across the counter to take her hand. "We've got this."

"I know. I just—" She stops and takes a breath. "What if I freeze up?"

"You won't." I squeeze her hand. "Remember why you're doing this. Not for him. Not for the panel. For you. For us."

"For us," she repeats. Something in her expression shifts. The fear doesn't disappear but it's joined by determination now. "You're right. This is our moment."

"Damn right it is."

We finish our coffee and load the supplies into my truck. The ingredients are already measured and packed in coolers. Everything is organized and ready to go. By seven fifteen, we're on the road.

The drive to the venue takes thirty minutes with the traffic. The event is being held outside the Merryville Community Center, the same place where the meeting was held weeks ago. Except now, the parking lot is packed with cars, news vans, and people setting up camera equipment.

"Holy shit." Holiday breathes as I park. "This is bigger than I thought."

"I can't believe they're live streaming it," I say.

"The whole world is watching," she whispers.

I kill the engine and turn to face her. "I'm going to be right there beside you during every single step. Ready?"

She takes a deep breath and nods. "Let's do this."

We get out and unload our supplies. The December morning is cold enough that our breath fogs in the air, but the sun is shining and the sky is clear. It's going to be a beautiful day. I can already tell.

The community center has been completely transformed. A massive tent has been erected in the parking lot, the kind used for weddings and festivals. Inside, it's been divided into three distinct areas.

The center area is where twelve baking stations are set up, each one equipped with a full kitchen setup. My eyes scan across the industrial ovens, burners, mixers, and prep space. It's everything we could possibly need and more. A massive Christmas tree stands in one corner, covered in lights and ornaments made by the kids from the elementary school.

White lights are strung everywhere across the tent ceiling, twinkling like stars. Giant snowflakes hang down. Red and gold ornaments spin in the draft. Evergreen garland wraps around every support beam. It looks like Christmas exploded in the best possible way.

To the left is the spectator section with rows of chairs set up theater style. Families are already claiming seats, holding signs, and wearing festive clothing. Cameras are positioned throughout to capture every angle.

To the right is the judging area with a long table draped in red cloth with five chairs, clipboards, and a centerpiece made of pine branches and ornaments. Behind that is a smaller media section with additional cameras and equipment for the live stream.

The whole space is open, so the crowd can see everything happening at the baking stations, and the panel can easily walk between stations during judging.

"I thought there were more people competing?" Holiday looks at me.

"I heard many people dropped out after eating your cookies," I tell her.

"Really?" she asks, chuckling.

"Yeah? Do you blame them? I'd be intimidated, too."

"Contestants!" A woman with a clipboard approaches us. She's wearing a Santa hat and a bright smile. "Names?"

"Lucas Jolly and Holiday Patterson," I say. "Team Jolly Holiday."

She checks her list. "Station seven. You've got ninety minutes to set up before we start. Bathrooms are in the back, water stations along the wall. Hot chocolate and cookies in the break area if you need a snack. Any questions?"

"We're good," Holiday says.

"Here, please wear these hats. We're asking everyone," she says, placing a green Santa hat on Holiday's head and a red one on mine. "Make sure to keep your name badges on, too."

"Yes, ma'am," I say as we walk toward station seven. It's in the middle of the room. That means no more hiding and no backing down. We're front and center.

Each station has a small Christmas tree on the corner of the prep table and a sprig of mistletoe hanging above. Someone really went all out with the holiday decorations.

Other contestants are already setting up their stations. I recognize some faces from town. Jake's friend Henry is here with his sister, both looking nervous but excited. A server from the diner is with her boyfriend, and they're wearing matching ugly Christmas sweaters. There are even some teenagers competing, too. One thing I love about this contest is that it brings people of all ages in to participate.

Christmas music drifts through the speakers. "Rockin' Around the Christmas Tree" transitions into "Jingle Bell Rock." The energy in the room is festive.

And then I see him.

Dominic Laurent stands near the panel table in full chef's whites, looking polished and professional. He's talking to the four other judges—Patty Morrison with her kind eyes and silver hair, Marcus Williams looking relaxed in his chef coat, Mary Carter with her warm smile, and Thomas Reeves with his tattooed arms crossed over his chest. They're all in formal attire, clipboards in hand, looking official and intimidating.

Dominic's eyes scan the room and land on Holiday. The look on his face, like he's looking at something that belongs to him, pisses me off.

"Ignore the judges' table," I say quietly to Holiday.

She nods, but I can see her hands shaking slightly as she unpacks our supplies. I move close enough that our shoulders touch, a silent reminder that I'm right here.

We spend the next hour organizing everything exactly how

we practiced. Ingredients laid out in order and tools are placed within reach. The timer is right in the center. To the side is the ice cream maker. Every detail matters when given only three hours to create a three-part dessert. What we're doing is next-level.

By nine o'clock, the twelve stations are set up, and the crowd is filing in. I see my entire family taking seats in the front row. Hudson is with Emma, who's holding one of the twins, while Hudson holds the other. Jake and Claire are wearing matching Santa hats. My parents are bundled up in their winter coats, looking excited. Mawmaw has a sign that says "Team Jolly Holiday!" with glitter and everything. Even Colby is here, bouncing with excitement and waving a candy cane.

Holiday's family is there, too. Her parents, Tricia with Bethany, and Sammy wearing a ridiculous Christmas sweater with our faces poorly photoshopped onto it. Half of Merryville seems to have shown up to watch, wearing festive clothing and holding signs for us.

The energy in the room is electric and joyful. Cameras are recording our every move, and the live stream has started. I can see us on the TVs. This is *really* happening.

At nine thirty, Mayor Thompson moves to the microphone in the center of the room. He's wearing a red suit and a Santa tie.

"Good morning, everyone, and welcome to the ninety-first annual Merryville Christmas Cookie Competition!" The crowd erupts in applause and cheers. "We have twelve amazing teams competing today for the grand prize of five thousand dollars and their names memorialized in the hall of fame display that's kept at town hall. Not to mention, someone will be going home with a beautiful trophy."

He holds the trophy in the air. It's a golden oven on a platform. Applause roars.

I glance over at Holiday and loop my pinky with hers under the table. I give her a smile and she returns it.

"Our panel today includes some of the finest culinary minds in the world. Let me introduce them very quickly," the mayor continues. "First, we have Patty Morrison, food critic for *Texas Monthly* and this year's James Beard Award winner."

The crowd gives polite applause.

"Second, Chef Marcus Williams, owner of Williams Steakhouse in Austin. He's been featured in *Bon Appétit*'s Top 50."

He stands and nods. The crowd grows more enthusiastic.

"Third, Chef Mary Carter, award-winning pastry chef and author of *Southern Sweets and Treats* and *Preparing the Perfect Cookie*."

Holiday's breath catches, and I know she owns Mary's cookbooks. This is a big deal for her.

"Fourth, Chef Thomas Reeves, last year's Texas Baking Champion and owner of Confetti Cupcakes in Houston."

He stands and grins at the crowd.

"And finally, Chef Dominic Laurent, Michelin-starred pastry chef from Paris."

The applause is mixed. Some people cheer enthusiastically, but I notice a lot of people in the Merryville section are quiet. Word must have spread about what he did to Holiday. And if there's one thing that's certain about our small town, it's that we stick together.

"The rules are simple," Mayor Thompson says. "You have exactly three hours to create your signature holiday dessert from scratch. Everything must be made here, in front of our panel and audience. If you finish early, present your creation to the judges. Everything will be scored on taste, presentation, creativity, and execution. The team with the highest combined score wins." He pauses for dramatic effect. "Contestants, are you ready?"

All twelve teams shout *yes*, including us. Holiday's voice is strong beside me.

"Then let the baking begin! Your three hours start...now!"

A loud buzzer sounds and "All I Want for Christmas Is You" starts blaring through the speakers. The crowd goes wild.

All around us, teams spring into action. Mixers whir to life as ovens preheat. People are measuring and moving around with nervous energy.

Holiday and I look at each other, and she's smiling now. Really smiling.

"Ready?" I ask.

"Ready," she says.

"Let's fuck 'em up," I tell her, singing along with Mariah.

We fall into our rhythm immediately. We start on the shortbread bases together. We've practiced this so many times that we could do it blindfolded. Every movement is like second nature.

"Two cups of flour," I say.

"One cup of butter," she responds, already moving to the mixer.

We work in sync, dancing around each other in the small space like we've been doing this together for years. Because in a way, we have. This is what we always talked about doing: baking together, creating together, and being together.

The Christmas music keeps the energy high. The crowd sings along. The whole atmosphere is festive and fun rather than cutthroat competition.

Fifteen minutes in, our shortbread dough is ready. I press it into our pans while Holiday starts melting chocolate for the fudge. Around us, other teams are struggling. Someone drops a bowl and it crashes against the ground, spilling eggs and flour everywhere. Another team argues about measurements. The couple in the ugly Christmas sweaters looks like they're on the verge of breaking up.

But we're good. We're solid. We're in our element.

"How's it looking?" Holiday asks, peeking over my shoulder at the shortbread.

"The best batch we've made. How's the chocolate?"

"Almost there." She stirs carefully. "Another minute."

I slide the shortbread onto the table next to her so she can easily pour the fudge on top.

Holiday hums while she works. It's soft, almost unconscious, but I hear it. A grin touches my lips and she smiles wide.

"What?" she whispers.

Suddenly, we're no longer in this tent, but we're teenagers baking in Mawmaw's kitchen.

"You're humming," I say.

She looks over at me, surprised. "Am I?"

A smile breaks across her face. "I didn't even realize."

"That's how I know you're happy." I lean in close enough so only she can hear me over the music. "You're incredible, you know that?"

She blushes. "You better stop."

"Never." I steal a quick kiss, right there under the mistletoe hanging above our station. The crowd goes wild, cheering and chanting our team name.

"Jolly Holiday! Jolly Holiday! Jolly Holiday!"

"Lucas!" Holiday laughs, swatting at me. "We're being watched!"

"Good. Let 'em see."

She shakes her head, but she's smirking as she goes back to stirring the chocolate. When it's done, she adds the nuts. The joy radiating from her is contagious.

This is exactly what I wanted for her, for us. I wanted to do this together and have fun. I wanted her to reclaim the joy that Dominic stole from her in Paris.

"Fudge is done!" Holiday announces, doing a little victory dance as she pours it on top of the shortbread. I can't help but laugh as we slide our pans into the fridge to let the pecan fudge with the sea salt topping cool.

Around us, everyone seems frantic, but we're having the time of our lives.

This is what Christmas should feel like. Joy. Love. Partnership. Magic.

And experiencing this Holiday is everything.

CHAPTER 33

❄

LUCAS

The first hour passes in a blur of precision and laughter. Once our pans of cookies are in the fridge setting, I relax. Everything is going exactly according to plan. Around us, other teams are starting to stress. Someone's oven isn't heating properly. Another team realizes they forgot a key ingredient. Henry and his sister are bickering about timing. But Holiday and I are in perfect sync.

"Ninety minutes left!" the mayor calls out.

"Time to make the ice cream," Holiday says, checking her watch.

"Almost." I grab her hand and pull her away from the prep table. "First, we celebrate."

"Lucas, what are you—"

I spin her around right there in our station, making her laugh. The crowd goes absolutely wild as we dance to "Jingle Bell Rock."

"Keep it up and they're going to think we're showing off," she says with a laugh.

"Babe, we are showing off. Who else can bake a masterpiece and dance like this?" I dip her dramatically and she squeals. "Might as well own it."

When I pull her back up, she's breathless as I spin her around. "You're ridiculous."

"And you still love it," I mutter.

"I really do."

"This song is only three minutes; take the break with me," I tell her.

I notice Dominic watching us from the judging table as we continue to dance. His expression has changed and his jaw is set. He's watched us laughing, dancing, and being completely ourselves, and it's eating him alive.

Good.

When the last guitar strum of the song plays out, she pulls away. "I needed that."

"I know," I say.

"Ice cream time," Holiday says, pulling out our ingredients.

"Heavy cream, whole milk, sugar, vanilla bean, and a pinch of salt. That's it. Simple and perfect."

She measures everything while I get the ice cream maker ready. We've tested this recipe a dozen times at home. It's foolproof.

She scrapes vanilla beans into the mixture, and I can't help but admire her as she works. Holiday makes it look easy. While she's concentrating, the confidence in her movements is undeniable.

This is what she was meant to do. Create. Bake. Bring joy to people through food.

We mix everything together and pour it into the ice cream maker. The machine hums to life, and Holiday sets a timer.

"Thirty minutes," she says. "Then we assemble and we're done."

"We're crushing this," I tell her.

"I'm so happy to be doing this with you," she confesses.

"Fuck, me too, Peaches."

I glance down at the clock, knowing we have plenty of time. We're right on schedule.

That's when I see Dominic stand from the judging table and he's heading straight toward us.

"Incoming," I mutter to Holiday.

She follows my gaze, and her shoulders tense, but she doesn't back down. She stands up straighter, lifting her chin.

Dominic stops in front of our table, looking at our setup. His eyes scan our ingredients, our timing sheet, and our ice cream maker churning away.

"Impressive," he says. His accent seems thicker when he's agitated. "You're ahead of everyone else."

"Aren't I usually?" Holiday asks.

His eyes finally meet hers. "You always were talented. I didn't give you enough credit."

"It's too late now," Holiday says. "I don't care what you think anymore."

Something flickers in his expression. Regret? Anger? I can't tell.

"Are you sure?" He leans against the edge of our station, too casual. Too familiar. "Or is he just making you believe that?"

"Don't," Holiday warns.

"I made you who you are," Dominic continues, his voice dropping lower. "Everything you know, everything you do is because I gave you that opportunity."

Holiday bursts into laughter, but she's laughing *at* him. In front of everyone. And I just stand back and let her give him exactly what he deserves. "That's hilarious. I was baking and winning competitions when I was a literal child. Try to steal someone else's credit, not mine."

His jaw clenches. "We had something special."

"We had nothing." Holiday's voice is steady, strong. "You had control. You had someone to manipulate and use. That's not love, Dominic. That's *abuse*."

The word hangs in the air between them. Around us, I can feel people watching, listening. I glance up at the TV and see that the cameras are focused on us. Did they catch every word?

"How dare you—" Dominic starts.

"Chef Laurent." Patty Morrison is suddenly there, her voice firm but professional. "You need to return to the judging table. This is *inappropriate*."

"I'm observing their technique," Dominic says, but his mask is cracking. "As a judge."

"You're harassing a contestant. You're wearing a microphone," Patty tells him, pointing to the label on his chef coat. "Return to the table. *Now*."

For a moment, I think he's going to argue. His hands are clenched at his sides, his face as red as a tomato. He looks at Holiday like she's something he lost and desperately wants back.

"This isn't over," he warns.

"Yes, it is," Holiday says.

He walks back to the judging table, but I can see him seething. Marcus and Thomas are talking to him in low voices, clearly addressing what just happened. Mary is watching with concern.

"You okay?" I ask Holiday.

"Yeah." She takes a deep breath and grins. "All is well in the world."

"Yes, it is."

The timer goes off, which means our ice cream is ready.

We work together to assemble everything. I pull the cookie bars from the fridge and they're perfectly set. Holiday cuts them into perfect fat squares. I arrange them on the plates, then she scoops the ice cream, making sure each portion is identical.

We drizzle a bit of extra fudge sauce for presentation. She adds a sprinkle of sea salt on top.

We're done with forty-five minutes to spare.

"Ready to turn it in?" Holiday asks.

"Let's do this."

We carry our plates carefully to the judging table. All five members of the panel stop what they're doing to watch us approach.

"Team Jolly Holiday," Mayor Thompson announces into the microphone. "First team to complete their dessert!"

The crowd applauds.

We set our five plates down in front of the panel. Patty, Marcus, Mary, and Thomas all look pleased and interested. Dominic's expression is unreadable.

"Tell us about your creation," Patty says, wearing a warm smile. She reminds me of Mawmaw.

Holiday takes a breath. "This is our signature holiday cookie bar called 'The One.' It's a buttery shortbread base topped with rich pecan chocolate fudge, finished with sea salt, and served with homemade Philadelphia-style vanilla bean ice cream."

"And the inspiration?" Mary asks.

"Holiday created it," I explain, giving credit where credit is due. "She perfected the ratios, added the fudge layer with pecans, and created the ice cream pairing. This is all her talent. I'm just her partner in crime." I waggle my brows at her.

"Lucas was my inspiration," Holiday says, winking at me.

The panel picks up their forks and begins tasting. I watch their faces, looking for any tells.

Marcus takes a bite and his eyebrows raise. "This shortbread is perfectly executed. The texture is ideal."

"The fudge layer," Mary says, taking another bite. "It's rich without being overwhelming. And the pecans add just the right amount of crunch."

Thomas is focused on the ice cream. "This is incredible. Simple but perfect. The vanilla doesn't overpower the other flavors."

Patty takes her time, tasting each component separately, then together. When she looks up, she's laughing. "This is *exceptional*. The balance of flavors, the textures, the temperature—everything works together beautifully. This is the work of someone who truly understands baking."

Holiday's face fills with pride. "Thank you so much."

Dominic clears his throat, then speaks. "It's rustic," he says, his accent sharp. "Simple. Not particularly innovative. A kitchen sink dessert."

The other four members of the panel turn to look at him like he's grown a third head.

"With all due respect," Marcus says carefully, "sometimes simple is exactly what's needed. This dessert is comforting, elevated, and perfectly executed. That's not a weakness."

"I agree," Mary adds. "Innovation for innovation's sake isn't always better. This is several classics with a twist and done exceptionally well."

Dominic's jaw tightens but he doesn't argue. He makes a mark on his clipboard and doesn't say anything else.

"Thank you for your presentation," Patty says to us. "You can return to your station. Feel free to pass out the rest to those watching the competition."

We walk back and I can see Holiday's hands shaking slightly. I grab her hand and squeeze her fingers.

"Proud of you," I whisper. Today, she stood up to Dominic twice. Our creation was praised by some of the best in the business.

"You were amazing," she whispers to me.

"We were amazing," I correct.

The two of us happily pass out the dessert with ice cream and people go wild for it.

"I want seconds," someone yells.

"Me too!" another woman says.

Everyone laughs.

"That's it! You know how it goes. Bakery is open tomorrow until we sell out," Holiday announces.

We begin cleaning up our mess while the other teams continue working. Some are just now pulling things from the ovens. A few look defeated already, like they know their desserts didn't turn out right.

"Thirty minutes left!" Mayor Thompson calls out over the speaker.

Right now, all I feel is relief. We did it.

Once our station looks pristine, all we can do is impatiently wait.

I pull her close, wrapping my arms around her from behind as we watch the chaos around us.

"No matter what happens," I say against her ear, "I'm so fucking proud of you."

"I owe Mawmaw a thank you," she says, leaning back against me.

Over at the judging table, the other teams are turning in their desserts. Henry and his sister present something that looks like it collapsed. The couple in the ugly Christmas sweaters has a dessert that's clearly burnt. The teenager team brings them a chunky chocolate cookie that looks pretty impressive.

Each team presents, the panel tastes, makes notes, and they move on to the next.

Through it all, Dominic is growing angrier. He's barely speaking during the tastings and doesn't smile at anyone. He's focused on Holiday and me, watching how obviously happy she is.

I'd be willing to bet that he's finally seeing the real Holiday. The version of her that exists when she's not being controlled or manipulated. The Holiday who hums while she works and does victory dances when something goes right.

I don't think he's ever known this version of her.

"Ten minutes remaining!" the mayor says.

The last few teams are rushing to plate their desserts and hurrying to the front before the timer buzzes.

"Time's up!" Mayor Thompson announces. "If you haven't presented your dessert, you're unfortunately out of the running. Thank you for participating."

The two teams that didn't finish look crushed, but they accept it gracefully. The judges continue to taste the desserts, and some of their faces say more than their words could have.

Once they've finished tasting everything, Mayor Thompson speaks up.

"Our panel will now take ten minutes to deliberate. And then we'll announce our winner."

The tent is filled with conversations of people speculating. Contestants are nervously waiting. The energy is electric.

"You ready for this?" I ask.

"With you? Always."

The judges huddle together. They're comparing notes, discussing, and debating. I can see Patty and Marcus having an animated conversation. Mary is nodding at something Thomas says. Dominic is standing with his arms crossed, barely participating.

Five minutes pass, then ten.

Finally, they break their meeting, and Mayor Thompson goes to the microphone again.

"Ladies and gentlemen," he says, and the tent falls silent. "Our panel has reached a decision."

Holiday's hand grabs mine and she interlocks our fingers together.

"This was an incredibly difficult choice. Every team here today showed remarkable skill and creativity. But there can only be one winner."

The pause feels like it lasts forever, and I swear, I can hear my own heartbeat. I feel Holiday's pulse racing where our hands are joined.

Dominic suddenly stands up from the judging table. His chair scrapes against the floor, the sound harsh in the silent tent.

"This is ridiculous," he says, his voice carrying over the crowd. "I can't be a part of this."

Everyone turns to look at him.

"Chef Laurent—" Patty starts.

"She doesn't deserve to win," Dominic says, pointing at Holiday. "She's—"

"Dominic." Holiday's voice cuts through the tent like a blade. She steps forward, pulling her hand from mine. "Stop."

"You think you can just leave me?" His voice is rising now, his professional mask completely gone. "After everything I gave you. Everything I did for you?"

"Everything you did *to* me," Holiday corrects. Her voice carries through the silent tent. "There's a difference."

"You're nothing!" Dominic shouts. The crowd gasps. "You will always be a small-town baker with no future! I gave you Paris! I gave you opportunities! I gave you *everything*!"

"Do you want to discuss what I gave you?" Holiday asks, and her voice doesn't waver. "Do you really want to go there?"

It's a threat. It's fierce. I watch the color drain from Dominic's face.

"You controlled me. You manipulated me. You made me believe I was nothing without you. That's not true."

Whispers echo through the tent.

Dominic's face goes pale, then beet red. "How dare you."

"How dare me?" Holiday interrupts. "Dominic Laurent, Michelin-starred chef, is a user. He makes people feel small so he can feel big."

"You're lying!" Dominic's voice cracks. "You're trying to ruin my rep—"

"You're ruining your own reputation," Patty says, standing. "Right now. In front of everyone."

"Chef Laurent, you need to leave," Marcus adds, also standing.

"I'm a judge!" Dominic protests. "You can't—"

"You're removed from the panel," Mayor Thompson says. "Effective immediately. Your behavior is completely unacceptable."

Two large men in black security shirts make their way toward the judging table.

Dominic sees them coming and something in him completely snaps.

"This is her fault!" he screams, pointing at Holiday. "All of this! She's——"

"Sir, you need to come with us," one of the security guards says, reaching for Dominic's arm.

"Don't touch me!" Dominic tries to pull away. "Holiday, please! Just listen to me! We can fix this! We can——"

"No," Holiday says. Her voice is calm. "I'm finally free from you."

Security has him by both arms now, physically escorting him toward the exit.

"You'll regret this!" Dominic shouts as they drag him away. "You'll never be anything without me! You'll——"

His voice cuts off as they get him outside the tent. The crowd parts to let them through. Cameras capture every second.

The silence that follows is deafening.

And then, slowly, someone starts clapping.

It's Mawmaw. Standing in the front row, applauding.

Jake joins her, and so does Claire. Both of my parents are standing, along with Holiday's entire family.

Matteo, Dean, and my elusive younger cousin Eli, are here. Next to them stands Bella and Wendy, and I see my little cousin Bristol, who's home from college for Christmas.

Seconds later, the entire tent erupts in cheers for us.

It's not polite. It's a thunderous standing ovation. People are cheering. Whistling. Shouting Holiday's name.

It's not because of her baking, but because of her courage. Because she stood up to her manipulator in front of hundreds of people. Because she chose herself.

Holiday's eyes fill with tears as she looks around the tent. At all these people supporting her. Believing in her. Celebrating her strength.

She buries her face in my chest, and I feel her shoulders shake.

"You did it," I say. "It's over."

When she pulls back, she's smiling through her tears. The crowd is still going wild.

Mayor Thompson approaches the microphone, looking stunned. "Well. That was…unprecedented." He clears his throat. "But the show must go on! Our remaining four panel members have reached a decision."

Everyone slowly settles back into their seats. Holiday wipes her eyes and stands up straighter, but I keep my arm around her waist.

"Without further interruption," the mayor says, "the winner of the ninety-first annual Merryville Christmas Cookie Competition is—"

CHAPTER 34

❄

HOLIDAY

The tent is so quiet, I think I could hear a pin drop.

Mayor Thompson stands at the microphone with the envelope in his hand. Every eye in the room is on him. Lucas holds me so tight, I swear I can feel both our pulses racing.

"Without further interruption," the mayor says, "the winner of the ninety-first annual Merryville Christmas Cookie Competition is—" He opens the envelope with agonizing slowness. "Team Jolly Holiday! Lucas Jolly and Holiday Patterson! Clear winners."

The cheers are so loud, I can't hear myself think. Lucas sweeps me up in his arms, spinning me around right here in the middle of the tent. I'm laughing and crying at the same time, my face buried in his neck.

"We did it!" I shout over the noise. "We actually did it!"

"You did it, Peaches!" He sets me down and cups my face in his hands. "You're so fucking talented."

Before I can respond, our families are rushing toward us. Mawmaw gets to me first, pulling me into a hug that smells like her perfume and Christmas cookies.

"I'm so proud of you, baby girl!" she says, tears streaming down her face.

My mom is next, then my dad, then Tricia, then Emma. Everyone is hugging and crying and celebrating. The twins are being passed around. Colby is jumping up and down, screaming, "You won! You won!"

Mayor Thompson approaches with the trophy and hands it to Lucas and me together. It's heavier than I expected, solid and real in my hands. He also gives us an oversized check for five grand.

"Congratulations," he says. "Very deserved."

Cameras are flashing. The live stream cameras are focused on us. Someone from the local news is trying to get our attention for an interview.

Lucas and I hold the trophy between us, both grinning.

This is real. After everything, we *actually* won.

"Speech!" someone in the crowd yells.

"Speech! Speech! Speech!" More people join in.

I look at Lucas, and he nods, squeezing my hand. We step toward the microphone together.

"Thank you so much," I say, my voice shaking with emotion. "This is—wow. This is incredible. I can't believe—"

My voice breaks, and Lucas takes over smoothly. "We're honored to represent Merryville. This town, these people, you are everything to us. Our family. And a huge thank you to everyone who supported and believed in us."

"Especially to Mawmaw," I add, finding her close. "None of this would've been possible without you entering us into the contest. You always encouraged me in your kitchen."

She blows me a kiss, still crying.

Patty Morrison approaches the microphone.

"If I may," she says, "I just want to add that what we witnessed today went far beyond baking. We saw courage. We saw someone stand up for themselves. And that matters more than any competition." She looks directly at me. "Holiday, you're not just a talented baker. You're an *inspiration*."

I'm crying so hard, I can barely see.

Marcus, Mary, and Thomas join us, congratulating us individually. Mary pulls me into a warm hug.

"You were exceptional," she says.

"Thank you so much. I own both your cookbooks. You're one of my heroes."

"And I'm honored to call you a colleague." She smiles. "Actually, I'd love to talk to you privately before I leave today. Do you have a few minutes?"

"Of course! Absolutely."

"Wonderful. Find me when things settle down."

She moves away, and I'm pulled into another round of hugs. Jake lifts me off the ground. Hudson kisses the top of my head. Emma is crying almost as much as I am.

Lucas and I are posing for photos with the trophy when I hear shouting from the entrance.

"Fuck you!"

My blood runs cold.

Dominic.

Everyone turns toward the commotion. The security guards who escorted him out are struggling with someone at the tent entrance.

Dominic's voice is hoarse, raw.

He's charging into the tent. His chef's whites are disheveled. His face is red and blotchy, and he looks completely unhinged.

"This is bullshit!" he screams, pointing at the judges' table.

Mayor Thompson steps forward. "Sir, you need to leave—"

"She belongs to me!" Dominic's voice cracks.

"Nah," Lucas says, shaking his head. "She doesn't."

His eyes land on Lucas, and something in his expression shifts to pure rage.

"You!" He charges toward us. "You ruined my life!"

Everything happens so fast.

Dominic lunges at Lucas with his fists raised. I scream. Lucas pushes me behind him. But before Dominic can reach us, two bodies intercept him.

Jake and Hudson.

Hudson catches Dominic's fist mid-swing, his face cold and terrifying. Jake has Dominic's other arm twisted behind his back in a hold that makes Dominic cry out.

"You're fucking done here," Hudson says, his voice deadly calm.

"Get off me!" Dominic thrashes against them, but it's no use. The Jolly brothers are huge. "She was mine! He stole everything from me!"

"Holiday was never yours," Jake says, tightening his grip. "And you need to leave before I break both your legs."

Seconds later, Sammy walks up, rears back his fist, and slams it into Dominic's face. "That's for stealing my sister's recipes."

Sammy's fist connects with Dominic's jaw again, and the sound echoes through the tent. Everyone gasps.

Blood trickles from Dominic's split lip. He's still struggling against Jake and Hudson's hold, but he's dazed now.

"And another thing." Sammy steps closer, his voice carrying through the silent tent. "I saw your Michelin-starred cookies. The ones you're so famous for? You didn't create them. My sister did when we were teenagers."

Whispers fill the area as the cameras capture every word.

"That's not—" Dominic starts.

"Don't lie," Sammy cuts him off. "I was there when she created those recipes in our parents' kitchen. Funny, they showed up on your menu with your name attached as the creator. Piece of shit."

Mary Carter is standing nearby, her eyes wide. Patty Morrison has pulled out her phone, recording the whole interaction. Marcus and Thomas are watching with identical expressions of disgust.

"The lavender shortbread," Sammy continues, counting on his fingers. "The brown butter snickerdoodles. The Earl Grey macarons. All Holiday's recipes. All credited to *you*. Care to explain why that is?"

"This is slander!" Dominic spits blood onto the ground. "I will sue you—"

"Sue me," Sammy says. "I have proof. There are photos of them from over a decade ago on social media."

"We all knew," Mary Carter says suddenly, her voice cutting through the chaos. Everyone turns to look at her. "Everyone in the industry knew Dominic was taking credit for other people's work. We just couldn't prove it or pinpoint who was feeding him recipes." She looks directly at Dominic. "But now we can."

Patty nods. "I've heard rumors for years. Noticed how so many young chefs he mentored left the industry entirely."

"This is ridiculous—" Dominic tries again.

"Is it?" Thomas Reeves steps forward. "Because I competed against you in Paris years ago. And the dessert you presented? I know it was one of your sous-chef's creations. She interned with me and you took credit for her work, too."

The tent has gone completely silent except for the sound of random gasps.

Security is rushing over now, along with two police officers.

"Assault," one officer says, looking at Dominic's bloody lip. "Who threw the punch?"

"I did," Sammy says immediately, holding up his hand. "And I'd do it again."

"Sir, you can't just—"

"He's been threatening my sister for weeks," Sammy says, but they arrest him, too.

"No, please do not take him," I say.

"That's the rules," the officer says.

"It's fine," Sammy says, laughing. "I'll beat his ass in jail, too."

The officer looks between Sammy and Dominic. "You two won't be together."

They cuff Dominic and my brother, then escort them out.

"This isn't over!" Dominic shouts as they drag him toward the exit. "I will destroy all of you! My lawyers will—"

"Your lawyers will what?" Mary Carter calls after him. "Defend you against theft? Against fraud? I'm sure every major food publication in the country will see this. By tomorrow morning, everyone will know exactly who Dominic Laurent really is. With proof."

Dominic's face goes white, then he starts screaming in French, thrashing against the officers as they force him out of the tent. This time, he doesn't return.

I'm shaking from the spike of adrenaline. My brother just punched someone. Mary Carter just destroyed Dominic's career on live stream.

Lucas wraps his arms around me. "Are you okay?"

"Yeah," I manage. "Holy shit."

My dad is already on his phone, probably calling a lawyer. Mom looks torn between being proud and horrified. Tricia is filming everything on her phone.

"Don't worry about me!" Sammy calls out as they lead him away. "Worth it!"

Somehow, through this disaster, I laugh because that's Sammy. He's always had my best interests in mind.

The crowd erupts again—this time in support of my brother. People are yelling his name. Someone starts a "Free Sammy" chant, and half the tent joins in.

Mayor Thompson looks completely overwhelmed. "Let's… let's get back to celebrating our winners, shall we?"

The energy shifts back to us. People congratulate us again, though now everyone wants to talk about Sammy punching Dominic. The local news is having a field day.

Lucas keeps me close, his arm around my waist. "Your brother is scary sometimes."

"I know. But he's not wrong."

"No, he's definitely not wrong."

"Did you see how Dominic flinched?"

"Yeah," he says. "Pussy."

Laughter falls from my mouth.

After twenty minutes, Mary Carter catches my eye from across the tent and gestures toward a quiet corner. I excuse myself from Lucas and make my way over to her.

"First," she says when I reach her, "is your brother going to be okay?"

"Yeah. My dad left to bail him out. Sammy knew what he was doing."

"Good." She glances around to make sure no one's listening. "I don't want to add to an already overwhelming day, but I have a time-sensitive opportunity I'd like to discuss with you."

My heart starts beating faster. "Okay."

"I'm opening a new bakery in Nashville in February. It's going to be a flagship location. Very upscale, innovative, and focused on elevating southern baking traditions." She looks at me intently. "I want you to be my partner."

The words don't register at first. "I'm sorry, what?"

"Partner. Equal ownership. Your recipes, your creative control, your name on the door alongside mine at Adorable Bakery." She pulls out a folder from her bag. "I've been following your career since Paris. I knew Dominic was taking credit for your work—everyone in the industry knew, but no one wanted to call him out. When I heard you were competing today, I had to see you in action. Everyone here did."

I stare at her, unable to form words.

"Your technical skill is exceptional," she continues. "But more than that, you have heart. You understand what makes people connect with food. That's *rare*. And now that the truth about Dominic is out there? Your reputation is going to skyrocket. People are going to want to support you, to taste your real work. This is perfect timing."

"I don't know what to say."

"Say you'll think about it." She hands me the folder. "Everything's in here. Salary, ownership percentage, creative control, along with timelines. It's a substantial offer, Holiday. This could launch you into a completely new level of your career. Your own bakery, your own recipes, in a major market. Nashville is exploding right now."

I take the folder with numb fingers. "Thank you. I'll think about it."

"I need to know by Christmas Eve," Mary says apologetically. "I have interviews scheduled the week after Christmas, and I don't want to waste anyone's time if you're interested in teaming up with me. If you have questions, call me. My number's in there."

"Christmas Eve," I repeat. That's ten days away.

"I know it's fast. And I understand today has been...*a lot*." She squeezes my arm gently. "But this is real, Holiday. This is your shot. Everything you've worked for. Think about it carefully."

She walks away to rejoin the other judges, and I'm left standing with the folder in my hand. My mind is blank.

My own bakery in Nashville. Partnering with *the* Mary Carter, one of the most respected names in southern baking. I'll have creative control, my name on the door, and equal ownership.

It's everything I've ever dreamed about. She's my baking hero.

I look across the tent and see Lucas laughing with Hudson and Jake, probably talking about the fight. His family surrounds him, celebrating. Mawmaw is showing the trophy to anyone who will look. My family is mixed in with his—my mom talking to his mom, my sister chats about Sammy, and everyone is together like they've always been.

I can't stop watching Lucas. This is his home. His life. His family's business spans generations. His roots go so deep here, they're practically part of the soil. And he's my home, too.

"Holiday?" Bella appears beside me. "How are you?"

"Just...processing."

"Yeah, Sammy punching Dominic was the most badass thing I've ever seen. Your brother is going to be a known *legend*."

"Yeah." I clutch the folder to my chest. "He already is."

"But you won!" She gives me a hug. "You actually won! And Dominic's career seems to be over. Everything worked out!"

"It's a day I'll never forget."

"Come on, everyone's going to Mawmaw's to celebrate. And apparently, to plan Sammy's breakout of jail strategy. You coming?"

"Yeah. I'll be right there."

She walks away, and I'm left standing alone with a folder that might change everything.

Lucas catches my eye from across the tent and gives me that dimpled smile that makes my heart skip.

He mouths *You okay?*

I nod, forcing a smile.

But I'm *not* okay because I just got offered my dream job. Everything I've worked toward my entire career, everything Dominic stole from me, I can finally have for myself. My own bakery in a big city with my name on the door alongside Mary Carter's. It would be my recipes, my vision, and my reputation restored.

The only problem?

Nashville is twelve hundred miles away from Merryville. That's twelve hundred miles between Lucas and me. It's an eighteen-hour drive away from this life we just started building together. And I have ten days to decide.

I watch him laugh with his brothers. I could never ask him to leave everything he's built. He's made it very clear he won't move away from his family, the home he built, his entire career. Merryville is in his blood.

But how can I turn down this opportunity? Especially after everything Dominic took from me.

I tuck the folder under my arm and plaster on a smile as Lucas walks over and pulls me close.

"Ready to go celebrate?" he asks, kissing my temple. "Mawmaw's making a feast."

"Yeah. Let's go."

He doesn't notice the folder, doesn't comment on how my hands are shaking. Lucas has no idea how much things have changed in the span of five minutes.

But tonight, we will celebrate our win and each other.

CHAPTER 35

❄

LUCAS

The caravan to Mawmaw's house is ten vehicles long. Cars are honking, people are hanging out of windows, shouting congratulations, and someone—probably Jake—is blasting Christmas music so loud, I can hear it from three cars back. We won. Today should feel perfect.

But something's off.

Holiday sits in my passenger seat, staring out the window. The trophy is in her lap, the oversized check folded carefully beside it. She hasn't said much since we left the venue. Just quiet responses.

"You sure you're alright?" I ask, glancing over at her.

"Yeah." She looks at me and smiles, but it doesn't quite reach her eyes. "Just processing everything. It's been a lot."

"That's an understatement." I reach over and take her hand. "Dominic showed his ass, your brother punched him and got arrested, Mary Carter destroyed Dominic's reputation on live stream, and we won five grand and a trophy. That's a hell of a day."

"One for the scrapbook," she says with a small laugh. "Very eventful."

I squeeze her hand and she squeezes back. Maybe she's just

exhausted. Maybe the adrenaline is wearing off. Maybe standing up to Dominic in front of hundreds of people took more out of her than she's letting on.

By the time we pull up to Mawmaw's house, there are already a dozen cars in the driveway and lining the street. Lights are on in every window. I can already smell food cooking. The truth is, Mawmaw's been preparing for this celebration all week. She knew we'd win.

Holiday and I walk in together, and the house erupts in cheers. Everyone's already here. My parents, Hudson and Emma, Jake and Claire, and Colby's bouncing around like he's had too much sugar. The twins are with Emma's dad at their house. Holiday's family is here, too—her parents, Tricia, and Bethany. And apparently, Sammy just got bailed out because he's sitting at the kitchen table with an ice pack on his hand, grinning like he won the baking contest.

"The champions!" Mawmaw announces, pulling Holiday and me into a double hug. "I'm so proud of you both!"

"Thanks, Mawmaw," I say, kissing her cheek.

"Come on, come on. I made all your favorites. We're celebrating properly tonight."

The next hour consists of us sitting around the table eating Mawmaw's famous fried chicken, mashed potatoes, green beans, biscuits, mac and cheese, and three different pies. Our family is eating and laughing and retelling stories from the past. Sammy is showing off his bruised knuckles like they're battle scars.

"Worth it," he keeps saying. "Totally worth it."

Holiday's dad claps him on the shoulder. "You did good, son. That bastard had it coming."

I watch Holiday from across the room as she chats with Emma, who's recovering from giving birth two weeks ago.

Holiday is smiling, hugging people, and accepting congratulations, but I notice the way she's being a little too careful. Her smile is just a fraction too forced.

After about an hour, she catches my eye and mouths *Can we talk?*

I nod, and she gestures toward the back door. We slip out while everyone's distracted by Colby trying to steal a third piece of pie.

The back porch is exactly how I remember it. String lights hanging from the eaves, the old porch swing Mawmaw refuses to replace, and hanging right above the steps—mistletoe. My grandma has hung that mistletoe there every Christmas for as long as I can remember.

It's where Holiday and I first kissed when we were sixteen. I used the mistletoe as an excuse. She did, too. I kissed her before I could overthink it. That was the moment everything changed between us.

Now, we're standing in the exact same spot, fifteen years later, and everything's about to change again. I can feel it in my bones.

"Hey," I say softly, pulling her close. "Talk to me."

She looks up at me and I can see tears threatening. "I needed a minute with just you."

"You've got me." I cup her face in my hands. "Always."

Then I kiss her. Right there under the mistletoe, where it all started. She kisses me back, and it's sweet and desperate and feels like something I can't quite name.

When we pull apart, she's crying.

"What's wrong?"

She reaches into her pocket and pulls out a piece of paper that's been folded. Her hands are shaking as she hands it to me.

"Please read it before you say anything."

My heart is pounding as I unfold it. I read the heading.

Partnership Proposal
Adorable Bakery
Nashville, Tennessee

A VERY MERRY ENEMY

. . .

I keep reading. Holiday is being offered an equal partnership and creative control with a substantial salary, working alongside Mary Carter. Everything is detailed with timelines, ownership percentages, and profit sharing.

"This is everything you've ever wanted," I whisper.

But it's Nashville. That's hours away from here. From me.

When I finally look up, Holiday is watching me with tears streaming down her face.

"Are you considering it?" My voice comes out broken.

"I don't know." She wipes her eyes. "I honestly don't know. She offered it to me today, right after everything happened with Dominic. I haven't had time to think. I haven't processed any of it."

"This is huge, Holiday." I hand the paper back to her. "This is everything you've worked so damn hard for."

"I know."

"Mary Carter is—she's a baking legend. This is a once-in-a-lifetime opportunity," I say, knowing Holiday has baked her way through Mary's cookbooks several times. "When does she need an answer?"

"Christmas Eve."

That's in ten days.

"You need to think this over," I tell her, even though every cell in my body is screaming at me to beg her to stay. "Really think about it. This could change your entire career."

"Lucas—"

"I'm serious." I take her hands. "Don't make this decision based on me. Or us. This is about *your* future. Your dream."

"You're my future, too," she whispers.

"Then we'll figure it out." I pull her against my chest even though I don't know how the hell we're going to figure this out. "Whatever you decide, I fully support you."

She cries into my shirt, and I hold her, staring at that

mistletoe hanging above us. This is the same spot where everything began. And maybe it's where everything ends, too.

We stand there, holding one another for a long time.

Inside, I can hear my family laughing and celebrating. Out here, it strangely feels like the world is ending.

"We should get back inside," Holiday finally says, pulling away and wiping her eyes. "Before someone notices we're gone."

"Yeah," I tell her.

We go back in, and I watch her plaster on that fake smile again. She hugs Mawmaw and laughs at Sammy and pretends everything's great. But I know the truth. She's not fine. Neither am I.

The party goes on until dark. My family starts filtering out, exhausted from the day. Holiday's family left not too long ago. Hudson and Emma went home after lunch. Jake and Claire have Colby with them.

"You coming?" Jake asks me.

"In a bit. Gonna help Mawmaw clean up."

He looks between me and Holiday, sees something in my face, but doesn't push. "All right. See you tomorrow at the farm."

"See you," I say.

After everyone's gone, it's just me, Holiday, and Mawmaw in the kitchen washing dishes.

"You two are quiet," Mawmaw observes.

"Just tired," Holiday says quickly. "Long day."

Mawmaw looks at me, and I can see her putting pieces together, but she just nods. "Well, you both did amazing today. I'm so proud."

"Thanks, Mawmaw," I say, kissing her cheek. "We're gonna head out."

"Drive safe. And Lucas?" She catches my arm and pulls me back into a hug. "Whatever it is, you'll figure it out."

How does she always know?

"I know," I whisper, hugging her tight.

Holiday and I walk to the truck in silence.

"You want to come over?" I ask, even though I'm terrified of her answer.

She looks at me for a long moment. "Yes. I do."

We drive to my house. The whole way, my mind is racing. Nashville. Eighteen hours away. Ten days to decide. How do I compete with her dream? How do I ask her to choose me over everything she's worked for?

I can't. I won't. But gosh, I should.

When we get to my house, Holiday follows me inside. I turn on the lights, start a fire, do all the normal things. But nothing feels normal.

"Lucas," she says, and her voice breaks on my name.

I turn around, and she's standing in the middle of my living room, crying again.

"Come here," I say, and she does.

I pull her close and just hold her. We stand there for a long time, not talking, just breathing together.

"I don't want to lose you," she finally whispers. "Not again."

"You won't." I tilt her chin up to look at me. "No matter what happens, you won't lose me."

"Promise?"

"Promise."

She kisses me then, and it's different from every other time. It's more urgent and desperate, like she's trying to memorize the taste of me and how we fit together.

I kiss her back with so much fervor, I steal her breath away. My hands slide into her hair, down her back, pulling her closer. She tugs at my shirt, and I help her pull it off. Her sweater follows. Then we're stumbling toward my bedroom, shedding clothes as we go.

When we fall into bed, everything slows down. I take my time touching her and kissing every inch of skin I can reach. She does the same, her hands trembling as they map my body.

"I love you," she whispers against my chest.

"I love you, too." I roll her beneath me and look into her eyes. "So much."

When I slide inside her, she gasps, and her eyes fill with tears. We move together, holding each other tight. It's not frantic or rushed. It's tender and heartbreaking and feels like we're trying to hold on to something that's slipping through our fingers.

It feels like goodbye, even though neither of us says it.

Afterward, we lie tangled together in my sheets. She's tracing the tattoos on my chest with her fingertip, and her breathing evens out as she drifts toward sleep.

I hold her and stare at the ceiling.

She has to decide again if it will be her dream or me. Nashville or Merryville. And just like before, I have no idea what she'll choose.

I think about asking her to stay without begging. I want to tell her I can't lose her again, that I need her here, that Merryville is her home. But that would be selfish, and she's already sacrificed so much. She's already given up years of her life and career to Dominic.

I won't be another person who asks her to give up her dreams, even if it destroys me.

Holiday's breathing deepens, and she's asleep in my arms.

I press a kiss to her hair and close my eyes as I inhale her scent.

Whatever happens, we'll figure it out.

We *have* to.

CHAPTER 36

HOLIDAY

A week has passed since we won the competition.
For seven days, Lucas has pretended everything's fine when I can see the worry painted in his green eyes. It feels like forced normalcy as we continue our routine. We've prepped dough in the afternoons, had dinner with our families, and I've slept in his bed while he holds me like I'll vanish. Lucas has been so damn supportive. It just breaks my heart that he thinks there is any choice other than him.

The day after the contest, he asked me to take the remaining nine days to consider my decision. It was important to him that I didn't rush into it, and he made me promise to think about what I want. Lucas has always been concerned about me regretting my choices. And I get it. I would never want to hold him back from true happiness, either.

The opportunity I've been offered is huge. It deserves serious consideration, so I get his concern. This one decision could change the trajectory of my entire career.

Lucas and I haven't talked about it recently. He doesn't want to influence my decision to stay or to go and is leaving it solely up to me. Yesterday at the bakery, he opened his mouth like he was going to ask, then closed it and turned away to measure flour. Even when I begged him to tell me what he was going to say, he made a joke and said he forgot. I know better, though. We grew up together, and I can read him like a book. He knows that.

My reflection stares back at me from the bathroom mirror. I'm wearing a red sweater, dark jeans, and my hair is down in loose waves, exactly how he likes it. I hear Lucas's boots on the hardwood floor as he gets dressed in his bedroom.

Tonight is the Winter Solstice celebration at the town festival. It's one of the biggest Christmas events that Merryville throws. There will be a tree lighting ceremony, a bonfire, carnival rides, and so much more. It's a time when the whole town comes together to celebrate the magic of Merryville. Myth has it that once people come here, they never want to leave.

I used to believe it was an old wives' tale until I left. My heart brought me back here. It's the only place that's ever felt like home.

"You ready?" Lucas appears in the doorway, wearing a dark green sweater that makes his eyes look like the same shade as an evergreen.

"Yeah." I give him a smile, admiring how handsome he is. "Just need to grab my coat."

I walk past him, trailing my fingers across his abs, feeling his muscles flex as I pass. Touching him, just because I can, is one of my favorite things. For so long, I felt like I was in prison, forced to keep my hands to myself. Now, I take every opportunity I can get. So does he.

Lucas watches me pull my jacket on, and he looks at me like he's trying to memorize this moment. Like we're running out of time.

We're not.

The drive to the fairgrounds takes fifteen minutes. One of his hands stays on the wheel while the other holds mine. Christmas music plays low on the radio, filling the silence, but neither of us sings along.

A VERY MERRY ENEMY

"You okay?" I ask.

"I'm better than okay, Peaches." Lucas squeezes my hand and kisses my knuckles. "Let's have fun tonight."

When we pull into the parking lot, I can see how packed it already is. We get out, and in the distance, the bonfire blazes against the night sky. It's massive. Christmas lights are strung everywhere, wrapped around trees, outlining buildings, and draped between lampposts. The Ferris wheel towers above it all, and it's lit up like a rainbow.

"Wow," I breathe out, closing my eyes. I feel like I'm being transported back in time. Lucas and I always went to the festival together. As we'd walk around, our fingers would lightly brush together, but even when we barely touched, I'd get warm fuzzies.

We walk toward the entrance, and I hook my finger with his. He turns and smiles at me, and I can't help but smile back. In the distance, I can hear a mixture of different songs, kids screaming on rides, and laughter. Then I smell the funnel cakes and wood smoke from the bonfire.

"I've always wanted this," I tell him, and he interlocks his fingers with mine, pulling me closer.

"Me too," he says, stealing a quick kiss.

"Holiday! Lucas!" Claire waves at us by the ticket booth while juggling hot chocolates. Jake is trying to keep Colby from running off as he stands in line at the ticket booth. "You made it!" she says to us as we move closer.

"Colby," Jake says, grabbing his shirt. Colby's face is blue from the cotton candy he must've already devoured.

"Aunt Holiday," he says, reaching toward me. Jake lets him go, and he rushes me, giving me a hug.

"Bee!" I bend down and give him a high five. The last time he came to the bakery, he told me to call him by his nickname.

He runs his hand down my hair. "Your hair looks so pretty today."

"Leave my woman alone," Lucas says to him.

Colby balls up his little fist. "No, she's not."

I chuckle at him. "Yes, actually. I'm dating your uncle Lucas."

"Oh." He looks between us. "Are you going to have babies? So Evan and Ella can have more friends?"

"Uh," I say, watching him. "Not any time soon. Ask Jake and Claire to bring you cousins first."

"Yes!" he says. "I'm going to be the oldest, too. Just like my daddy!"

Jake walks over with a ton of tickets and takes one of the hot chocolates from Claire. She hands Colby one. They've been spoiling him rotten since the twins were born so he doesn't feel left out. Plus, Emma and Hudson have their hands full at the moment, taking care of two newborns. He's a fun kid and is always happy.

"How are you?" Claire asks as Jake and Lucas entertain Colby.

"I'm doing great," I tell her with a smile.

Claire doesn't look convinced, but she also doesn't push.

We walk through the festival grounds, past the winter wonderland and elf village, over to the bonfire. The flames reach toward the sky, and sparks float upward to the stars. A huge crowd is gathered around, with most sitting on logs. Among tourists and townsfolk, I find my family and the Jollys sprinkled throughout.

Everyone wants to talk about the competition and what's next for us. Each question feels loaded, like they're really asking about our entire future. It's added pressure we don't need.

"Dad, please. We're enjoying the moment," I say.

Lucas grabs my hand and lightly brushes his thumb against mine. "We'll see everyone later," he says, waving goodbye to our families.

Seconds later, he's leading me over to where the band is playing some slow country music.

"Wanted to be alone with you," he says, pulling me close.

I wrap my arms around his neck, and we sway slowly to the music. His hands rest on my waist, then slide lower to my hips, pulling me against him. There's no space between us now. I can feel the heat of his body through our clothes, the steady rhythm of his heartbeat against my chest.

"I love this," I whisper against his neck, breathing him in.

"Me too." His voice is strained. One hand moves up to tangle in my hair.

He's not looking at me like we have forever, but more like he's preparing to let me go.

His green eyes seem darker than usual under these dim lights, and they're filled with something I can't explain. I have to tell him right now. No more of this uncertainty.

"Lucas—"

He kisses me before I can finish. Not gentle or sweet, but desperate, like he's claiming me for the entire world to see. His hand tightens in my hair, and I press closer, opening for him. The music fades away. The crowd around us disappears. There's only this—his mouth on mine and his hands gripping me like I'm the only thing keeping his feet on the ground.

When we break apart, we're both breathing hard. His forehead rests against mine, and his eyes are closed.

"Get out of your head," he whispers, his lips curving into a small smile. "I can tell you're thinking."

I let out a surprised laugh against his mouth. "Is that so?"

"Mm-hmm." His hands slide down to my hips again, pulling me closer as we sway. "Also, I'm positive you looking this damn pretty should be criminal."

"Lucas Jolly, are you saying I'm torturing you?"

"Absolutely. You always have." His eyes are full of that familiar mischief I'm used to.

Laughter bursts out of me. "Hush."

"Make me," he says, and something about the way he says it makes my heart do a little flip.

This. This is what I've been missing for fifteen years. No one else can make me laugh, even when emotions are running high. Only his touch sends electricity through my entire body.

"Well," I say, trailing my fingers down his neck, "maybe I will."

I press up on my toes and kiss him again, slower this time. His hands tighten on my hips, and he makes that sound in the back of his throat that drives me wild.

"You're killing me." He breathes against my lips when we break apart.

"It's mutual."

He spins me, pulling my back against his chest as we continue dancing. His arms wrap around my waist, and his lips find that spot just below my ear that makes me shiver.

"Do you have any idea what I want to do to you right now?" he asks, but there's amusement in his voice because he knows I do.

He turns me back around to face him.

"Yes," I say, meeting his eyes.

His brow pops up. "Ferris wheel?"

I nod and bite my lower lip.

We sway like this for a moment, and I tilt my head back to look up at the stars.

This is home. Not a place or a building or a city. This feeling right here.

"What are you thinking?" Lucas asks.

"That I'm exactly where I'm supposed to be."

When he speaks again, his voice has a vulnerable edge to it. "Yes, you are."

The song ends, but we stay planted.

"Dance with me a little longer," I say, rubbing my hand across his scruff. "We can talk on the Ferris wheel."

This time when we sway, it's more intimate. His hand slides up my back and tangles in my hair. I press my face into his neck and breathe him in.

When the song ends, he takes my hand, and we weave

through the festival. His thumb traces circles on my palm and every touch sends little sparks up my arm. When he glances back at me with that smile—the one that's just for me—I can't help but blush.

Lucas Jolly is looking at me like I'm his everything. The way he's always looked at me.

We reach the Ferris wheel and wait in the short line. Lucas pulls me against his side, and I rest my head on his shoulder, fitting against him perfectly like I always have.

"Remember the last time we rode this?" he asks.

"And I kissed you?" I ask innocently. When we were seventeen, I kissed him and he kissed me back. Then I took things too far by sliding his hand under my shirt to touch me. He pulled away and told me *no*.

"Yeah, that's what we'll call it." He leans in and whispers, "I had a hard-on for a week."

I turn to look at him. "Proof I've always crushed on you."

"Whatever, I crushed on you harder. Don't start this argument, you will never win it," he tells me. "I'll kick your ass from here to next Christmas with that one, HoHo."

Laughter releases from me again, and my heart swells. "I tried to kiss you when we were twelve, and you pushed me away. I always made the first move, Jolly."

"Yeah, because Sammy threatened to kick my ass for having a crush on you, and he was bigger than me," he explains, and it's true. Sammy used to tower over all the kids our age because he hit a growth spurt early. "I had to wait until I could defend myself."

"Yeah, yeah," I tell him, loving that we have so much history together. "Wait, you told my brother you had a crush on me way back then?" My mouth falls open.

"Don't act shocked. You knew. You could feel it," he says.

"I could," I say as the operator waves us into a gondola.

We climb in, and the safety door clicks shut. As the wheel starts moving, Lucas pulls me close to his side. We lift up into the air, and the fairground spreads out below us. The bonfire is blazing, the Christmas lights are twinkling, and so many people are celebrating together. It's beautiful and magical and exactly what I remember.

Almost at the very top, everything stops.

The wheel comes to a stop and our bucket sways in the cold breeze.

I turn to look at him, really look at him. His green eyes catch the light from below and above. His smile is soft now, genuine. "I was hoping we'd get stuck up here."

He searches my face, and some of that playfulness fades into something deeper. "The view is incredible."

"It is," I whisper as he leans in and kisses me. His hand slides up my shirt and across my breasts. I gasp.

"Making up for lost time," he whispers, kissing my neck.

I laugh, running my fingers through his hair. He pulls away. "What would you have done if that was my response?"

"Oh, I'd have given you my virginity then," I admit. "It was only ever going to be you."

He smirks, and I look out at the festival. All of the grounds being lit up like this makes it feel like a dream. Merryville sparkles with Christmas lights. I turn back to him and shiver.

Lucas immediately shrugs his coat off. "Here. Take this."

"No way. You'll freeze. Put it back on."

"I'll survive. I'm used to this." He drapes it over my shoulders and pulls me against him. "Just want you warm."

I snuggle into his side, breathing in his scent lingering on the collar of his jacket. We sit in comfortable silence for a moment, just swaying in the breeze. I can hear faint carousel music from below. Kids are laughing, and someone's singing "Jingle Bells" off-key.

Lucas stares out at the view, and I watch his expression shift. The playfulness fades and something more serious takes its place. "I've been thinking a lot this week. About Nashville. About what you should do."

"I—"

"Fifteen years ago, I let you leave because I thought it was the right thing to do. Because I thought you needed to figure out who you were without me. So you knew that I was who you wanted. And I lost you because I didn't speak up."

"Lucas—"

"This time, I'm not letting you go." His voice cracks. "I'm so fucking aware that Mary Carter is offering you everything you've ever worked for. I know it's a chance for you to build something that's completely yours in a city that's exploding with opportunities."

Tears stream down my face, hot against my cold cheeks.

Lucas cups my face in his hands. "I won't be another person who controls you or holds you back or makes you choose between your dreams and your home. You deserve Nashville. You deserve everything. But I want to be selfish because I'm so fucking in love with you that it hurts."

"I'm in love with you, too." My voice comes out shaky. I kiss him, pouring everything I have into it. "I'm not going anywhere. I already turned down the offer."

Lucas goes completely still. "When? You promised you'd think about it. You said—"

"The morning after the contest. I kept that promise, but I didn't need ten days to know you're everything I want in my life. You're it for me, Lucas. I can't imagine a future without you. That decision was one of the *easiest* ones I've ever made."

The words hang in the freezing air between us. Our breath fogs in the space separating us. Lucas stares at me like I just spoke a different language.

"You…" The sentence dies before he can finish it.

"I choose you, Lucas Jolly. Because I'm already living my dream. Right now. At this moment." I take his face in my hands to make sure his gaze stays on me. "I want to wake up next to you every morning. I want to build a life that's ours. You're what I choose. And I always will, every single time."

Lucas kisses me so passionately that he steals my breath away. "You're staying," Lucas says between kisses and tears, like he needs me to confirm it. "But what about the job opportunity? What about—"

"I already get to create badass recipes that sell out like crazy. Emma's already agreed to expand the bakery. I wanted people to eat my pastries and love every single one of them. I already have that. And I have you. I can have my cake and eat it, too."

Lucas pulls me against him so tightly, I can barely breathe. His face is buried in my neck, and I can feel him shaking.

"I love you so much," he murmurs against my skin.

"You're my home," I whisper.

The Ferris wheel lurches back to life and we descend. Lucas pulls back to look at me, and he's happier than I've seen him in days.

"Move in with me," he mutters against my ear after leaning in close again.

"What?"

"If you want to fall asleep with me every night and wake up to me every morning, you have to move in with me," he says.

My breath catches. "Really? You don't think we're rush—"

"I built that house for us, Peaches," Lucas says, confirming what I've always thought. It was too close to the dream house we planned. "You're basically living with me now. Make it official."

"Okay."

"The door code is zero-seven-zero-four," he says.

Everything inside me melts. "You chose *that* date?"

"Unforgettable," Lucas says. "That day confirmed for me that you were the love of my entire life. It felt right."

Speaking is impossible. I'm nodding and crying and kissing him. It's all I can manage.

"Is that a yes?" Lucas asks against my mouth.

"Yes. Gosh, yes. Yes to everything."

The gondola reaches the ground, and the operator opens the gate for us. We stumble out and he grabs my hand.

"Want to go *home*?" he asks, like it's already ours.

"That sounds nice," I say, not knowing what I did to deserve him.

As Lucas wraps his arms around me, my heart flutters. Excitement radiates off us both.

"Promise there are no regrets?" he asks.

"Not a damn one."

And I mean it with everything in me.

Being here with Lucas in Merryville, living this beautiful life together, is pure happiness.

This Christmas, I learned that home is love. Home is Lucas. Home is *us*. And I'm never leaving this again.

As we drive back to the Christmas tree farm, I glance over at Lucas and know, without a single doubt, I made the right decision.

CHAPTER 37

LUCAS

Mawmaw's house is packed this afternoon. Every seat at the dining table is taken, and folding chairs are squeezed in wherever they'll fit. Colby is under the table with a sweet roll, making engine noises as he plays. Conversations overlap each other from every direction as Holiday's dad and mine argue about whether we'll actually get a dusting of snow this year or not. Her mom asks Claire about married life, and Sammy and Jake place bets on tomorrow's football games. Hudson stopped by quickly to give their love and make plates but left to get back to Emma and the babies.

The smells and sounds of Christmas fill the house. Mawmaw made ham, glazed with brown sugar and pineapple, her famous mac and cheese that she only makes for special occasions, green bean casserole, and sweet rolls so fresh that steam rises when they're broken open. Three different pies are cooling on the counter, and of course, we brought *The One* because my family begged for it.

Holiday sits beside me, so close that our legs touch and our arms brush together. Every few minutes, I reach under the table and squeeze her thigh just to remind her that she's here, and she's mine.

"Where's Colby?" Holiday asks, looking around the table.

Mawmaw points under the table. "I don't know where he is."

He giggles from below. I make a fart noise with my mouth, and he rushes out, pretending like it stunk.

"Yeah, yeah. Time to eat, kid," I say as he climbs into the chair next to Mawmaw. When Hudson tried to take him home earlier, Colby cried and clung to Mawmaw's dress until Jake offered to keep him. My brothers are so good with kids. They make it look easy.

Mawmaw scans over the table from her spot at the end, and she looks satisfied as she gazes at everyone. "I love Christmas Eve."

My dad says grace, and then we pass around plates, family style. Rolls are passed, turkey and cranberries are slid onto plates, and I run out of room.

"So, I heard you and Holiday are living together?" Mawmaw asks.

I nearly choke on the bite of macaroni I was swallowing. "I do not want to be the center of conversation tonight. Thank you."

"That's not an answer," Mawmaw pushes.

Everyone stops eating, and their forks pause mid-bite. All eyes turn to us and wait for an answer.

"It's true," Holiday says as her cheeks turn pink.

"Well, it's about time," Mawmaw says.

I kiss Holiday's temple and smile. "That's what I said."

"So, when are you two getting married?" Mawmaw asks suddenly, looking right at us with that knowing smile of hers.

Holiday's eyes go wide at the question.

"Mawmaw," I say, trying to keep my voice casual. "Holiday isn't even fully moved in yet. It's been three days, so you might want to slow down a bit."

"When you know, you know." Mawmaw winks at me.

"We've got plenty of time," I say.

Holiday laughs. "Maybe we should just elope right now?"

"Honey, now don't be ridiculous," Mawmaw says. "Not the night Santa is coming to town."

She gets the hint that we don't want to discuss this and drops the conversation. Or so we think.

"But just know that I'm not getting any younger, and I want to see my grandbabies settled down."

The conversation shifts to other topics, but my heart is still racing.

Dinner stretches on for hours with too much food and too much laughter filling the house. After dessert, Mawmaw moves us all to the living room where she prepares to read *'Twas the Night Before Christmas*.

Mawmaw makes us all a glass of her famous, but dangerous, eggnog as we gather.

She pulls out a worn book with a red cover that's been passed down through the generations. She settles into her rocking chair and opens it up. When we were kids, Mawmaw always insisted on reading this classic story with the dramatic pauses and inflections. Holiday's hand finds mine and she squeezes. Colby stirs on the couch, and I realize he's asleep. When Mawmaw finishes, she closes the book and looks around. "Now, time to get home and snuggle into bed before Santa arrives. Merry Christmas, my babies."

"Merry Christmas, Mawmaw," we all say in unison.

People start gathering their coats and heading toward the door around seven. The sun has set, and the Christmas lights on her house are twinkling.

Jake carries a still-sleeping Colby to the car while Claire follows with leftover pie. My parents hug us both and head out into the cold.

Holiday and I stay behind to help Mawmaw clean up the kitchen. She tells stories about past Christmases while we wash the dishes. It ranges from tales of me and my brothers fighting

A VERY MERRY ENEMY

over toys, to Hudson eating all the cookies, to Jake knocking over the tree when he was five.

"You two better get home," Mawmaw finally says, shooing us toward the door. She hugs us both. "Merry Christmas, my babies. See you tomorrow."

The drive home is quiet, but we're both smiling. I love having her with me at family events. Tomorrow we're visiting her folks. My hand rests on Holiday's thigh. When we pull into our driveway, I look at the house I built. It's lit up with the lights my brothers strung when I was spiraling. So much has changed since November first. So much I never could've predicted.

Inside the house, the tree glows in the corner. I start a fire in the fireplace while Holiday makes hot chocolate in the kitchen. We settle on the couch together with her head resting on my shoulder.

"I can't believe I'm spending Christmas with you," she says. "When I initially showed up at the bakery, and you were so angry to see me, I just…I didn't think we'd ever have a chance again."

"I tried to fight it." I kiss the top of her head while my heart races. "I lost."

"Ready to exchange our sentimental gifts?" I ask. We'd agreed to share one special gift, something that money can't really buy, on Christmas Eve, then open the other gifts in the morning, in our matching pajamas. I immediately agreed, because all season, I've been working on something for her.

"Sure." She smiles at me. "You'll *never* guess what I got you. But you're gonna love it."

I walk to the tree and pull out the box I wrapped last week. Holiday grabs something flat from behind the couch, where she must've hidden it earlier.

We sit facing each other by the fire.

"You should open yours first," I say, wanting to see her reaction.

Holiday carefully tears the paper to reveal a hand-carved

wooden recipe box I made for her. She gasps out loud. Her fingers trace the carvings on the lid that illustrate rolling pins, whisks, and measuring spoons.

"Lucas," she breathes out. "You made this?"

"Yeah. Anytime I thought about you over the season, I carved." I watch her open the box. "I wanted you to have a special place to keep all the recipes we're going to create."

She pulls out the top card where I wrote our winning recipe in my messy handwriting. "You wrote it down."

"I figured we should start the collection with the thing that helped bring you back to me."

Holiday's crying now as she looks at me. "This is the most beautiful thing anyone's ever given me in my entire life."

"Aw. I'm happy you like it," I tell her.

She slides her lips across mine and then pulls back. "I love it so much. Now, please, open yours."

I open the lid of the box, and inside is a diary. "What is this?"

A laugh releases from her. "Open it."

Inside, it's full of pages in her handwriting. Some are recipes, and then I come across different entries from when we were teenagers.

Dear Diary,

Today I saw Lucas. He was wearing that black hoodie that made him look so cute. We were lying on the trampoline together, and when he looked at me, I almost kissed him. I didn't, which is a good thing because Sammy came back outside right after that. I blushed, and I couldn't help it. I don't know what to do. We're friends and will always be friends, but I like

> him. Like <u>like</u> him. And I can't tell anyone. Ugh. This sucks! Not to mention I have this HUGE pimple on my chin.
>
> H

I chuckle. "This is the best gift you could've ever given me."

"I was cleaning out my closet at my parents' house and came across a box with every note you ever wrote me, and years of journals full of me confessing how I felt about you."

"Years?"

"Literally," she says.

We sit there for a moment, both of us emotional over gifts that mean more than anything expensive ever could.

"Thank you so much for this," she whispers against my mouth.

"Thank you, Peaches."

Holiday stands to turn off the overhead light so we can sit in the dark by the fire, and my heart starts pounding harder in my chest.

When her back is to me, I drop down to the floor on one knee and pull out the small velvet box that's been burning a hole in my pocket all night. My hands are shaking as I open it.

The firelight catches on the diamond.

When she turns around and sees me on one knee for her, all I can do is smile.

This is it.

This is the moment I've been waiting for my entire life.

CHAPTER 38

❄

HOLIDAY

I turn around from switching off the light and freeze when I see Lucas on one knee in front of the Christmas tree.

Time stops.

My heart stops.

Everything stops.

In his hands, he's holding a small velvet box, and inside sits a ring, sparkling in the firelight. It's a round diamond on a delicate gold band—simple and timeless and absolutely breathtaking. It's the exact ring I told him I'd want if anyone were to ever propose to me.

My knees go weak, and I have to steady myself.

"Lucas," I breathe out, my hand flying to my mouth.

"Hi." He's grinning at me, wearing a sexy expression.

"Hi," I manage to choke out.

This is happening.

This is really happening.

"So, I have something to ask you." His voice is rough with emotion, but there's that playful edge that I adore.

A surprised laugh bursts out of me even as I start trembling.

"I've been in love with you since we were literal kids." Lucas takes a shaky breath. "Since I kissed you under Mawmaw's mistletoe when we were sixteen. Since you held my hand at the lake. Since the time at the carnival when you tried to get me to touch your boob. Since July Fourth, when we gave each other everything that we were."

I can barely breathe as tears stream down my cheeks.

This man. This beautiful, incredible man.

"I stayed in love with you when you left. Every day you were gone, I wondered if you were happy, if you were safe, if you ever thought about me. When you came back broken, I promised myself that I'd help put you back together. That I wouldn't let you be the girl who got away and haunted me for my entire existence." His voice cracks, and he takes in another breath.

"You choosing me was the greatest gift I've ever been given. And I want to keep choosing you, too. Every single day for the rest of my life."

I can't help but sniffle as I wipe my tears away.

"I want to keep conserving water with you. I want to have babies with you and teach them how to cut down Christmas trees and make gingerbread houses. I want to sit on our porch and watch the seasons change. I want to bake cookies with you when we're eighty. I want a lifetime with you, Holiday."

He looks up at me with so much emotion in his green eyes that it steals what's left of my breath completely away.

"I want to have as much fun growing old with you as I had growing up with you." He smiles, giving me that dimple. "I want fifty more years of arguing about who crushed harder or who loves the other more. I want to laugh until we can't breathe and make love until we're too tired to move. I want every ordinary weekday and every big milestone. I want all of it. And I promise to always make you laugh, even when you're mad. I promise to support every single one of your dreams. I want you exactly as you are, and I will never, ever try to change you. And I promise to never let a day go by without showing you how much you mean to me."

He pulls the ring from the box with shaking hands and holds it up.

"Holiday Patterson, will you please marry me? Will you be my wife and let me spend the rest of my life making you as happy as you make me?"

I try to speak but no sound comes out.

My throat is too tight.

This is Lucas asking me to be his forever.

The boy I've always loved is on one knee, asking me to marry him. I feel like I'm dreaming.

I drop to my knees in front of him so we're face-to-face, both of us shaking with happiness.

"Yes," I choke out. "Yes, Lucas! Yes, yes, a thousand times, yes!"

His hands tremble from adrenaline as he slides the ring onto my finger.

I hold out my hand, watching it sparkle and send little rainbows dancing across the room.

"This is exactly how I dreamed it would be," I say, unable to look away from the gem.

"I bought it fifteen years ago." He wipes moisture from my cheeks with his thumbs.

"What?" I ask.

He nods. "Yeah."

More tears stream down my face. "This is exactly how I dreamed it, too."

I laugh through the emotion overwhelming me. "You were going to propose to me back then?"

"Yes." He cups my face in his hands. "You were always supposed to be my wife."

"I really, really like the sound of that," I confess.

Our lips crash together, and it's full of love and promise.

He takes my hand and we stand. He places his other hand on my waist and we sway back and forth, dancing without music.

I rest my head on his chest and close my eyes, letting myself live in this moment. The fire crackles beside us, and the tree lights twinkle. I've never felt more complete in my life.

"I love you so much," he whispers against my hair.

"I love you, too." I pull back to look up at him. "This has been the best Christmas I've ever had."

He spins me around. "Big agree."

We sway like that for a few more minutes, just holding each other, both of us smiling and laughing.

As his hands slide down to my hips, the energy shifts.

The playfulness melts into something hotter and more urgent.

"Take me upstairs," I whisper against his mouth.

He doesn't need to be told twice. Lucas carries me up the stairs to our bedroom. He flicks on the bedside lamp and golden light fills the room.

For a moment, we just stand there looking at each other. Then he slowly pulls my sweater over my head. I reach for his shirt, and we undress each other piece by piece until we're both naked.

"You're so beautiful," he says, his voice full of want.

"So are you."

He guides me to the bed, and I pull him down with me. His weight settles over me, and I wrap my legs around his waist.

Our eyes stay locked on each other, and it feels different when he slides deep inside me. It's more intense, full of emotion, like we're sealing this promise between us. He lowers his forehead to mine, our noses brushing, our breath tangled in the same small space. We just look at each other, every second stretching longer until the whole world seems to fit between our hearts as he thrusts deeper inside me.

The kiss that follows isn't rushed. It's like we've waited our whole lives for this one chance. Every place his hands touch feels like a promise for our time ahead.

Everything around us fades away. It's only us, finally letting go of all the years that kept us apart.

When we move together, it isn't about need. It's about finding home. It's about forgiveness and having the kind of love that can survive everything.

Lucas whispers my name like a prayer. All I can do is hold him tighter, afraid that if I let go, the moment will disappear.

We make love until we're both trembling and shaking with satisfaction. Lucas collapses beside me and pulls me into his arms. We lie there tangled together, breathing hard, staring upward.

"Can we add glow-in-the-dark stars to your ceiling?"

He shifts to his side and grins, pulling me closer so he can steal a kiss. "Absolutely."

We stay wrapped in each other's arms, hearts pounding, our bodies sticking together. The firelight from the fireplace in the bedroom dances against the ring on my finger, scattering sparks across the room like tiny stars.

He strokes my hair and breathes against my temple. "Merry Christmas, HoHo."

"Merry Christmas, my fiancé."

"Oh, I love the sound of that," he says, leaning forward to kiss my shoulder.

"Really? Just wait until you're my husband."

"I can't wait," he admits. "Because honestly, I'd marry you right now if I could."

"What about the Fourth of July?" I smile against his lips. "Make it super special."

"Love the sound of that," he says as I trace his jaw with my lips.

I rest my head on his chest and close my eyes as he draws circles on my back.

All the pieces of my life have finally clicked into place.

"I can't wait to see everyone's faces when we tell them," I say. "Mawmaw is going to lose her mind."

"They all will." Lucas chuckles. "Let's tell them tomorrow."

"Sounds good." I let myself live in this moment with him, memorizing the way his strong arms feel around me. "Lucas?"

"Mm-hmm?"

"Thank you for waiting for me and never giving up on us. Thank you for accepting me and loving me exactly as I am." My voice gets thick with emotion. "And for asking me to marry you."

"You don't have to thank me for any of that," he says as he keeps holding on to me. "Being with you has always been the easiest choice I've ever made, and the only thing I've ever wanted. You make everything in my life better."

I press a kiss to his chest. "Good night, future hubby."

"Good night, Peaches."

I snuggle into his arms and let my eyes drift closed. His breathing evens out, and I know he's close to sleep.

But I stay awake a little longer, just taking in how right this feels.

I'm marrying Lucas Jolly. The boy I fell in love with at sixteen. The man who waited years for me. The person who makes me laugh and challenges me and accepts me unconditionally.

This is what happiness feels like. It's not a big city or a fancy career or a prestigious partnership.

The magic of Merryville brought me back, and there is no other place I'd rather be.

Lucas is my home.

Lucas is my future.

And he's my proof that wishes upon stars come true, too.

EPILOGUE

LUCAS

Jake and Claire's house is packed when we arrive.

The living room has been transformed, with gold and silver decorations hanging from every surface. Balloons cluster in the corners and a massive "Happy New Year" banner stretches across the fireplace. Music pumps through the speakers, and at least thirty people are already here, dancing and drinking and celebrating.

"There they are!" Jake shouts when he spots Holiday and me walking through the door. He's wearing a ridiculous gold party hat that says "New Year, New Me" in glittery letters.

Holiday grins at me. She looks incredible tonight in a black dress that hugs her curves and makes my mouth go dry. Her hair is down in those waves I love, and the ring on her left hand catches every light in the room.

I can't stop staring at her. Can't stop thinking about how, two months ago, I was angry and hurt when she walked back into my life. Now we're living together and planning our future.

"Stop looking at me like that," I whisper in her ear.

"I can't," she admits.

Even though the entire town practically knows by now, we decided to officially announce our engagement tonight.

A VERY MERRY ENEMY

Christmas Day was spent telling our families. Now that those who are most important to us know, we no longer have to keep our love a secret.

We make our way through the crowd. I recognize people from high school and friends from town. Claire has outdone herself with the food. There's a massive cheese board, sliders, and about five different dips spread across the dining table and counter.

"Lucas! Holiday!" Claire rushes over with two champagne flutes, her own party hat slightly crooked on her head. "You're here!"

"Thanks for hosting," Holiday says, taking a glass.

"Are you kidding? I love New Year's." Claire beams.

"I love it, too, wifey." Jake appears beside us with a beer in hand. "Ready to tell everyone?"

"I guess," I mutter.

Jake climbs onto a barstool so he towers over everyone, and Claire yells at him to be careful. My brother cups his hands around his mouth. "Everyone! Shut up for, like, ten seconds!"

The music gets turned down and conversations die out as people turn to look.

"My baby brother has an announcement," Jake says, gesturing to us.

All eyes turn in our direction. Holiday's hand finds mine, and I give it a squeeze.

"So," I start, pulling Holiday closer to my side. "We've got some news."

Holiday holds up her left hand and the diamond catches the light. "We're engaged!"

The room explodes with cheers.

Even though Wendy and Bella already know, they rush over. So do Sammy, Eli, Matteo, and Dean. Everyone is talking at once. The girls surround Holiday, squealing and demanding to see the ring up close. I catch snippets of their conversations. The guys slap me on the back, and Jake makes a joke about me finally settling down.

"Dude, I knew you were waiting for Holiday," Marcus, one of my old high school friends, says.

"That obvious?" I ask, watching her just a few feet away from me. Our eyes catch each other, and she grins.

I love that we can hold a full-ass conversation without saying a single word.

"Yeah, everyone knew you two had it bad." He smirks.

Another friend, Ryan, hands me a beer. "Did you cry?"

"Like a baby," I say with a chuckle.

Everyone laughs, and someone starts a round of congratulatory shots. Within minutes, Holiday and I are bombarded with the same questions over and over.

When's the wedding?

Who's in the wedding party?

Am I invited?

Holiday tucks some hair behind her ear as she shows off the ring. She's glowing.

Every few seconds, she glances over at me. When our eyes meet, she smiles like we're sharing a secret.

About twenty minutes into the celebration, I feel a hand on my shoulder. I turn to find Hudson standing there, looking slightly out of breath.

"Hey, man. Didn't think you'd make it," I say.

"I'm not staying." He glances around, making sure no one's paying attention. "Can I talk to you for a second? Outside?"

"Yeah, sure."

I follow him out to the back porch. It's freezing compared to the party inside. Hudson reaches into his jacket and pulls out a cream-colored envelope. It's thick, bulging with something more substantial than just a letter.

"Emma wanted me to bring this to you." He hands it to me. "Give it to Holiday at midnight. Not before. She was very specific about that. And trust me when I say, you do not want to piss her off regarding this, okay?"

I turn the envelope over in my hands. It's heavier than I expected. "What is it?"

"If I told you, it would be a death wish." Hudson grins, but there's something in his expression I can't read. "But seriously, don't give it to her early. Right after midnight, got it?"

"Why would she care—" I stop.

He claps me on the shoulder. "Don't be a stubborn ass and just listen to me. Congrats on the engagement. You two are so good together. You always have been."

"Thanks. You sure you can't stay? Even for one drink?"

"Nah, I need to get back. Emma's handling three kids under six by herself right now, including a very energetic Colby, who's convinced he can stay up until midnight. Doesn't help that Mawmaw sent him home with a candy basket." He laughs. "I just promised I'd deliver that. Midnight, remember. Not a second before."

"Got it. Midnight."

Hudson just grins and heads back through the house. I hear the front door close a minute later.

I look down at the envelope, then tuck it inside my jacket pocket and head back to the party.

When I go back inside, Holiday's laughing near Claire and Jake at the food table. One of Wendy's friends—Tara, I think—is holding Holiday's hand up to examine the ring in the light.

"It's exactly what I would've picked," Holiday explains. "Simple, classic."

"Lucas has good taste," Tara says.

"He does." Holiday looks over and catches me watching her. She excuses herself and makes her way over to me. "Where'd you go?"

"Hudson stopped by real quick."

"Is everything okay? Emma and the twins? Colby?"

"Everything's fine. He just had to drop something off."

"Oh." She wraps her arms around my waist. "Good. I'm having the best time. Everyone's so happy for us."

"Me too." I kiss the top of her head.

The party continues, and we dance in Jake's living room to everything from Beyoncé to old country songs. Holiday requests a few songs and pulls me close, and we sway together while our friends whistle and cheer.

Someone starts a game of beer pong in the kitchen as Claire sings to the music. Her voice is slightly off-key from the champagne, but she's having so much fun that nobody cares. When she finishes, everyone cheers, and she takes an exaggerated bow.

The night blurs together. We have more drinks, more dancing, and more celebrating. At one point, Holiday pulls out her phone and snaps a photo of us kissing and tells me it's going on our fridge.

After eleven, I pull Holiday onto the back porch for some air. It's freezing outside, but we're both overheated from dancing and drinking. The stars are out, and I can hear fireworks already going off in the distance as people celebrate early.

"I think this might be the best week of my life," Holiday says, leaning against the railing. Her cheeks are flushed from the champagne, and she's never looked more beautiful.

I wrap my arms around her from behind. "I have to agree."

She turns in my arms to face me. "Did you think this was possible?"

"In my dreams." I brush hair away from her face. "It's what I wished for."

"I feel so lucky," she says.

"Me too." I kiss her softly. "You're the best thing that ever happened to me."

She laughs and wraps her arms around my neck. "I love you."

"I love you, too, Peaches."

We stay out there for a few more minutes, just holding each

A VERY MERRY ENEMY

other under the stars. One skips across the sky and she points up at it.

"Did you see it?" she asks excitedly.

"I did. Did you make your wish?"

"Of course," she tells me, and I notice how her expression softens.

"It's eleven forty-five!" someone yells from inside.

We head back in, and the living room is packed now. Someone's passing out more champagne and noisemakers. The TV is on with the New Year's coverage from Times Square, the massive ball glowing against the night sky.

Everyone's laughing and talking, the energy building as midnight approaches. I keep my arm around Holiday's waist, wanting her close. She leans into me and I feel the ring on her finger brush against my hand.

My fiancée. My future wife.

The countdown starts with ten minutes to go. Everyone begins taking pictures, making last-minute resolutions, hugging friends they haven't seen in a while.

"Five minutes!" Jake announces, turning up the TV volume.

Holiday looks up at me. "This is it. New year. New life."

"Same old us," I say, stealing a quick kiss.

The room gets louder as everyone gathers around, champagne glasses raised.

Everyone starts counting down from sixty seconds.

"Fifty seconds!"

"Forty seconds!"

Holiday's hand finds mine. She's grinning up at me, and I see our whole future in her eyes.

"Twenty seconds!"

"Ten! Nine! Eight!"

"Seven! Six! Five!"

"Four! Three! Two! One!"

"Happy New Year!"

The room explodes with cheers. Confetti cannons are

popped and gold and silver paper rains down. The TV displays the ball dropping in Times Square, and "Auld Lang Syne" starts playing through the speakers.

I pull Holiday into my arms and kiss her like it's the first time and the last time and every time in between. She tastes like champagne and happiness and home.

"Happy New Year, Peaches," I say against her lips.

"Happy New Year, future husband."

Around us, our friends are hugging and kissing and celebrating. Confetti is everywhere. Bella's crying happy tears. Jake and Claire are taking Polaroids of the crowd.

Then I remember.

"Oh, wait! I have something for you."

Holiday pulls back, confused. "What?"

I reach into my jacket pocket and pull out the envelope Hudson gave me earlier. The cream-colored paper is slightly warm from being against my chest all night.

"Hudson dropped this off earlier. It's from Emma. She said to give it to you at midnight."

Holiday's eyes go wide as she takes the envelope. She turns it over, examining it like it might have answers on the outside.

"What is it?"

I chuckle, realizing how alike we are. "Funny enough, I asked the same question. But I have no idea. Hudson wouldn't tell me."

EPILOGUE

HOLIDAY

I stare down at the cream-colored envelope in my hands.

It's heavier than it looks, bulging with whatever's inside. My name is written across the front in Emma's neat handwriting.

"What do you think it is?" I ask Lucas.

"Only one way to find out."

Around us, the party continues. People are hugging and celebrating the new year. Confetti is still floating down from the ceiling. But I'm frozen, staring at this envelope like it might contain the secrets of the universe.

"Come on. The anticipation might fucking kill me at this point." Lucas takes my hand and leads me down the hallway to Jake and Claire's guest bedroom. He closes the door behind us, muffling the noise from the party.

I carefully tear open the envelope.

A folded letter slides out first. I unfold it and recognize Emma's handwriting immediately.

Holiday,

> It was never my dream to own a bakery, but I've been told that it was always yours. You've poured your heart and soul into the place over the season. You created recipes that had people lining up for hours to try. You turned a small-town bakery into something magical. And you made it what it is today. That's why I've decided to transfer the ownership of the bakery to you. Congratulations. You're now the proud owner of Jolly Cookie Shop. The paperwork and title are enclosed.
>
> And don't tell me it's too much. You've earned this, and you deserve it.
>
> Welcome to the family.
>
> Oh, I just have one small request—unlimited pastries for life? Happy New Year, sister!
>
> Love,
> Emma

I lose my balance, and my ass bounces against the mattress.

I read the letter again, wondering if I'm dreaming or if I've had too much champagne. This doesn't make sense.

My hands start shaking as I reach back into the envelope and pull out the rest of the contents. It's full of official documents with gold seals and embossed lettering. Title documents. LLC transfer paperwork. Business licenses.

"Oh my goodness." I breathe out.

"What?" Lucas moves closer, kneeling in front of me so we're eye level. "What is it? Tell me."

I can't speak. My entire body is trembling as I flip through the papers, each one confirming what the letter said.

"She gave me the bakery," I whisper. "Emma gave me the bakery."

I hand the letter to Lucas, and his eyes scan the page. His face changes from confusion, then to shock, then to something that looks like awe.

"Holy shit," he mutters. "Congrats, HoHo. This is what you've always wanted."

It hits me all at once, and I burst into tears. I'm not crying because I'm sad, but because I'm so overwhelmed with joy, I can't control it. Too many emotions hit me, all at the same time.

"Aw, sweetheart," Lucas says, wiping my tears away.

"I can't accept this." I pull back, wiping my face. "I need to call her right now and tell her she can't do this."

"It's late."

"I don't care!" With shaking hands, I grab my phone from my pocket.

Lucas stops me. "Listen to me. Emma isn't going to let you give it back to her. I know her."

"It's too much," I whisper.

"She's a billionaire," Lucas says. "Her dream was to be a mom. I'm sure the twins made her realize that owning the bakery isn't something she wants. You're the best choice, and it helps that you're family. She could build a thousand bakeries if she wanted. The recipes you created, the way you light up every morning when you walk through those doors—that's all you. You made it special, and Emma—hell, the whole town—saw that."

I'm so full of emotion, I can barely speak. "I don't know what to say."

"Tomorrow, or actually, later today, you'll call Emma and tell her thank you."

A laugh bursts out of me. "Is this real?"

"Based on this paperwork? Fuck, yeah."

I wipe away more tears. "I get to have it all. The man I love, my dream business, and a loving family."

"Lucky girl," he whispers in awe.

I collapse back onto the bed, still holding the documents. Lucas sits beside me and takes my hand. "I am so happy for you."

"Thank you. I think I'm in shock."

"Me too." He captures my lips. "We should go home and ring in the new year the right way."

"Thought you'd never ask," I say.

We walk back into the living room, hand in hand. The party is still going strong. The music is pumping, people are dancing, and the champagne is still flowing.

We say quick goodbyes to Jake and Claire, making excuses about being tired. Nobody questions it because it's almost one in the morning and everyone is winding down.

The drive home is quiet. I clutch the documents in my lap, still trying to wrap my head around what just happened. Lucas keeps one hand on my thigh, making sure I know he's right there with me.

When we pull into our driveway, I look at the house he built for us, how he planned for a future he wasn't sure he'd ever get. This is our house. And in the morning, I'll wake up as the owner of Jolly Cookie Shop.

This doesn't feel like real life.

Inside, Lucas locks the door behind us and turns to me with that look in his eyes that makes my stomach flip.

"Come here," he says.

He leads me upstairs, and we take our time undressing each other. His lips find my neck, my collarbone, and my shoulder. Every touch feels more meaningful. Like we're celebrating, not just the new year, but everything our future holds.

When we finally make love, it's slow and full of emotion. Our breaths and panting mix together until we chase our end. We lie in bed, looking up at the glow-in-the-dark stars.

"I'm so proud of you," he whispers as we lie tangled in the sheets.

"You know what's wild?" I say into the darkness.

"Tell me."

"I have everything now. You, the bakery, this life we're building." I trace patterns on his chest. "The only thing that would make it complete is a baby."

Lucas is quiet for a moment, then I feel his chest rumble with laughter.

"What?" I lift my head to look at him.

"Well," he says while grinning, that dimple appearing, "the way we just went at it, we might've made one."

I burst out laughing and swat his chest. "Lucas!"

"Or two! I'm just saying, Peaches. That was some pretty solid baby-making right there."

"You're absolutely ridiculous. Don't you dare wish twins on me."

"Aw, you love it." He slides his lips across mine, taking my bottom lip into his mouth and sucking. "But for real, when you're ready, I'm ready. I want everything with you."

"Me too." I smile against his mouth.

He yawns. "We've got time, sweetheart. No need to rush. Damn, I love you."

"I love you more."

"No, you fucking don't," he mutters, but I can tell he's grinning.

"I guess I get to have my cake and eat it too," I whisper.

"Enjoy the buffet, babe. It all worked out exactly how it was supposed to." Lucas kisses my forehead.

I close my eyes, wrapped in his arms, knowing I'm living my ultimate dream.

Two months ago, I came home a broken woman.

Tonight, I'm engaged to the love of my life and I own a bakery.

I have no doubts that I'm exactly where I'm supposed to be.

Lucas is my home.

**Want to see more of Merryville and Mawmaw Jolly?
Read The Friend Situation
<u>books2read.com/thefriendsituation</u>**

LUCAS & HOLIDAY BONUS SCENE

CHAPTER 1 (BONUS)

❄

LUCAS

ONE YEAR LATER

The tree lot is absolute chaos.

Customers are everywhere—picking out trees, asking questions, dragging kids away from the hot chocolate stand at the snack shack. It's opening day of tree season and we've been slammed all day. A family of five is arguing over whether they want a seven-foot or a nine-foot tree. Two teenagers are taking selfies in front of one of the biggest tree on the lot. An old man is lecturing Jake about proper tree care like my brother hasn't been doing this his entire life. But Jake just smiles and nods.

This is exactly how it was a year ago when Holiday walked back into my life.

It's been one year. Somehow it feels like yesterday and forever ago all at the same time.

Jake is helping a family wrestle a ten-footer onto their car roof while Hudson deals with the payment line that's wrapped around the barn. The air smells like fresh-cut pine and the coffee Claire brought earlier. Christmas music plays from the speakers we set up, competing with the sound of chainsaws and laughter.

A VERY MERRY ENEMY

I'm in the middle of explaining to an older couple why Jolly Cookies are the best in the state of Texas when I see her.

Holiday carries two large boxes with the Jolly Cookies logo printed on the side. She's wearing jeans and a flannel over a white t-shirt, her dark hair is pulled back into a high ponytail. Even from here, I can see the sparkling diamond on her left hand catching the sunlight.

My wife.

My heart does that skip thing every time I see her. Even after having a crush for decades, us living together for almost a year, and being married for four months, the sight of her still gets me. It's the one thing that's never changed. She owns Jolly Cookies now and when Emma made the announcement at the Valentine Day Festival, Merryville went crazy.

She added a coffee bar, hired a manager and more employees, and expanded the building. The place is thriving. We wake up at five every morning and have coffee together, then we ride to the farm together.

Our lives are busy as hell. Some days they're exhausting, but I wouldn't change a damn thing. I'm living my dream.

We got married on July fourth under the trees on this very property where we used to play as kids. Holiday wore a simple white dress that made my breath catch when I saw her walking toward me with her dad. We said our vows as the sun set, and I barely got through mine without kissing her. As our lips finally touched, fireworks went off in the distance, giving our guests a show.

The reception was at our house. We had dinner and dancing and Mawmaw's famous punch that got everyone drunk. Jake gave a speech about how he always knew we'd end up together. Hudson cried, which shocked everyone. Sammy threatened me in the most loving way possible.

It was perfect. Small and intimate and exactly us.

"Excuse me," I tell the guy I was chatting with.

I make my way over to the cookie shop.

"Hey, Peaches," I say, sliding my arm around her waist from behind.

She leans back against me and I feel her body relax. "Need some cookies?"

"Just need you, HoHo." I kiss her neck, breathing in the scent of vanilla and cinnamon that always clings to her skin.

She turns in my arms and there's a twinkle her eyes. "Then let's go."

My stomach does a weird flip. "Right now?"

"Why not?"

I glance around the lot. It's packed with at least fifty people browsing trees, but Jake and Hudson have it under control. Dean, Matteo, and Eli are also helping. It's all hands on deck today and I think they can survive without me for a bit.

Holiday steps closer, her hands sliding up my chest. "I need you." Her voice drops lower and heat floods her eyes. "Can we go home? Right now?"

My brain short-circuits for a second. "The lot is crazy busy. You know what? Fuck it."

With how she's looking at me, I couldn't say no if I tried.

"I need to tell Jake. The bakery good for now?"

She chuckles. "They can handle it."

I take her hand and we weave through the customers toward the old barn where my brother is. It's same barn where we hooked up during our wild summer. I remember pushing her against the wall and kissing her like I'd been waiting my whole life to do it. Because I had been.

When I'm close to him, he stops his conversation and glances at me.

"What's up?" he asks.

"I need to leave for like an hour. Can you and Hudson handle it?"

Jake looks over at Holiday. "Seriously? Right now? Opening day?"

"Shut up," I tell him. "I'll be back in an hour. I'm not asking."

"Fine. But you owe me!"

I flip him off and he laughs so loud a few customers turn to look.

Holiday's already walking toward my truck. I follow her, my heart pounding harder with each step.

The drive home takes ten minutes but feels like forever. She keeps her hand on my thigh, and her fingers trace patterns that make it hard to concentrate on the road. I can feel the tension radiating off her in waves.

She's out of the truck before I've even turned it off. Inside the house, we don't make it past the living room. Holiday pulls me toward the couch and we're kissing before I can even close the front door. It's desperate and urgent and full of need and want.

Her hands are everywhere—pulling at my shirt, my belt, her own clothes. The flannel she's wearing hits the floor, then my shirt, her jeans, until we're both naked.

"I love you," I say against her mouth as I lower her onto the couch.

"I love you too. So much."

When I finally slide inside her, we both groan. She wraps her legs around me and pulls me deeper, her nails digging into my back. I bury my face in her neck and breathe her in.

This never gets old. Being with her, loving her, the way our bodies fit together like they were designed for this.

We move together, starting slow then building faster, chasing that edge. Her breath comes in gasps against my ear. My name falls from her lips like a prayer. When we both finish, it's together.

I collapse beside her on the couch, and we're breathing hard. Sweat cools on my skin as my heart pounds in my chest.

"That was—" I can't even finish my sentence.

"Yeah."

We lie there for a few minutes, tangled together, my arm around her and her head on my chest. Our breathing slowly returns to normal.

Then Holiday sits up and looks at me with an expression I can't read. Nervous. Scared. Hopeful. All at once.

"Lucas?"

"Yeah, Peaches?"

She studies me. "I think I might be be pregnant."

I blink, still half-dazed from sex. "What?"

"Well…" She swallows hard. "I can't remember the last time I had my period."

My brain takes a second to catch up. Then it hits me like a freight train.

"Wait." I sit up fully and can't help but smile. "You think you're pregnant?"

She chuckles. "I don't know. I was chatting with Wendy about period cramps and realized I'm late, by weeks."

My heart is pounding so hard I can hear it in my ears. "Holy shit."

"I think I should take a pregnancy tests." She looks at me with those pretty eyes.

"Shit, yes." I pull her into my arms, holding her tight. My mind is racing. A baby. We could be having a baby. We've talked about it, obviously. About wanting kids someday. About how many we want, what we'd name them, what kind of parents we'd be. But someday always felt far away. Not now. Not four months into our marriage. But as I study my beautiful wife, seeing the hope and fear mixing together, I realize I want this. Right now. With her.

"I have some tests upstairs." She bites her lip.

"Let's go right now," I say, standing up, handing over her clothes.

I'm pulling on my jeans and hunting for my shirt.

"You look like a kid on Christmas morning," Holiday says as

she quickly gets dressed. Her hands shake as she buttons her jeans. We rush upstairs together and move into the bathroom.

She holds the stick in her hand and I lean against the counter reading the instructions. Holiday does her business then we set a timer and wait. I run my fingers through her hair, and kiss her softly.

"No matter what happens, I'm happy."

"Me too," she says, but it's not lost on either of us that we might be having a baby.

CHAPTER 2 (BONUS)

❄

HOLIDAY

The timer on Lucas's phone feels like it's slowing down even though I know that's not reality.

We sit on the bathroom floor, my back against the tub and Lucas beside me with his arm around my shoulders. The pregnancy test sits on the counter, face down, waiting.

Three minutes feels like three hours.

My heart won't stop racing. What if it's positive? What if I'm actually pregnant? I just took over the bakery less than a year ago. We're still figuring out our routine together.

But God, I want this. I want it so much it scares me.

"What if it's positive?" I ask.

"Then we're having a baby." Lucas kisses the top of my head. "Are you excited?"

"Ridiculously excited," I admit. "After helping Emma with the twins, it's just, I want that, you know?"

When the timer goes off, we both freeze.

My stomach flips. This is it. Everything could change in the next ten seconds.

Neither of us moves.

After another minute, Lucas stands and reaches for the test. His hand is shaking as he picks it up.

I hold my breath, watching his face, waiting for any reaction.

His eyes go wide. Then a massive grin spreads across his face—the one that shows his cute little dimple.

"Holiday." His voice cracks as he reaches out for me. He pulls me toward him and hands me the test.

I'm on my feet instantly, looking at the window that shows the results.

Two pink lines. Clear as day. *Positive.*

I'm pregnant.

"Oh my God," I breathe out. A laugh bubbles up from my chest, mixed with a sob. "Lucas, we're pregnant."

"We're having a baby!" He's laughing now, pulling me into his arms and spinning me around. "We're having a baby!"

Tears stream down my face and I don't even try to stop them. Lucas sets me down and cups my face in his hands, his own eyes wet.

"We're going to be parents," he says, like he needs to hear it out loud to believe it.

"Yes, we are." The reality crashes over me. There's a tiny human inside me. Lucas's baby. Our baby. "Baby Jolly."

Lucas kisses me hard, then pulls back. "This is the best day of my life. Well, second best. Marrying you was first."

"Smooth recovery." I laugh through my tears. "I can't believe this is real."

"I wished for this." He drops to his knees and lifts my shift, kissing my stomach. "I love you baby Jolly."

I run my fingers through his hair, and something shifts inside me. A feeling I can't quite name. Love, maybe. Or fierce protectiveness. Or just…everything.

I try to do the math in my head and think about my last period. "I think we're going to have a July baby"

Lucas's face lights up. "Around our anniversary?"

"If my math is correct," I whisper, and a fresh wave of emotion hits me. "Our baby could be born right around the time we celebrate our first year of marriage."

"That's perfect." He stands, pulling me close again. "You're perfect."

We stand there for a long moment, just holding each other, then reality sets in.

"What do we do now?" I ask.

"Um, we go back to the tree lot and pretend like everything's normal."

I laugh. "There is nothing normal about me having a human growing inside me."

"Should we keep it to ourselves for a bit?" He touches my stomach again. "Just us. Our secret."

"Yeah. I think that's best for now." The thought of telling everyone makes me anxious. "I want to go to the doctor and make sure everything is okay before we make an announcement."

"I'm following your lead, Peaches." He kisses me.

"Maybe we can tell everyone at Thanksgiving? Make it a thing."

I take a deep breath, and feel happiness wash over me. But then I think about everything that needs to be done. I have to make a doctor's appointment and figure out maternity leave. I need to eventually tell Helena, my store manager, eventually. I need to—

"Hey." Lucas tilts my chin up to look at him. "You're doing that overthinking thing you do. We'll take it one day at a time. Right now, we just go back to work."

I nod. "You're right. Don't want to be late."

We head downstairs and Lucas reaches for my hand as we leave.

"Is it safe for you to be working, like lifting boxes and stuff?"

I laugh. "Lucas, I'm like five or six weeks pregnant. I'm fine."

"But what if—"

"No heavy lifting, okay? I'll take care of myself, I promise."

A VERY MERRY ENEMY

He still looks worried. "Okay. But if you feel tired or sick or anything—"

"I'll tell you first."

The drive back to the tree lot feels surreal. I'm trying to wrap my head around what's happening inside me. I think about all the wishes I made on stars when I was younger. I wished for my own bakery. Wished Lucas would love me back. Wished for a life that felt like home.

I have all of it.

And now we're growing our family.

When I was a kid, I used to believe in the magic of Merryville. Somewhere I stopped believing in it. I thought magic was for children and fairy tales.

But I was wrong.

The magic of Merryville is real and it brought me home. It gave me Lucas. It gave me everything I ever wanted and things I didn't even know I needed.

"You okay over there?" Lucas asks.

"Yeah. Just thinking."

"About?"

"How everything I've ever wanted, I've gotten." My voice cracks and emotion overtakes me. "Every single one. The bakery, you, and now a baby. I'm so happy, Lucas."

He squeezes my hand. "Me too, peaches. Me too."

When we pull in, I swear the amount of customers doubled. Hudson spots us and walks over.

"Where have you been?" He studies our faces. "You both look weird."

"Everything's great," Lucas says, and I can hear the barely contained excitement in his voice.

Please don't give it away, I think.

"What's going on? You look like you just won the lottery or something."

"It's a beautiful day," I say quickly. "Perfect reason to be so happy."

Hudson doesn't look convinced. "Jake needs help at the pre-cut line."

Before Lucas heads off, he pulls me into his arms and kisses me. I make my way inside the bakery and my legs feel shaky. The smile on my face might be permanent. I'm pregnant and it's our little secret.

I keep myself busy in the back, prepping dough while the ladies run the front, but it doesn't stop my mind from racing.

As I look around, it's almost as if I see the world differently. My child will grow up playing on the Christmas Tree farm, eating yummy cookies, and experiencing family traditions. He or she will have the twins and Colby to play with.

Helena walks into the kitchen, humming with the music.

"You okay, boss?" she asks.

"Amazing." I throw dough into the fridge. "Having a really good day where everything just seems to go my way."

If only she knew that in a few months, we'll need to have a very different conversation about coverage and schedules.

"Great! Cookies are flying out of here today," she says, then rushes back to the front.

My chest fills with warmth as I imagine our entire future together.

For the first time in my life, I'm not scared of what comes next.

I'm looking forward to our future.

This is my dream. Not Paris or Michelin stars or fancy restaurants.

This. Right here. Right now.

Later that evening, when the tree lot finally closes and we drive home together, exhaustion hits me all at once. Lucas makes us spaghetti and afterward we curl up on the couch with carb comas.

I rest my head on his chest.

"You know what I was thinking?" Lucas says, running his fingers through my hair.

"What?"

"What if it's twins?"

I lift my head to look at him. "Do not jinx me."

"I mean, Emma had twins. It does skip a generation."

"Oh my God, don't even joke about that." But I'm laughing.

He grins and touches my stomach. "Maybe it's triplets?"

"I would never forgive you."

"You would." He kisses my forehead. "But it would be kind of perfect, wouldn't it? Us, several babies, this life."

I settle back against him, his hand resting on my stomach where our baby—or babies—is growing.

"It's already perfect," I tell him. "But it keeps getting better, doesn't it?"

Through the window, stars scatter across the November sky. The same stars we used to wish on as teenagers. I still can't believe every single one of them came true.

And this? This is just the beginning.

THE END

This concludes the Very Merry series.
Thank you so much!

WANT MORE OF LYRA?

The Billionaire Situation Series
The Wife Situation
The Friend Situation
The Boss Situation
The Bodyguard Situation
The Hookup Situation
The Hockey Situation
The Royal Situation
Fall I Want (connects with this world)

Valentine Texas Series
Bless Your Heart
Spill the Sweet Tea
Butter My Biscuit
Smooth as Whiskey
Fixing to be Mine
Hold Your Horses
You Can Call Me Honey

Very Merry Series
A Very Merry Mistake
A Very Merry Nanny
A Very Merry Enemy

Every book can be read as a standalone, but for the full Lyra Parish experience, start with book 1 of the series, as they do interconnect.

ACKNOWLEDGMENTS

I thought about what I'd write here because ***this*** series saved me. It's been happiness in a bottle, something I've really enjoyed writing. For the past three years, so many of you have returned, wanting more of the magic of Merryville and the Jollys. My heart is so full, and I can't say thank you enough for loving it as much as me.

Can't wrap this baby up without giving a big thank you to my ARC and content team who have been so gracious to me while I've navigated one of the busiest years of my career. I am forever grateful and will never forget my OG readers, the ones who screamed through the rooftops about this series back in 2023. It's been a wild ride, hasn't it? Thank you!

It seriously takes a village to keep me on track and I am so freaking grateful to be working with people who are understanding, who push me to continue to keep going. Big thanks to Erica Rogers (my lovely assistant), Amber (for making beautiful images), CM Wheary for keeping up with timeline better than I ever could, Marla Esposito for giving her a shine! Can't wrap this up without thanking Dee Garcia at Black Widow Designs for designing the covers for the entire series. Also thanks to Qamber Designs for making these super cute characters too.

Thank you to all the writers who joined me on 4thewords while I finished this book. If it weren't for you, I don't think I would've seen the end. LFG!

Cannot end this without giving a gigantic thank you to my

hubby, Will Young (@deepskydude), for always encouraging me to keep going, but also for reminding me to take breaks when I won't stop. I love you to the moon and back. Funny enough, you'd know exactly how many miles that is. I'll leave it to Google for everyone else.

This is the final book in the Very Merry series, and wow, it's so bittersweet. Happy holidays! Thank you for being on this journey with me. MAGIC IS HAPPENING!

KEEP IN TOUCH

Want to stay up to date with all things Lyra Parish? Join her newsletter! You'll get special access to cover reveals, teasers, and giveaways.

lyraparish.com/newsletter

Let's be friends on social media:
TikTok 🖤 Instagram 🖤 Facebook
@lyraparish everywhere

Searching for the Lyra Parish hangout?
Join Lyra Parish's Reader Lounge on Facebook:
https://bit.ly/lyrareadergroup

ABOUT LYRA PARISH

Lyra Parish is a hopeless romantic obsessed with writing spicy Hallmark-like romances. When she isn't immersed in fictional worlds, you can find her pretending to be a Vanlifer with her hubby and taking selfies with pumpkins. Lyra loves iced coffee, memes, authentic people, and living her best life. She is represented by Lesley Sabga at The Seymour Agency.

Made in the USA
Las Vegas, NV
27 November 2025